*To Sid. —
Good friend and confidant —
and also one fine writer —
Best always to you!*

ALLEYMANDEROUS AND OTHER MAGICAL REALITIES

*with appreciation —
Bruce Taylor*

Bruce Taylor

27 May 2017

ReAnimus Press
Breathing Life into Great Books

ReAnimus Press
1100 Johnson Road #16-143
Golden, CO 80402
www.ReAnimus.com

Cover Art by Carl and Lida Sloan

ISBN-13: 978-1545536391

First ReAnimus Press print edition: May, 2017

10 9 8 7 6 5 4 3 2 1

To Carl Sloan and in memoriam to his wife, Lida, whose work graces the cover of this book: two of the most creative, visual artists I have ever met and whose interest in my work with magic realism sparked their imaginations and certainly fed mine. Thank you for your support, your wonderful art and years of friendship.

Also to all the furry, four-footed "mew-ses" who have padded through my life, and especially to Flak who, when I was a child, was often there when no one else was. I learned a lot from you. Thank you, my little gray and white, yellow-eyed bodhisattva.

"To sleep: perchance to dream—"
 —Shakespeare, *Hamlet*

"In Dreams Begin Responsibilities"
 —Delmore Schwartz

"To not respond to a dream is like not answering a letter."
 —Arabic proverb

"Dream? Waking up from a dream? Since when?"
 —Alleymanderous

Alleymanderous

12:46 am

...you get home, pooped from the New Year's celebration. But it wasn't the celebration that wore you out. It was being with your family, your grandmother, your father, sister and mother. You keep hoping each year it will be different but it never is. You remember the words of your therapist: "You always hope that it will change, don't you?" Somehow, this evening, you get it. You truly *get* it: it ain't *ever* gonna change. But you know, way down deep inside, *something* is *gonna change. But what?* Your mind swims at all the possible and alternate realities but out of all the possibilities: which one is the one you're going to finally wake up to?

You sigh, go to bed, and in a few minutes, your Maine coon cat, Alleymanderous, hops upon the bed, crawls beneath the covers, flops against you and purrs and purrs and you begin to drift...

...and then the fun begins...

12:56 am

...you are in a bathtub and you look up to the blue tiled walls with the clouds floating in it and out from them, looking a bit like white shelf fungi that you find on trees in the Great Damp Northwest. You are in your clothes, and your cat, Alleymanderous, is sitting on the side of the bathtub with a giant black tarantula in his mouth. You do not like this. The water is beginning to harden like it's Jello™. You cannot move. You look up at Alleymanderous and you say, "Don't. Please don't."

7

In the background, Beethoven's *Eroica* is playing and when the music nears its crescendo, Alleymanderous drops the spider. It scrambles up your stomach, your chest, your chin, up to your nose, then up to your eyes. You want to close your eyes but you cannot. "No," you scream. "No! Please!" The tarantula comes closer and...

...darkness. You are aware that it is growing light again. This time you are aware that you are covered by sand. You look around. The sky is pink and everything is covered by a light frost. "Mars?" you whisper. "What am I doing on Mars?"

You also notice that your penis is exposed and you see a little point of light above. A minute later, a little spidery craft lands right near your penis. For a long minute, it is quiet, still. Then movement—a mechanical hand with a strange fixture at the end of it approaches your penis—to take a sample, you assume. You imagine the machine thinking, "Is it alive? Is there life in that strange, thick log?" You close your eyes. This is a dream. This just *must* be a dream. You want to wake up. Any minute you will wake up. You hope. And...

...darkness. The light. And you are sitting in the bathtub and are sitting in what appears to be red wine or strawberry juice or something. Alleymanderous sits on the edge of the tub with a book that has no title. He sits up like a rabbit and says, "Life is but a dream..."

You smile. "...filled with sound and fury..."

"Signifying everything," says Alleymanderous.

"Nothing," you reply.

"A tale told by idiots."

"Well," you finally say, "have it your way. Just what *is* this dream trying to say?"

"That this is life," says Alleymanderous.

"It is?"

Alleymanderous nods. "The bathtub. The constancy."

"How do I wake up?" you ask.

But Alleymanderous turns the page and does not answer.

"Maybe all these dreams are incarnations," you say. "I have to go through all these life dreams until I come back to the dream that is reality. Is *that* it?"

"Out, out brief candle," says Alleymanderous.

"So what am I to do?" you ask.

Alleymanderous hands you a straw. "Eat, drink, and be merry."

Dumbly, you look at the straw, then bending forward, you drink and become drowsy, sleepy, and dimly hope that maybe *next* time...darkness...

...and slowly, the darkness becomes lighter and you finally realize that you are still in the bathtub and you feel a sense of relief—either you are still in the dream or you have awakened from the dream and are, in reality, in a bathtub where you must have fallen asleep. But you notice Alleymanderous dressed in flippers and an ingeniously designed face mask. He points with a paw to the water in your bathtub. You stare. "How'd the floor get tilted?" you ask, noticing that the water level dips down in the direction of Alleymanderous. Alleymanderous shakes his head and points up with his paw. High above, on what you thought was the wall, is an overflow. "What?" you ask. "*What?*" You're in a bathtub *in a bathtub*?

Alleymanderous nods and manages to get the cleverly designed snorkel out of his mouth. "A bathtub in a bathtub, a dream within a dream. Boy you can't help but get clean. Awesome, no?"

"No. No, not awesome at all. How do I wake from a dream and back to reality and not into another dream?"

Alleymanderous flips water up from outside the tub that you are in and says, "Some things are not known. Or knowable. Yet."

With dismay, you now indeed recognize the vastness of the tub that surrounds your tub. You even notice the bathtub ring high above. You vaguely wonder about the size of the creature that must bathe in this tub. Suddenly feeling very modest, you put your hand over your privates and ask Alleymanderous, "Aren't you concerned about any of this? How can you be so calm?"

"Because," says Alleymanderous, "it's not my dream. Besides," he adds, as if all of this makes perfect sense, "I'm not the one taking a bath, although I don't mind snorkeling or scuba diving."

"Then why the hell do you raise such a fit whenever I try to bathe you?"

"Simple," says Alleymanderous, "I can't stand baths." With that, he somehow manages to get the snorkel back in his mouth and flips over backwards into the water outside your tub.

"Alleymanderous," you yell, "how do I get *out* of this?" But he doesn't answer and you close your eyes really tight, hoping that when you open them again, things will be different. And when you *do* open them again, even though you don't notice any difference in physical sensation, you rejoice. You are not in a bathtub. You are outside of it, sitting in a chair reading a book and you rejoice. You look out the bathroom window and your heart freezes. Mars is impossibly huge in the sky. You look to the book you are reading. "Nope," is printed on the page. You flip the pages. "No," "Nyet," "Uh-uh," you read. You sigh. This does not look good. Then Alleymanderous walks in wearing Adidas running shoes, purple running shorts and a pale purple towel over his shoulders. He looks like he has been jogging, his fur wet and dripping, and you don't think cats can sweat, so you then assume he ran through a lawn sprinkler. You look at Alleymanderous. "Now what?" you ask.

Alleymanderous looks up. "Care to join me in a fifty yard sprint?"

"This is insane," you say.

"Maybe it's life." Alleymanderous shrugs.

"Life is insane?"

"Life is a dream."

"Is dreaming insane?"

"Maybe it's life."

"This isn't helpful."

Alleymanderous takes off a front shoe and licks his paw. He then puts it back in the running shoe and yanks the Velcro strip over with his teeth and anchors it. "Interesting," he says, "how strangely logical dreams are. That you would even think of a detail like the Velcro strap to give credence to something like a cat wearing running shoes. Clever. Cunning."

"Diabolical," you say, "very diabolical."

"Oh," says Alleymanderous, "you don't *know* how diabolical it *truly* is."

Suddenly, and with great foreboding, you turn and look into the bathtub. There is a large version of yourself, floating in the bathtub. On the head of that image, which has one eye gone, withered, sucked out like an egg, sits the tarantula. *"Get me out of here!"* screams the version of yourself. *"Get this fucking dream over with! This is crazy!"*

"I'm trying," you say. "I'm trying. I don't like this any more than you do, but it's like I can't get out of it. It's like I have to go through this damn thing to get *past* it!"

"Do something!" yells the you in the bathtub. "This is fucking *dreadful!"*

You look at Alleymanderous. "So what do I do?" you ask.

"Like I said," says Alleymanderous toweling himself off, "fifty yard dash?"

"Maybe we can dash out of this dream?"

"I don't know."

"I don't care *what* you do," says the you in the bathtub, "but for God's sake, do *something* before my visitor gets hungry again."

So you stand, take a step and...

...darkness. And slowly light returns and you are in another bathtub, but it is filled with steaming water. And that's good, because the sky is real black, the stars are bright and there is a very bright point of light and you look around to a snowy landscape. Alleymanderous leaps up on the side of that bathtub. He is dressed in a space suit.

"Uh, you know," you say, "this doesn't look like Earth. Pluto, a moon of Uranus, maybe, but not Earth."

Alleymanderous lifts his face visor. "True," he says, "away from the bathtub, the air is a mite thin."

"When does this end?" you ask.

"Are you sure you want it to end? How do you know that, if it ends, it won't be worse than before? Maybe this dream is better than what your real life really is."

You shake your head. "I can't believe that my life is, in reality, *any* worse than what my life now appears to be. Besides, I have to be dreaming all of this... I just *have* to be."

"Oh?" says Alleymanderous.

"What do you know about all of this?" you ask. "Do you dream?"

"Of chasing mice, yes."

"Doesn't help me much," you reply, sulking, looking around to the bleak landscape. "I just want to go back to where I was before."

Alleymanderous laughs. "Don't we all? Oh, don't we all? Oh, don't we all have memories of those good times?" He laughs again and pulls his face shield down, securing it. And with that, Alleymanderous leaps from the side of the bathtub and you watch him walk away—soon to vanish in the vast snows and unending silent shadows.

1:17 am

...you close your eyes and when you open them, you discover that you are sitting in a chair on the front porch. Alleymanderous is nearby, still dressed in a spacesuit. "Dream," he says. His voice crackles as if coming from a two-way radio.

"Dream what?" you ask.

"Dream of the way it could be."

You laugh. "Good try, cat," you say. "Good try. The dream ended in the 70s when Vice-President Spiro Agnew said we could be on Mars in 1986 and was either laughed at or told to shut up. Hard to say which."

But Alleymanderous stands on his hind legs, sitting as a rabbit might, puts his paw up and, pointing to the sky, says again, "Dream."

"Dream?" you ask. "The dream is dead, cat. The dream is—" A weird feeling comes over you and you shake your head. "What—" You close your eyes tight and then you feel a crushing force and a rough shaking. Just when you think you can't stand it any more, you open your eyes and looking down, you see you, too, are dressed in a space suit. Nearby, Alleymanderous has already removed his helmet and without really thinking how, you reach up and remove yours. A door opens to another compartment.

"Enjoy the ride?" asks Alleymanderous.

"Whew," you respond. "Space flight? Lift off?"

"Yup," says Alleymanderous. "You didn't get sick."

You shake your head. "Actually, I don't remember much."

"Just as well," says Alleymanderous. "Can be a messy ride."

You both step through the doorway, and before you, a vast window and the scene is that of the Earth below, all blue and white and brown with land masses and water and clouds. Then, looking up, you see directly ahead and not far away, two vast arms of what appears to be a space station, extending outward from a central hub. And not far away, and also looking out the window, a painter, painting the view of the Earth below. He turns.

"Like it?" he asks.

Alleymanderous, still holding his specially-designed space helmet, looks to the painter, then at you, to whom he points. "Convince him."

You look to the painter. The art looks familiar—"Uh—" you begin. "Not Chesley Bonstell—"

He smiles. "I know, I'm supposed to be dead, but—"

You look to his art. "—uh—" you say.

He points. "Where we are, is 1955. My art has always been considered very realistic. Photo-realism is the term used."

You look around. "—uh—" you say again, "—uh—sure the hell is."

He returns to his painting. "My art ran in *Colliers Magazine*, 1954-1955. The public couldn't handle the art and articles on space exploration and called me, Willy Ley, and Wernher Von Braun, 'space cowboys'. People couldn't believe space travel could or would happen." He looks back up, a sad smile on his round face. "If the political will had been there, we would have been first in space, not the Soviets. And all that you see here would have been up and running between 1965 and 1975."

Alleymanderous sighs, sits on a stool bolted to the floor and looks out the window, feet up against the wall, suit-encased tail twitching. " — and Mars by 1986 — "

"Sooner," says Bonstell, "much sooner. 1976, at the latest."

Alleymanderous nods. "Mars base in the early 80s."

Bonstell holds up a painting, *Saturn as Seen from Titan*.

You nod. "I've seen that. It was in the Astronomy section of the *Encyclopedia Americana* I had when I was growing up. I used to stare at those pictures and dream — "

Alleymanderous looks at you. "So you did dream."

You nod. "But I knew it was a dream."

"Even when we landed on the moon?"

You nod. "Sure. We beat the Russians, but then we had Viet Nam — and when Vice President Agnew said we could be on Mars — "

You watch. Chesley Bonstell puts his hands to his face. "It didn't happen as I dreamed it — did it?" he whispers.

You sigh. "No, it did not — and it's probably not going to for a very, very long time — we live in a time of wars, wars, never ending, never ceasing wars — "

Abruptly, his picture changes; the oils begin to run, then around you, the walls begin to sag, to melt, the plastiglass in the windows begins to bulge outward. Instantly, Alleymanderous snaps on his helmet, as do you. Then both of you are blown out the suddenly ruptured window, blown out a long, long ways away, and you watch the nearly completed Mars ship sag and melt and then dissolve, as does the wheel of the space station and the Bonstell-designed rockets and rocket cruisers. All melt, and then it's as if they become like taffy — pulling apart, becoming unglued, then just evaporating.

And you start falling, falling toward Earth.

"Whose fault?" you hear in your earphones.

"I don't know," you say. "Ignorance? Bad PR job? Space as entertainment? Contest? Not a glorious new frontier? Viet Nam?"

"A pity," says Alleymanderous, "where it could have taken — " then, surrounded by plasma, you are out of radio contact and in the searing light, you see nothing. You are glad that the suit you wear seems to have remarkable properties, like, not burning up. And somewhere, at about 10,000 feet up, your parachutes pop open. And you both land. Somewhere.

Taking off your helmet, you are struck by how corrosive the air, how hot it is. "Alleymanderous," you say, "Alleymanderous—where are we?"

Alleymanderous, having landed just a few yards away, looks at some sort of readout device on his right paw. "Just a minute," he says, then, "solar radiation is intense, no ozone, it's one hundred fifteen degrees and we are at—" he looks at his readout, this way, that, as if trying to make sense of it, "not far from Nome, Alaska."

Not far away, a bright light erupts, the ground shakes, "Whoa," says Alleymanderous, "sure looks like a bomb to me." You dive for cover in what appears to be a bomb crater, and feel a wave of heat pass overhead. In a few minutes, you look up, around.

"Nothing growing," you say.

"Yup," says Alleymanderous, and he sits on his haunches, looking away.

"There is still—" you gulp, "Isn't there still—this doesn't have to be the future," you say, and you can't help but hear the pleading in your voice.

But Alleymanderous doesn't answer.

And you begin to feel incredibly ill.

Alleymanderous looks to you, eyes filled with what you guess to be pity. Finally he says, "Why the dreams of what could be get so easily replaced by the nightmare of what is—" and he shakes his head. On the horizon, sudden, staccato, searing white lights and the ground shakes, shakes again, again and again...

1:41 am

...the light is blinding and you think, "Oh, fuck, this is it." Suddenly, it's dark. In the dream you open your eyes, and you are looking out a window, with a view of a vast star field and you recognize constellations. Then you turn around; you are in a room with people you don't recognize. Sitting beside you is a large version of Alleymanderous, remarkably human-looking but still, Alleymanderous. He wears a black shirt and woven in the fabric, little stars; they twinkle and form—constellations.

You focus on Gemini and Alleymanderous, looking through glasses with small, rectangular lenses, studies you. Abruptly you realize that the lenses are just glass.

"I know," says Alleymanderous, "these are for looks, but first impressions are everything."

He then picks up a cup of coffee and you see the logo on the outside, CATBUCKS, and the image is that of a feline form with its tail going up one side of the body, around the neck and then down the other side.

You squirm. This, you intuit, is going to be so fucking weird. You brace yourself.

"You're tense," says Alleymanderous. He sucks on a straw and you get the scent of intensely sweet, vanilla flavored hot milk.

"No shit," you say.

"It's OK," says Alleymanderous.

"I don't want to be here," you say.

"That's true," says Alleymanderous. He looks at you with green eyes that are strangely luminous, like two glowing spirits are sitting in the irises. You can't take your eyes off those eyes. He continues, "But here you are."

"Where's the door?" you ask.

"There." Alleymanderous points.

You look up. It's in the ceiling. Ten feet above you.

"This won't hurt you."

You keep staring at the ceiling, to the door and you say, "I'm not so sure."

Alleymanderous says, "That's true."

"Which," you ask, "that this won't hurt me, or my being not so sure means that they might hurt me?"

Alleymanderous simply stares at you with those luminous eyes and says, "This is true."

"What?" you ask, "What's true?"

"Shall we begin?" asks Alleymanderous.

"Begin what?" you ask.

"Examining more deeply your family of origin. That's why you can't get out of the dream."

"What's this got to do with my family of origin?"

"Everything."

"What?"

"You'll see. After this, you might have better dreams."

"But it might not help me get out of this dream?"

"Or dreams," says Alleymanderous. He takes another long suck on the straw. You notice he wears a wrist watch around his furry wrist and you realize that the hands are going backwards. You are beginning to dread this more and more. Alleymanderous then says, "Tell me about your family. Brothers? Sisters?"

You stare longingly at the door in the ceiling. "Sister. Kathy."

"Mother, father?"

You nod.

Then he points to the group of twenty or so individuals in the room. "Pick out people to represent your family. Without thinking, just physically move them to a place that feels right in the room."

"Why?" you ask. "What's this about?"

"Generational Field Energy. These people are going to represent your family and will show you your family dynamics."

You can't help it. You start crying. "I wanna go home," you wail.

"This will help you."

You look at Alleymanderous, sitting there, with his constellation-designed shirt, those glasses and, even though his image is tear-blurred, you have to admit, in this dream, he looks distinguished. You sigh miserably. "So these people will act out the field energy of my family that I've internalized?"

"That's true," says Alleymanderous.

"Do you have life insurance? Medical coverage?" you ask.

"Of course," he replies, "also malpractice insurance. Think I'll need it?"

"Probably," you reply, "especially if this is really accurate."

"It is," says Alleymanderous.

"Then you'll need all the coverage you can get." You then take on a "what the hell" attitude and get brave. You go to the strongest looking fellow you can find and you motion him to stand. He smiles. He's the most not-looking-like-your-father guy there. His whole attitude is of interest, curiosity, attentiveness. You sigh internally; *So unlike my father,* you muse. You set him up in the center of the room. You then go toward a kindly-looking woman; her demeanor is sweet, engaging. *Good choice,* you think; *no one could be more different from my mother.* You then go for a representative of your sister. You locate someone petite, with long brown hair, who is quite lovely, and again, as different from your sister as you can imagine. You place her not far from your father. You place your mother figure next to your father.

"Now," says Alleymanderous, "choose someone who represents you."

You pick a young man, calm, pleasant; his demeanor is the exact opposite of yours right now. You set him up next to your mother. In your head, you hear the theme music of *Leave It to Beaver* and *Father Knows Best*.

You turn back to Alleymanderous.

"Through?" he asks. He takes another sip of his drink.

You nod. You look back. The fellow who represents your father has *become* your father; he stands on his head, in his Metro uniform, steering wheel in hand. He moves it like he's actually driving a bus; his feet move in the air as if braking and accelerating. "Vroom," he says. "Vroom, vrooooom."

Your sister hangs by her feet from the ceiling by a chain. Her dress is over her head and she's got on stainless steel underwear with such things as, "Come and get me, baby," "fuck me," "I'm yours" written all over them.

The representative of your mother becomes your mother; she somehow stands as though anchored rigidly perpendicular to the wall. She has her eyes closed, and is snapping her fingers like she's listening to a rock concert in her head and you? You see yourself scrunched in a corner, sitting on the floor, with your arms wrapped around your legs, looking around as if you're in mortal danger and have to be on guard every moment.

Alleymanderous gets up, goes to your father and asks, "And how does the father feel?"

He grins and yells out, "Fourth and Blanchard. Free ride zone!"

Then, he goes to your sister. "Hello, sister," says Alleymanderous, "what's the sister feel?"

"Hornier 'n shit!" she screams.

Alleymanderous contemplates the stainless steel underwear and says, "That's true."

You watch Alleymanderous move. You don't how he does it—you've never seen cats walk upright—but in this dream—you then rivet your attention on Alleymanderous going over to your mother, and part of you says, "Oh, boy, is *this* is going to be good."

"And how is the mother feeling?" asks Alleymanderous.

"I'M FUCKING FINE," she screeches, "JUST FUCKING FINE YOU MISERABLE EXCUSE FOR A FELINE!"

As she says this, she continues to smile, snapping her fingers.

"That's true," says Alleymanderous. Then, looking to your representative, he asks, "and how does ___ feel?"

You notice he doesn't have a name for you but somehow, at a time like this, you don't give a crap. You see yourself cowering and simply saying, "I'm scared out of my fucking mind." It comes out almost as a high pitched squeak.

Alleymanderous looks to you and says, "Well, for this interesting family constellation, there must be a powerful ancestor who is still disturbing the field. Who's missing?" He looks at you for a long minute. "Oh," he says, "I know who it is —"

"Don't," you say.

"Don't," says your representative.

"Oblivion and James Street," calls out your father.

"Someone get this God damn stainless steel underwear off me! The bolts have quarter inch heads, it unbolts from the front and you can use this 3/8ths socket wrench which I have in my hand!" yells your sister.

"I'VE NEVER FELT BETTER IN MY LIFE!" screams your mother.

Alleymanderous looks to you again. "The field must manifest itself. You must let all aspects of your field be represented —"

"No!" you wail.

"No," says your representative.

"NO!" yells everyone in the room in a panicked chorus.

Alleymanderous goes over to a grandmotherly-looking woman, and has her come forward, saying, "The field *must* be healed."

Alleymanderous lets go of her; abruptly, the representative turns into your grandmother; she smokes a cigar, carries a whip in one hand, an AK-47 in the other and is dressed as a Nazi SS officer. She looks to Alleymanderous, then to you and says, "You shoulda listened! You shoulda let me remain unconscious —" and then she screams, "BUT IT'S TOO LATE NOW AND THE FIELD HAS MANIFESTED ITSELF. COVER YOUR ASSES, PUSSIES!"

Alleymanderous, now beside you, says, "Ooops."

And the next thing you see is that the room has exploded in pandemonium. People are running pell mell as your Grandmother lets off a few rounds from her AK-47. Then she morphs into a black widow spider and looking at you, hisses, "I devoured your grandfather; I destroyed your father—"

You get it.

Abruptly the floor gives way, you're falling though space, Alleymanderous right beside you, and he yells, "TOLD YOU THIS WORK WAS POWERFUL!"

All you can think of to say is, "NO SHIT!"

2:05 am

...you fall for a long, long time. You keep falling. Then, somehow, it's like you hit something dense. You turn to look at Alleymanderous. He holds a mask up to his face: you recognize it's your sister to whom you've always felt inferior, but you think, well, hell, it's just a mask, and Alleymanderous is behind the mask, so you feel safe enough to ask, "Why are we slowing down?"

"Gawd," comes the voice of Alleymanderous, which suddenly changes and sounds exactly like your sister, "how can you be so dumb? We've hit invisible matter."

You immediately go into deep shame and you recognize, gee, you feel the same way now as you used to around your sister. You don't know what to say.

"I bet you don't know what to say," says Alleymanderous in his familiar voice.

You don't say anything. Instead you try real hard to admire the place through which you are falling; yellow stars burn in a deep blue background and it's like you and Alleymanderous are feathers, just drifting.

Alleymanderous says, "Admiring the place through which you are falling doesn't change the fact that you don't know what to say."

You turn and this time Alleymanderous is holding a mask of your father up to his face.

You turn away again to be dazzled by a golden-hued galaxy drifting past you; you love the glowing, spiral arms.

"Admiring a golden-hued galaxy drifting past you and loving the glowing spiral arms just distracts you from the task at hand."

You look at the mask of your father that Alleymanderous holds up before his face like some weird, existential all-day sucker. "Geeze," you say, "if I say something, to whom do I talk? The mask or you, Alleymanderous, the Cat Behind The Mask?"

"That's the dilemma, isn't it?" says Alleymanderous. "When we talk to people, who is it we really talk to? Who is it we're really with?"

"Well," you say, "right now I'm talking to you, Alleymanderous."

"Fourth and Blanchard. Free ride zone. Are you sure?"

You look at Alleymanderous; there is no mask. You see Alleymanderous, but the voice is that of your father. Same inflection, same tone, same everything.

You close your eyes. *This is a dream*, you think. *This is a dream. Just a very, very —*

"And who's to say that dreams aren't their own reality?"

You look. Alleymanderous has another mask up in front of his face—a mask of your mother.

You sigh.

"Different people bring out different aspects of our personality," says Alleymanderous. "So who are we, really?"

"Oh, God," you say, "if that's true—" suddenly, you feel feverish, pouty, and, in the worst sense, childish.

"You don't look well," says Alleymanderous in your mother's voice as he floats gently down in tandem with you. "Maybe you should go to bed."

You feel like you are five years old. Suddenly, you get it: You not only see who you are in your mother's eyes, but—

"Stop," you say in a weird, childish voice. "Just *stop!*"

"OK," says Alleymanderous. It's quiet for a minute, and you savor the momentary peace of this falling, falling, forever falling. Falling past those blazing yellow suns, occasional slow motion bluish-white comets, ghostly glowing galaxies, and when you look to Alleymanderous again, he's holding up a mask of—

—you instantly turn away; you want to run, but you can't; you want to do something but you can't, for floating right along with you is Alleymanderous, holding up like an existential lollypop a mask of—your grandmother. You're freaking out and you can't believe it—she's dead. She's gone. She's harmless. And you're freaking out. It's like your unconscious hasn't heard the news and your memories have become reality and you again feel the hatred she had for her husband and her hatred of everything male, including your father, including...you gulp, and you want to scream. Then you really begin to lose it when you see yourself dissolving, see suns shining through your hands, your arms—the right word comes to your mind: oblivion. You see how your grandmother saw you—hating males into infinity, oblivion, hatred, hatred, never-ending hatred. You see yourself becoming even more ephemeral and yet somehow something in you awakens, fights and on some cellular level you hear the very DNA essence of your life force screaming, "It's not me who has the problem! It's *her*!"

Suddenly, you stop fading away; slowly you come back. You look at the face of your grandmother and you hear Alleymanderous say, "Hey, that was pretty cool."

You're stunned for a moment; you're still drifting in wherever it is you're at, but somehow—it's OK. You reach over to grab your grandmother's mask away from Alleymanderous, but he says, "Ah, ah, ah. Mustn't touch the merchandise."

"Listen, you feline Marquis de Sade, give me that fucking mask so I can be done with this once and for all." You grab for it again. "Come on—let go of it!"

Alleymanderous waves his paws about and says innocently, "I *have* let go of it."

You grab the mask by its handle but, "It won't budge," you say, clearly aware of the fear and frustration in your voice. So you look at the mask and knowing what you're feeling, you watch with horror as the mask's eyes light up, the mouth works.

Then, you get it. "Whatever this mask brings out in me, my fear of it animates it, creates it, gives it power."

Abruptly the mask drops away and behind that, you see another mask, that of the wretched countenance of a man; face twisted in rage, fear, insanity. You don't know how you know it—

Alleymanderous just continues to drift with you, drifting, down, down, deeper, into wherever it is you are going, and finally he says, "For your grandmother to be so mean and nasty to the men she chose to have in her life, and to whom she gave birth, can only mean one thing—"

You inwardly shudder at the implication. You look to the twisted, contorted mask behind which is the face of your grandmother's father and you simply say, "God in heaven, why, why, why did you do it? Did you think that my grandmother, your daughter, would forget what you did? Forgive you?"

You watch the mask twist in anguish and agony and you see the lips move and you hear the mask whisper, "Oh, gods, I don't know why but do know this: my pain is absolute, eternal, for I see the damage it has done for generations to come and to you.... am so sorry." Tears well up, flow over the mask and it slowly dissolves until you can see your grandmother's mask reappear. You still have fear but now you know why. You let the fear go, replaced by compassion, sorrow, grieving, for all the pointless pain and the lost generations.

But! It's *really* more like *this*:
Tug. Tug. Tug.
You feel something insistently pulling at your shirt sleeve. "Huh?" you say, "wha—?"

You open your eyes. You're still drifting, but much more slowly now. You see Alleymanderous looking at you from behind a mask of Buddha. "Wake up," he says. "It's time to go to sleep."

"Huh?" you say again.

"Sleep on this: 'infinite wisdom, infinite compassion.'"

"What else is there?" you ask, feeling yourself begin to drift off again.

"Good try," says Alleymanderous, "but, unconsciously, you're still scared shitless of her, ain'tcha?" And he holds up the mask of your cigar-smoking, abusive, Nazi grandmother.

You wince. "Not as bad," you say, "and someday, I'll get over her entirely."

"In your dreams, my friend," says Alleymanderous in the voice of your grandmother, "only in your dreams."

Instantly you feel hope. "Since this is a dream, I'm over you."

"What if this dream is reality?" says Alleymanderous.

Right then, you hate Alleymanderous. Now you feel dread. Since you've tried in vain to wake up and since that hasn't worked, this is the reality. And as you ponder your despair, you notice that you are entering a darker realm of space and you slow even more.

"Dark matter," says Alleymanderous.

"Dark indeed," you muse, aware of the irony. Yet you are also aware of being so tired, so very, very tired.

The stars suddenly begin to expand, then blowing off shells of matter, they collapse in on themselves and abruptly, their light winks out and you feel the space around you distort.

"Black holes," you whimper.

Alleymanderous holds up a mask of Newton; it caves in on itself, turns inside out, collapses into a neutron star and zips away.

Alleymanderous looks wistfully in the direction the star has gone and says, "End of the masks. They simply don't work anymore, now that you have seen the real face of the Universe." Alleymanderous drifts with you, now looking like the cat that he is, all black and white and gray fur, but, upon closer inspection, the black fur creates patterns of galaxies. And he looks at you through glasses; his eyes appear very large and green, his stare absolute, somewhat unnerving. He's on his back, front paws folded upon his chest, but his stare is of vast serenity and a mild curiosity.

You look at him and you say, "How can you be so calm? We could be engulfed by a black hole at any moment."

"That is true," says Alleymanderous. "Not much we can do about it."

"There must be something," you say, feeling yourself a bit petulant and put out by all this.

"There is," says Alleymanderous.

"What?"

"Sleep."

"Huh?"

"Sleep. Three, two, one, *sleep deeply*."

Bang. You're gone. You are gone, gone, and deeper into that goneness you go and you have the sense of floating, drifting and this endless sense of just going deeper, deeper asleep. Images come to you.

You are on the planet Mars. It's a 1950s Mars with canals, blue sky, cities. You see a figure sitting at an easel on the sidewalk, painting. The sidewalk tops a levee that contains the water of a canal. It's the artist Chesley Bonstell again.

You say to him, "Hello. I didn't get a chance to say that I thought you did great photo-realistic space art. I've always wanted to tell you how much I enjoyed looking at the snowscape picture you painted called, '*Saturn As Seen From Titan*.' So familiar yet so strange." Almost breathlessly you ask, "What are you painting now?"

Chesley, young, bright eager, gets up so you can better see his latest creation: You gulp. It's Alleymanderous, dressed like your grandmother, holding out, in an outstretched paw, a Mars Bar.

The scene changes to third person viewpoint where you see yourself running down that sidewalk, with the sky filled with meteors, asteroids, smashing into the surface, exploding around you. You come to a cliff and the Great Northern Ocean of Mars is seething, roiling and steaming from the heat of the impacts and looking down, beside you, Alleymanderous is there. He is dressed up as Buck Rogers and he points, saying, "Not science fiction but science fact."

"What does it mean?" you ask.

"What Ray Bradbury could not know: so right, so wrong. Mars was but a canvas for our fantasies that the Universe really was a nice place and we really weren't alone and there wasn't really any violence anywhere."

When you look to Alleymanderous again, he momentarily changes to a feline Beaver Cleaver from *Leave It to Beaver*. And he looks up imploring. "Can we go to Mars? I hear i's really neat. Can we, huh? Can we? Can we?"

You look out to the chaos before you, of a Mars not terraforming but martianforming and your heart wants to break.

Abruptly night falls, and just as abruptly, it is daylight: the Northern Sea has vanished, the sky is pink and Alleymanderous, now in a space suit, looks out over the scene.

You abruptly realize that you, too, are wearing a space suit and you wonder, more to yourself, *What happened*?

You hear Alleymanderous in your earphones: "The Mars equivalent to Reaganomics."

"What?" you ask.

"Or," says Alleymanderous, "what happened to you at the hands of your grandmother."

Night again, then day dawns. But it's a world you do not recognize. A great sea is before you, and you stand in what appears to be grass. The sky is a deep and wonderful blue. Before you, an ocean, the waves crashing upon a rocky shore with a mighty and slow rhythm like the slow, powerful and ponderous heartbeat of the world, *Ka-woomph, ka-woomph, Ka-woomph.*

You turn around; not too far off in the distance, you see a great cliff and beyond that, the gentle slope of a great volcano with icy white summit.

And beside you, dressed in child's clothing, blue shorts, red, short sleeve shirt, there is Alleymanderous, a child-sized kitten, and you can tell he's excited at what he sees. Somehow, he is able to smile, his green eyes so dilated that they look as if they're taking in the entire world.

He looks up to you, face filled with delight and wonder, and says, "You as Mars; the way you would have been without your grandmother." He looks back to the scene and you watch a moon, *Deimos? Pho-*

bos? tumble, fall, through the sky. Alleymanderous looks back up to you again and says, "You as Mars, as you could still be, in spite of your grandmother."

You reach down and gently stroke Alleymanderous on the head, and you can feel his whole body vibrate, thunder with his purring. You feel the wonder, the power and nature of the dream that can yet become—the reality. But—

2:30 am

—of course, it all changes. And the next thing you know, you're sitting in a bright blue lawn chair. Above you, a starless sky, at the horizon, brightness, like the sun rising but appearing to be stuck and the light is unchanging. It's neither warm, nor cold; you look down and touching the ground, you feel the texture of the surface: slightly coarse, not hard, not soft; it almost reminds you of a dark gray sheet of asphalt stretching off into infinity. Abruptly, you turn your head and there is Alleymanderous, sitting in a lawn chair, a laptop computer on his lap. You didn't think it was anatomically possible for cats to have laps, but there sits Alleymanderous, diligently tapping away on his computer. You aren't even going to guess how a cat can type on a keyboard. But he does: *tap-tappy-click-clikkity click – tap —*

You look at him. He's dressed in a blue shirt with red flowers printed on it in all shapes, sizes. He's got on red shorts and you can make out lettering on one lower left side of the shorts, just above the opening, in yellow lettering: *CatzMeYow.*

"I'd hate to guess what you're writing," you say.

Alleymanderous stops, then reads aloud. "—of course, it all changes. And the next thing you know, you're sitting in a bright blue lawn chair. Above you, a starless sky, at the horizon, a brightness—"

"Stop," you say. "It kinda feels like *déjà vu.*"

"I was just getting to the good part," says Alleymanderous.

"That's OK," you say.

Alleymanderous looks at you for a moment more, then continues writing.

"Well?" you finally ask.

Alleymanderous keeps on typing, *tik-tikka-tappy-click-click*—He stops, picks up a cup of coffee. There's the "Catbucks" logo again.

"Where'd you get that?"

Alleymanderous points to his right; off a ways is an espresso stand. You get up and walk toward it, but as you walk, it appears you don't get any closer to it. Finally, you stop, think better of it and when you turn to go back—you frown. No chairs, no Alleymanderous, no nothing. So, you decide to keep on going and, turning around again, you notice that the espresso stand is even farther away. A song comes to mind, *Who was it?* you think, *Who was it—oh, yeah, yeah, Paul Simon,* "...nearer your destination/The more you slip slidin' away."

So, you stop. You sit. You close your eyes.

"Is that one shot or two?"

You open your eyes; right before you, the espresso stand. You get up, reach into your pocket but—nothing. Beseechingly, you look at the person behind the counter. You suddenly realize who it is.

It's your grandmother—but she's, what, you figure, seventeen? Eighteen?

"Surprised?" she asks, "that I was once a young girl who had dreams?"

She's sensual, her hair blonde, curled, her eyes green, dressed in a red dress with bright blue flowers.

"Two shots," you mumble.

"Soy? Rice Milk? Whole milk? Two percent? One percent? Non-fat?"

"Rice," you say.

"We don't have that," she replies.

"Then why did you say you had it?"

"Because we usually carry it. And I never *said* I had it."

"What do you have?"

"Everything else."

She serves you up a double shot latte. You sip it and you spit it out. "This tastes dreadful," you say. "What did you make it out of?"

Your grandmother, dressed in a blue shirt with red flowers and blue shorts and who now looks to be about age ten, says, "Apple juice." Then she says, "You just said you wanted 'everything else,' so what I had was apple juice. Not good, huh?"

"Dreadful," you reply.

"Did it ever occur to you people make mistakes?" she asks.

You look at your drink, pour it on the ground. "Apparently."

When you look back, you find yourself staring at the girl who slowly changes into—Alleymanderous. "Just having fun," he says, "but the principle really is the same."

"What's that?" you ask. "You can't get what you want?"

"No," says Alleymanderous, coming out of the espresso stand and then sitting back in the lawn chair. "People are messed up. It's up to you to decide how much you want them to affect you."

You look at Alleymanderous, then you sit down onto your blue lounge chair which has magically appeared. Then it dawns on you: *how much power do we have in how we let others affect us?*

As if answering your question, Alleymanderous says, "Maybe the issue is, why do we keep trusting people who hurt us?"

You laugh. "It's like a child thinking that somehow, some way, it will eventually be different, even though the results are always the same. That's a good definition of being nuts, isn't it?"

Alleymanderous goes back to typing on his computer. *Tick-tick-tap, tap, tappy-click—*

"What are you writing now?" you ask.

Alleymanderous looks up, green eyes shining. "God, this is fun," he says. "Even I learn something."

"Like—?" you begin.

"Get this: maybe it has to do with expectations of trust being generated, then not followed up on. So, whose problem is it really?"

Alleymanderous looks at you like this is the most obvious thing in the world and you feel as obtuse as ever, but you think you get it. "The person who does that has the problem," you say slowly. "It becomes your problem if you keep on believing someone who you know doesn't follow through—"

"—but you keep expecting them to—*then* who has the problem?"

You know the answer to that. *Boy,* you think, *boy, do* you *know the answer to* that. And as you sit there, under that pale sky, on that dark plain with the sun almost rising but not rising, as you sit there, pondering, knowing the answer to that question—you discover, to your dismay, all the implications of that answer. And...

2:49 am

...when you open your eyes again in the dream, you find yourself looking at a television. Alleymanderous is in a space costume complete with silver plastic helmet with little antennas sprouting out of it on either side, each ending in a small red ball. He sits there. His tunic has a picture on the front of it, a cat, soaring up to the heavens, face with an expression of purposefulness, one arm out-stretched, the other, folded in front of his chest, his paw, balled into a fist, and a caption beneath it reads, "Mighty Cat."

Alleymanderous points to the television. "Watch," he says, "this is where it gets good."

Dumbly, you stare at the screen. It shows a group of men in security uniforms addressing a man in a suit and tie who you recognize as your father.

"Dad —" you begin.

"Be quiet," says Alleymanderous, "you gotta *hear* this."

You look to your dad. He looks composed, but there's that edge of nervousness — you see it in his eyes — that you've always recognized about him, ever since you could remember. Then you remember him always saying to you, "Save your sanity — drive a bus for a living."

You begin to understand why he never talked much about his work.

Alleymanderous reaches over and turns up the sound. You look at one guy, tall, with dark hair. He's looking at your father harshly. "Are you *sure* you're not an alien?"

"No," your father says, "I am not now nor have I ever been an alien."

The guy who asked the question — his head abruptly turns into the head of *The Fly*, from the movie of the same name.

Another man asks your father, "It's OK if you are an alien. We're here to help you. We want to know about your saucer technology."

"I tell you," says your father, "I know nothing! I am not an alien."

"Are you sure?" asks the man. Abruptly his head turns into the head of the creature from the movie, *The Creature from the Black Lagoon*.

"I'm positive. Why do you think I'm an alien?"

A fat fellow, with a big nose and dark little eyes says, "Just answer the questions."

Suddenly, his head turns into that of the Monster from the Id from the movie, *Forbidden Planet*.

And the heads of other men change: one turns into that of a spider, another into the Metaluna Monster from the movie, *This Island Earth*. Finally your father, who remains unchanged, asks, "Why? Why are you asking me these questions? How many times must I tell you that I am not an alien?"

Another man, before his head changes to that of Frankenstein's Monster says, "We know you are not like us."

"Thank God," says your father.

The T.V. goes blank.

Alleymanderous says, "Not very good years, that McCarthy era."

You sniff. "Any better now?"

"Define now," says Alleymanderous.

"11 January, 2004."

Alleymanderous nods. "Point well taken. Some say it's even worse."

"Sure looks like that," you sigh.

"But," says Alleymanderous, "be that as it may, and given that it has happened before, what are you to make of all of this?"

You shrug. "My father had guts?"

"Did he?" Alleymanderous removes his space helmet.

"Guess so."

"What happened to him?"

"He got a job driving a bus after he got out of the security business—took his own advice. But—"

"But?"

"I'd rather not—"

"But—?"

You look at Alleymanderous for a long time. "You know what happened," you finally say.

"Yes," says Alleymanderous, "but I want to hear it from you."

"He and his bus and five passengers never got to their destinations one night."

"Oh?" Alleymanderous sits on his haunches, out of costume, sitting there in his now resplendent brown and white fur, those yellow-green eyes, so alien, boring into your soul. You stop, not wanting to continue.

"Oh?" says Alleymanderous, "and were they abducted by aliens?"

"—can't rule that out." You grimace as you say this, because it's so idiotic, but you continue, "No sign of the bus, my father, nobody. Just—gone. No trace. Zero, zilch, nada."

"So," says Alleymanderous, "as far-fetched as it seems—"

You sigh. "You can't know everything, and in the end, you can't be sure of anything, even as unlikely as it is—"

Alleymanderous sedately licks a paw. "Can't know everything. For to know everything—"

You can't *stand* where this conversation is going. "I know," you say, "I know. It's the same argument for why one shouldn't give up, because to give up means you know the future and there is only one entity that knows that, knows everything—"

"God," says Alleymanderous.

"Yeah, you become God because you know all, you know the future and therefore no matter how bad things seem, no matter how off the wall things are—"

"There's hope," says Alleymanderous. "String Theory says that there may be eleven dimensions and the universe may be but a bubble in a fabric of bubbles, the extent of which is beyond comprehension; in such a scheme of things, even death is called into question—"

You close your eyes. You hate this dialogue. You hate Alleymanderous. You don't know where your daddy has gone but it sure the hell can't be because of alien abduction—that's—

Woooooosh—you feel a tremendous sucking sound then you are buffeted, pummeled, pushed and then everything is still. You open your eyes just in time to see a bus that has roared on by. The dust settles. You look up—the sky is pale green; a giant moon looms in the sky and over the horizon, a ringed moon rises. Coming out of the distance, you see a rooster tail of dust and then within seconds, a car pulls up to you. In front of the car and built into it——Robbie, the Robot from *Forbidden Planet*. He says in that Robbie-the-Robot voice, "Sir, please get in."

You shake your head, go around to the side and in the passenger seat, Morbius' daughter, Altaira, sits—but it isn't really his daughter; it's Alleymanderous dressed up like his daughter.

"Better hurry up," says Alleymanderous. "If we step on it, we might be able to catch up to the bus and—"

"My father," you sigh as you get in. You sit, buckle your seat belt and Robbie says, "Hang on gentleman." He pauses, then adds, "and gentle cat."

3:11 am

...you're speeding along with Alleymanderous at your side, dressed as Altaira, from the movie, *Forbidden Planet*. You're speeding across the landscape of what you assume to be the surface of a planet that, if it isn't Altair IV, it's a close approximation. You hang on and you wonder how fast you're going—you suspect it's over 200 mph—and you wonder why Robbie doesn't trip or run into something; you can't see a road. Ahead, you see a bus; you draw closer, closer, then—it becomes airborne and becomes infinitesimally small.

Then *you* become airborne and although you're moving, it feels like you're drifting.

"Can't you go faster, Robbie?" you ask.

"Siw," the robot says, "my name isn't weally as you pwonounce it. It's Wobbie."

You blank. "Wobbie? Wobbie, the Robot?"

"Siw. Wobbie the Wobot."

You shake your head. "Just a while ago, you could pronounce 'r's,' so what's changed?"

"We have entewed a section of the time wawp continuum. Pawt of the pwoblem is that wobots can no longerw pwonounce ewtain lettews like—" Wobbie shortcircuits; blue and red electrical discharges blast through the circuitry that is visible through the clear plastic that encases it.

Alleymanderous sits there, now no longer dressed as Altaira—matter of fact, you realize that Alleymanderous doesn't even really look like a cat anymore, but like something created by Picasso: he's two dimensional and speaks somehow out of a mouth on his left cheek. "Going through different dimensions is tough on appearances," he says.

This is getting so bizarre, you think, and then it dawns on you, "Um—" you say, "I guess I'm affected—"

As if on cue, Alleymanderous holds up a mirror. You shriek. You look as if out of a painted nightmare, a combination of Dali and Picasso: a hand sticks out of your head, your leg is bent up, like that part of you is part bird. Your nose is flattened to one side, and your wristwatch is melting. The last thing you remember thinking about was asking Wobbie if this Universe where robots can't pronounce "r" has something to do with avoiding legal issues of copyright infringement from Walt Disney Studios, but now it's the farthest thing from your mind. You have this deep feeling of nausea and you feel like you could throw up, but you know you don't dare, because you don't think you could stand what the experience would be like here, much less how it would all look. Besides, you realize that you are approaching the bus driven by your father—but the closer you get, the smaller the bus becomes—"or," says Alleymanderous, as if able to read your thoughts, "the larger we grow—"

"Oh, geeze," you say, "I grow infinitely huge and the bus grows infinitely small—"

"Something like that."

"So the closer we get—"

"The farther you grow apart."

"This isn't going to work, is it?" you say.

"Not likely," says Alleymanderous. His mouth has now moved to the place where it should be, and his nose, in the middle of his forehead, is upside down. He still holds a mirror up to you with a weirdly splayed paw, and even though the mirror ripples and slowly begins to melt, you can now see an ear where your nose should be and your eyes are fluorescent blue. You avoid looking at the rest of your body, but looking ahead, you notice that Wobbie hasn't changed.

"So, how do you stop being weirded out by this dimensional stuff?" you ask.

"Kwell technology," he replies. Then, "Instwuctions, siw?"

You look to your father's bus ahead of you: it's now so small it could fit in your hand. "Bummer," you say, "That his infinite smallness will be a function of my infinite vastness."

"Or," says Alleymanderous, now glowing pale orange, "your infinite vastness is a function of his infinite smallness."

"Same thing," you say.

"Yes," says Alleymanderous.

"And at the point of touching—" you muse.

"To each other, the other vanishes."

"Destroy each other?" you ask.

"No, just pop into different universes."

"Instwuctions?" asks Wobbie.

You sigh. "Well, I'll sure never get to talk to him this way. Can we go to a different dimensionality?"

"As you wish, siw."

Wobbie backs off and you notice the bus getting larger, larger and you can finally read the destination of it on the back display above the windows: ROUTE 11, LONGING. Then you notice Alleymanderous begins to look like his old self; still strapped into the seat. You now see him with glasses, smoking a specially-made pipe, with a beard and dressed in a natty suit from what appears to be the late 1800s. "Cheer up," he says, "we'll get that connection with your father," he pauses, "or *some* sort of connection;" then shrugging, "at least a resolution." He pauses again. "Maybe."

"You sound like Freud," you say.

Alleymanderous smiles. "Freud E. Cat."

"E?" you ask.

"Existential."

"I don't know—" you begin.

"Nothing to worry about, you don't have to be a fraidy cat. Now. Tell me about your mother."

You begin to say something, but suddenly—

"Hang on Gentlemen," says Wobbie. Before you, a wall of light; light everywhere, pulsing, shimmering brightly. You slam through it and it's not unlike plunging into a pool of warm water except that you don't get wet. When you get to the other side, you find yourself driving your old 1965 Blue Dodge Coronet, and it's a beautiful day. You're driving somewhere—it looks like a mountain pass in the Cascades. You glance over and there is Alleymanderous, still in a seat belt, but now dressed up in hiking shorts, boots—you don't even begin to wonder how he can wear them—and he's got a hat on like you see folks wearing in the Alps.

"Well," you say, "this is sort of more normal." Up ahead, you see a bus coming at you, barreling at you, and you think you see your father in the driver's seat as he passes you going in the opposite direction, upside down, right over the top of you, and you watch him, in your rearview mirror, vanish—into infinity.

3:22 am

...you're driving that blue, 1965 Dodge Coronet and you realize that you've missed another chance to connect with your father. Alleymanderous, noticing your despair, simply says, "Well, maybe it's not meant to be after all."

You hate that thought, as you keep driving in this dreamscape.

Alleymanderous, who knows you really, really well, says, "I bet you hate that thought."

You cop to it. "Yeah. I do."

Alleymanderous, still in his hiking attire, pulls out a granola bar for cats. You glance to the gay packaging; you've seen it before, little images of muscular cats, scaring rats and dogs. You know the brand: POWER-CAT—"With catnip protein for extra energy." You watch Alleymanderous' paws morph so the toes become more like fingers and he can not only dig it out of his hiking shorts, but peel off the wrapper as well. Doing so, he then tosses the wrapper out the window.

"Don't litter," you say.

"It's a dream," says Alleymanderous. "Remember?"

In your rearview mirror you watch the wrapper abruptly transform into a huge blue butterfly and flap wildly away.

"Oh, yeah—" you say. "That's—"

Before you can finish and as if on cue, the trees on either side of you sort of blur, and vertically run as if melting. The road lifts as if detaching from the earth. And you say, "Oh, God, now what?"

Alleymanderous is no longer wearing hiking clothes, but saffron robes like a Buddhist monk. He says nothing for a minute, and finally he looks at you and says, "Dream."

You look around. "But I'm already dreaming."

"Dream again—"

You blink.

You are on the bus. Your father is driving. Alleymanderous is dressed up in granny glasses, an old-timey printed skirt and looks like a little grandmother—just like—your mother's mother. You sit next to him? Her? You're not sure, but you sit on the seat next to the door and you can look at your dad from the right side.

"Dad?" you ask, "Dad, is that—"

"Fourth and Blanchard," he says, "still the ride free zone."

You look around. It looks like you're in Seattle, but all the buildings are gutted, dark, and above, a massive galaxy slowly turns. You are filled with foreboding. You notice that Alleymanderous has taken up knitting and he/she says, "Might be a tad cold out there, honey—I'm knitting you a space blanket made out of NASA spin-off technology."

You don't know what to make of this; outside, the streets are deserted. You try again. "Dad—can we talk? I want to say—"

"Fourth and Pike," says your father, "Movie district. The movie *Big Fish* is still playing as it has for centuries. The eternal quest of connection between father and son."

"I don't wanna watch a movie," you say, "I want—"

"And, of course, between mother and daughter. No difference."

The bus lurches forward.

"Hold on," your father says, "leaving Earth, next stop, *The Twilight Zone*."

Alleymanderous throws a ball of silver, spin-off-from-space-technology yarn at your father. "Hold up, sonny, you have to let a passenger on before you go there."

The bus slams to a stop, and on clambers Rod Serling, but he isn't really there, he's like a holographic projection; he's dressed in a 1962 suit and smoking a cigarette. He doesn't look at you, he looks off, like he's talking to a camera or to an unseen audience. The bus lurches forward again and Serling says, "A man, a strange cat, on a bus, trying to connect with someone. Will they finally do that? Or is this connection something that can only happen—in *The Twilight Zone*?"

Your father leans forward, touches a toggle switch on the console and *click*—Serling vanishes.

"Doesn't look good," observes Alleymanderous.

You try again. "Dad!"

He ignores you.

You touch him.

He vanishes.

Anguished, you wail, "Why? Why? Why?"

"I don't know," says Alleymanderous, continuing to knit, "and he probably doesn't know either, but *you're* driving this bus now."

"What? I don't wanna drive a bus."

"Like it or not," says Alleymanderous, "you can't get away from driving his bus." He/she looks at the garment with approval, then says, "Just do a better job of it."

"But—but—but—" And you find yourself in the driver's seat. A mighty galaxy swims toward you. "But—but—what about my father? How do I connect with my father?"

Alleymanderous puts down his/her knitting and looks at you through those granny glasses. "Just because you want to connect with him doesn't mean he can, or will, or is able to connect with you. It's all very generational, you know."

You watch the massive galaxy draw closer and then you have a flash of memory: how your father and *his* father couldn't connect either. You feel a rush of great sadness as you drive your father's bus on, on, on-ward—to the burning heart of the galaxy before you.

But—you abruptly stop.

You see your father drift by in front of the bus. He is in what appears to be a glass casket that is shaped like a bus. He wears his blue Metro uniform, and his hands hold a steering wheel.

"Bus driver to the end," you muse.

Alleymanderous, beside you, peers out though his/her granny glasses. "Maybe that was the problem," she/he says. "so identified with his job that he didn't know who he was and couldn't relate to anyone else."

"Least of all, me," you say.

"Generational," says Alleymanderous, "but—"

And your tears come.

"Doesn't help much, does it?" Alleymanderous looks at you with great sympathy.

You sit there sobbing your heart out for what wasn't, what could never be. And seeing him in that coffin—the finality of it hits you like a lightning bolt of searing ice rippling through your soul. Even now, no connection. *Nope. Nada. Zip. Zilch. Nothing.* God, how you *get* it and it breaks your heart.

"Just remember," says Alleymanderous, "it's about him, not you. Let go of the guilt, the shame that tells you that somehow it's your fault."

"I know," you wail, "I know, but still—"

Alleymanderous stands nearby, paw on the coin box, that has a fee schedule pasted on the front telling you how much it costs to ride this bus, and Alleymanderous softly says, "I know. I know."

Abruptly the bus lurches forward and you again drive on, on, on-ward—to the burning heart of the galaxy before you.

3:37 am

...in the dream you cover your eyes with your hands, but when noth-ing happens, you dare to slowly peek between your fingers. No bus. No galaxy. Now you're standing on a vast, gray, gritty plain; the pale blue sky above fades to a white line at the horizon, as if sunrise is coming, but is somehow—stuck. It isn't warm, it isn't cold—you wonder, *Is there such a thing as a neutral temperature?* You don't know what you are doing here—the last thing you remember—you think back. You can't remember *what* you were doing before you discovered yourself here. *Great,* you think, *fucking great. Where the hell am I?* But there is something else, a sense of *déjà vu*—somehow, this is familiar—not the scene, but *something.* It's like you're re-dreaming a dream.

Off in the distance, you see something coming toward you; there is a rooster tail of dust behind it. *A car?* you wonder. What the hell—it comes at you and then you recognize it for what it is—it's the ground car piloted by Robbie the Robot out of the 1956 movie, *Forbidden Planet.* It pulls up to you, stops. "Get in please," Robbie requests.

"Didn't we just—" you begin. You shake your head but somehow you just can't remember, even though this feels so familiar. You go around to the side and, strapped into one seat is Alleymanderous, your cat, dressed in the uniform of the crew of the saucer from the movie.

You ponder this. You don't know where you were before now, but you sure as hell recognize some things.

You look at Alleymanderous. "You sure don't look like Captain Adams."

"I'm not," says Alleymanderous.

"Haven't we—" you begin. "Weren't you wearing—I keep thinking your name is Altaira."

"I don't confirm it," says Alleymanderous, "but I don't deny it."

"So what's all this about? Where the hell am I?"

You get in the car and Alleymanderous looks at you and says, "It's not Altair IV."

"That's supposed to help?" you ask.

"Fasten your seat belts, gentlemen," says Robbie.

You do. You want to ask Alleymanderous more questions, but suddenly the car accelerates and you don't know how fast you're going, but you suspect it's close to 300 mph. It's impossible to talk. You notice the direction you are going; it's away from the bright horizon; it's in the opposite direction, like you are headed into the dark edge of an oncoming night and you know you don't like this and sure enough, it grows darker, darker and in all of this you keep wondering, *what the hell am I doing here?*

Suddenly, it's pitch black and you abruptly stop moving.

Then you hear, *tinka-tinka-tinka-tinka* and you know what that is—it's the theme music to *The Twilight Zone*. Again, that sense of *déjà vu*. Just as suddenly, it's light again, and standing before you is Alleymanderous, in an early 1960s suit, somehow standing perfectly erect, paws folded in front of him just the way Rod Serling looked; a cigarette resting between two toes. Alleymanderous even has the fur on the top of his head combed and looking like the hair style of Serling.

"What—" you say, "didn't we just—"

Alleymanderous says, in a voice almost exactly like Serling, "Meet Mr. _____."

You gulp. No name again.

"Mr. _____," Alleymanderous continues, "leads a quiet life, or so he thought, until he awoke into a dream—and now he must go where the dream takes him—to another dimension? To his subconscious? Maybe— but to understand where he is, he first must travel through—*The Twilight Zone*."

You don't like this.

"Alleymanderous," you say, "Alleymanderous—"

Alleymanderous-turned-Serling, walks away and you stand there, as if standing before a blank wall. Suddenly, the wall becomes an image and the image sharpens—it is your family at Christmas time and there is your grandmother, the one who smacked you for wanting another helping of oatmeal, your dad, angry, and your mother, looking apprehensive, your sister looking away, vacant. Suddenly the scene becomes three dimensional; they all turn to you and suddenly you get this *gestalt* of them: you somehow suddenly "see" them—your grandmother's face becomes that of a scorpion; her son, your father, his head becomes a black hole from being stung so much by his mother that he has collapsed in on himself. Your mother's head becomes that of a leech and your sister's head just vanishes.

Then you hear screaming—you wonder—then you abruptly know who it is who's screaming.

It's you.

3:41 am

...and you scare yourself almost awake. You're vaguely aware of the covers: Alleymanderous stirs, purrs. It's dark, you drift and *flash* a scene comes to you and you go to a different sort of dream. You find yourself sitting... somewhere... sitting on your butt, rocking, rocking, and you hear, "That's the way it was, wasn't it?"

In the darkness, you feel yourself nodding, then whispering, "That's the way it was."

It's quiet for a minute: then you hear a purring and you feel Alleymanderous rubbing against you.

"And the only one there for you —"

" — was my cat."

Purrrrrrr —

" — and the only one you truly felt safe with was —"

" — my cat."

Purrrrr – and you feel Alleymanderous moving against you, nuzzling you, so affectionate.

" — and the only one you really felt connected to was —"

" — my cat," and suddenly you break down and sob. "Oh, God," you whisper, "that *is* the way it was — what might have been — where would I be had my family been healthy and loving and not so fucked up?" and you sob and rock, sob and rock and then you hear again: *Purrrr. Purrrr. Purrrr.*

A memory comes to you — when you were four, in the wooded lot next door, sitting on a log, your cat coming up to you, putting his paws on your knee and looking into your eyes so intently and you then realized, you were not alone. On some unconscious level you realized then that gods and angels and the beauty and magic of the universe and life could present itself in so many forms and you felt this immense sense of gratitude, that you, too, had a right to be here. You would be safe, and love can come in so many forms and so many ways. And in that moment, you understood faith as the universe opened to you and filled your eyes with light.

You feel Alleymanderous rubbing against you, feel the rumble of his purr; you reach and there he is; his fur soft and silky. You drift into a dream where you see the sky slowly lighten and Alleymanderous coming to you again, putting his paws on your knee. You look into those eyes, understanding again the forms and ways in which gods and angels appear, and you now understand that your task is to remember that, to look for that in all life around you in this stunning and wonderful world in which you were born.

"And remember," says Alleymanderous, "compassion."

"Even to those people I was born to," you whisper.

"Even them," says Alleymanderous, "especially them. Particularly, them — for they died so early in their lives, and having died, could only pass on to you the pain of their dying long before their death. What greater tragedy? For you, what greater hope. You have not forgotten the magic. And you have kept it alive."

And in this dream you sit there, in sadness yet wonder, in grief yet hope, and Alleymanderous sits beside you as the heavens fill with light; your hand stroking his head, his back and Alleymanderous fills you with his song, his experience of the beauty and wonder of his being: *Purrrr. Purrrrr. Purrrr.*

Then it becomes quiet and...

3:53 am

...something goes *snap* and the next thing you know, you're in Red Square, in Moscow. There is a massive parade underway; you see Soviet citizens waving red flags with the hammer and sickle; with a sick feeling, you realize that this has to be the pre-collapse Soviet Union. But what year? Nothing, of course, is familiar, except you see a modern ZiL limousine flash by, and through the crowd, you can see a parade of the military might of the Soviet Union; huge missiles parade by and you can make out Lenin's tomb.

"Impressive, comrade, no?" And, right there, beside you, is a big version of — Alleymanderous. He's got on a cap that looks like a bulky baseball cap and there's a red star on the front of it. He wears glasses and almost looks a bit like a feline Chekhov. He's dressed in clean, but dated, plain clothing: blue shirt, dark brown slacks, serviceable, but drab. On the collar of the shirt, a little pin of — you look closely —

"Trotsky," says Alleymanderous.

"Trotsky?" you ask. "That's impossible." You know your history well enough. "Trotsky is an unperson."

Alleymanderous looks to you for a minute. "Who are we talking about?" he asks.

"Leon Trotsky," you point to the pin that Alleymanderous is wearing, then you look again. "Stalin?"

Alleymanderous nods. "The Great Helmsman himself."

There is thunderous music, a pause, and then the somewhat mournful dirge of the Soviet National anthem. You don't know what to do with your hands, but Alleymanderous stands there, paw up to his furry white forehead, as if saluting. Tears come to his eyes. "Praise the Motherland," he says. "Death to all counter-revolutionary scum. Down with U.S. hegemony and imperialism."

You still don't know what to do with your hands, so you put one up to your chest, but not over your heart, because you think America has the corner on that patriotic gesture, as you hope that somehow this looks reverent and Socially Realistic enough that you won't get in hot water for not looking sufficiently patriotic. Apparently, it works. No one seems to be paying much attention to you or Alleymanderous.

A valise appears in Alleymanderous' paws. "Want to see some cool photos?" he asks.

You aren't exactly sure why you don't find this odd, but you nod.

Alleymanderous hands you a picture. You recognize it as Seattle, Washington. You know this place very well and, though you can't place the date, it looks contemporary. It's a scene looking westward: there is the Space Needle, Elliot Bay, the Olympic Mountains. You look at it blankly and say, "That's just how it looks." You hand the photo back to Alleymanderous.

"You sure?" he asks. He hands it back to you.

You look at it again. The foreground is the same, there's the Space Needle but the Olympics now look as mighty as the Himalayas.

"Stunning," you say, "but someone has been playing with foreshortening the shot. That's not the way the Olympics *really* look."

Alleymanderous somehow smiles and you get the idea that there is great humor in this for him. "But if you'd never been to Seattle, how would you know that they didn't look like that?" He gives you another photograph. It's a scene of Mt. Rushmore. There's Lincoln, Jefferson, Roosevelt, Washington.

You shrug. "So?" You give it back to him.

Alleymanderous looks at it, gives it back to you. Wordlessly, you look at it: Lincoln, Jefferson — you stare — Reagan and Gorbachev?

"Gorbachev?" you say, "*Gorbachev*? He wasn't an American president." But looking at it closely — it looks like it's absolutely real.

Alleymanderous produces yet another picture. It's a picture of Lenin's mausoleum, and standing atop it, in the viewing area, you see Khrushchev, Beria, Stalin. The three of them wave to the masses of proletarians who have turned out for some event. You look at the picture for a long time. You then hand it back to Alleymanderous who, again, looks at it, then hands it back to you. You stare. It's Khrushchev, a young Leonid Brezhnev and Stalin. "What happened to Beria?" you ask.

Alleymanderous takes the picture back without saying anything and instead, gives you a picture of President Bill Clinton at a Cabinet meeting. You commit this to memory. You are absolutely sure of what you are seeing. You give it back to Alleymanderous. You take in the surrealness of the scene, standing on bricks in Red Square, in Moscow on a clear and sunny day with a military parade going by and you feel very much as if you're in a Lewis Carroll story, or else *1984*, and you have to admit, given the politics of the last thing you remember about the U.S., it sure feels like it's *1984*. Alleymanderous hands back the photograph of Bill Clinton sitting at a Cabinet meeting, but this time, a young lady is sitting on his lap, giving his ear a tongue job and the President's hand is up her blue dress.

"This is *dreadful*," you say.

"Oh—" says Alleymanderous, "'scuse me—I feel a New Soviet Cat-spell coming over me—excuse me—I have to transform my identity for the state. Don't worry," he says, "you'll get used to it in your time, your place."

You watch Alleymanderous transform: he rolls up his sleeves, puts one foot forward as though boldly striding into the future; puffs out his chest, his jaws set in a firm line, the eyes fixed upon a Grand Socialist Future and from somewhere, a wind comes up, blows back his hair, ruffles his shirt as if he's standing in a field of wheat, gazing at a collective farm's tractor. He holds that pose for a moment then—he's back. "Have to do that every so often," he says. "Have to get into that thought/physical-mind-frame to go forward into the future when the state will wither away and we'll all be truly socialist." He sighs. "Wow. Wotta rush. Free catnip for everyone."

You sigh and say, "But what has this got to do with me?"

"Comrade," says Alleymanderous, "it's like Stalin said; 'Those who cast the votes decide nothing; those who count the votes decide everything.' Power, power, power. If you challenge the status quo, the status quo will do everything it can to maintain its power—" Alleymanderous stops for a minute, then, eyes bright, he continues, "—after all, you have nothing to lose and everything to gain; those in power have nothing to gain and everything to lose, so you have to expect they will do all sorts of things — like rigging elections, lying, doctoring photographs. Absolute power tends to corrupt absolutely and — " Alleymanderous looks at you like your intelligence is just a notch above that of a tree frog, " — it's really no surprise what those in power will do to alter the reality of those they deem inferior." Alleymanderous smiles. "Need proof?"

"Um — " you say, "the photographs are obviously doctored."

"But," says Alleymanderous, "you have only your memory to prove that and memories are notoriously unreliable. Remember Winston Smith, in *1984*, working in the Ministry of Truth, rewriting history?"

"I know what I know — " you say.

"So thought Winston Smith," says Alleymanderous. "Do you?" he asks, "Do you? Do you know what you know?"

Flash

When you open your eyes, you are in a room, the television is on; it looks like some sort of travelogue — there is Mt. Rushmore and you stare: Lincoln, Jefferson, Reagan and Gorbachev stare stern and granite-eyed to the horizon. The next thing you see is a news item about the impeachment of Bill Clinton, and there's that damning photograph of him, in a cabinet meeting, with a woman on his lap giving his ear a tongue job while his hand is up her blue dress. Then you glance out the window and — beyond the Space Needle, the Olympic Mountains rise majestically, as high as the Himalayas.

"But," says Alleymanderous, "you're missing the best part of all — what this is really all about — " and he points to the walls.

Photographs. Photographs of your family; there: a family portrait of your mother, father, your sister, you, all grinning, happy, and in a separate photograph, your grandmother, in pale blue dress, the tones of color done so softly, she smiling and, at the bottom of the photograph, a note, "To my beloved grandson, how I treasure you."

4:21 am

...and the next thing you know, it's New Year's Eve. You look out the window to the Tower from where the fireworks will be fired off at midnight and glancing at the calendar on the nearby wall, you suddenly notice that the year following the word, "December" is gone. You stare at it and you think, somewhat dumbly, *geeze — it was there a minute ago —* You look to the photograph for December and instead of a picture of a snow-clad Mt. Rainier, it's a picture of Mt. Rainier — erupting.

"Irritating, isn't it?"

You turn and there is Alleymanderous, wearing a Hawaiian grass skirt, his ears protruding from a black wig. From somewhere, soft and sensuous Hawaiian music begins and Alleymanderous, with great dexterity, although it looks really strange, puts his paws behind his head and, standing on his hind legs, gyrates his hips with a sensuality that you are embarrassed to look at. You turn away.

"Getting turned on?" asks Alleymanderous.

You continue to look out through the window, and, where the Tower was, where the city was — it's now a vast, still-steaming, lava plain below you.

The music abruptly stops.

"Cat's can't do the hula," you say.

"This one can," says Alleymanderous. "Care for some *poi*?"

You find yourself fretful. "What happened to New Year's? What happened to the Tower? Where's my city? Why is Mt. Rainier erupting? What year is it?"

You sit hard on the chair. To make things even worse, you notice a moon rising in the *western* sky. You also notice it has rings.

"Picky, picky, picky," says Alleymanderous, sitting now on his haunches beside you. He's smoking something — you smell —

"Oh shit, you damn cat — you trying to get me busted?"

Alleymanderous takes in a deep drag, holds it, then offers the joint to you.

"No, I can't smoke it — "

Alleymanderous breathes out slowly and says, "Too bad. It's good shit. Besides, who's to bust us?"

You hear a furious pounding at the door; "Oh, my God — " you whimper. The door flies open and one after another, Alleymanderouses fill the room, all dressed in grass skirts, with black wigs, and when the room is packed, they all yell, "Who's to bust us? We're not in Kansas anymore, dodo!" The Hawaiian music starts up again, savage, energetic and the room, filled with what you assume to be clones of Alleymanderous, stand on their hind legs and begin to dance and shake their hips violently and you can't stand it. You close your eyes and suddenly, it's quiet.

You want to open your eyes but *God*, you think, *do I dare*?

And for whatever reason, you remember a line from a poem by T.S. Eliot, *The Love Song of J. Alfred Prufrock*: "Do I dare/Disturb the Universe?" *Better not,* you decide. *Besides, isn't the Universe disturbing me?*

Ka-chink, ka-chink, ka-chink—

God, you think, *I don't want to know—I don't want to have to open my eyes—I want to just sit here—*

Ka-chink, ka-chink—

You don't want to open your eyes, but you know you have to. You do. You immediately close them again. It's worse than you can possibly imagine. In the snapshot peek, you see:

1. You are sitting naked in a black plastic chair on

2. the tippy-top of a spire of rock and

3. it's thousands of feet down on all sides and

4. Alleymanderous is laboriously rock-climbing up to you, carefully and meticulously driving pitons in the rock and

5. A huge blimp is coming toward you and you catch the message on the side, a giant flashing sign that reads, "Channel 8, International/Intercosmos/Interdimensional Telecast, THE SHAME GAME, 24/7."

You cannot fathom why you don't jump. And you have this awful sense of what's coming and—it does. You hear the blimp coming closer and you hear a voice blaring out, and you gulp.

"AS THE ENTIRE WORLD CAN SEE, MY SON IS SO STUPID AND THOUGHTLESS THAT HE GETS HIMSELF IN THESE RIDICULOUS SITUATIONS THAT HE CAN'T GET OUT OF AND HE JUST GETS PARALYZED. BESIDES THAT, HE'S LAZY, AND WHILE I USED TO EXPECT GREAT THINGS OF HIM, I ALWAYS KNEW HE COULDN'T DO THEM." You know whose voice that is: it's your grandmother yelling about your father. You swallow hard. You can guess what's coming next and it does: the message is repeated verbatim, and this time, it's your father yelling the exact same thing, *at you.*

You hear laughter, and mixed in with it are jeers and horn blasts and you know your ears are so red hot you could fry eggs on them. You hear shouts of "LOSER!" and you can hear the voice of your ex-lover yell, "YOU ALWAYS WERE LOUSY AT PEOPLE SKILLS AND ROTTEN IN BED AND I GOTTA STUD NOW WHO FUCKS ME TWENTY TIMES TO SUNDAY AND I COME EVERY TIME!"

More laughter, and the amped sound is horrendously loud; you feel your body vibrate with the sound. You don't dare look up; you know the blimp is right there and you can just imagine who else is on it and sure enough, you hear your mother, "YOU POOR THING I WAS AFRAID THIS WAS GOING TO HAPPEN I KNEW YOU COULDN'T DO IT YOU BETTER COME HOME AND GO TO BED YOU'RE NOT LOOKING WELL I'LL BRING YOU COOKIES AND A DAMP WASHCLOTH FOR YOUR FEVERED BROW YOU POOR SICKLY THING!"

Then your sister comes in: "YOU LITTLE FUCKER, YOU LITTLE WEENIE: EVERYONE FELT SORRY FOR YOU AND I'M THE ONE THAT GOT DIDDLED AND SMACKED AROUND AND IT'S ALL YOUR FAULT."

More laughter, horn blasts, applause and cheering and you just sit there, head down, not knowing who you hate more: your entire family, or yourself. And then you hear, *Ka-chink, ka-chink* – and then the voice of Alleymanderous: "It's understandable you'd feel hatred of your family, but the only reason you feel devastated, and so much self-hatred—"

You open your eyes to see Alleymanderous in his climbing outfit, the ropes and yellow climber's hard hat—and you look at him. You still hear the blimp, the commotion, the laughter, the derisive slurs, but you can still make out what Alleymanderous says: "Come on, you get it. You have to get it and until you get it—"

What Alleymanderous is saying is interrupted by your father lambasting you again. "I CAN'T TELL YOU HOW DISAPPOINTED I AM IN MY SON AND I EXPECTED GREAT THINGS OF HIM, AS LONG AS HE DIDN'T SHOW ME UP."

You look at Alleymanderous for a long time, and in spite of the ache and pain, dimly, somewhere, something in you goes, *click* and you numbly say to Alleymanderous, "—is because, unconsciously, I believe *they* are more right about me than *I* am about me."

"Whew!" says Alleymanderous.

"AHHHHHHHHHHHHHH!" comes the combined scream of your family, "YOU LITTLE BASTARD!"

You look over; the blimp has caught fire and almost instantly it's engulfed in flames, then falls like a rock.

Alleymanderous hands you a rope and as soon as you grab it—darkness.

When you can see again, you are back in your place, looking out the window. It's near midnight. You glance over to the calendar and—you sigh. "The year is still missing," you say.

In the background, you hear sitar music softly playing, and Alley-manderous, sitting beside you, has a joint in his paw. He's got sandals on and wears a saffron colored robe and looks something like a guru. Finally, he says, "Maybe there is no year that one's internal torment officially ends, just years that it becomes less intrusive." He looks thoughtful and then says, "Maybe it really does come down to what one chooses to believe about oneself — consciously — "

"That," you say, "and — "

Alleymanderous takes a long drag of his joint and looks at you expectantly. " — and — ?" he asks, breathing out sweet, blue smoke.

"And," you say, "compassion. Forgiveness."

Alleymanderous continues to look at you. "There's more. And? What's the rest of it?"

"I guess — " The memory of being on that pinnacle of rock, the horror of it, the shame of it still burns and with it the sense of injustice but you continue on, almost unbelieving of the words coming out of your mouth, " — guess I have to remember that those who treat others badly are simply showing how badly they treat themselves and how badly they were treated."

"Does that help?" says Alleymanderous.

You sigh, "Still feels crappy — but — yeah, yeah, it does help." You pause. "A lot, actually."

Alleymanderous says nothing. You look to the calendar again; in this dream, you realize, the year, the time, is meaningless, but this moment is timeless.

You take a sip of wine. He takes another hit off his joint; suddenly the fireworks are fired off from the Tower and the sky is alive, crackling, booming, thundering with fire and light.

BUT — it's probably more like —

...in the background, you hear sitar music playing softly. Alleyman-derous sits there, with a joint in his paw and says, "How forgiving you are."

"I'm trying," you reply. "It's hard."

"Yes," says Alleymanderous, "it is. How hard is it, really?"

"*Very* hard," you reply.

"Very hard as in — "

You get it. You sigh. "Almost impossible."

"Almost impossible as in —"

You get it again. Worse. Oh, shit. Do you *get* it — you want to believe the words, you really do — but what comes out of your mouth makes you sound like a Tourette's victim in full disease process: "THOSE MEAN GOD DAMN MOTHERFUCKERS I CAN NEVER FORGIVE THEM THOSE SLIMY COCKSUCKING —" You stop. Internally you say, *Oooops.*

"Well," says Alleymanderous with a look that, you swear, would look doleful on anyone else, "you get Brownie points for being truthful, but —"

"I know," you sigh, "I know."

And you *know* what is coming next. *God*, you think, *how do I change that which I cannot change even though I know I have to*? You close your eyes for a second and when you open them, you're back on that pinnacle of rock in a plastic chair again and you're chained to it. "Oh, holy shit," you whimper. You watch the sun set, and turning, you can see the shadow of the night coming — along the eastern sky, you see the shadow of the night approaching, that long dark shadow that stretches north to south and as it approaches, you notice something — you feel your muscles tense, your jaws clamp, the hair rising on the back of your neck — because the approaching shadow has eyes and, flashing orange in the light of the setting sun, you also know that the night — has teeth.

" — but wait — there's more." You *know* whose voice that is, and as you see the night approaching, you think weirdly of the Jabberwocky, "The jaws that bite/ the claws that catch..."

You wonder just *where* Alleymanderous is.

"You called?"

Alleymanderous appears wearing a rocket pack, a red helmet, and a blue flying suit with a hole for his tail, which, encased by flame retardant material, is between the two rockets attached like green inverted fire extinguishers to his back.

You see the night approach, the eyes and the flashing teeth and you say in a voice so high pitched and squeaky that you can't imagine that it is yours, you say, "Help me! Heeeeelp me!" and you have this weird image in your head of the last scene of the 50's movie, *The Fly*, where the fellow is caught in a spider's web, shrieking "Help me! Heeeeelp me!" as the spider is ready to do its nasty mandibular deed.

"Well," says Alleymanderous, hovering nearby, "you think you deserve help?"

"Yes!" you squeak.

Alleymanderous continues to bob about, pale blue flames issuing from his rocket pack. You are amazed at how quiet it is.

"Can you accept that which you cannot accept?"

"I don't know—" you wail.

The night comes closer.

"What's the solution?" asks Alleymanderous.

"I don't know—"

The night descends with a vengeance, and it's dark; you know you've fallen into the mouth, been swallowed up, and man, it's black. Then, curiously, you see light, and before you know it, you ponder what you see—a vast, slowly spinning, spiral galaxy.

Click. "Awesome, no?" You hear Alleymanderous' voice as though coming through earphones. Alleymanderous is again in a space suit and you realize that you are in one as well, but you also find yourself wondering if somehow the spacesuit had been there all along, or if you created yourself wearing one as soon as you realized you were in space.

Alleymanderous looks at you. "Don't wonder about things of no consequence," he says. "In a dream, some things make sense, others don't. However, right now, your main task—"

You guess what that is as you see yourself drifting to the galaxy, to the bright central hub of it. You say to Alleymanderous, "There's a black hole at the center of that galaxy and that's where I'm going isn't it? I may well die—"

"Picky, picky, picky," says Alleymanderous. "Now, the question—" His suit is bathed in the faintly yellowed light of the galaxy, now seemingly coming faster toward you, or you are moving faster toward it.

"I'm going to be stretched to infinity and pulled apart atom by atom, aren't I?" you ask wonderingly.

"More like quark by quark," says Alleymanderous. "But your time is happily infinitely finite. In the meantime, about the question—"

"—at the center of that galaxy is a black hole," you continue numbly. "I'll be destroyed."

"The question—" says Alleymanderous, as his tail switches. He rotates slowly about and looks at you upside down.

"How do I answer such a question?" you ask. "How do I accept that which I cannot accept?"

Alleymanderous laughs. "But that's the way it is; how does mortality accept the knowledge of its own mortality? How does one accept aging?

How do we accept our no longer being here? How does anyone accept anything that he/she cannot accept?"

Right now, you can't tell which you hate more, Alleymanderous, or you feeling fully the horror of your annihilation at the center of the galaxy. You idly wonder if the stretch socks you're wearing will be of any help. You smile stupidly to yourself. What an *insane* concern at *this* moment.

Click. You hear Alleymanderous on your helmet radio, "Now, are you *sure* there are some things you cannot accept?"

"I don't—" You remember the taunts, the insults, of all those who hurt *you* but then it dawns on you that just maybe you've hurt others.

"Maybe I can forgive—" you say meekly.

"No," says Alleymanderous, "maybe you *have* to forgive."

You still hate that idea: why *should* those who have hurt you be forgiven?

You look down. Your feet are being pulled toward the bright hub which conceals the black core of that galaxy. No, you think, no, your stretch socks aren't doing a fucking bit of good. But then the question again: *how do you accept that which you cannot accept?*

Oh, God, you think, you simply *have* to, because if you don't—your body is beginning to stretch to infinity and it is getting a mite warm near your feet.

"Time is getting tight," says Alleymanderous. "I have no choice *but* to accept that which I cannot accept—there is no other way."

Abruptly the central disk of the galaxy contracts, the gravity releases, and *snap*, the force of the stretching of your body releasing is like a cosmic rubber band and you're flung off to God Knows Where.

4:44 am

...and "God Knows Where" turns out to be a vast pile of popcorn, into which you have been flung. You look around, somewhat distracted, sink down a bit in the pile and nibble some. "Fresh," you say.

"Shh!" You look and there is your cat, Alleymanderous, sitting in a theater seat, his back to you. "This is the good part," he says. "This is where Dr. Morbius talks about the Id."

You look, and there is a movie screen, with *Forbidden Planet* playing and sure enough, Commander Adams is asking Dr. Morbius, "Dr. Morbius, what is the Id?"

"Id! Id! Id!" shouts Dr. Morbius, and then he launches into his big explanation of the Id, "an outdated term." Yes, yes, you know all about Freud, the Id as the seat of all the violent, carnal, lustful and primitive instincts which, now subdued by Prozac, weren't supposed to exist any more but—

"Yeowwwwl," howls Alleymanderous in a voice that sort of reminds you of Godzilla in heat. "Would you listen to that? 'Outdated concept'!"

Still a bit dazed, you listen to what Alleymanderous says, and you have the feeling that he's not real pleased. But above all, right now, you cannot fathom what you are doing in a huge pile of popcorn.

"Alleymanderous," you say, aware of a pitiful pleading in your voice, "what is this?"

Alleymanderous leaps out of his chair, becomes invisible, but you can see the popcorn flatten in the outline his paws leave as he walks, just like in the movie when the Monster from the Id walked. Then the projectionist plays a light ahead of you and you look up; outlined by the play of light, Alleymanderous towers over you, his howl deafening and you say, "Oh, holy shit!" as you scrunch down to bury yourself in the popcorn.

—and suddenly it's quiet. You wonder if it's OK to look. Is the Monster from the (Feline) Id still towering above you, ready to grab you in its mouth along with all the popcorn? You want to stay buried, it feels safe, but since it's so quiet, slowly you let yourself plow upward through the popcorn until it falls away and—nothing. You see, nothing.

Everything is blank. You're still surrounded by popcorn but you sense you are drifting, like you are peeking out from a popcorn ball in space and you want to rejoice, but at the same time, you're terrified. *Where the hell am I?* you wonder.

"Be not afraid." You look to your right and drifting on a cloud, comes Alleymanderous with tiger-striped wings and furry orange halo.

"Are you dead?" you ask.

"Alas," says Alleymanderous, "my Higher Executive Functions, Ego and Inner Child, all devoured by my Monster from my Id."

You don't quite know what to say. You do the best you can. "I'm sorry."

He plucks a string on the harp. *Plink.*

You look at Alleymanderous, floating there. "I never thought of you having an inner child," you say, "maybe an inner kitten."

Plink. Another string plucked. Alleymanderous stares soulfully at you. "Not very good at playing a harp," he muses.

You nod. "I always thought cats were better at purring or chasing wads of paper. You never cease to amaze me."

Plink. Alleymanderous stops. "This is too difficult. My claws keep getting caught in the string."

"So," you say, "I guess you're dead."

"No. The concepts of my inner psyche are. I'm still OK."

You shake your head. "You got wings."

"Special effects," says Alleymanderous.

"You're floating."

"Local gravity null-field." Abruptly, he falls, landing on all fours. "Local gravity null-field nullified." He smiles brightly. You're not quite sure how he does that, but he does. Then you think, in this *reality/dream/nightmare, anything is...* "Had you worried," he abruptly continues, sedately licking a paw.

"Yes and no," you say. "Before you were an angel, angelic rather, you had me terrified. *Were* you the Monster from the Id?"

Alleymanderous' stare is withering. "You don't get it," he says. "You just do not get it, do you? Listen! We're all *still* Monsters from the Id; we cats are *all* Id, but you people just try to cover it up with a light frosting of civilization. And lots of suppression. And," his tail lashes wildly, "denial."

"Jeeeze," you say, "cynical or what?"

Suddenly there is a searing light and a rumble and a shaking and you're knocked off your feet. You cover your head when suddenly a shock wave hits and you're lifted off the ground and blasted to someplace else. When you can see again, you're looking at a blasted, shattered landscape; you can barely breathe.

Alleymanderous appears in a military uniform, little beret on his head, gun at his side, his furry face covered by a gas mask.

It's dark. "What happened?" You look about with fear; nothing looks familiar at all.

"That was supposed to be Hiroshima but it kinda looks like the blast kept on going."

It's cold. It's terribly, *terribly* cold. You stand, hopping from one foot to the other. "Cold," you say, "why the hell is it so cold?"

Alleymanderous looks around. "'Tis a mite chilly, isn't it?" He looks at a watch he wears on his furry white right paw. "July 17th." From his left breast pocket, he pulls out a little gizmo which sort of looks like a cell phone; magically, again, his claws have become more like fingers and he can manipulate the device easily. "My GPS unit says we're supposed to be somewhere in India; the bomb sort of knocked us off a ways and—uh—also looks like it knocked us into the future as well."

You keep hopping about. "The future? What year is it?"

"2019."

"Why the hell is it so cold? I thought India had a hot climate and all." You look to the horizon but you see nothing, no mountains, just a vast, dark field that stretches off into a deeper darkness.

"Well," says Alleymanderous, "a guess. I bet the global warming kept on going, the Greenland Ice Sheet melted and dumped a mass of cold water into the North Atlantic, and the Deep Ocean Current shut down."

"So?" you ask.

"No heat exchange from the tropics to the northern latitudes." He puts the GPS unit back in his pocket.

You put it together. "The northern hemisphere is going into another ice age and the tropics are—"

"Heat stroke city," muses Alleymanderous.

It begins to snow. "Oh, shit!" you say. "How'd we do this anyway?"

Alleymanderous says, "Violence comes in many forms; maybe violence is as violence does." In a mewling voice, not altogether unpleasant, Alleymanderous begins a chorus line routine while singing a distorted version of a silly little song that you remember hearing on the Mickey Mouse Club so long ago:

"Violence is as violence does
What else is there to say?
So if you wanna be vi-o-lent,
Do this every day:
Flip off all your neighbors,
Drive an S.U.V.
Use up all the fossil fuels,
Pollute the air and sea...."

He stops singing, then gazes wistfully off into the distance. "Bummer," he says, "no more catnip."

It snows like crazy and you become buried in drifts and then, strangely, the snow falling around you becomes sort of crystallized, then puffy, and you realize it's—"Popcorn," you say with great wonder. You lift your head; the popcorn falls from your face and you look around— popcorn everywhere. It's like the popcorn is a vast blanket of snow, but it's all—popcorn.

You hear a crunching behind you and you turn and look. A shiny red, white and blue Hummer grunts its way to you through the deep pop- corn. You see the driver is—Alleymanderous.

You notice something else: sticking out of the popcorn are vast bill- boards and suddenly they light up.

Alleymanderous gets out of the Hummer; his fur is thick, and he sits on the hood in shorts and a Hawaiian shirt. Between his paws, he holds a microbrew, a Black Rat Stout, which he sucks on through a straw. "Hey," he says, "get comfy. The show is about to begin."

"Which show?" You ask.

"Any one you want."

The display is bewildering: simultaneously you're presented with pic- tures of everything from *The Beverly Hillbillies* to scenes of Iraqi soldiers being buried alive in trenches by American troops in the first Gulf War.

"What the hell am I supposed to be paying attention to?" you ask.

"Everything," says Alleymanderous.

"How can I?"

"You can't handle information overload? What kind of unpatriotic consumer are you?"

"Turn if off!" you plead.

"Can't," says Alleymanderous. "Bad for the economy."

"Who thought up this madness?" you ask.

Alleymanderous smiles benignly. "Monsters. Monsters from the Id."

It begins to snow again, and the images on the billboards begin to speed up, the sound is amped, you can't understand anything and the snow is flying. You turn to Alleymanderous getting into his Hummer and you yell, "What do I do?"

Alleymanderous yells back, "What did Morbius have to do?"

You think back to the Id-Monster getting ready to bust through the thick Krell steel which is glowing red hot, and you remember Morbius going from denial that the Monster from the Id was his, to accepting that it was.

"But," you say, "others are responsible for this mess, not me."

Alleymanderous tosses the microbrew bottle out into the popcorn and snow, the wind dies down and you can hear him again. "You still don't get it—no, maybe it's not your personal monster from the Id that did this, but nonetheless—" and as he climbs into the Hummer he stares at you. The wind has picked up and it's harder and harder to see him through the blowing snow, but you hear him yell, "—it's still Monsters, Monsters from—" and he pauses looks at you again for a long time and says, "the *collective* Id."

With that, he slams the Hummer's door closed and you watch Alleymanderous drive off, into the snow, the popcorn, the night.

5:01 am

...you are blinded by a blizzard of popcorn; but it abruptly stops. Dazed, you look around, only to find you are in a tavern, a pint of Deimos Dark Porter and a huge bowl of popcorn in front of you on the highly polished cherry counter. Alleymanderous sits beside you, wearing a red derby hat with holes for his ears, and blue coveralls with a hole in the back from which hangs out the brown fluffy tail of his Maine coon heritage. He drinks through an ingenious straw, stealing glances at the TV above the bar.

"Yowl," he says. "Look at that. What do you call that move that everyone is so excited about?"

"Touchdown," you say.

"What's that?" His tail switches.

"I don't really know. Never got into football. Never got into sports."

"Yowl," says Alleymanderous, yellow eyes narrowing, "looks like everyone is on a testosterone high. Maybe this activity should be called 'spurts' instead of 'sports'."

"Maybe," you say. Looking through an enormous window you dumbly stare at a huge volcano and something tells you it sure ain't Mt. Rainier. The view gets lost in what looks like a snowstorm, but you suspect it's not a storm made of "snow."

Alleymanderous follows your gaze. "Atmosphere precipitating out," he says. "Nothing like a little Martian carbon dioxide blizzard."

You suspected you were on Mars, but didn't really want to know, because you don't have a clue *what* you're doing there, in a bar, having a

Deimos Dark and talking to your cat, Alleymanderous, dressed as strangely as he is.

He glances over to you. "You still don't get it, do you?" he asks, then, finishing his drink, gets served another bottle labeled Old Catnip, and somehow manipulates it to refill his glass. "Since when does reality make sense? But you're trying to make sense of it, aren't you? I just bet you're wondering what you're doing on Mars, in a bar, having a Deimos Dark and talking to me, dressed as strangely as I am."

You nod. "You are perceptive. I am indeed wondering that."

"Hmm," says Alleymanderous. "You left out a detail."

"What?"

"The carbon dioxide snow."

"Hmm," you reply.

You close your eyes for a minute and when you open them— Alleymanderous and you are in a huge rubber raft, like the kind you would use for river rafting, and around you billow clouds of red, tan, and brown. The winds howl and the air stinks. You frown.

"OK," you say, and you suddenly discover you're speaking though a microphone at chin level, like you see astronauts using. "OK. I betcha—" and up ahead you see a horizon, red, swirling. "Don't tell me; we're on Jupiter and that's the Giant Red Spot up ahead."

"Sure ain't *The Twilight Zone,*" he says through his own microphone. He's now dressed in a tight-fitting, silvery suit with a rebreather cleverly designed to fit over his face. You suddenly discover you're wearing earphones. "Alleymanderous to his crewmember. This is Alleymanderous to his crewmember. Come in, crewmember."

Crewmember? you think. *I thought I was Alleymanderous' owner,* but somehow out there, things are strange.

"Come in crewmember," says Alleymanderous. "Do you copy?" This is followed by a high pitched "beep" and you're reminded of film clips of space flights and conversations of astronauts with each other and mission control.

You're surprised at what comes out of your mouth as you speak into the microphone. "This is crewmember. Roger, oh-niner. Do we have a go for EVA excursion on winds of Jupiter? Do you copy?" *(beep)* You can't fathom what you just said. *EVA on the winds of Jupiter?*

"Roger," says Alleymanderous. "We are traveling at three hundred miles per hour on the south longitude jet stream. Methane and helium levels within normal limits; roger-dodger we are affirmative for go on excursion. Over." *(beep)*

"Copy that." *(beep)*

You flash back to your memory of walkin street in the town of S. by the mountains by the sea and seeing a woman that you knew who had treated you badly in the past, remembering your despair and loneliness after she left you for the guy she was screwing while she was with you. And then, seeing her those many years later, she passed you by, not recognizing you, but from her you picked up this grief, this sadness so profound that whatever anger you had toward her vanished as you realized the despair, the immense pain she exuded. Then, *blam*, you're back on Mars.

A particularly strong current pushes you closer to the maelstrom of the Great Red Spot and you hear Alleymanderous saying, "feel your pain." *(beep)*

"Roger," you say. "I copy that." *(beep)*

"This is Alleymanderous to crewmember. We are approaching the Great Red Spot; the maelstrom of what we thought was real is often—not." *(beep)*

You watch the Red Spot, the gigantic storm, draw near. "She really hurt me." *(beep)* And you can feel those old emotions surfacing, buffeting you from inside; the heat and reds of rage boil up from deep within your core.

"Copy that," says Alleymanderous, "and now *she's* hurting." *(beep)*

"Roger dodger," you say, "and I don't know what to think—can you uplink data for a personal course correction? Over." *(beep)*

"Negative." *(beep)*

Hanging on to the raft, you head into the Red Spot, and Alleymanderous says, "Think nothing; just understand." *(beep)*

You are whipped along, caught up in the 600 mile per hour windwall of the Great Red Spot and suddenly—

—you're rafting over something deep blue—Neptune's atmosphere? You begin to sink deeper, deeper until the atmosphere, the blueness, is all around you and then it's as if you are not so much floating, but sliding, skating across a semi-solid surface.

Alleymanderous removes his mask.

"Why did I not need a mask, and you did?" you ask.

Alleymanderous looks about in the blue murk, not looking at you and says, "Allergic to helium."

You drift for a while in the quiet blue murk, not saying anything. And oddly, you don't feel particularly cold.

Alleymanderous opens up a plastic foil pouch of catnip and uses it like snuff. He offers you some.

You shake your head. "Never touch the stuff," you say.

"Do you know where we are?" Alleymanderous asks, still dressed in his silver suit and, this time, even his tail is encased in the garment.

"I guess we're drifting on the atmosphere turned sea or ice or slush of Neptune," you say, "or maybe Uranus."

But Alleymanderous shakes his head. "No, no."

"Then what—" you say.

"No," says Alleymanderous. "Who."

You think for a minute then—yeah—yeah, you get it. "OK," you say. "I get it."

"Well?" asks Alleymanderous. He sneezes out the catnip and, from somewhere, pulls out a handkerchief with a picture of Tweety-Bird on it. He blows his nose deftly.

"We're drifting and floating over—" you swallow—"someone so lost in her despair; lost so deeply, she can never come out. Lost and blue and cold, so cold—" You feel your heart beginning to break.

"All the anger you felt toward her—" muses Alleymanderous, putting his handkerchief back in a heretofore concealed opening of a pocket in his suit.

"I didn't deserve it," you say.

"But for her to do what she did to you—"

The tears come now. You nod. "Simply a mirror of what she did to herself—"

"As was done to her." He pauses. "As those who did it to her—"

"Did it to themselves as it was done to them." You look to the blue-green murk, feel the raft half-skating, half-floating on whatever surface you are on. "That unconscious?" you ask, "that unconscious?"

Alleymanderous shakes his head, turns away, looking through the dark blue air of Neptune, or Uranus, wherever it is that you are. "You've always been so conscious yourself?"

And then you sigh and finally say, "Just as joy is my teacher, pain is my guide." Then you just sit there, sit there, both of you drifting, on this cold planet, drifting, knowing the maelstrom of Jupiter is far away, and letting go of the turbulence of all that pain that you felt, only to find yourself, in this sad, blue, cold place, drifting. You realize you can indeed have compassion for the one who hurt you so, just as those, whom *you* have hurt, had, in the end, compassion—for you.

5:25 am

...you stay in the Sad Blue Murk a while longer, then you pass through another barrier and discover yourself sitting in your favorite soft chair, a glass of wine in your hand. In the corner of the room, Christmas tree lights blaze red, yellow and blue and a fire burns in the fireplace. You smile. Christmas. Right now, you don't care how or why it's Christmas; it is, and that's fine. Something you like, something familiar. You close your eyes and in your mind, the image of the fire burning brightly in the fireplace.

"Ho-ho-ho-*yowl*." You look. The fire is gone. *Uh oh,* you think, *oh, crap—*

Scuffle-scuffle-scuffle Something is coming down the chimney and before you can say, "rottenfiggypudding," *thump*, there is Alleymanderous, in the now dark fireplace, bearded, in a Santa suit, ears poking through holes in his Santa hat. He hops out of the fireplace. *Tinkle*, a bright green bell dangles from the end of his Maine coon tail.

"Yowl," he says, "yowl-tide greetings! Ho, ho, ho." He pulls out from the fireplace a red bag, blackened by soot. "Boy," he continues, "tight fit. You gotta clean out your chimney—creosote buildup can result in a chimney fire."

You look at Alleymanderous. "What happened to the fire?"

Alleymanderous moves his lips in what you know to be a smile, even though he wears a beard. "Bet you're wondering what happened to the fire," he says. "The fireplace with the fire is in the *other* dream."

You gulp. You happen to glance down to your wine glass; the wine has changed into a seething mass of little, itty-bitty red spiders. You throw it into the fireplace, the glass shatters and in a second there appears a ghostly, deep red vaporous form in the shape of a spider, with angel's wings, drifting, floating in the fireplace, then vanishing up the chimney.

You stare for a minute at the fireplace, then back at Alleymanderous. You hear the plaintiveness in your voice when you ask, "OK, so what dream am I in *now*?"

Alleymanderous says nothing; his tail switches and every time it does, the bell flashes and goes *tinkle-tinkle-tinkle*.

Then you ask, "How do I get back to reality?"

"What reality?" asks Alleymanderous. He turns to open his bulky sack, then starts pawing through the packages.

"The reality I was in when I was drinking wine and sitting in front of the fireplace with the fire in it."

Alleymanderous picks out a package, but in trying to toss it to you, the ribbon catches on his claws and dances there, mid-air. Alleymanderous vigorously shakes his paw, and he laughs. "Looks like this gift has a hard time letting go of Santa's claws." Finally the gift lets go and you catch it. "For you," says Alleymanderous.

"What about that other reality—" you begin.

"Open the package," says Alleymanderous.

You do. You tear off the red ribbon, the blue wrapping paper with pictures of candy canes, and inside is another package done up in blue ribbon with little pictures of candy canes on red paper.

You look up. In front of you, an image of yourself sitting in front of the fireplace, glass of wine in your hand, and through the window you see—"Jupiter?" you ask. "Is that the planet Jupiter?"

"None other," says Alleymanderous. He sits on his haunches, Santa hat cocked to one side, staring at you intently with eyes that have the thinnest slit for a pupil, as if he's staring into bright light, but—there's no bright light. You can't help but think his eyes look a bit reptilian. You can't fathom how his pupils can be so narrow.

"Rather than focus on my eyes, a smart pupil would focus on the big picture."

You look out the window, trying to ignore Alleymanderous'—what you assume to be—humor, and you say, "That can't be Jupiter."

Alleymanderous shrugs. "Did you look out the window when you were drinking wine and sitting in front of the fireplace in that other place?"

"Well, no. But I don't remember seeing Jupiter—"

"But," says Alleymanderous, raising a paw, "since you didn't look out the window, you can't know, can you?"

You ponder the memory of the other scene for a minute.

"Why don't you open your other gift?" asks Alleymanderous.

Hesitantly, you turn away from the scene, and looking at the package at hand, you begin to open it. You then dumbly stare at another wrapped package—one with bright red and white candy canes on pale red ribbon over blue wrapping paper.

This is bad, you think. *This is very, very bad.*

"Well?" asks Alleymanderous, as he lights up a cigar and holds it in a cleverly-designed holder that looks like it's specially designed for, you muse, furry-pawed, diabolical entities.

You look at Alleymanderous and then, glancing out the window, you see in the distance a mighty cliff face and a gentle upward slope beyond, and pink sky. You're not quite sure how you know this, but you say, "—um—that's not the Olympus Mons volcano on Mars, is it?"

Alleymanderous blows out smoke and you then realize what the cigar is made of: catnip. Burning catnip. You are not quite sure what to make of the odor; it almost reminds you, for some reason, of stir-fried sweat socks.

"Of course that's Olympus Mons," says Alleymanderous. "After all, if you're celebrating Christmas here, it must be Christmas everywhere at the same time in the cosmos, including Mars."

You ponder the—what appears to be flawed logic in this as you stare back at the package in your hand. You wonder, do you really want to open this?

"It's your choice," says Alleymanderous, "whether or not you wish to open it."

"What if I open it and it's another package that's wrapped?"

"Might be," says Alleymanderous. He sits on haunches, smoking his catnip cigar. He looks calm, but you can see a wildness in his eyes, which have now totally dilated. This is weird, because sunlight from the weaker, but still bright, Martian sun is flooding in through a southern-facing window behind you, which Alleymanderous faces.

You look back to the package. "And if I don't open it—?"

"You're still making a choice," says Alleymanderous.

"No matter what I do—" you say, "—you make a choice—even if I choose to do nothing—"

"Still a choice," says Alleymanderous.

"—but if I keep opening these packages—"

"—might get you to where you want to go—"

"—and if I don't keep opening them—"

"—never know."

Stuck. You think, *I know what stuck is. I now know the full meaning of stuck. Damned if you do, damned if you don't; between a rock and a hard place.*

Stuck. Stuck. Stuck. No matter what you do, no matter what action you take, even if it means doing nothing —

As if reading your mind, Alleymanderous blows out a blue cloud of catnip smoke, and says, "You choose."

"Well," you say, "maybe the best course of action is to give up on this —" you give the gift back to Alleymanderous, "and do nothing."

"You're sure?" asks Alleymanderous.

"No," you say, "but I don't feel real positive this is taking me anywhere. Especially back to what I call reality."

"Okay," says Alleymanderous, "but maybe reality, as you call it, isn't such a good place to be. Maybe opening packages is the better reality, even if it means it's a dream." With that, he tosses the gift back in the bag, turns around and heads to the chimney, and, shoving his bag ahead of him, he then pushes it up the chimney and disappears behind it. You hear a muffled, "Ho, ho, ho yowl — Merry Christmas, happy yowl-tide."

You sigh. Quiet again. You're glad you made what you think is, under the circumstances, the right choice.

You look to the window again, to see what you think will be a view of the Martian landscape, but instead, what you see is yourself, running, and coming after you, swooping after you, is a huge red spider, giant wings flapping wildly.

5:55 am

...running wildly from that flapping, nightmarish thing, though scared out of your wits, suddenly, part of you suspects what that thing is. And you find that there is a calm part of you that says, "The power of the beast is based on your —" You understand. It's like you trip a switch, and then you are falling over a cliff, falling, falling and then, oddly, your fall slows and gently, you land on a chess board. The light is grim; low clouds move overhead. The mountain range curves with ragged summits around you. You smell something.

"Pretty bad isn't it?" Alleymanderous stands there, in robes of lavender and blue.

You look at him. "Bishop?" you ask.

Alleymanderous nods. "Bishop I am."

You sniff. "What is that *nasty* smell?" you ask.

Alleymanderous, standing right beside you, sniffs as well. "Rotten, burning catnip," he says. "What an awful waste of such fine stuff."

"Hmm," you say, "it smells to me more like rotten plumbing and garlic."

"*And* burning catnip," says Alleymanderous.

You kneel down. The red and black squares, about a foot in length and width are cool to the touch. "Like jade, obsidian," you muse. You stand again, and look and the chessboard goes off into the darkness. You ask, "If you're a bishop, what am I, a pawn?"

"Maybe," says Alleymanderous, "but maybe you're more than that."

You say, "A rook? A knight?"

Alleymanderous simply stands there. "Maybe, but maybe more than that."

"Another bishop? A king?"

A wind comes up and the fabric of Alleymanderous' clothes billows, flutters. "Maybe," he says, "but maybe more than that."

You look at Alleymanderous, who stares straight ahead. "Have I missed something? What other pieces are there in a chess game?"

"Maybe more than you think there are."

You smile and say, though you don't know why, "This can also be used for all sorts of games, checkers, for one."

Alleymanderous simply stands there and says, "Checkers this ain't. Chess it is."

Something in his tone, you think, *the way he says this—This* is *about chess and it's* also *about something*—movement, you see movement way off in the distance.

"What—" you whisper.

"Remember the power of bishops," says Alleymanderous.

You strain to see what is moving down the board—to the left, to the right, forward, right, forward, left. You suddenly understand. "It's the queen."

The figure draws closer. And you recognize it as, indeed, the queen. The head is that of a spider and you know, you know who it is. Alleymanderous stands there with you. "What are you going to do?"

"I don't know what to do," you say, knowing that you're becoming a bit uncomfortable, "I don't know what I am in this game."

"How about being what you want to be?" You look down at Alleymanderous with robes fluttering, billowing in the wind. Dust is kicked up and the smell now is that of rotten eggs, burning grease and old blood.

"And don't forget the power of the bishop."

The queen comes dancing down the board and you realize that the way she moves is not only the way the queen can move, it's a move of play, of arrogance, that she can move any way she pleases, because she's gonna *getcha*.

Or so she thinks, you muse. As she draws closer, you suddenly find yourself calm; wondering, idly, how she moves like that, eight little legs under that mantle, that robe around her body? Is her head on the body of a person? And is she sliding on a self-lubricating sheen of arachnid slime? Pre-silk stuff? You wonder how she moves, and in the gloom of the scene, with the clouds torn, shredded, moving as though slowly being pulled like a ragged blanket across the sky, with a few of the mountains beginning to erupt as volcanoes, you wonder, wonder how she moves. And suddenly you realize something—why would you be focusing on something like this? Where's the fear? What has changed? You stop again. No, not what *has* changed, what *is* changing—something is happening. It's as if, somehow, things are OK; it's like you are on the edge of something terribly sad, tremendously beautiful and the image of a soldier, triumphant and proud, comes to you.

Alleymanderous abruptly looks up. "You're using your bishop."

You shake your head. "I guess I am—why not a knight?"

Alleymanderous somehow smiles. "Maybe I'm a knight in disguise." He pauses. "Maybe we're all knights becoming bishops."

You don't quite know what to think, and you turn to watch the beast come toward you. As you watch this curious play, she abruptly tries to slow, because the closer she gets to you, the smaller she becomes, and the larger you grow. And she has been moving, skating over the surface with such arrogance and so quickly—that she cannot stop.

You hear her *hiss, screech* as she comes closer, closer, smaller, smaller. In your head you see yourself stick your foot out. You see her go flying, and you see yourself doubled over with laughter, but in this reality you just abruptly step aside.

Where she once lorded over you, now, she is half your size. You watch her pass and you simply say, "Good-bye, grandmother. Be at peace." You turn to watch her as she goes on, becoming infinitely smaller on the chessboard that now stretches off into oblivion in the other direction.

You turn to Alleymanderous. "Game over?"

Alleymanderous nods. "*This* game over."

"Thanks," you say, "I didn't know bishops had such strange power to shift events that way."

"It's amazing what can happen when you choose the right bishop," Alleymanderous muses. "Amazing what can happen."

You turn to look at the place to where your grandmother/spider disappeared. "Guess it's all over."

"Nope," says Alleymanderous. "This part is over but it never is really over, just changed."

You find yourself looking down the chessboard again. Movement in the distance; you cannot know what or why, but something moving, something coming.

"Just remember," says Alleymanderous, robes billowing in the wind, "remember the power of the bishop."

6:18 am

...the scene around you fades, fades, fades away and you think that maybe, hopefully, all will return to normal, or you'll wake up. At least you hope you will. *Well*—you ponder, *you thought you did other times, too, but you ended up*—you gulp. A new reality begins to materialize and before you know it, you're staring at Alleymanderous, floating in a blue, translucent inner tube on the wine-dark sea. He wears reflective sunglasses and drinks from a bottle of Mousedrool beer via a cleverly designed straw. And you? You're lying on an air mattress the color and design of an American flag, which, over-inflated, has begun to leak. "Oh, oh," you say. You don't see any land nearby; just the dark sea, the intense blue sky, and on the horizon, the billowy, white-gray cumulonimbus thunderheads rapidly building, as though you're watching them through time lapse photography.

You look to Alleymanderous. "I dealt with my grandmother; I dealt with my family; I thought I woke up."

Alleymanderous takes a long drink. "You thought you did."

"But I didn't, did I?"

Alleymanderous takes another long drink and looks at you for a minute. "You, seeing me, a cat that hates water and cannot drink beer, sitting in a blue inner tube, and you wonder if you've woken up."

"I thought I did." You pause. "I hoped I would." You sigh. "I wish to fuck I would." You look up to the blue sky. The starship *Enterprise* appears, in *very* low Earth orbit and, towed behind it, an advertising banner flutters. You read it. "You are not awake, Voyager," it says.

"Well," you try, as Alleymanderous' blue inner tube slips closer to your air mattress, that continues to slowly lose air, "um—" you continue, "maybe I awoke from one dream into this dream?"

Alleymanderous' inner tube is right next to yours; *flash*, his paw arcs out and you see sun flash on the claws as he slashes at your air mattress. *Pa-woof*—the air blasts out of the tear and you slide all over the sea, only to finally become airborne, ending up in the black gut of a thunderhead. *Flash*, lightning explodes around you. You alternately cover your eyes then your ears, as the thunder crashes. Still hanging onto what's left of your American flag air mattress, the next thing you know, you've landed somewhere and it's cold. You have the sense that you are teetering; wondering, you look down. The air mattress has abruptly turned into a toboggan and you see things written on it: "Good Luck" and "Bon Voyage" and "Get 'em, Tiger." And a poignant note, "I know you can do it, Son." But before you can ponder this further, the clouds vanish and you see where you are. "Oh my God," you squeak. You want to get off the toboggan but to your horror, you discover you are chained to it. And you notice movement to your right. There is Alleymanderous, dressed in a snazzy outfit of black and red checkerboard design pants, matching vest and hat. He holds a feline-friendly stop watch, a starting gun and says, "Get ready—"

"Wait—" you say. You look down to the icy cliffs below you. "Where am I?"

You really do know where you are, you just hope that somehow you're wrong.

"Hellas Basin Freestyle Toboggan Demolition Derby, Mars. Get set—" says Alleymanderous, cocking the gun.

You *knew* it! *Oh, shit!* you say to yourself. "Th-that's 25,000 feet down," you whimper.

Alleymanderous has gotten behind the toboggan. "25,496 feet to the bottom, to be exact," he says. "Go!" He fires the gun and the "bang" sounds like an airy and hollow "pop" in the thin atmosphere. Then he kicks the rear of the toboggan and you're flying, sliding down the slopes, but it's in slow motion, and within seconds, Alleymanderous, now in casual clothes, floats down beside you on some sort of cushion. He has a camcorder with him and he's speaking into a microphone on his lapel like he's broadcasting to an audience. "1000 feet down in this First Annual Hellas Basin Toboggan Demolition Derby and would our brave pilot care to say a few words—"

"Ahhhhhhhhhhhhh!" is all you hear coming out of your mouth.

"Ahhhhhhh, it is," laughs Alleymanderous. "Our hero has always been known for his humor and his pithy commentary. We're now 4000 feet down—"

In spite of your slow motion, you nonetheless hit an outcrop of rock on the wall of the vast crater, grinding, scraping, skidding momentarily over CO_2 ice and snow before you launch again into the air on the downward slide. About this time, a sudden memory of a recent and even deeper realization comes to you, of just how it felt that the connection you *so* wanted between you and your father wasn't to be, and how you went down, down, down into the cold misery and frigid dismay of the Hellas Basin of your heart.

"Pilot," says Alleymanderous, "does this ride remind you of your descent into—"

Then you *really* scream, "AHHHHHHHHHHH!"

Before you, still some 20,000 feet down, you see the black shadows, the deep shade, hiding the floor of the immense crater. But more urgent, immediately before you, the wall of the basin slopes out once more and you are heading toward it. You hit it, slide again on the CO_2 ice, then smash into a rock; the toboggan disintegrates. From somewhere, you hear a tremendous and rousing cheer and applause as you launch again into space, into the shadows, heading with sudden velocity into the darkest, deepest part of Hellas Basin—

—you stop moving. Suddenly still, so quiet. You open your eyes. In bed. The covers are thrown about as if you've been thrashing. But that's sunshine coming in through the open window; you hear birds singing and you are grateful. You have woken from a dream into another dream, and now you are waking up from *that* dream—

—rustle of paper. You look over. Alleymanderous sits, in slacks, golf shoes, and white tee shirt with little red letters above a breast pocket that spell out, "FeLinz." He wears glasses and looks up from a newspaper called, *The New York Times, Evening Feline Edition.* You can read some of the headlines, "Dreams, Nightmares, Be Glad You're Alive."

"Feeling well?" Alleymanderous puts the paper down.

"I was," you say, "until I realized I was in a dream again."

Alleymanderous moves his lips in what you want to believe is a smile. "And when are we not in a dream?" he asks. "Be glad of it."

You look out the window. Aside from Alleymanderous, you really could be, you think, in a state of mind called "being awake."

"Be glad of it?" you ask. "Be glad of these nightmares?"

Alleymanderous laughs. "Dreams and nightmares. Be glad of them. Dreams tell you where you want to go, nightmares tell you your worst fears — where you *don't* want to go."

"I don't care," you say, "I just want to wake up. I want to wake up from this dream."

"No, you don't," says Alleymanderous, "because you will wake up," and he pauses, "soon enough." And he looks at you for a long, *long* time.

6:31 am

#1: *Alleymanderous Obnoxiousfelinus*

...then you look again at Alleymanderous and he is now dressed in a clown costume. He has a bulbous red nose, wears a green and purple checkered suit billowed out at the upper arms, the thighs. But he doesn't have shoes on. For whatever reason, you focus on that, rather than the strangeness of the blank landscape around you. You say, "Every good clown I know wears big floppy shoes. Goes with the image."

Alleymanderous looks at you. "Not this clown." As soon as he says that, some of the background of the scene fills in. You notice that the floor, which has suddenly appeared, is highly polished, blond hardwood.

You look closer at Alleymanderous and you realize something very unsettling. "The colors on your face, that really *is* the color of your fur, isn't it?" Alleymanderous just stares blankly at you. "I thought clowns used greasepaint."

"Not this clown," says Alleymanderous. You notice the background fills in a little more. The floor seems to go off to infinity. To your left, a rugged black outline of a mountain range — you follow it with your eyes — in the distance it seems to curve to the right, then, looking to your right, you see it there as well. It's like you're standing in a cul-de-sac. Behind the mountains, a glow and you realize how impossible that is: that the sun is rising not only on your left, but directly in front of you and to your right, as well.

Alleymanderous continues to look up at you. The look is at once intense, calm, and knowing, and he looks as if he could take your soul apart, atom by atom.

You say, "Aren't you supposed to be cracking jokes, jumping up and down and doing funny things?"

You have the sense that Alleymanderous is somehow smiling, like what he is doing is magnificent fun. "Not this clown," he finally says. His eyes narrow.

For whatever reason, you look up, the pale and featureless sky now becomes black, and stars appear.

You look back to Alleymanderous. "Somehow, some way, I remember that if one likes the colors of purple and green, it means an over-riding concern that others see you favorably."

Alleymanderous strips off the clown costume, but you see his fur, indeed, has the same green and purple pattern, and Alleymanderous says in a low voice, "Not this clown."

You look from Alleymanderous up to the stars and beseechingly, you say, "Is there something I am to learn? Something I am to understand?"

The stars rearrange themselves into a message: "Not this, clown."

#2 Alternatus Realitus Wayoutum Finalius 32.0 F

...the floor has changed to a brilliant checkerboard pattern of red and green tile, and it stretches off away from you.

The mountain range still exists, but many of the peaks have become volcanoes and are erupting furiously. To the left, straight ahead, and to your right, the sun is cresting the mountains. There is a slight vibration from the erupting volcanoes. Alleymanderous floats in space, no costume, just him and his purple and green-colored fur again. And before you know it, it has changed to red and green. "Ummm—" you say, "if I remember correctly, according to color psychology, you go after your goals with intensity, and you don't let yourself be distracted from your purpose."

Alleymanderous floats in the air. "You left out the fact that I want to achieve special recognition and social standing from my success."

"Sorry," you say. Then, "I appreciate you talking to me more. Your previous comments weren't too helpful," you smile, "clown."

"Am I trying to be helpful?" Alleymanderous says.

You frown. "Why shouldn't you be?"

Alleymanderous shrugs. "Why *should* I be?"

"Are we enemies?" you ask.

"Are we friends?" he asks, in return.

"Well," you say with more than a little exasperation, "if we aren't enemies, and if we aren't friends, what *are* we?"

"I don't know," says Alleymanderous. "A puzzle, no?"

And he looks at you with those green eyes.

You sigh. "Isn't there anything certain in the world?"

Alleymanderous continues to float before you, on his side; his tail, red and green checkerboard as well, hangs languidly down. "String Theory talks about alternative universes and multiple dimensions," he says. "Looks like the hallowed truths on which we based our consensual grasp of reality are just plain wrong. What is to be done? Nothing is certain, nothing is sure after all."

You notice movement, and looking up, you notice the clouds have vanished and the stars have arranged another message for you: "Nothing certain. What a pisser, huh?"

You notice the ground shaking. All the volcanoes are erupting more forcefully, and ash is blasted high into the air. It's like you're surrounded by countless exploding Mt. St. Helens.

"So," says Alleymanderous, "what is to be done? What is to be done?"

Not far away, a crack appears in the tile, and a curtain of lava shoots up 500 to 600 feet; the heat feels like a blast furnace, the roar is almost deafening. You look up to the sky; another message in the stars: "Think fast." You look at Alleymanderous who continues to float there. "Think fast, faster," he says.

You see a flaming wall of lava approaching you from all sides. "I'm thinking as fast as I can," you say.

"Well, you better think as fast as you can even faster."

"How the hell can I think faster than I can think if I'm thinking as fast as I can?"

"Dunno," says Alleymanderous, "but you'd better think of *something*."

"*You* think of something!" you say, backing away from the approaching lava.

"I can't think of anything," says Alleymanderous.

"Why?"

"Because I'm a cat, and cats don't think."

For a second you wonder at the madness of dreams: that they can make perfect sense even though they don't. The wall of lava approaches; you can't get away and then suddenly you feel an overwhelming sense of gratitude. "Not that I'm dying," you whisper, "but that I lived." *That DNA, the unknowable forces about me,* you think, *sought to combine and create a conscious and sentient me.* "And in spite of my impending death," you say, "I feel glad and am able to let go."

#3 *Mea Fibbus Maximus*

"That's the biggest piece of shit I've *ever* heard." Alleymanderous continues to float; you notice the checkerboard pattern of his fur, purple and black. You find yourself recoiling at the color combination. Alleymanderous still looks to you with that intense eye contact.

You gulp. "This isn't about you, is it?"

"Smart," says Alleymanderous. "Of course it's not about me."

"You're on to me, aren't you?"

"No," says Alleymanderous, "you're on to yourself. Come on, what do the colors say?"

As you have so many other times, you hate Alleymanderous, not for who or what he is, but for what it is he says about you.

"Come on," says Alleymanderous, "out with it."

He drifts right there, and you look about to the scene around you. Nothing has changed, really, except it's like on freeze mode. It's as if you're in, and surrounded by, a 3-D holograph. And Alleymanderous just serenely floats there, on his side, paws splayed out now in front of him and you say, "Purple and black, I guess that means an imperative need for some kind of bond or fusing with another which will be sensually fulfilling, but won't conflict with my convictions."

"Having said that," continues Alleymanderous, "let's replay this scene. Honesty, please?"

#4 Coppus Crappus

...the scene comes to life. The lava approaches, it's hotter than hell, you can't get away and you scream, "Oh, my God, I'll never get a chance to fuck my high school lust object, Dianne, because I'll die and lose all chances! Oh, my God, I haven't done my will and my family's gonna be so pissed that I left my estate in such a mess! Oh, my God, I didn't get to New Zealand and I wanted to hike there more than anything! Oh, my God, I never told Annie how much I loved her! Oh, shit, I never paid back that debt to my best buddy, Stan; I'll never see it snow again; I don't wanna die—wahhhhhhhh!"

"*That's better*," says Alleymanderous, and the scene freezes again. "Who is ever prepared to die, when death unexpectedly presents itself?"

You gulp. "As it often does." You look to Alleymanderous. He's back in a clown suit, but the colors of the checkerboard design are blue and red. You look to those colors. You nervously laugh. "I know we are going to die and have time to prepare—"

"But," says Alleymanderous, "we all know we are going to die, and no matter how unprepared we are, we can still be prepared."

"In spite of all the regrets?"

"Can't change that. But can change—"

"—living now to have as few regrets as possible—I guess." You study the colors of the clown suit Alleymanderous wears. "Why do we clown around with that which we seek the most? Affectionate, fulfilling and harmonious relationships—an intimate union in which there is love, self-sacrifice and mutual trust."

At that point you see a character walking through the lava curtain and you know who he is: it's Anslenot from the book, *Kafka's Uncle* and he points up to the sky and says, "I didn't get the message; maybe you can."

You look up, and suddenly, the smoke from the volcanoes turns transparent and you watch the stars arrange themselves in that message once again, "Only love makes tolerable the knowledge of our mortality."

#5 *Maximum Noblus Afterallus*

...you watch Anslenot surrounded by light and smoke, walk away now, through a dark landscape. The lava has solidified into a vast, flat sheet and you know that Anslenot will walk on until he vanishes in the land beyond the mountains, in the land beyond the ice.

You want to cry. "He never knew love," you say. "He'll die without love."

Alleymanderous stands with you, now in soldier's outfit: helmet, khaki clothes, and boots. "What was it that Victor Hugo said?" muses Alleymanderous, "Oh, yes, 'Lack of sex is an inconvenience; lack of love is a tragedy.' We have to be soldiers in life," he says. "We have to battle the enemy of fear, of beliefs that love means being hit, abandoned, abused yet again, and the fear that if we are attracted to someone it is because they are so familiar—"

"Of the family?" you ask.

Alleymanderous looks out over the landscape and moves on and you follow him and soon, soon, so soon, you come to the edge of the world, and before you all the stars and galaxies you can't even begin to dream of lie before you. With Alleymanderous you sit on the edge and you look out and you say, "Well, what is—"

"Shhhh," says Alleymanderous, "for even I am a student now. Watch."

You do. And slowly the stars and galaxies stop streaming past and begin to form a pattern that you can recognize: stretching in front of you, the shining, shimmering double helix of DNA, without beginning, without end. Before you it slowly rotates and then you hear a voice—a fervent whisper—time? The Universe? The past? Being? God? Gods? The DNA itself? You don't know, but you listen. "Courage," pause, "courage it is to exist, to live and love in the face of our mortality." A long pause, the DNA rotates, shimmers; you shiver and tears come to your eyes at the loveliness, the heartbreaking beauty of what you see. "Courage, courage to get up every day, knowing that it is one day closer to your dying and the dying of your parents, of friends and loved ones. Courage to know that you are dying but choose nonetheless to live, to create purpose, and ultimately to love."

You and Alleymanderous are bathed in the pale blue light of the glowing helix, the star stuff of life, and ultimately, sentiency, and with that sentiency, that terrible, terrible knowledge—"We are all soldiers," the fervent voice again, "we are all soldiers, as good as the Greeks, as great as the soldiers in the greatest battles ever described, ever fought in antiquity. Oh, soldiers, soldiers, soldiers are we all. Such fine, fine soldiers are we all, fighting the greatest battle we can fight: the knowledge of our dying while we live. What brave, brave soldiers are we all. What brave soldiers are we all. To have love and purpose to live knowing the strength of the enemy and who will eventually win, but, oh, what brave soldiers are we all."

And you and Alleymanderous sit there, sit there in that pale light, in the light of the same star stuff of that glowing double helix which is in you. You sit there with Alleymanderous, sitting there on the edge of the world and you whisper, "And die we must."

Alleymanderous' eyes are large as he takes in the spectacle and he finally says, "And die we must. Leave this form we must. On some level, all life, all being knows it. From the trees shedding their leaves in autumn to my kind seeking a time and a quiet place that we may lay down our lives alone, undisturbed and with dignity."

"And yet," you say.

"And yet," says Alleymanderous, "we cannot know what we do not know." A pause. "String Theory. Multiple universes. Maybe in some universe that we cannot see, two characters are having this same conversation."

"And," you say, "to die is to —?"

"Cannot know. But maybe the Buddhists have it right about life and reincarnation. All the more reason to, as St. Augustine said, 'Love and do what thou wilt'."

When you look again at Alleymanderous, he is kid-sized, and instantly you understand that he is Everyone — as are you. You put an arm around his shoulders, his around yours. The voice again, "Though in a dream, though different beings, the understanding is yet the same." You look at that magnificent spiral of DNA and you watch as planets, suns, stars and galaxies move and turn majestically before you. "And with this," the voice continues, and you feel the love in the voice, "and with this, admire the courage it takes to live, the courage it takes to move past fear, pain and to finally love, to be loved, yet to die, and still be the soldiers, soldiers, the brave, brave soldiers that you *truly* are."

With that, you see a glowing filament of white star stuff from that double helix move toward you and Alleymanderous. When it touches you, your mind explodes with a white and burning light of the exquisite joy of being and being the proud, brave and noble soldier that you truly, *truly* are.

31:14.72.4 xit.z

...your eyes fly open and you lie there, exhilarated but anxious, eager but cautious. You glance out of what appears to be a window and your breath stops. A red and white ringed planet looms close and huge in the sky. You look down. Four pale blue fingers to each hand. In your head, you want to scream out, "Alleymanderous! What the hell happened?!" but it comes out a hissy, "Ekammmshhius! Swaazhhnil futtzy pa'ta'ka?!"

You stare at a three-eyed creature, sitting on a luminous blue cube. The eyes are pale green, the skin, scaly and deep magenta. You hear a high-pitched voice, "Eeekk rubb-but-ter ska na flop floop pe'de'ra kna pa reekle," which you understand to mean, "Hey, what's your problem? Be glad that what you learned last time has been so powerful that it stayed with you. It will make it easier this time around. Oh, yeah, by the way— Happy New Year!"

"Eeeeeeeeeeee—!" A new sound. You. Screaming.

...and other magical realities

Bats

Now Edward and Roy had this thing about Frankenstein, Dracula and castles and all. And you know how it goes when you're all of fourteen, and it's Saturday night during the great month of August, and you're sitting outside on the front steps right after dinner beneath a dusk-colored sky with Venus burning like a molten pearl in the sky, and Edward says, "Hey, on TV tonight—Dracula!"

And Roy said, "Oh, geeze, gotta see that—what time is it on?"

Edward squints at the fading glow of the just-set sun and says, "11:00—Horror Theatre, Channel Ten."

"Yeah," said Roy, "hey, I'm up for that—"

And they sat on that front step admiring the evening, the wonderful color of the sky going to rest and Roy said, "You ever really believe in vampires? Ghosts? Things that go 'Boo' and suck all your blood?"

Edward grinned, "Nah, I once saw a bat. It was at Lake Serene; we were sitting at a campfire and this thing kept fluttering and fluttering by—my dad said it was a bat."

"Did it land on your neck and snack on your juice?" And Roy, a sly grin on his lips, pulled them back, pretending he had fangs that were now bared. "Hah," he said, "Type 'O' please. And can I have a straw?"

"G'wan!" said Edward, "It just fluttered around and that's all it did."

"Yeah?"

"Yeah. Kind of disappointing."

"Didn't go for your neck? Didn't suck on your blood?"

"Nah, not a drop. Dad said they ate insects and that's about it."

"Do you suppose there ever were vampires?" said Roy. "You know, like Dracula?"

"Ah, who knows," said Edward. "I think it's farfetched. Those kinda things don't ever happen. People don't turn into bats and suck others' blood. I really don't think that it's true; you don't believe it, do you?"

And Roy thought for just a minute and said, "I don't *think* I do—but maybe in some way, somehow they exist—"

"Oh, man," said Edward, "oh, wow, you *are* bats!" And he laughed.

And Roy grinned, "Yeah, maybe so, I dunno. But wouldn't it be spooky if they really did? Wow, wouldn't that be weird?"

"Yeah," said Edward, "but I think I'd rather watch it on TV."

And they didn't talk for a time; they just sat on those steps, with an after-supper calm in their guts and peace in their minds and they admired the evening as the darkness of trees became one with the sky, and a few more stars peered out from the on-coming blanket of night, and after a minute Edward said, "Hey, you feel like going up to Jack's Hamburger De Lux for some ice cream?"

Roy thought for a minute and smiled and said as he fished in a pocket, "Yeah, I've got fifty cents. Why don't we do that?"

So they got up for an easy wander to Jack's Hamburger De Lux, maybe four blocks away. They walked in that evening, hearing the chirp of the crickets and the *ba-roomph* of a frog in a swamp not far away, in that neighborhood that wasn't entirely paved over with roads and shopping malls just yet, a place where some trees still grew with a primitive sense of the rotting and damp, of things multitudinous-legged scampering beneath logs, and where multi-eyed things fixed on the blackness beneath rocks; a wooded lot now, by night and imagination, a place of strange chlorophyll castles with cellulose belfries in which perhaps fluttered bats, or in whose stickery rooms lived other creatures loving of night.

And so they walked on past this particular place, a place of darkness and the smell of leaf mold and a dampness that sighed like a fetid breath from the brush-thickened lot, and Edward whispered as they walked by, "See that shape? Maybe it's Frankenstein's monster."

Roy said, "Aw, geeze." But he *did* turn his head. Then he nudged Edward. "Heavy breathing, do you hear?"

"Naw," said Edward, looking to see if Jack's was close by.

"Woo-hoooo," said Roy. "Dracula's around. Ssh. Listen!"

Edward stopped.

Roy said, "The flapping of wings."

"That's you slapping your coat."

"I ain't got a coat."

"C'mon," Edward said, "let's get some ice cream."

And perhaps both of them knew, or perhaps they did not, that they were walking faster past that wooded lot, but then they stopped in front of the old Macklewitz place, set back from the road and surrounded by trees. And you know how it is when you get into a certain frame of mind, and Roy poked Edward. "Dracula's castle. You can see his beady red eyes in that window over there."

"Cannot," said Edward, fearfully hoping that it wasn't so, but sort of hoping it might be true, so he'd have some sort of reason to feel afraid.

"Psst," said Roy, edging closer to the dimly lit house. "You can see the werewolf hiding in the bushes there. See? He's changing into a wolf right now, can't you tell?"

Fsst and *rustle*, a cat hissed and dashed out from the brush. Edward said, "God! Scared me to death! Hey, let's go on."

"Getting scared?" Roy asked. "Thoughtcha didn't believe in this sort of stuff. You're beginning to look scared."

"I want some ice cream," Edward said. "Let's go on."

And the next house they passed was well lit, but the curtains were drawn. "Ssst," said Edward, "betcha don't know what goes on in there."

They stopped by the fir tree so that they could hide. "In the basement, that scientist now has the head of a fly."

"God," Roy said, "God, why'dja say that! In the movie when the lady took the towel off the fly's head, you think I was happy about wanting to puke? God, I'll take Dracula any old day."

"Nah," said Edward, "I was just pulling your leg. Actually what goes on in there is that they dismember guys who have crewcuts—oops, oh, wow, I'm sorry pal—"

"Yeah, you are. Come on, let's go."

And they passed another house which was dark and where high un-cut grass grew for the lawn. "Hey," said Roy, "remember the movie called *The Thing*? It was about this vegetable creature—maybe he's hiding in that house over there. Remember how no one ever knew where it was?" And just then Roy suddenly reached and grabbed Edward on the arm, "Boo!"

Edward jerked and said, "Gawd, would you cut it out?"

"Whatcha scared of? You don't believe in any of this stuff, so why're you so tense?"

Edward didn't say anything and they walked for a ways in silence down those darkened streets. Then to himself, Edward smiled. "Something is following us; a giant spider, you suppose?"

"Darn you," whispered Roy, "you know I hate spiders."

"Ever notice how they get their bugs? The bug gets caught in that silky web—"

"Would you shut up—"

"—and then the spider comes down and grabs the bug—"

"—Edward—" and Roy looked around behind him.

"—and bites the bug—" and Edward this time landed a hand on Roy's shoulder but Roy jerked away and said, "Darn it, would you stop—?"

Abruptly they came to yet another wooded lot and both of them stopped. Edward gulped. "You know we've just been having fun; I mean, there aren't really such things as bats like Dracula or creatures from the Black Lagoon—"

They began to approach the wooded lot through which the road went, and just beyond they could see the blue and white sign of Jack's Hamburger De Lux. Roy said, "Naw, naw, there aren't really any ghosts or anything like that."

And they walked slowly on. "That noise in the brush is probably just a cat," Edward said.

"Yeah," said Roy, "and that shape over there is just a weeping willow, not a giant spider that's ready to pounce on us and wrap us in silk and drain us just a little bit at a time."

"Right," said Edward, "and I don't really believe that mutant from Metaluna is gonna come out from the brush to grab us in the guts—"

And as they walked, the darker it became, as the night merged with the dark of the trees, but Jack's Hamburger De Lux seemed no closer at all. And Edward said, "We saw *Sound of Music* last week; man, that was such a fun show."

Roy said, "Yeah, I've heard good things about it. I saw a Marx Brothers movie, *Horsefeathers,* last week—"

Abruptly both broke into a run and in minutes emerged puffing from the wooded lot. "There's only one problem," Edward said, "we gotta go back through that."

"Ah," grinned Roy, "we'll be OK. You know that Dracula and Frankenstein—well, even if they do exist, they won't have nothing to do with us—"

Edward nodded. "That doesn't make a lotta sense, but I'm gonna guess that maybe you're right. Boy I can't wait for that ice cream..." At that point, they passed yet another house, the house where the Cranston family lived, and just then they heard Mr. Cranston yell in a drunken rage, "Get the fuck outa here you little son of a bitch!" He shoved his son Tommy, aged eight, down the front steps, and Tommy sat there and cried.

Stunned, and wanting to do something but not knowing what, Roy and Edward stared and then they walked on in silence beneath that black wing of sky, feeling the unbounded fright when there are no vampires to blame — for the screams in the night.

The Bauble

Now as was customary in this time of year, in the southern lands, Juan was given to wander along the sandy shores of that immense river beneath the pale, blank sky of late evening. He, all of thirteen years of age, dark eyed and inappropriately muscular for his age was, perhaps because of this, calm, strong, assured, hence a very keen observer of the world around him. Not much missed his attention; not the Dark Things swooping through the air nor the sour smell of river, the pungent odor of water-soaked wood, the distant brilliant blue blasts of lightning or the flowering and black blossoms of the grasses on the shore and...and...? Juan stopped and looked out to the water. Something was bobbing in the slow current...something dark floating in the water, dark, yet sparkling, but there were no lights shining nearby, so nothing could be making it sparkle like that. Juan rolled up his pants and waded out, out to his knees, up to his waist and he lunged for the object—it felt like it was glass and terribly cold. He waded back to shore, gingerly tossing the object back and forth between his hands, and then sat on the shore with the object on the sand in front of him.

It was then that his father, Mr. Diaz, stomped out from the house nearby and the screen door slammed shut. "Juan," he yelled, "it's the middle of the night! Why are you still up? You must come back to bed."

Juan grinned, and ran a quick comb of fingers through his pale hair as if this gesture might do something to justify his being out so late or perhaps it was a nervous gesture at his father's irritation. But he smiled and said, "Look, Papa. Look what I found floating down the river."

Mr. Diaz, short with big stomach, and a round face, with dark intelligent eyes that had a way of focusing in on you as if you were a specimen on a slide, came over and looked and then he pulled on the right side of his long mustache and said, "A float, obviously, my son. Off some net, probably." He looked even closer; all you could hear was the *slip-slap-slap* of water licking the shore, and as Juan's father studied it, he got down on his hands and knees and then, hesitantly, he touched it. "Yows!" he said, yanking his finger away. "Cold, my *God*, that's cold! I've never seen a float like *that* before."

Both he and Juan stared at the round object which was black inside but speckled with brilliant white dots and elliptical objects with hazy arms that almost looked like bright whirlpools.

Mr. Diaz sighed and looked upstream. "This river brings the darndest things," he said, "the *darndest* things." He looked across to the far shore of the river in the light of the night as if there might be some answer over there. Then he looked upriver. "That Country Up North," he said, "probably their doing. Lord knows what they dump into this river." He sighed. Standing, he went over and finding an old shirt washed up on the shore, he wrapped the object up and said, "It's interesting. Maybe we'll use it as a paperweight. Right now, I want you to come home, clean up and for heaven's sake, get some sleep."

"But Papa," said Juan, "I don't have school tomorrow, and I'm not sleepy—"

"It's night," said Juan's father, holding the now wrapped sphere in its cloth cocoon. "Time to sleep."

Juan kicked at the brown, fine sand but said nothing, then walked beside his father toward home. Once inside, Juan's father put the object next to the bowl of fruit on the table in the kitchen and unwrapped it again. Gazing at it, he said, "Well, maybe Dr. Sanchez will look at it tomorrow." He shook his head again. "The river brings the strangest things...once saw a refrigerator floating downstream. Don't know how it floated but it did. The river is strange. Once saw a dog walking on the water—clear to the other side—when he reached the other side, he exploded—"

Juan looked up at his father in awe and horror. His father smiled. "No blood, not messy—the animal exploded in light and color—beautiful. Strange. But the river is like that. Strange. The river *is* strange." It was at that point that Blue Dwarf, the cat, leaped onto the table and, sniffing the globe filled with darkness, began sneezing violently then leaped off the table. "Hmm," said Juan's father. "The mystery deepens." He pulled at his mustache. "Hmm," he said. Then, "To bed."

Juan looked at the object a few more seconds, then turned and went to his room.

In the paler light and sky of day, Dr. Sanchez dropped by. An older man, with white hair like a half collar from one ear around the back of his head to the other ear, he always looked to Juan like a religious man. He walked with a stoop and a bit of a shuffle and he put his black satchel down on the table and sat. "Any whisky?" he asked.

Juan poured him a glass, being trained to take care of guests that came the way of the George Diaz family, and after the doctor took a sip, he looked at the globe. "Ho," he said, rather unimpressed, "Well, it's interesting but probably not real useful to medical science." He sat back and looked as if this pronouncement was sufficient.

"Would you care for a sandwich?" Juan's mother asked.

"More whisky?" said Juan's father.

"Both," smiled Dr. Sanchez. He then looked at the globe again as if the object barely deserved a second opinion. "Interesting that it's so black in there and those white objects are so bright." Abruptly he pulled back. "Ho. One exploded. Ho. Yes, it's like you always say, George—that river does bring down the strangest things."

"I wonder," said George, sitting down at the table and filling Dr. Sanchez's glass again, "if it might be something from that Country Up North."

"Could be," said Dr. Sanchez. "If it is, you'd best be very careful of it. Hard to say what they put into the things they dump into the river. Hard to say. May even explode, but that's doubtful."

Mrs. Diaz brought over a plateful of sandwiches and pickles and they ate in silence, contemplating the globe. "Attractive paperweight," said Mrs. Diaz.

"Indeed," said Dr. Sanchez, then, to Juan, "Where did you say you found this?"

Juan, mouth full of sandwich, just pointed out to the river.

"Ho," said Dr. Sanchez, munching a pickle. Then, "Well, I wish I could stay longer, but I have to take care of that family down the road— Mrs. Alvarez has had the flu recently." Then, "I take it—aside from interesting things that the river brings to you, your family has been blessed with good health?"

"Yes," said George, "we are well."

The doctor nodded. "'First wealth is health,' I always say." He stood, then stared at the globe once again. "Try the priest, Father Carlos. Maybe he might know what that thing is—gift of God, or the Devil's handiwork."

And he left. That afternoon, Father Carlos arrived. He was properly polite and reverent, and walked as though in the Grace of God, though to Juan, he always looked like a doctor.

Mr. Diaz pointed to the object on the table. "Dr. Sanchez thought that maybe you might know what this might be."

"I found it floating in the river last night," volunteered Juan with pride.

The priest stared at it for a long, long time. He sat down and continued to stare at it and finally said, "My." Then he looked at it very closely and said, "My, oh, my." Another pause. "A divine gift," he said, "certainly useful as a paperweight but also extraordinarily beautiful. Such a find, I would say, such a find."

Mrs. Diaz, looking both a bit hopeful and a little wary, said, "It is holy?"

The priest smiled. "All that God does is holy and this is just a manifestation of His Power and Grace," he said.

"Look," said Juan, pointing.

A bright point of light appeared and, perhaps due to the optics of the "glass," nine dimmer points of light seemed to be circling it.

"How strange," said Mrs. Diaz.

The priest shook his head. "Well, whatever you have, it's very, very unusual. I'd say enjoy it."

After he left, Juan said, "We still don't know what it is."

George pulled at his mustache and said, "Well, whatever it is, it's ours."

And everyone seemed satisfied with that. For a long time, it sat on the table where it made a most unusual conversation piece. Sometimes Mrs. Diaz moved it and put it on top of the television or in the bookcase along with her small vases and knick knacks. Once, in a fit of catnip-induced frenzy, Blue Dwarf leaped about the room, his great tail hitting the sphere of darkness, and it crashed to the tile floor...and in a wobbling roll came to a stop some feet away. Amazed that it did not break, Juan shook his head and then picked it up gingerly, not because of fragility but from the coldness of it and put it on top of the shelf where it would be out of the way of future antics by the cat. Sometimes, Mrs. Diaz would dust it, or Juan would, and then he might sit, staring at it as if he had rediscovered it.

Once in a while, those who had heard about the find might drop by and ask to look. A couple from the Country Up North dropped in and wanted to buy it, saying how they could set up some sort of business where people would pay to see it and, of course, the Diazes would get a certain percentage if they claimed a certain right to it but that would be such a bother and why not just sell it outright and be done with it and have a quiet life and don't these tourists bother you and so forth and so on and the Diazes said, "No."

And so. That was the state of the Dark Glass Globe as everyone in the little village came to know the treasure of the Diaz family. But one day things changed when lean and silver-eyed Antonio from down the street came to visit Juan.

"Let's do something," said Antonio.

"What?" asked Juan.

"Baseball."

"Yeah," said Juan, "you got a bat?"

"Yeah," said Antonio. "You got a ball?"

" —uh—" said Juan, "I don't have a baseball—guess we can't—" He stopped for a minute. He looked to the dark globe now sitting on the television. *What harm?* he wondered, *it was indestructible.* "We can use this—playing with it won't hurt it—nothing can hurt it."

Antonio hesitated. "You sure?"

Juan hesitated also, but then smiled. "Sure."

So, they went out along the river, with their catcher's mitts, and tossed that black and sparking ball back and forth, back and forth. Then Antonio picked up the baseball bat.

"Don't hit it too hard," said Juan, "I don't want to lose it."

"Don't worry, friend," said Antonio.

Juan tossed the small black globe.

Crack!

Juan yelled, "Not so hard—you said—"

"Sorry," said Antonio, grinning.

Juan watched the black globe, go up, up, up, then it came down, down, and about half way down, Juan noticed that it was streaming black stuff, looking like it had a tail. "Darn it, Antonio! You cracked it—"

Plop. The globe fell into the river not far away.

Antonio came over, trying to frown, swinging his bat like a pendulum. "Well, you said—"

Blinding flash of black light then, *ka-whoomph!*

"Oh, no!" yelled Juan, after he could see again, "what has—" he looked to the river and stared. Antonio dropped his bat and stepped back. The entire river was black, with bright points of light.

"Wow," said Antonio, "that's really—*wow*..."

"Yeah," said Juan in a whisper.

And both stood, awestruck, amazed, dumbfounded. Then Antonio pointed and slowly began to walk backwards up the bank—and then broke into a run.

"Oh-oh," said Juan, suddenly backing up as well—then running after Antonio—as the beach, boats and shoreline began slowly sinking, crumbing, caving-in and vanishing—into the black and sparkling river...

The Little Black Box of San Manuel

Now in our southern lands, there lived a shop keeper with a very long first name that everyone soon forgot and so they named him San Manuel. He was a fiftyish man, hair dusty white, and his eyes were a fragile and crystal blue; almost turquoise, actually, which made them appear as gems set in his leathery brown face. He seemed to have an affinity for faded denims and blue shirts with pearl buttons. He walked with a limp which he never talked about and, though some of the townspeople speculated about it, no one ever came to any conclusion. People loved to keep the mystery going. Some said he had been hurt in a car accident. Others said it was due to That Big Disaster many years ago in the Great Country Up North — which was no longer so great. Or habitable. Others thought it was due to a disease. But no one knew for certain. Probably because everyone knew that the truth was either very disappointing or worse than anyone could possibly imagine.

Now San Manuel had a most interesting shop, curious, you might say. Tourists passing though could find almost anything they wanted which might have had something to do with the area, but more often did not. Ashtrays made of green glazed clay, authentic beer steins imported from what was once Germany, small ancient pewter cars from the No-Longer-So-Great-Country-Up-North, flags from the robust and booming country Down South, and, of course, the usual fare of agates and precious, semi-precious and interesting, shiny but not particularly precious, stones. And San Manuel was always interested in new things that might establish him as the person with the most interesting or unusual items in the area, and since his store was the *only* store of that kind *in* the area, it was easy for the items that he carried to be considered interesting or unusual, although they might be common in places where stores like his were many.

It must be said that San Manuel did not do a great business. Not that many tourists came though the little town. But somehow, as many in these parts can testify, people got by. And so did San Manuel. He wasn't overly friendly; he'd stand behind the counter and smile but said little. Never seemed to move much. Kind of quiet, still, almost an embodiment of the warm dry air that is the rule in this southern land. But, had anyone been in the shop on a certain day in a certain recent year, they might have seen a very different person. That was the day that little Anastascio, regarded by some in the town as a jokester or resident devil, brought in a black, glass cube for San Manuel. Little Anastascio, with great reverence and a smile, put the glass cube on the counter. He looked up at San Manuel. San Manuel did not move. His eyes, however, focused in like two little blue camera lenses on the glass box. Then he looked to little Anastascio with his black hair over his forehead; the eyes, brown, bright, mischievous. "Well?" he asked.

Little Anastascio shrugged, and smiled.

Finally, San Manuel moved closer and picked up the black glass box. He shook it. Silence. He looked at it closely. "Well," he finally said, "a mystery. Any more?"

Little Anastascio shook his head, his eyes searching San Manuel's face.

"I assume, little urchin, that you want a lot for this. Still—" he pondered the cube, "it might be worth a great deal to someone," and he smiled, "but most likely not. It's going to sit on my shelf and gather dust, so I'm afraid you'll have little position on which to barter or argue."

Little Anastascio just smiled, nodded.

San Manuel produced a five-note, suspecting that he might likely sell it for ten times as much or more. Stuff like this sold. Why, was beyond him.

He gave the five-note to Little Anastascio, who grinned and bounded out of the store like he had received a hundred-note. San Manuel just smiled and put the cube on a shelf near the cash register. He turned away to do something else; when he turned around, he looked at the cube for a long time. It was no longer black but a deep shade of maroon. "Hmm," mused San Manuel, "it must be the light." He watched it a few more minutes, but it remained maroon. He smiled to himself, went about the store dusting, and rearranging items that didn't really need to be rearranged since they hadn't been moved much since his last rearrangement. In a few minutes, he returned to the counter and stared at the cube. It was now a deep blue. San Manuel picked it up and considered it. His hand trembled just a bit; the cube also felt decidedly warmer. San

Manuel cleared his throat, put the cube back down and again stared at it for a long time. No changes. He glanced away. Still no changes. He turned his head—then looked back. The cube was now pale green. San Manuel sucked in a deep breath, held it for a second, then let it out slowly. "Little Anastascio, what is it you have left me with? What is this?" He picked up the cube again. And as he did so, the green faded to white and, as though entranced, he kept watching. Abruptly, the white dissolved and there was a scene of a strange world—he could see a three dimensional view of his shop in the cube, but there were several moons in the sky and the sky was a deep blue-purple. "Little Anastascio," said San Manuel again, "what *is* it you have given me?" He felt a sudden urge to put it down, but it was as though his hands and vision were frozen. And as he watched the scene in the cube, he saw a figure come out of the store and walk toward him, gaining in size. Abruptly, he sucked in another breath. "Mariana—can it be you? How can it be—?"

The figure in the cube, dark haired, with hazel eyes, smiled. And he saw her lips move and somehow heard her voice. "Dear San Manuel, I've never forgotten you—we were so young then and so foolish. But I've changed and I know you have too—can we start over?"

Stunned, San Manuel stepped back until he bumped into the counter and still he could not take his gaze off the vision in the cube and still he could not let go of the cube. "Mariana," he whispered, "this cannot be— you died in a car accident—I went to your funeral—"

Mariana shook her head. "Say what you want, think what you will. Maybe this is a little heaven you are holding in your hands. Maybe in the end it makes little difference what this is. But know this, dearest San Manuel, I love you, I miss you and I want you—do you want me?"

And the composed, controlled facade of San Manuel crumbled. "I always wanted you... to be with you...but your father—I wasn't rich enough—"

And Mariana shook her head. "That was a long time ago in a different time and different reality. This is where we are now. I want you;" she said, "do you want me?"

"More than anything," said San Manuel. "I've always dreamed of you and thought of you often—"

"Then that is all that is needed—"

Flash—white light burst from the cube, engulfing San Manuel.

Crash and the cube hit the floor. Almost immediately, Little Anastascio dashed into the shop, and picking up the cube, saw two figures stroll toward the open doorway of the strange curio shop in the cube. The scene then vanished and the cube went black. Little Anastascio gave a squeal of delight — and bounded out the door.

And of the fate of San Manuel? Who is to know why or how this all happened; suffice it to say, it did. But most important, wherever San Manuel went, it is most likely that he is a very, very happy man.

Spiders

A part of me must think they're cute, you know, the spiders in my bathtub. I've grown to call them 'pie-ders'. I'm not sure if spiders are cute enough to call them a cute name. I mean, if you don't like spiders, then a bathtub filled with them is hardly cute. Also, it's difficult to take a shower or a bath.

Pussy Galore, my huge tiger cat, frequently wanders in, and standing with paws on top of the bathtub, looks down; his gaze darts about as he contemplates the writhing mass of black spiders that fill the bathtub halfway up. His tail switches wildly, his mouth twitches and he makes noises like *shk-shk-shk-shk*. If he could think, I would fantasize him saying, "What are you doing? What are you doing? Keeping a tub filled with spiders. What are you *doing*?"

If I had to answer Pussy, I confess, I would not know *what* to say.

"You do have a problem, don't you?" says Sally, my next door neighbor. "How many times have you hauled them out?" She's fiftyish and stands back away from the tub. She even pulls her long, grey hair back around her shoulder as if somehow the spiders are going to erupt *en masse* from the tub up to her hair and maybe weave her to death or dump silk on her and put her into some sort of cocoon.

"Kind of like a vein of live coal," I say. "No matter how much I excavate, I can never excavate enough."

"They come up through the drain or what?" she asks.

"Damn if I know. Maybe they drop through the ceiling, but," and I look up to the bare ceiling, "no place they can drop from."

"Hmm," she says, "and you just moved in here," her blue eyes scrutinize the mass in the bathtub, "because you had problems at you last place with—"

"Scorpions—"

"Um."

"And before that—sow bugs—"

"Bathroom sink?"

"Toilet."

Sally gazes a few minutes more. "There's a pattern."

"You could say that."

"You know what I think?"

"I've already made an appointment."

Dr. Glazier has something of a cool temperament and maybe it is just as well. His mind is as intricate as a snowflake and with insight equally well-designed. He is a moderately heavy man and I have the sense that he has been much heavier. He doesn't wear glasses, or a tie, neither is he bald. Rather, he has thick grey hair, wears a green shirt open at the neck, and grey trousers. He does his therapy on a patio with the pool in the background and an absolute *whammo* view of Mt. Rainier towering above him like a big blunted Freudian *dong* getting a slow, cold blowjob from the glaciers. Counseling has been good to Dr. Glazier. *Very good.* "So," he says, "you got spiders in the bathtub."

"Yeah."

"Lots?"

"Yeah."

"You get rid of them—"

"They come back."

"And if it's not spiders—"

"Scorpions."

"And if not scorpions—"

"Some other god-forsaken creature."

"Bug."

(Pause) "Yeah. Bug."

Dr. Glazier nods. "Ya know," he says, "in some clients I see, they either can't face their feelings or their past issues and it comes out as a fear of something—being locked in the closet as a kid comes out as a fear of the night, of closed doors, a habit of giving away clothing; sometimes a fear of a parent which was never expressed comes out as some unfortunate bug. Betcha you were either abused or stuck in a place with lots of bugs—as punishment, locked in the cellar, perhaps."

He looks directly at me. Matter-of-fact look of pride—he's done this for a long time. Years. A decade. A thousand years. Maybe since humankind began wandering this rock and first learned Fear, and, for the most part, how not to take responsibility for it. Paste the Fear Picture on mommy, daddy, the Democrats, the Environmentalists and make them the enemy. You know. Glazier has been around for a long time, therapeutically inching down the incredibly unending incline of the Human Condition.

Like a monkey putting two sticks together and thus able to reach for the metaphysical banana, I say, "My bathtub filled with spiders is a symbol of my unfinished business/fear regarding my father—a sort of three dimensional creation of my fears—"

"Did you see your father as a spider?"

"No."

"How did you see him?"

"I didn't."

"Why?"

"He was never there."

Dr. Glazier looks at me. On his slow journey down the Incredible Incline of the Human Condition, he has just hit a rock. I look over his shoulder. I point. He looks. He stands.

The entire swimming pool is filled with spiders. Big ones. Small ones. Black ones. Brown ones. Pretty ones. Poisonous ones.

He whistles through his teeth and says, "Holy shit." A long pause, then, softly, "Ho-lee shh-it—!"

I offer to pay him. He shakes his head and I leave him standing by the swimming pool, hands on his hips. I don't hear him whistling.

On the way home, I have to admit, what Dr. Glazier said hit something. My father wasn't around. *Where was he?* *Where was that son of a gun? Where was that son of a bitch? Where was that prick!* I catch myself. Anger? *Come to think of it, where was my mother? Where was—where was—*I squeeze my eyes shut; suddenly, a hot blade of pain—no, *rage*—skewers my guts from my anus to my throat and inside something burns and blisters and I have an uncontrollable need to sneeze—*achoo*—and there on my lap, a little spider. It turns, waves a leg in greeting, and scampers off my leg.

I muse. I think I'd like to tell Dr. Glazier of my experience but I don't think he'd be too happy to hear from me right now.

And when I get home, I go to the bathroom, only to see what appears to be a Martian or an alien sitting on the toilet.

"You're out of toilet paper!" it screeches.

"Tough shit," I say. I have an idea of what *this* is about. Later. Later. Inwardly, I sigh at the other work that I now know needs to be done, but right now, the spiders, the spiders—my attention is drawn to the bathtub. The spiders are gone—or—melted? For what is in there looks like a slowly moving black pool of India ink.

"*Toilet paper!*" shrieks the alien. "How can you be so cruel as to put me through this? How can you *do* this to me, the one who cared for you? How can you *do* this to me?"

I don't reply. I kinda gotta hunch who *that* is. But right now, I retrieve a fountain pen from a desk drawer, go to the bathtub and fill the barrel of the pen.

"You *never* treated me well," says the alien writhing on the toilet. "You never could do anything right...what a rotten grandson—(and blah, blah, blah—)"

I've more important things to do. I go to the desk and taking out a stack of paper, I write, long, long, into the night, each letter becoming a spider, running, hiding from the light.

Dilly of a Dally of a Day

Yes sir, yes, sir, we've all had days like that, yes sir; that goddamn perfect dilly of a dally of a day where you wake up in the morning and it's summer, my God, that sunlight is so white and bright, and it makes trees and grass (especially if it's all May young and not yet July old) all bright green—my goodness, and you wonder how it is that all the plants right here and now can be all so bright as if the very juice of them is somehow on fire with the burning green of growth. And now it was on that kind of day, a perfect dilly of a dally of a day that Edward, all of perhaps age ten, decided that he and his best friend Roy would go out and explore that perfect day.

So. Now. Just how do you go about exploring a perfect day? Why, of course, you go to a movie. And so Edward and Roy, they sat down right after breakfast (after sleeping out in Roy's back yard and having for breakfast sausages and waffles and eggs over easy and hot cocoa, too, and they sat at the table while Roy's thin mom with the black hair streaked with grey hummed to herself and cleared away the dishes with a delightful homey clatter placing them in the sink, and ran the sink full of suds and water) and Roy said, "Hey! Looky here!"

And Edward, still munching on a sausage and delighting in its squirting, salty droolingness grinned, and looked and said, "Huh?"

"Looky," said Roy, pointing to an ad for the local theater, the View, (Oh, don'tcha wonder where names come from? View? The only view it had, at least from the front, was the new 1956-built Texaco station across the street with the Coke machine out front that, when it worked, delivered those awesome thick bottles of Coke that you had to pry the lid off of. View? Musta meant the view inside the theater maybe, or maybe the view of the apartment near the Texaco station, the second floor of which frequently had the drapes open with a wide man in tee shirt and red and white striped underwear looking out at the lines that formed in front of the View about noon on Saturdays, rain or shine, to watch the show and

99

maybe never really realizing that he, himself, was a show but no mat-ter — the View was the View and that's all that matters here) and Roy said again, "Hey, a double feature! *Creature from the Black Lagoon* and *Zorro.*"

And Edward took another bite of sausage and said, "Wow!" and in the background the clatter of dishes. Outside Edward saw a willow wave and weave as if somehow a vast and vertical sphere and pool of green water rippling in the wind, and he said, "Hey, let's do that. What time?"

"Noon," said Roy.

"Let's do it," said Edward.

"More cocoa?" asked Roy's mom.

"Yeah," said Roy.

"Please," said Edward.

"Marshmallows again?"

"Yeah," they both said and in a minute they were drinking hot cocoa, delighting in the chocolate-slicked marshmallows and ah, yes, it seemed as if it was to be a perfect dilly of a dally of a day, yes, yes indeed and so, from breakfast table and the sighing at the wonder of hot chocolate, they went outside and felt the coolness of the air and admired the shadows of the trees, the blue sky and the sunlight coming through leaves and Roy said, "What'll we do?"

"Let's go for a walk," said Edward.

So, they went for a walk to a so-called vacant lot that was supposed to be developed — that is, cut and leveled and paved over with a building dumped right there, right in the middle of a flat of black asphalt.

So. They walked through this vacant lot and saw: from a fallen and rotting tree with exposed deep and rusted red bark (the color soil and close to being soil) white, oh, so pale and white delicate mushrooms. "Ah," said Edward pointing, "aren't those neat?"

"Yeah," said Roy and he stopped. "Hey, look."

Edward did. A fly struggled in a web and a spider danced down to the insect and grappled with it and spun it about, then knelt and bit the fly and the fly became so still and the spider became busy wrapping, wrapping, wrapping the fly in a sticky silky package and then hauled it to the center of the silken web.

Roy said, "Geeze."

Edward gulped.

And they continued on, on a pathway that was somehow, it seemed, just used by kids and Edward could never, but never figure out why older people never used it and they kept on through that vacant lot and something rustled in the leaves on the ground.

"Sh," whispered Edward.

Roy stopped.

Edward looked around, oh, carefully this way, that, then pointing. Roy looked where a very large toad sat, warty as could be, brown skin the color of old leaves and delicate yellow lines down its back with eyes as dark as soil.

Edward leaned over and picking it up, the toad was suddenly wet and made soft and frightened pleading sounds.

"Hey," said Roy, "it peed on you."

"Yeah, it did," and Edward laughed.

"You'll get warts."

"Nah, I won't." And for a minute, fumbling toad and Edward's hands stopped their mutual dancing grapple and the toad appeared to be looking at Edward and Edward smiled again and put the toad down and it crawled away to blend and hide in leaves and earth and Edward wiped his hands on his pants.

"I hear they make good pets," said Roy.

"Never had one," said Edward, "but I've had turtles." He shrugged. "Not very exciting pets."

"My brother had a turtle, but he let the water evaporate from the bowl."

"Yeah?"

"Yeah. He found it all shriveled up like a prune a week later and tossed it in the bathroom sink and apologized to it for an hour."

"Yeah?"

"Yeah."

"Then what?"

Roy shrugged. "Frankie felt better but the turtle didn't seem to benefit too much."

They continued on, they continued on through the rich and damp smell of sour soil and leaf mold, through the dampness and cool of the so-called vacant lot and by the side of the path—

"Oh-oh," said Edward.

"Yeah, doesn't that look like Mrs. Ellsworth's cat? She's been looking for him for a week."

The cat was a tiger cat, but now it lay close to the earth, eyes closed, and fur matted and very dirty as it lay, lay close, close to the earth.

"Been there for a while."

"Yeah," said Roy, "probably some jerk ran over it and threw it in the woods—"

And who knows why, but Edward took a stick and moved the cat.

"Oh, God," he said, and the maggots squirmed and twisted and danced in their interrupted feeding and Edward had an urge to vomit; he looked away and took a breath.

"God," he said, "God."

Roy shook his head. What could be said at the spectacle of life returning to the earth? Not much. No, sir, not much at all and on that dilly of a dally of a day, the flow of life moving up from the soil into trees and into the leaves to dance as chlorophyll and photosynthesis and water vapor and sunlight and air and life, moved down from things once living now dying, now maggoty and returning to the soil and Edward and Roy just stared again at Mrs. Ellsworth's cat that now was more and more belonging to the earth and finally Edward said, "God, that's really weird. Let's go."

And they did. And they moved on through that vacant lot; they moved on beside a marsh and heard the plop of a frog and on the shore of that marsh that was most likely going to be moist mud in several weeks and after that, dry caked earth—but for right now, that was water, and that water was marsh and in that marsh: "Pollywogs!" said Roy. "Hey, why don't we come back later with some jars—?"

"Yeah," said Edward, "that'd be fun."

And the pollywogs, like large black sperm, wiggled and waggled to the deeper water, waiting to be caught and watched or, escaping, waiting to transform. And they had just a short time to do it before the water would be gone, but Edward and Roy knew that they would do it in just the right time. Edward secretly wondered how it was that those pollywogs *would* do it in just the right time, just before the final water turned to air, but he knew and the pollywogs too, that it would be done, everything done as if a road map were somehow laid out and everything was arriving to every important destination right on time, the journey going along so well that no one, nothing, no pollywog nor maple tree nor maggot nor spider ever had to consult a travel clock or set a second hand or even glance at the position of the sun in the sky. Everything knew what time it was and where they ought to be.

And Edward finally said, as they came to a point where the path led out of the woods up an embankment of new dirt, "Hey, I bet we have time to stop at Jackson's Drugstore," and as soon as he said it, they were up over the embankment and there was the drugstore sitting right there.

"Yeah," said Roy, "let's do that!"

And they walked in.

They walked into Jackson's drugstore and sniffed the alcohol and chocolate scented air. They went to the magazine section and glanced through the comics on that dilly of a dally of a day and they had only been there a few minutes when old Mr. Jackson walked in; old Mr. Jackson, owner of the drugstore, came walking in, tired looking with his brown hair now turned white and his face lined and jowled and his suit brown and a little baggy, and he went to the cashier, young Karen Thompson, maybe nineteen, with her brown hair pulled back in a ponytail and braces on her teeth and she tried to smile and keep her upper lip down so that, she probably thought, no one would notice her braces although everyone knew she was trying not to show them because she thought it might be detracting from her looks and everyone loved her anyway, and Mr. Jackson told her, "I'm expecting a call from the Bax Brothers Construction Company—they're supposed to fill in the rest of the vacant lot today."

"Oh," said Karen, "they already called—they'll be here at one to fill in the lot."

Edward looked at Roy and Roy looked at Edward, the mutual look of, "Oh crap!"

Then Mr. Jackson looked over to Edward and Roy and frowned and said, "You kids *know* you aren't supposed to read the comics—buy or be on your way."

And Edward and Roy looked at each other, put down *Superman* and *Little Lulu* and went back and followed the path past the marsh past Mrs. Ellsworth's cat, past the place where to toad pleaded and peed, past the spider's web and they sat on a log near the place where the pale white mushrooms fed off the old log returning to earth and there, amidst cool and dark shadows, they sat on a log; they sat and watched sunlight shift in the trees and looked up to the blue sky high above, and on this perfect dilly of a dally of a day, Edward and Roy sat. They sat on that log in the so-called vacant lot, knowing that they would not be going to see *Creature from the Black Lagoon* or *Zorro*. No, on that dilly of a dally of a day, they knew that even the finest of days brought with it monsters, and as they sat in the theater of earth and life, they sighed, felt sad and wanted to cry as they waited for the sad, sad show to begin.

Eggs

You know how it is. You've probably had mornings like that where you wake up and wish to hell you hadn't. That's how Edward felt as he sat up in bed and wondered, *Jesus! Hangover! Just* how *am I gonna get through* this *day?* He glanced at the clock. *Nine! Feels like five!* He stood and with one foot, managed to step on the bottom of the other leg of his pajamas, stumbled, and caught himself on the dresser. He yanked up his pajamas, made it to the bathroom and studiously avoided the mirror. *I'm doing okay*, he thought, *now, the kitchen. Just a few feet to go.* He kept a hand on his pajama bottoms, turned the stove on, put water on to boil, thinking, *Yeah, it's gonna take a lot of coffee.* He reached into the refrigerator, pulled out a carton of eggs that he had bought yesterday and, setting the carton down on the kitchen table, he picked up an egg, held it in his hand as he looked around for the frying pan—which was in the sink. *Great*, he said to himself, *real great—sloppy housekeeper.* He stopped. The egg. Something was moving inside. *Oh, shit*, he thought, *no wonder the eggs were on special. Fuck. They're hatching!* With both dismay and surprise, he looked at the egg in his hand. *Well, well, well*, he mused, *isn't this just dandy? A miracle of birth is occurring right in my little alcohol-stained hand and I'm too hung over to cry at the beauty, the wonder, of birth.*

Pow! The side of the shell flew off as though it had been blasted.

Edward pulled back. *Little chickies are brought into the world with dynamite? Are shells that tough?* A little head poked out through the opening. A little blue head looked cautiously around. Then it looked up at Edward. "Are they gone?"

Edward gulped. "Are who gone?"

"The Klorts."

Edward stared. "You aren't a chicken, are you?"

"No," said the little figure. "I'm from the Certa Empire."

Edward was feeling a trifle upset. "Why are you in my egg? I can't scramble you. Why are you in my egg? Are you really in my egg? Am I having alcohol withdrawal?" Edward looked very pathetic, like he really wanted to have someone suddenly appear with all the answers.

The little Certan climbed out of the egg and sat on Edward's thumb. "I really can explain."

Edward went over to the table and sat down. "Please do."

"It's like this—oh—wait a minute." The little Certan jumped off Edward's hand and scampered to the opened egg carton. He ran up and down both rows knocking on each egg and yelling, "Okay! It's okay! We're safe here."

Seven eggs burst open and seven other little blue Certans crawled out. They went to the last four remaining eggs, cut them open with something that looked like a miniature laser, and began to haul out equipment. The first Certan returned to Edward's hand and, climbing back into it, returned to his former position on Edward's thumb. "By the way," he said, "I'm Erlk."

Edward shrugged. "Hello. I'm Edward."

"Hi," said the alien, smiling. Edward noted that the alien was actually very nice. Erlk was bald, had little yellow eyes which were quite attractive with the blue skin and he wore a kind of one-piece body suit made of some material that was orange and looked like spun metal. Erlk wore little black boots and there was some sort of insignia on the lapel of the suit—something like an emblem that astronauts wore on their suit signifying the mission. But then, Edward thought, it might be a political slogan: "Vote Erlk for High Command" or even an advertising claim: "Healthy Certans drink Plook."

"What are you looking at?" asked Erlk.

"That," said Edward, pointing to the button. "What's it mean?"

Erlk shrugged. "Who knows? I just like the way it looks."

"Oh," replied Edward, suddenly embarrassed that he had not considered something as simple as that.

The alien smiled. "Don't be embarrassed. I hardly expected you to know that. After all, I don't know what that thing is around your neck."

Edward looked down. "That. Oh, that's a crucifix."

Erlk looked puzzled. "A what?"

"Crucifix. It's a symbol. A man, long, long ago, was nailed to a wooden cross—"

"Oh," said Erlk, making a vile face. "Do you people still do that?"

"No," said Edward, then, after thinking for a minute, "yeah, I guess we do."

Erlk looked aghast. "Really? You still nail people to crosses?"

"No," said Edward, "we nail ourselves to our own crosses."

"Ah," said Erlk. "I think I understand."

"Oh," said Edward, looking a bit askance, "then tell me about it."

Erlk gave Edward a very, *very* penetrating look. "You *know* what *your* cross is."

"Look," said Edward, feeling incredibly uneasy. *How, how, how*, he thought to himself, *could these little bastards know so much*? "how was it you ended up in my eggs?"

Erlk smiled. "In response to your unspoken question, we are semi-telepathic. In response to your second question, we came because we were attacked by the Klorts: we tried to lose them by dashing into a Safeway, they had locked us onto their scanners and no matter where we tried to hide—be it behind the S & W peas or the toilet paper, they came right after us. Of course, we made it difficult for them to get us and that's what saved us. While we hid behind those nice, thick cans of MJB coffee, we had already discovered that eggs were the perfect hiding place. So," and Erlk smiled in obvious pride, "we had a simultaneous matter exchange. While eight of us and tools and the Perkle Drive beamed and occupied the dozen eggs, one dozen yolks beamed aboard our ship." Erlk laughed and rubbed his chin with a four fingered hand. "Wonder what the Klorts thought when they opened the ship and all those yolks poured out?"

Edward smiled. "If they blasted your ship, they'd have one hell of a big omelet to contend with." Then, thoughtfully, "Incidentally, what is the Perkle Drive?"

"Our world exists in a different dimension; the Perkle Drive enables us to detect and travel different dimensions. You see, that is why the Klorts are after us—we have an advanced model and we can skip around to various dimensions while the Klorts have to go through one at a time. The only reason they got us was that they have a new system of masking their presence—we were attacked and the shock caused damage to the drive—" Then the alien looked a bit sheepish, "Ah—do you mind if we repair it on the counter? Next to the sink? We'll clean up afterwards."

Edward smiled. "You considerate beasties," he said, "sure."

It was then that a commotion took place up counter toward the stove, sink and refrigerator. Four little blue Certans were pointing and yelling at something. *God*, thought Edward, *what if they're pointing to a dirty towel? How embarrassing.* But as he looked, he discovered that was not what the aliens were pointing at, at all. No. Stacked along the end of the counter, right next to the refrigerator, were spice bottles that Melissa, Edward's now ex-wife, kept there. Edward frowned. *So what's to get excited over about a squat bottle of mustard, a giant size bottle of Heinz ketchup, a big, round cardboard cylinder of iodized salt and small glass jars of cinnamon, nutmeg, cocoa and pepper?*

Erlk jumped down from Edward's hand, ran across the table, jumped up to the counter and ran over to the others, then stopped, stared— obviously awestruck.

Edward did not know what to think. He shrugged, stood, pulled his pajamas up higher and wandered over. "You guys like ketchup? I can give you a large tablespoon of it but I really don't have anything you can eat it with—"

"What?" Erlk said. "Oh, no—we're not talking about what's in the bottle—we're talking about the bottle—it's a perfect replica of an Andron Star Cruiser!" Erlk looked at Edward entreatingly. "Can we have it? Please? We'll give you anything for it—we can put the Perkle Drive in it, Polyhedratetranize the exterior for external and structural strength—it— it's perfect!"

"Well," said Edward picking up the bottle, "I could put the ketchup in another bottle—I take it you want the label off—unless you want to call your ship 'Star Cruiser Heinz 57 Varieties'—"

But before either of them could say another word, more ruckus. This time several aliens were gleefully pointing at the coffee pot. Erlk gave a gasp and went scampering over to it. "Oh, Stars!" he whispered. "A Botollean Battle Cruiser!"

Edward was reluctant to offer that, but he also thought, *Hell, what was five bucks compared to getting these little critters on their way?* At that, Erlk turned and smiled. "That was indeed a kind thought. Have no fear; you shall be well reimbursed for whatever way you help us. You are a kind person."

Edward sighed. "Thank you," he replied. "I wish I could believe that."

Erlk looked at Edward sympathetically. Edward felt very self-conscious and looked away. He got the ketchup bottle, thunked the contents into a large jar, then washed out the inside of the bottle with hot water and managed to get the label off. He shook it and got most of the water out. "Do you guys want the bottle on its side or upright?"

"Upright," said Erlk. "We have our clingboots on." He turned to join the others as they brought over from the egg carton a device that looked like a miniature vacuum tube.

Edward stretched. "You guys use what ever you want; take what you need."

Erlk turned and bowed. "Thank you."

Edward yawned. "I'm gonna take a shower and get dressed. Oh, and yeah, when the water boils would you cut off the burner?"

"You bet," said Erlk.

And after Edward left the room, another blue alien, this one by the name of Yum, who was dressed in a yellow suit, came up to Erlk. "That man is very nice; we should do something delightful for him."

"I know," said Erlk, nodding, "and I think I know what we can do." He nodded again and looked at Yum. "We're going to leave him a surprise." He smiled. "Yes, a nice, *nice* surprise." Then, "All right, let's install the Perkle Drive in the coffee pot first and see how it works before we decide."

And while all this was going on, Edward was standing in the shower. *What time was he supposed to meet Janice? Oh, oh, yeah, right*, he thought, *11:30 for coffee. She's probably going to say goodbye—just like Marsha did, just like Connie did, just like my wife. Might as well prepare for the worst*, he thought, *I'm just a loser.* He sighed and even thought about calling Janice and telling her that he was sick and couldn't make it. *No*, he thought, *no, hell, I'll go. What a hassle.* He dried, shaved, put on his bathrobe. He peeked into the kitchen; the coffee pot, with three Certans sitting on the bottom along with what he assumed was the Perkle Drive, circled about the kitchen, then landed back on the stove like some ungainly aircraft.

Erlk called to Edward, "We decided on the ketchup bottle."

"Great," said Edward, "hope it works."

Edward went to get dressed. He was gone, perhaps, ten minutes and when he returned to the kitchen, the Certans were gone. But, there on the table—"Well, I'll be damned," Edward said, "breakfast!" Two pieces of toast with jam, bacon, scrambled eggs and there was a full dozen eggs sitting in the carton. Near the plate, a note that Edward had to squint to read: "Thank you Edward. Hope you enjoy your breakfast; our matter analyzer created it for you and we put in some special vitamins and minerals that will be helpful to you. The eggs are fresh. Enjoy your meal. In particular, enjoy how you will feel afterwards. Thanks again for your help. Your friends, The Certans, Captain Erlk."

Edward sat and almost felt like crying. *That was nice of them*, he thought, *now that was* really *nice of them.* He ate slowly, savoring the food—even if it was artificially produced, it nonetheless looked like food and tasted great. He sipped the coffee. "Ah, perfect," he sighed. Yes, he felt better. Much better. He stood, stretched. Then he thought about Janice. His feelings turned dark and he thought again, *Oh, hell. I'm going to call and cancel*—and just as he thought that, he froze. *What the*—he thought. He could not move. He looked at his hands; they were white, hard, like eggshell. Involuntarily, his arms rose until they stuck out perpendicularly from him and he looked like a cross. His whole body became encased in the shell and he had just enough room to breathe. *If I don't get out of this*, he thought, *I will suffocate.* He raged at the Certans. *You little fuckers*, he thought, *you trapped me in my shell of*—he thought for a minute—*of-oh-oh. Oh, dear. Oh, God.* Edward suddenly became frenzied. *I want out, I want out of this shell! I want out of this misery! I do want to live! I want to see Janice, God damn it!* Somehow, he freed a hand from the mold; he had barely enough room to pull his arm back, form a fist and punch the shell from the inside. It broke. One arm free. Then the other. *God damn it!* he screamed in his mind, *I want out!* He punched, squirmed, fought—more of the shell cracked, broke and hurriedly he shucked off the other pieces, gasping, panting from the exertion. The shell that had covered his face was intact and looking at the molded expression, Edward gulped. "Oh, God," he whispered, "I had no idea I looked so hurt and angry. Why did they *do* this—" and then the thought occurred to him: *the Certans cared enough about me to show me that.* Slowly, he went to open the kitchen window, looked out to the sky and said, "Erlk, if you ever need a friend, you *got* one." Then, quickly, Edward broke apart the rest of the shell and threw the pieces in the wastebasket. And he hustled about, not wanting to be late to meet Janice, for after all, it looked like it was going to be a fine, fine day indeed.

You Can Hardly Wait

In your youth, life looks long, unending, before you. You turn ten and your parents are *so* cool. You turn thirteen, and your parents are *so* stupid. You turn eighteen and God, you can't wait to get away. Twenty-one! Celebrate with a hangover the next day. On and on. Thirty, great job, making lots of money, swell wife, forty, been having trouble with the kids and you and your wife—well, it feels like you're kinda going your separate ways, fifty, geeze, time sure is going *sixty* whoa, how did that— *seventy*—I can barely remember where I put—*eighty* and you know the rest. Yeah, yeah, you *know* the rest. You *know* how it's fuckin' gonna be. And it is. And it is.

"Mr. Taylor? Mr. Taylor? Time to get up now. We're gonna get you shaved and cleaned up—"

—*what*? you think. *Where—where am—what*? You open your eyes. The room swims into focus. You look at the girl. She's dressed in pale blue and she's got blonde hair in a ponytail and she must be what, sixteen— no, eighteen, maybe. You were that young once. For some reason, you really like her nose—proud, Roman. She's pretty. You can still feel your dong get stiff.

"Let me help you," she says. She puts her arms around your back and gently helps you sit while also helping you swing your legs over the edge of the bed. It's warm in the room. "You know where you are?" she asks.

"Har-Harbor—Harborbay—" Fucking words won't come out.

"That's right," she says. "Harborbay Nursing Home. You know the date?"

"October—uh—September—uh—um—25th, 2025—"

"Almost," she laughs. "27th of September. Do you have to pee?"

Pee, you think. *Pee. Do I haveta pee*? *Yeah,* yeah, *I gotta pee.* You nod your head.

"You want the urinal or can you make it to the bathroom?"

God damn, you think, *at least* some *shred of dignity.* "Bathroom."

You stand. These legs. These legs that took you to the Andes in 2010. These legs that took you backpacking in the Wind River Range in 2000. These legs that don't move worth Jack shit now. But you somehow get to the bathroom and it takes forever to pee. Through the open bathroom door, you can hear the sounds of the unit: someone laughing, the distant clink of silverware on ceramic. The television in the dining room is suddenly turned up. You catch some of the news —

"—colony on Mars destroyed—unknown organism or virus to blame—survivors en route back to space station—question of quarantine major issue—in other news, riots continue to flare up in Cape Town as more emergency food shipments are discovered stolen—" You get a little sliver of pee and you continue to listen: "—Mary Mathis here with the weather report. Temperatures continue hot for this time of year in many places; the high in Fairbanks will be 95 today, Seattle, 107, Los Angeles, 118 as more records are shattered—many dying of heat stroke." You then hear someone yell, "Turn that damn thing down or turn it off—" The sound drops.

You're finally able to pee and glad the place is air conditioned. You finish your task and turn: is that you, shuffling across the floor? Is that your hand shaking as you hold your pajamas up? You look at the pjs: pale green with alternating vertical bands of dark green stripes. Nursing home issue. You open the door and the nurse's aide is there. Your eyes can focus better and you look at her name tag. Jenny. Yes. Jenny.

"Did you pee?" she says.

You nod.

"Did you poop?"

You shake your head and try to smile. "Nope. Not in my britches either."

"That's good," she says. She takes you by the arm and you shuffle down to breakfast. You sit at the table across from Mrs. Whatshername— you think you knew it yesterday but today—well, maybe you'll remember it later. She looks blankly at you, then looks away. The wallscreen continues to present the news and you can't imagine why no one changes the channel, as if you really want to hear about all the disasters in the world—at breakfast.

Jenny brings your tray for you. "Looks good," she says brightly, "scrambled eggs, ham, and Malt-o-Meal. Mmmmm—mmm."

"Thanks," you say. She's trying.

Mrs. Pickins sits at the table over there. She constantly moves, twitches. Anxiety. You know that's anxiety. No matter how much the distraction, the stimulation, she knows what she's here for. She wrings her hands, so anxious that she can't focus on her eating. Mr. Smathers over there, you recognize him and a while back, you actually had a lucid conversation with him. He used to be a big shot at Macrosoft before it crashed. "Lost everything," but he was philosophical. "Just glad I paid off my house. Can't believe it would happen to me. What? Macrosoft crashing? Delayed Electromagnetic-Induced Neurodegenerative Syndrome—DEINS—what? Linked also to the onset of Parkinson's and Alzheimer's disease? *What?*" You pay attention to your food, to the eggs and it actually tastes pretty good. The big SonyFord wallscreen still presents the news, now—*Breaking News* flashes on the screen—"Katy Durant here—a special on the Mars Colony Disaster or the MCD—unknown contamination—"

You really can't hear that well with the plug of wax in your right ear and with the increase in noise in the dining room as more folks come in for breakfast: the movement, the voices, Mrs. Halsey over there crying as she has been doing all the time she's been there—you nudge your table closer to the screen to better listen to what Durant, the newscaster has to say. You don't suspect it's to cheer everyone up. "—apparently the contamination—and that's what we're calling it now—on Mars was transferred to the survivors—all now confirmed dead en route to Earth—question has come up about the safety of the Martian samples sent back in 2006—under quarantine in Mars Sealed Environment or MSE in Houston and no expected problems—makes the situation so perplexing—we go live to Mr. Shuster from NASA in Houston, head of the Mars Return Sample Mission—MRSM—Mr. Shuster, why is the *mumblemumble* showing up now and are the samples safe?"

Mr. Shuster's picture is on the screen—he's an older guy, white hair and that *terribly* pained expression that such folks get when they have to say something and they really don't know what to say, except they have to say something OK, bland, reassuring and ultimately stupid so the audience won't panic and stop looking at the commercial breaks for MaytagTimeWarner washing machines.

"—well, Katy—"

You're aware of a nurse's aide right next to you at Mrs. Halsey's table. "There, there, Mrs. Halsey—just try to eat—everything will be just fine—"

You're suddenly really irritated at the aide because you realize that you've been really trying to follow this newscast; you realize—maybe no one else does—*this* is serious, but you know something else that is—calming—what? After a few minutes, you can hear Mr. Shuster, apparently responding to a question Katy has asked him, "...theories that it has just taken this long...*mumblemumble*...prolonged exposure to water vapor, heat—possible that it has taken years for the virus—if that's what it is—nothing like we've seen before—not even the confirmed fossils in the ALH84001 Martian meteorite from Antarctica—"

Screeech—a chair screeches across the floor in the dining room and Mr. Artsworthy stands up, sways like he's going to faint, then sits down again, puts his locked hands up to his forehead like he's praying.

"—so, Katy—" continues Shuster, and the scene is that of a reaction shot of Katy, and God, you think, she's striking: straight copper blonde hair, dressed in the latest: a blue blazer with a metallic sheen, and an iridescent jewel at the closed collar of her white blouse, "—current speculation, if it is viral—was that it wasn't dead, but dormant, slowly genetically altering to adapt to just enough water vapor, warmth, air at the colony site—"

"—but that's just theory—" says Katy.

And, of course, someone changes the channel to a gardening show, showing where you can get desert plants for the Puget Sound region. You look around. On the pink walls, pictures. There's the cone of Mt. Rainier—it's a picture of the way it looked before all the glaciers went.

Jenny comes over. "Are you through, Mr. Taylor?" she asks. She tries to look cheerful, but you know she's really worried about something.

And so you say, "There's something—going on—something—bad—"

She looks startled. She wasn't expecting that. "Oh, no, no," she says. "You know the news, all gloom and doom. Would you like to go back to bed for a while? Remember, there's Occupational Therapy at 10:30 and it's going to be music today—you get to play an instrument. Won't that be fun?"

You don't say anything. Diversion. Oh, well, but you do feel better, more alert and—for some strange reason, *incredibly* calm. You get help shuffling back to bed and you nap and you dream of something—coming. You don't know what but it brings you something, a message, and it feels like it's from very, *very* far away. As you drift off to sleep, you think you hear, *I bring you peace. I bring you peace from fear, suffering, pain. I bring you peace,* and your head fills with this pink glow and you find it so — soothing, so very, very — soothing.

"O.T.," says Jenny. "Time to get up, Mr. Taylor. Do you need to pee? To poop?"

You shake your head; you feel like you're back from — somewhere — the room swims for a minute. You look to Jenny. She's having a real hard time trying not to look worried. "What's —" you begin.

"Let's get up." She comes over to the side of the bed, ready to slip her hands under your arm to help you stand; you're struck with the awareness that she must think that because you're old, you're oblivious and she's not going to answer your question. But you *know* something has happened. With her help, you stand and she takes you down the hallway and you get a view of the wallscreen, a picture of a tense newscaster, black hair plastered at an angle across his forehead, speaking directly to the camera. " — officials here at the Houston Mars Sample Containment Center urge calm — contrary to earlier reports, there is no evidence —"

Suddenly, commotion in the background, and you get a glimpse of what appears to be an explosion in a building — a — *pink* — explosion and someone is yelling, "Get back, *get back* — get the fucking media — the cameras — *turn them* —"

The wallscreen goes blank.

Another nurse comes up to Jenny. It's Dana, beautiful, black haired, and in spite of everything, you feel your dong getting stiff again and Dana looks really scared. "Have you heard —" she says to Jenny.

Jenny just nods and it's obvious she *knows* something and wants to say something to Dana, but fears you overhearing and she doesn't want to worry you, totally oblivious that you already know something wicked is going on. Abruptly, you look up. "What is going on?" you say in a very clear and, you're surprised, a strong voice.

Both Dana and Jenny look startled then look at you. They hesitate. They make a decision. "We don't know," Jenny says. "Some kind of contamination — an accident —"

You smile. They just can't tell you the truth and it's probably because what it means is just too awful for them to handle, but you realize that you're not too old to get it after all, even if it is awful. You've followed this Mars thing for years before you came here, the fascination everyone had with the return soil samples that indicated that there was indeed evidence that not only confirmed the minute forms in the ALH meteorite to be fossils, but also hinted of other forms of past life as well — only, you smile, looks like it wasn't so past after all. And here you've been wondering how your life was going to end. Now you know. Do you have to poop? Do you have to pee? You just *have* to smile. Probably won't be hearing *that* much longer. And you can *hardly* wait.

Icebergs

You think of icebergs when you see them. They are the ones who do not care. They are the ones above it all. You see them on the streets, cell phones crammed against their ears like they are trying to make their ears eat them, like they want the phones to be a part of them, like they only want to hear what is on the other end, not the farting buses, crying babies, squawking gulls and the, "Hey mister, c'n you afford 42 cents for a cuppa coffee—"

You think of monsters when you see them; giant insects in shiny chitin clothing; the only thing they're missing are the compound eyes; the insect mind is already there. Maybe they need a few more legs; the exoskeleton is certainly there and like bugs, they carry their armor because they are so squishy inside, but unlike insects, they *know* it, and the knowledge of that makes their armor even thicker, makes them even colder, like ice.

You know them. You've watched them on TV. The Jeb Bushes, the Kathleen Harrises, the Supreme Court Justices. They are bought and sold and they don't seem to care, or it's not in their interests to care—much less yours. You've seen them before throughout history: the brownshirts in Nazi Germany, the folks who gave Native Americans blankets infected with smallpox, the Stalins: one of whom in particular was said to have remarked, "They who cast the votes decide nothing. They who count the votes decide everything."

You go to bed and you dream of them. Of a vast army on insects, cold, mindless, surviving, eating everything, trampling everything. You dream of them, you dread them because you are just in the way; you don't matter; you can be stopped; you can be silenced. It is very easy. You aren't shot these days. You just can't pay your electric bill. Or your property taxes become overwhelming. Or your rent goes through the roof. Or the IRS comes *tap-tap-tapping* on your door. Or just months before you retire, your pension gets yanked. Or you get fired before you retire. Or your medications get too expensive and you have to choose between them and food. That, or you end up eating dog food. Or, you hear, cat food isn't too bad. Or you get sick and your insurance drops you.

In your worst nightmares, Kafka is there to comfort you, to help you understand. "See?" he whispers, "see? My father appeared in all my works as a bureaucracy, something overwhelming, indifferent, crushing. Is it any different now, here, this place? In my time, the fascists were gaining power, shoving their beliefs down everyone's throats whether they wanted it or not. Is it any different this time, this place, now?"

You lay there in bed, it's four a.m., and you realize how *right* he is. But you also know that, in the quest for absolute power, it has most likely always been this way. And it was that way in Mao Tse Tung's Little Red Book Land and it was that way in Soviet Socialist Realism Land and there is nothing that stops it from being that way here, wherever here is at whatever time or place you just happen to be born.

"Where is it safe," you wonder. "Where is it safe?"

"Where there is a quest and love of power, of domination of others, there is never safety," says Kafka.

"Why such a quest?" you ask.

"Such a question," Kafka says. "Why was my father so abusive? He doesn't know. I don't know."

"It's as if," you ponder, hearing the rain rattle against the window, hearing the wind howl, "it's as if—the more powerless one feels in one's life, the more they seek power to make up for what they never had?"

"Or," Kafka says, "maybe their father was powerful and to make their father proud, they became even more powerful. Who knows? Or perhaps the one who gets the power understands all too well who has the position of power in the families of the culture."

You lay there in the dark, wondering. You are aware that Kafka is no longer there. You also become aware of the distant sound of millions of busy feet—then silence, then the feet marching in a rhythm, a cadence, and you wonder where the army is going next, who is to be dominated next? Who is to be exterminated next?

And all the while, you are aware of those cold, insect minds—minds that become more and more like ice, each mind in a body cold as an iceberg; those bodies becoming like icebergs, all those icebergs becoming thicker, creating yet breaking off of an immense growing chitinous ice sheet, slowly, again, as it has in the past, freezing the world in yet another ice age, the depth of which, the duration of which is unknown. And outside, the rain has turned to snow, and everything is going to a soft and numbing cold, and in the distance you hear the low moan and rumble of the coming of the ice.

Mother, Mother, Burning Bright

My mother was on fire. But then, come to think of it, she always had been for as long as I can remember. It was, as I recall, very difficult to be close to her, but I remember how, at least, she'd smile from behind the shimmering hot wall of yellow and red. Sometimes she'd wave, so I knew she cared. She just couldn't do much about those flames.

Needless to say, we traveled a lot: couldn't stay in many places because she'd end up burning houses down, even the ones with big hearths — she simply couldn't stay put in the fireplace too long because she'd get bored and start walking around and of course, there went the floor, the walls or the roof. I even have a memory of a fireman trying to put her out with water — but she just steamed a lot and as soon as the water evaporated, she reignited. Even carbon dioxide fire extinguishers didn't work. I don't really know why or how my father stayed with her. How we were born, my sister Sally and myself (much less conceived) is something we never could figure out except that father, an exasperated, dark little man with sunken eyes and hair that was bituminously black, once said, "She wasn't always this way."

Guess not.

What changed?

"Don't know," said father, bleakly, "don't know."

So, like I said, we traveled a lot — had to stay out of forests because my mother had a tendency to start brush and forest fires — so we were pretty much confined to traveling gravel roads, (asphalt we couldn't do because my mother, obviously, would melt the asphalt, but we never really got in trouble for it). As one minister, walking beside us one day, said, "Your mother, she's a prize of the devil she is. She is, she is, she is, yes, she is." He sounded like a wizened old fellow, but he was as young and as robust as they come, in his twenties, I believe, but with the countenance of someone far, far older who knew the ways of darkness very well. "She is not to blame," he said to me and my sister and to my father who tried to appear polite, but just kept looking away, like he really needed more than advice, he needed some sort of divine fire extinguisher or at least *some* explanation which would somehow make this intolerable situation somewhat more tolerable. I think, on that day, he really wanted to ask the priest about this 'til death do us part' business—like he wondered if fire might qualify—but he just didn't have the heart to say it. He was a good man, dark and cool as he was, who really wanted to do the right thing, but had utterly no idea what the right thing was in this case, as did nobody else. And on this day, the priest went on, oh, *my*, how he went *on* as we walked that rainy day. "God speaks to us in strange ways," the priest was saying, "and why He chooses to speak this way, is only up to Him, and who is to say what His divine plan is."

I think my father muttered, "It would sure help to know."

My mother, of course, surrounded in her vertical, shimmering cocoon of yellow and red with faint hints of blue, as if she was fed by some natural gas pipeline in there somewhere, she, of course, had nothing to say. She just smiled. She wasn't naked or anything; in spite of the flames, she somehow wore something that didn't burn, like a shimmering white robe. Maybe it was made of asbestos or some Miracle Space Age Substance, a Direct Spin Off of Space Research. It's terribly hard to say. But she walked along with us, and every step she made, there was a slight "hisss" of water evaporating and when you looked down, you saw little puffs of steam coming up and the earth was dry where she had walked. I can't remember too much else the priest said. Maybe it was because it was getting repetitive. After a while, people tended to get somehow repetitive regarding my mother because there wasn't anything they could really say that really *was* different. But it really wasn't all bad. Different, yes, but all bad? Not really. Sometimes little street urchins might come up and roast marshmallows or weenies in my mother's flames. And she'd grin and humor them. She'd put her hands around the hot dog or the marshmallow and even one time, a game hen—she seemed to have this uncanny knack of directing just the right amount of heat to the item: marshmallows never burned but came out wonderfully browned; weenies were plump and sizzling, as were sausages. Eggs were magically hardboiled and chicken was broiled to perfection. I guess my mother majored in home economics and really took it to heart. During those times, she was a perfect cook and a most gracious hostess. She certainly had, at other times, a sense of humor about her plight, if, indeed, she saw it as a plight. And when we weren't being bothered by urchins, we were accompanied by the curious, who, after offering their own suggestions about what to do and, of course, after failing to find any cause, much less any solution, handed my father wonderful recipes for breads, cakes and meat dishes. I suppose, given my mother's creativity, she probably could have sat in a certain way as to create with her body a space that might be considered an oven and I suppose she could indeed sit that way for some hours or however long it took to "bake" whatever it was that the recipe called for. All this was certainly a wonderful way to meet all sorts of people in life.

I do remember when we were walking down a road; a group of picnickers who, astonished and delighted and cursing at the sight of my mother, invited her over to the picnic table. My mother wisely waved them away, and suddenly the picnickers knew what the problem was. But my mother stood by the side of the road, pointing to the meat dishes left on the table. The host somehow understood immediately what she was doing. He brought over the dishes, and my mother sat in the road, keeping the dishes warm in her lap. At times, her generosity was indeed humbling. And though my father's needs went largely unmet, maybe he was gratified in some way that his wife was meeting others' needs in a strange way. At times he looked proud of her, at times. At times. But more often his look was that of, "Dear God, why *me!*" Except of, course, when it was raining and my mother could somehow extend that flaming aura over us and keep us dry. My father looked very appreciative at those times. Or when it was cold. "Well," he said once, as we sat in a warm circle of heat and light while just beyond it was a field of white, "City Light and Utilities can go fuck themselves." I do recall him smiling hugely when he said that. Of course, the temperature outside the aura of heat and light must have been way below freezing. Not long afterwards the lights of the city on the horizon suddenly went black from over-loaded power circuits, and we all sat there laughing. We couldn't hear my mother laugh because those flames seemed to act as a sound barrier as well, but she waved as she extended her warm aura over us. And in many respects, we did have it good. In the mornings, she'd extend her hands and we'd put slices of bread on them; she always made *perfect* toast. The same with the bacon as well, and never any dishes to wash or mess to clean up. But it would have been nice to have been able to touch her, but that of, course, was impossible. All of us would simply have gotten third degree burns and I know she would have liked to have been able to touch us, but, for obvious reasons, that wouldn't have worked either because she would have just inflicted pain. But we could feel her warmth. We just couldn't *touch* her, was all. And this was particularly apparent when, one morning, we awoke on a bright warm spring day and my mother was lying down on the grass — the area singed and blackened about her — and the flames still shimmering yellow and red and hot. Usually she'd be sitting on a stone or on the bare earth; always awake. She never slept and why this was I still don't know, just as it was a mystery that she didn't eat. We tried to rouse her by tossing pebbles at her feet but she was either deeply asleep or,

"...dead," said Doctor Rotcod. "I guess —" he added. He was a very bright fellow, fetched by Sally when, no matter what we did, our mother did not wake up. Rotcod was very analytical and thought a long time, asked a lot of questions, wondering out loud about a "fever," "hot flashes," "hot tempered" and the like, but in the end, he simply said, "All clinical signs point to death — of course," he smiled ruefully, "without taking her pulse and feeling her forehead and examining her more closely, it's awfully difficult to know if she's dead, much less how she died." He looked for a few more minutes. "The dead must be, of course, disposed of."

"Burial?" asked my father.

"Only natural," said Doctor Rotcod, "but that necessitates moving the body."

"Difficult," said my father.

"Very," replied the doctor.

"Impossible," said Sally.

"Definitely," I said.

"Only other alternative," said Rotcod, "is to build a funeral pyre. It may get so hot that the body will finally consume itself and put the flames out."

"A reverse pyre," said my father.

Doctor Rotcod merely nodded.

So we gathered branches, logs, newspapers, Styrofoam cups and we worked on building a pyre and before long, the fire was indeed respectable. We let it burn, far, far into the night until it was just a heap of glowing coals.

"What a shame," said Doctor Rotcod, wiping his glasses on his blue tie with the picture of Marilyn Monroe on it and letters below her figure saying, "Some Like It Hot." "To never know just what happened to her.

What a pity. Such a use to science she could have been." In the firelight my father said nothing; but his expression was that strange mixture of extreme grief and utter joy — that maybe this whole damn thing was over and he could have a more sane life. And I think Sally and I decided about that time that, yes, mother was dead and it was certain and we both wept but more from not ever really knowing her, even though she cared and was always there. The coals continued to burn down, yet, even when most of the coals became ashes and the fire burned with that sullen heat and dim light of fires reluctantly dying, abruptly the ashes stirred. My mother sat up and looked around, still encased in her shimmering robe of yellow and red fire. She looked amazed, touched her body and looked suddenly disappointed. It was obvious to us then, that she had wanted to die, that she had wanted us to do *exactly* what we had done. But alas, she did not die. With great weariness, she stood, looked down at herself, shook her head. She looked at us, shook her head again, then turning away and burning, burning bright, she wandered off — into the night.

Planetary Loves

(A Solar System of the many Ways and Means of Love. Not all good. De-scribed by beings who might be Spirits or Gods, but then again, maybe not.)

We stand on Mercury and have our argument, there, in the 800 degree heat, shattered crater walls and dried pools of once-molten rock and I say, with the sunlight blinding, brilliant in my eyes, "That's horsepucky. Yes, I like Linda, but we've known each other for years and she's just a friend — I knew her before I met you and why would I stop going out for coffee with her?"

You stand there, your black hair frizzed by the heat, the sun and solar wind, with hands on your hips and your blue shirt looking a bit charred, "Well, it wouldn't be so bad if it weren't three times a week and if you didn't call her 'honey'. How'd you like it if I had Fred over all the time and he called me 'honey'?"

I look down and kick at the scorched rock. "Wouldn't bother me a bit."

"Look me in the eye."

I do. But the massive sun is behind you and I have to squint.

"I said, 'It wouldn't bother me a bit.'"

You stare at me. "I don't believe you," you say. "I think the only rea-son it doesn't bother you is that it isn't a reality. Linda *is* a reality and yes it bugs me and I am sure it would bug you."

"Why?" I say, "Why does it bug you? She's just a friend — "

"Is her friendship more important than our relationship — ?"

"No — " God, the sunlight is hot and bright. "I mean yes — I mean — "

You sigh. "Yeah," you say, "I guess I know what you mean — "

"Would you please listen — "

You walk away.

" —it's sick to put friends out of your life just because you have a relationship."

You walk to a rise of a crater, turn, and say, "Priorities, dipshit. Priorities." You walk to the top of the crater wall, then down the other side. I stand, angry, hot, and smelling the odor of burning cotton and then leather and looking down I notice my shoes have burst into flame. I do a tap dance to try to put out the fire. "Shit," I mutter, "if it isn't my God damn love life, then it's my fucking shoes..."

... but on Venus, planet of love, we walk, sweltering, as the corrosive sulfuric acid rain nibbles and chews through our shirts and the 90 atmospheres of atmospheric pressure makes the humidity of Kentucky feel like a spring day on an asteroid. We slog along and I say, "Jesus, why the hell are you so jealous?"

You wipe your hand across your forehead. "Jesus, why are you so insensitive?"

"Insensitive? How am I insensitive? Christ, don't I have needs? You can't meet them all. Two people end up drowning each other —"

"Not asking that," you say, "but you sure have a fuck of a time putting yourself in my shoes."

"Look, I'm trying to understand..."

You sigh. We come to a cliff and look out through the yellow light and look to the cracked and rock-strewn landscape below. In the distance, we can see the upsweep of Ishtar Terra and brilliant blasts of lightning explode around the higher slopes. A sulfuric acid rain squall dims the slopes of the immense, yellow-grey upwell of cliffs and mountain.

"If you'd just be more reasonable," you say. You pull your hair back with your hand and I see sweat trickling down your temple, your cheeks. Your shirt is soaked by sweat, by rain, and I am much the same—I feel the sweat down my neck, my shirt. It's sticky and it itches and it's damn hard to breathe.

I let out a sigh. "I thought I *was* being reasonable."

"Hardly."

"Well, suppose you define 'reasonable' for me —"

You don't say anything. Right now, we're too much on the edge of corrosive comments for us to say anything that feels like an opening, and for right now, we skip Earth, put that aside for later, to either return to it or dismiss it depending on the outcome of our differences. And...

...on Mars, we sit on the top of the great volcano, Olympus Mons, eighty-nine thousand feet up and on this planet, the great, pink, (actually) God of war, you say, "God, it's cold here."

"I know," I say. "But on the Goddess of love, we weren't getting too far."

"Heat and humidity make me a lot more irritable," you say.

"They do me too. But it's a little windy up here. Let's go down into the caldera so we can get a windbreak."

You don't say anything. So we slide down those ancient, blackened cinders, and we can faintly, faintly, hear them clink as we walk. Grey dust rises when we slide and there's a musty, vaguely burned smell as we drop down into the caldera. We find, before long, a large, reddish-brown angular boulder to sit on and I finally say, "Okay. Define reasonable."

"I don't mind that you have friends," you say, "but I feel crowded out—"

"I'm not crowding you out—"

You look at me with those brown eyes, your thin lips in a line and you almost look pouty. You sigh. "I didn't say you crowded me out—I said that's what it *feels* like—"

I look to the caldera, to the opposite rim 43 miles away, to the varying colors and depths of layers of deposit of volcanic stuff and I say, "...uh...I don't mean to do that, but...uh...is there something else going on?"

You look surprised. "What?"

I point. "Look."

In the late, pink-tainted blue of the sky, Jupiter rises...

...and we sail on the turbulent winds; in the brilliant blasts of lightning, the colors of yellow, red and white explode around us and I yell to be heard over the winds and crash of thunder, "Hold on to my hand!"

The wind rips at your shirt and your jeans flap around your legs and you say, "Why'd we have to come here? This place smells like a sewer! We were doing fine on Mars."

"No," I say, "there's something else—"

"JULIA!" A voice booms out from the clouds. You look around. "JULIA!"

I point. Before us a huge face appears in Jupiter's clouds.

"Father!" you mouth, but I can't hear the words.

"I told you I can't be at your play tonight—no, I can't come to your meeting either!"

"Father," you cry, "please! I'm not asking that much—"

"I'm sorry! Can't do it! My schedule's filled for the next three weeks!"

"Jesus Christ, Daddy—" and you shake your fist. "Don't I account for anything in your life?"

"Why, you ungrateful—I sent you to school—I worked my tail-end off for you—I've got these bills to pay—"

"But I want to see *you*! It's been this way all of our lives!"

"I know. It's sad. But that's the way it is. Don't call me at the office anymore! I'll be in Detroit all next week! Goodbye and take care!" And the face vanishes and a particularly strong updraft lands us on Io, plopping us in a warm pool of fresh sulfur from a bubbling geyser not far way. In the distance a volcanic eruption throws a pizza-colored umbrella of material ten thousand meters into the black sky and we sit in the pool and you look at me and say, "Oh."

I nod. I say, "Oh."

You nod and say, "Uh—guess I see where some of my issues come from. Oh."

I sigh. "Guess I see how I fit into some of your stuff. Oh."

We scoot down into the bath of warm sulfur, ignoring the rotten-egg odor, and lie in the pool for a long time, then we sit on an outcrop of pepperoni-colored rock and watch the volcano fountaining out the guts of this moon Io. Our clothes, though tattered, somehow stay remarkably serviceable and rather clean in spite of it all. And I shake my head. "Ahem. Well, what's fair is fair."

"Your turn?" you ask.

"Guess so," I reply.

We take a deep breath and dive into the sky and...

... glide past the rings and to Saturn we go, into the orange and yellow atmosphere, way down deep in it, we go. "Well," you say, "it's a little better than that Jovian crap."

"For you," I reply, and I want to say more but, oh, my god, from the Saturnian depths, the pale face of my mother appears.

"Oh, you're so sickly, are you all right?"

I sigh. "I'm fine, Mother, really I am!"

"You don't sound like it. Do you have a cold?"

"No, Mother, just a case of hay fever is all."

Her face lords over me like a vast moon. "You better stay here tonight. I'll fix you your lunch."

"No, that's OK."

"You should move out of that apartment and move back with me."

"No, Mother, I have a girlfriend—"

The vast moon face doesn't acknowledge that you even exist; she just stares at me. "I know that you're not taking good care of yourself."

"Mother, I'm fine." I grab your hand. "I have to go now."

"Oh, you just got here—" and her face now fills the entire sky.

"It's been a nice visit," I say.

"You can sleep in your own bed..."

"*Mother!*"

"You don't look well. I need to take care of you."

"Oh, no, no you don't. Oh, *no way* in hell!"

"You need me—"

"Oh, holy *God!*"

"Come back. It's so terribly lonely here without you—"

"*Agh!*" And with that, we leap...

... and land in the cool and dark and quiet regions, the bottom depths of the planet Uranus. I hear my mother calling down through the murk of the atmosphere, "Where are you? Your dinner's getting cold! I'll pack a lunch for you—do you like turkey?"

"Whoa—" you say.

"I just bought you some new underwear!" I hear my mother distantly call.

"Yeah—" I say.

"Where are yooooooouuuuuu?"

"Lonely old lady—" You shake your head.

"Mik-ieeeeeeee."

"Treats me like I'm five years old. I was her only purpose in life. Felt guilty as hell when I left. She even had me climbing into bed with her 'til I was twelve. Oh, it was sick, oh, man it was *bad*. I hate it how she always tries to track me down. Jesus Christ!" We sit in the darkness for a long time; then it is quiet. And you finally say, "So when I start wanting more time—"

"Yeah."

"Ooh."

"Uh-huh."

When the coast is clear, we don't say much. We go and—

...raft on the gentle warm currents of the Neptunian sea and watch pale blue pastel clouds drift over head. We drift on rafts of organic matter blasted up by the violence far below and we drift and we float, both contemplating, where, where, where do we go from here?

"Lots of problems between us," you say at last.

"Yeah," I respond, "funny how we found each other."

"Is it?" you ask. "Is it really so strange?"

We float a while longer and after a few minutes, a mighty current surges from below and we are spun high, high above and the next thing we know...

...we shiver and stamp our feet. "Pluto's cold," you say.

"Not too neat," I reply.

"So is this then the way it is for us? Lifeless and bleak like this dirty ice ball?"

"We sure got our problems," I say. I look to the snow drifts, to distant mountains etched in ice, of an atmosphere frozen out or perhaps never formed and the sun is a bright marble in the cold black of space. "Maybe we'd better go our separate ways — even though we understand — could it possibly work?"

"Well," I say, "guess the test is — does each of us feel better or worse without the other?"

You flap your arms around you to stay warm and you stare at the snow. "I don't know."

"Well —" I say, "shall we say goodbye and see how it goes?"

You sigh. "I suppose."

We shake each other's hands and then turn away and begin to walk that frozen white waste and I walk around a snow drift — and there you are.

"Couldn't resist. It was rotten without you."

"I know," I say. "I turned so that I could double back. Really felt bad." And we take each other's hands, admiring each for the work that love is and smiling, I say, "I think it's time to celebrate our decision, this revision, this willingness to try it again."

You smile. "To Earth?"

I laugh. "Oh, yes, to Earth. Place of simultaneous calm and storms, beauty and fear, the grand and the strange — all rolled into one."

"Just like our love," you reply.

"No better place to honor the difficulties and the triumph of love, of life. No better place to know the day and the night, or to feel the essence of life: to fight for the light."

We both laugh, embrace, gently kiss and then joining hands, we leap, leap, leap into the sky, and we fly —

...ah, to walk 'neath the snowy crowns of mountains high, to splash in the oceans, feeling the surge of the surf; to celebrate love — 'neath the blue skies of Earth.

Growing Up, Rocked and Rolled

A thanks to Rock Stars, dead and alive, for they helped me realize that times, they were a changin'.

Dear Elvis Presley,

It was 1956 and the only song, when I was that age—let's see— nine?...the only other song that, until then, grabbed me in the imagination or heart or wherever the place is that stops you from what you're doing and makes you listen, that was *Canadian Sunset* and don't ask me who did it because I remember someone singing it and also an instrumental rendition of it that made my pre-pubescent hair stand on end. But Elvis, with your hips going every which way and your guitar strobing the air like a penis looking for something warm, moist and close by, yeah, you may have been singing about a houn' dawg, but to see the way you moved, you were talking about something else and even at age nine, even though I didn't put it together in my head, my body knew exactly what you were saying. Houn' dawg my butt. But thanks anyway for letting me know that at some point in my future, my hips would be gyrating every bit as well as yours as I played my own guitar. So, Elvis, thank you.

Dear Pat Boone:

Oh, you crooning sweetheart. Musta been 1957? Gee, what a year, you know? Fords with their tail fins and Chevrolet had designed a car that would be popular to infinity and you, Pat, sang about love letters in the sand. I had just recovered from Elvis and, at age ten, was madly in love with a lady named Sandy. What a sweetheart she was: dark eyes and hair, and even now my broken heart aches/with every wave that breaks and does something to the love letters in the sand. We never did write in the sand, but I used to think and imagine how we might and, at age ten,

135

my broken heart didn't ache too long, but the fact was that Sandy left on a trip that summer and gee, was it lonely. No, Pat, I didn't see letters erased, but I knew, oh, yes, I knew what you were talking about. Loss is a son of a bitch, isn't it? Why bother getting close if it all ends in loss? But even then, even if love letters do get washed away, it doesn't wash away the magic of writing them in the first place, does it? So, thanks, Pat, for telling me that magic can't exist without risk. I realize that now, some 28 years later; I guess I knew it 28 years ago but you said it better. Oh, by the way, that sax that carried the song was haunting and sad. I think I cried when I first heard that. Yes, that was lovely indeed.

Anyway, thank you. You sort of balanced out what Elvis was doing, like you were saying, "Cocks and balls and slit are fine, but let's not forget the heart, risk and love, hey?" Good message, you clean-cut young man. My. What a nice role model you were.

Note to all rock stars: I'm sorry, I don't remember too much between my ages of ten and fourteen. I don't know why. Maybe it was because the "turf" had already been defined, groups singing about "Norman" and "go-un to the cha-a-pel of love" on one hand and folks like Jerry Lee Lewis yelling about "a whole lot of shaking goin' on." Yes, sir. From a Macrobiotic standpoint, we had songs about the Yin and we had roaring wham-crash Yang music: each seemed to celebrate itself without too much concern about getting the two sides in some sort of balance. So, at times I was totally Yin and at times utterly Yang, at times all heart and soul, at times all balls. But dear rock stars, when it's time for a change and the Earth says that it's time and the heavens agree, then events in the lives of men change and I remember Liverpool...

Dear John, Paul, George and Ringo,

Well, guys, you did it. It wasn't one man climbing the pinnacle of success—there was room for four to do it cooperatively. What happened to "me against them?" Oh, true, other groups had been successful, but somehow, somehow, you were more successful as you, it seems, gently balanced out the extremes. Was it my misconception or did you troubadours of heart really *know* what love was? Or maybe it was all fake but God, you faked it well.

And you appeared at a time when, I believe, I was trying to put my mind and heart together. "All your lovin'" helped. And how dare you sing a song about needing help? And how dare you explore so many feelings. How dare you sing about lonely people — how dare you be real and not just entertaining? How dare you be gentle and tough? How dare you try to remove the masks and you know what? People loved you for it; girls climaxed at the mere thought of you and young guys, myself included, knew that what they thought manhood was all about was just a pile of lies smelling like week-old shit. Daddy was wrong.

Why the hell was it that virtually *every* song you did rang true with me? Did you guys know yourselves so well that you made the right assumptions that experiences and feelings that you had were pretty much like everyone else's? How presumptuous! How accurate! How much we all have in common: how similar we are rather than different. God, you guys! How *much* you knew. How much you *trusted* what you knew. Even when you reached for the dope and the drugs, your message, at the dismay of so many parents, seemed to be "trust yourselves to do what's right." You musta drove parents everywhere crazy. And me? At age fifteen, me? I was listening to classical music and thought rock and roll was crap, except when I heard *your* music I noticed my heart rate jumping and my hand sneaking over to the radio to turn up the music and hey, roll over Beethoven and give Tchaikovsky the news.

Sadly, the bad news came later, but for now, thank you, John, Paul, George and Ringo.

Dear Bob Dylan,

And thank you. Were you the thin man that you wrote the ballad about? Were times a changin' for you too? They musta been. I always wondered when I heard your music, God, where had you been? What horrors had you seen? What alleyways had you walked down that everyone else didn't want to know about, but listened to you anyway because — because — because they — me — secretly admired the guts that it takes to forever put yourself on the line — to dance with the devil and to reach up and grab the balls of God. You were out there walking the line between hope and despair, life neverending and utter oblivion, creating your reality, your line, your direction and not being told what to do. And how we all secretly admire those that do that because that is what we long to do and yet fear to do because...because...ah, Bob, you made me focus on my deepest fears that somehow, out there, if I did what you did, lived as you did, I wouldn't survive, the fear too great, the responsibility too awesome, the loneliness too immense. What can I say, you bastard, thanks? Thanks for making me look at my deepest fear of mortality? Of vulnerability? Thank you for *this*? How dare you? Yet I listened to you and oh, *how* I listened to you. And dreamed. The madness you sang about was also immense and glorious courage and even now I love you as I hate you for making me look at me. Yet, I thank you anyway.

And Dear So Many Rock Stars That I Have Missed:

Hey, Elton John—yeah, wouldn't want to miss you and your Yellow Brick Road—at the time I heard that, I was in a relationship with a wonderful lady who never had much to say except that I know she cared a lot for me when I didn't care for me at all and I was frightened as hell that once she discovered how horrible I was (because I *felt* that way about me, I assumed that everyone else felt that way about me, the word of the day: Projection) I would be rejected as much as I rejected myself, so I had to keep her at a distance, see *her* as the cause of all the problems in the relationship so I wouldn't have to look at *my* problems. Ah, the Yellow Brick Road, Elton, I remember singing that song a lot because, like everyone else, I wanted a way out that was free and golden and always hopeful and dream-like because I didn't want to look. And you know what, Elton? She left. She got involved with someone else who knew that Yellow Brick Roads had a lot to do with what we wanted things to be rather than what they really were and even now, Elton, I see a lot of Yellow Brick Roads, but I don't set foot on them anymore because they come from a record and to step on a Yellow Brick Road is just to go around and around at thirty three and a third RPM and it's hard to get off and you get motion sickness and want to puke all the time. And so thank you too for showing me the nature of reality when I didn't want to see it for what it was.

And of course, Dear Rolling Stones,

...angry as hell, or trying to be, and I could never tell which, but I always did appreciate the song about spending the night together—there you go—doing my talking for me and even when I did spend the night together with someone, I was so scared that I couldn't do anything even though I bet her a bottle of plum wine and a six pack of Fresca that I could give her an orgasm and we both ended up falling asleep at the effort.

So thank you Elton, thank you Stones. You were there when I needed you. You were there making those connections just by the fact that you had your radar out, your sensitivity up, your hearing extended far enough, wide enough, long enough to hear the joy, the scream, the howl of everyone, of me, of those who smiled a lot but wailed deep inside. Strange, isn't it...to howl and not know it. To hurt and not feel it. To cause damage but not be aware of it. Strange and beyond strange...Gods, how do we survive? Elton, Stones, and So Many Others, you helped with some answers and yet, there was One in Particular who helped. One in Particular.

And maybe it's because of this One that I don't pay that much attention to Rock and Roll any more. Maybe it was because of this One In Particular that it all came too close to home. Maybe it was because it was all madness and horror that evening when I sat with a young lady who didn't want to talk about anything major and who was scared shitless of her own anger toward her parents and who hated yet admired me because I refused to fit her image of what I should be and right during the "discussion" of this—yeah, John Lennon gets shot.

It may sound trite, but that wasn't supposed to happen. The bards of the age, the troubadours who helped us connect; they of the visceral culture—they are to live forever, or at least die when we're ready for them to die and not before. And there, in the tavern, wrestling with a relationship that was my last for a long, long time, realizing that something had died between us—we stop and hear about Lennon. Dreams shatter. Hope breaks. Why try? Why go on when it is so fragile and so easily ripped away? Why? Absurd but the song Pat Boone sang came back about how they passed the time of day/writing love letters in the sand. And then he was crying because the tide had erased the message. The message? To live is to die? To live is to be out there, heart, soul and mind on the firing line of life—never, but *never* to die a single death, much less a thousand. Thank you John for being out there, living every second as if it were your last. I am reminded of the time that I have wasted as if it is abundant. And then I realize there is no guarantee for anything. Of anything. Thank you, John. Even when your death brought my own death closer—I had to realize just how I was to live my life, my time, before I, too, met your fate: your mortality. Maybe that was why I stopped listening to rock and roll: it was all a dance around the most fundamental issue that John Lennon had to embrace—and he embraced it far, far better than so many. And it had nothing to do with rock and roll—but everything to do with The Dance.

Thank you, John. By your misfortune, I guess you helped teach me all there ultimately is to know. Such a dance, John, such a dance this is, and while Rock and Roll pointed a finger—ultimately the finger pointed to me, it is up to me to determine how to dance this dance.

Thank you John—for you, a special thanks: may I dance as well.

Sincerely,

Bruce Taylor

Safeway Passion

I see you in the candy section near the M & Ms. You are wrapped up in a gay façade and I wonder who you are. Your sticker price says "59¢" and you are tempting. I want to talk to you but you move on to the bread section. There I stand beside you and breathlessly mutter, "Two loaves for 99 cents."

You look at me through your wrapper. You say nothing. You turn away. I swallow and stay behind. You go to the frozen meats. I smile again and bravely say, "Chuck steak."

You nod. "On sale today." Then shrug. "Take some home to the family."

Encouraged, I grin. Your wrapper is very bright and I think I like what I suspect is inside but I am not sure. After all, all you see of me is my Hostess Twinkie package and I know I'm marshmallow soft inside, but if it weren't for the lettering on my package, how would you know? And I look at you—ah, your bright package prevents me from seeing a lot, but that's the way it is, isn't it? Mysterious. Are you chewy caramel or hard on the inside?

But me? Yes, yes, you can look through my wrapper. See? It's clear plastic. And it says on the outside, "Marshmallow filling."

No, no, I'll not hide behind a heavy plastic wrapper or come at you from behind a wall of tin or look at you from behind hard, unyielding glass or cardboard, gaily decorated though it may be.

But you do not hear my silent plea. And in the pickle section, I stare at the pickles who look back at me with dumb and liquid smiles, and you look at a jar of yellow, yelling mustard. I want to tell you how curious I am about you, but I am vulnerable and easily hurt all the way down to my soft, cream core and I fear I must be oh, so careful lest you really look at my core and reject it for what it is and yet, yet, I'm so attracted. And I follow you and I know that you know I'm interested. You go to the beer section and the spirits are talking. You point to the beer. "One dollar-sixty-five."

But I proudly point to the ale. "One eighty-three."

You nod. I bring it down for you and place it in your cart, but I guess it's too close too fast and you hurry off. Oh, how the mystery remains, your packaging so well done, and I turn on myself for being so obvious and wish that I could at least be in an opaque wrapper with splashes of color so that I might look as intriguing as you, but I am what I am and in this vast store of competing prices, shouting colors and lots of untruth, I realize so acutely that packaging is *everything*. And I turn on myself again: *Oh, gods of packaging design, why did you make me so obvious? With all other products so obscured and shouting with misleading colors, I look like I cannot be real; there must be something behind the lie of clear plastic. Why, why, why could I not have some outlandish badge that I could hide behind and, around the sides of which I could probe with my tendrils of sensitivity — something behind which I could maneuver and not be so obvious so that if you rejected me, I'd have a label to hide behind and not risk being wounded to my soft cream core?*

I sigh and go past the spice rack and only distantly hear the strange and exotic languages spoken and the sneezing of the pepper. I walk past the coffee perking joyfully to itself and I see you by the noodles, talking to yourself, "Sixty-eight cents, seventy-five cents, a dollar-ten." Then you look at me. "Macaroni!"

I shrug. "Noodles. Italian spaghetti."

"Two for a dollar twenty," you say.

"Sixty cents each," I smile, charmed at my own cleverness.

"Four for two-forty," you smile back.

A put down? Attempt at humor? I don't know. God, how, how I wish I could see beyond the wrapper! It seems so unfair that some of us are born, oh, so well concealed. Is it strength or weakness that some of us are not so fortunate? Is to be well-concealed fortunate? Or cowardly? I do not know but with my basket under my thin, plastic wrapped arm, I am nearby, wondering, wondering. But in the cracker and cereal aisle, my thoughts are disrupted. The cereal boxes are hopping about. It's those secret prizes inside: those strange things that make the boxes jump out at you to get your attention. I pick out an ostentatious box that is especially noisy, for I like my breakfasts no dull affairs. But I notice that you pick the oatmeal with the picture on the front of Quakers looking so stern and allowing no nonsense, just plain, hard food, and I nod. You look at my cereal jumping about in my basket. I shrug. "Sixty-four cents."

You point to yours. "*Fifty-nine* cents." I suddenly feel as though I should buy what you bought, but no, no, I like noisy cereal. The top of my package erupts open and the cereal flies out, popping and banging up through the air. I smile ruefully, and as I walk, the cereal crunches under my feet. The religious men on your cereal box frown and scowl at me and you continue on, hurrying, like you don't want to be near me or know me. And I want to say, "But it's the cereal! It's the cereal! Just because I like noisy breakfasts, does that mean I am not worth your while? Listen, I don't think much of your sodden porridge!" And the religious men on the box hiss. My cereal explodes again and something in the box goes, "*Fweet! Fweet! Fweet!*"

And then I walk by the cosmetic section and cough and sneeze for the aerosols are fighting each other even though they all do the same thing.

And the toothpaste tubes rear back like snakes before striking and they spit gobs of toothpaste at each other. Oh, some gets on your wrapper — I come to wipe it off but you shrug and wipe it off yourself. Again, I chastise myself; *Oh, too much too soon again*, and I see my desperation drives you away. In the stinging mist of the aerosol truth, I feel my eyes burn and I try to blame it all on the antiperspirants, but the creamy core of me knows otherwise.

I turn away and walk past the wines in the third aisle. I listen to the soft sonorous sounds, the seductive whispers of the most expensive wines, and see their darkness, dark, dark as lovers' dilated eyes. From the less expensive wines, I hear babble and laughter and finally just giggling — then snoring.

And what, I reflect, *what kind of mood am I in right now? Ah*, I think, *ah, acute melancholia*. I pick out a very expensive wine with which to luxuriate in my martyred complexity and then you, you draw near and you point to the most expensive wines and I wonder, *what is this?* I read the price: "Eight thirty-five."

You nod. I reach for it and in so doing, drop it and the wine screams in pain and runs 'cross the floor. I swallow. My carelessness. Oh, oh, how I am not good enough and surely you will run from me now. But you do not. Delicately, carefully, I reach for another bottle and politely hand it to you. And softly you accept it; you accept it so well, that your wrapper does not crinkle oh, no, not at all.

I walk behind you, past the pop snapping their lids and their joyous merriment bubbling out, fizzing delightfully. What shall I do? What shall I do? Move up beside you? Look as though I happen to be shopping co-incidentally in the same place as you? As a compromise, I decide to simply walk nearby and look as though I'm actually interested in the products around me: to the soaps blowing bubbles, to the hand lotions trying to soften the coarseness of the world, past the sugar and cake mix trying to sweeten the various harshnesses of the bitter routines of reality and you turn to me and ask, pointing to the sugar, "Four pounds for two fifty?"

I nod. "A good buy, that pure cane sugar from Hawaii." I put a package in your cart and the tartness between us lessens a bit. We pass the raisins busily withering and wrinkling, their little puckered faces lined at the effort. And I walk with you and somehow your wrapper becomes more transparent; why I cannot possibly say.

Indeed, the colors are still loud and you are as opaque as ever—yet, beyond your label, I feel something coming out. What is it? What is it? Certainly you are hermetically sealed, your freshness insured and indeed, so am I, our freshness preserved just as we left the factory where we were melted, mixed, shaped and congealed. Yet, yet—it is as though you allow me to sense your inner goodness, though your wrapper remains intact.

And we turn down an aisle, and there in the fruits and vegetables—the magic occurs. Can I remember the time exactly? No, no, but I do remember you pointing. "Corn?" you asked.

I shook my head.

You held up a bag of bright red apples in a clear plastic bag and I could hear the muffled shrieks of their bright redness.

I shook my head again. I went to the freshly cut watermelon and peeled back the polyethylene cover to reveal the moistness, the redness, the rawness of fruit.

There was nothing, nothing I could say at the time. Instead, I paced a bit of the red fruit on your tongue and I, I placed some on my own.

And the sweetness! Oh, sweetness! And yes, yes, illegal the act most certainly was: the manager came and accused us of stealing his precious fruit.

"It was only twenty-five cents a pound!" I said.

But the manager burned red in the face. "Spoiled!" he shouted, "tainted for others! Out! Out! Out of my store!"

We had to leave our groceries behind — it seemed so unfair. So we suffered together and the doors of the Safeway opened for us. Yet, on the parking lot asphalt, our wrappers touched, and while beer cans blown by wind clanked up the street, I knew, yes, I knew that you knew too that what we had found in the store had left us far richer — and hungry no more.

One Afternoon in the Sears Catalog

"Insanity is not 'being insane and knowing that you're insane'. That's the 'Human Condition'. Insanity is being insane and not knowing you're insane. Evil is being insane – and not caring."
the Author

The father opens his new Sears catalog, the one that came today, and there she is, on page 13, modeling pantyhose. Her hands are folded across her naked breasts as though of innocence! *Oh, shameful thing!*

In his rage, he loses his place in the catalog. Angrily, he flips back the pages, but the woman who is modeling pantyhose on page 13 – no, no, she is not his daughter.

"Oh, excuse me. I was looking for my daughter. The one who ran from me and my bed – she ran to the city, the little whore." The pantyhose model looks horrified; she tries to keep smiling but her look betrays her. Impatiently, the father starts flipping through the pages; he tries it randomly so that the daughter does not know where or what page the father will pick.

"There you are! Think you can get lost in a fur coat, eh? Do you think I'll pay the price of the coat to have you scrub my back, you little wretch? How dare you leave your daddy behind! You're just like your mother. But now I have you; I've got you in the catalog. I see you in the fur coat section. Go ahead. Run."

The figure in the fur coat looks blankly out. If she is afraid, she does not show it. She has one hand across her chest as though clutching at the coat to keep it closed.

The father laughs. "Ho, ho, you think you can hide from me? Ho, ho, little daughter!" He closes his eyes and laughs again and, when he looks once more, he is certain that the daughter has changed. She looks somewhat distracted, as though watching something going on to her right—

147

something of interest that has caught her attention. If she hears the father, she does not let on. She simply stands, a sign with the price of the coat and hat at her feet and an eloquent but brisk statement of the fur's grandeur below the price.

The father smiles and quickly turns the pages. He comes to a color advertisement for quilts and pauses to admire them. He notices a woman is leaning, making the bed. She has the covers turned back, her hands flat on the bottom sheet as though smoothing out wrinkles. The father stares for a time, unable to decide if that is his daughter. Idly, he scratches his scruffy beard as he looks at the description:

"...for those cold winter nights, heavy quilts in delightful patterns. Filled with ENDURA-FLUFF, these quilts last a lifetime. 5-year guarantee against unraveling or lumping of fibers. Don't spend another cold evening..."

The father laughs bitterly. He remembers that the evenings have been cold only recently. He does not need a quilt, not when he can have his daughter.

He looks at the woman leaning over the bed. His loins ache.

He abruptly realizes that the woman has a different face. He finds himself with mixed feelings—he rather enjoys chasing his daughter through the catalog. He likes her fear; it excites him. It will make the payoff even greater. Yet, oh, he is impatient and decides the woman is not his daughter and again, he begins looking and realizes that ever since his daughter ran away, the bed has been cold, so cold. Oh, how good she was to her father, how good. And then to realize one morning that she had broken the locks on the inside of the house and, like her mother, escaped.

Then all those God damn people came prying. It must have been his wife. God damn her! She had no right doing that. And no one said where his daughter was. But he denied everything. They weren't going to put him in a nuthouse! But now he knew where she was: right here. Right here in the new Sears Catalog. Yes, yes, he will chase her. That is good fun.

And he flips through the pages: there! In the fireplace accessories! His blood boils! He is enraged! *Look at that! The little whore!* She is sitting in front of the fireplace drinking—something—maybe something *alcoholic!* There is a fire in the fireplace; the flames roar high. In front of the fireplace is a glass door firescreen, the doors folded back to let out the heat. And sitting right next to her is a young man wearing a white sweater with a zig-zag blue and yellow design in the middle, going all the way around. He has a guitar and his hair is blond. He is looking at the woman, *Oh,* thinks the father, *how innocent he looks, but I know what's there. I know what he's up to, the scoundrel. I told my daughter about men like that. I told her that she had to be protected against those kinds of men, men who would use her, soil her; only I could protect her and love her like she ought to be loved.* He realizes the man in the picture is probably going to get her drunk, seduce her. "I told you never to leave, that you would be hurt, but you didn't believe. I will rescue you. I will punish you for not believing me."

But if the woman in the picture is aware of the father, she does not acknowledge it. She continues to sit on the red, shag-carpeted floor, with the drink in her hand, and she smiles at the handsome young man sitting beside her with the guitar.

The father becomes so enraged that, for an instant, his vision blurs. He shakes his head. Suddenly the woman is gone, replaced by someone who looks very similar, but who is obviously not the daughter. No, the hair length is the same, down to her shoulders, the color is the same, dark brown, but she is somehow different. *See? Even the expression of the fellow is altered; oh, you have to look carefully, but there's a bit of a frown there now, a look of disappointment. Of course the bastard is disappointed. Yeah, he didn't get her into bed like he'd planned. Serves you right, you shit. You smooth talking bastard with rape in your eyes. She belongs to me. She can love only me. Only me. Her father knows what is best.* And he flips the pages again to find his daughter. He looks and looks but cannot find her. He looks in the index:

"*...Dado sets...853, 854. Darkroom supplies...1060 – Also see page 695 for Sears Camera Catalog. Day beds...*"

But Daughters are not listed. Idly, he flips the pages and stops. The undergarment section; a woman there, wearing a blue bra (B, C cups, each $10.00, 2 for $19.99. D cup, each $11.00, 2 for $21.99.) Her face is tilted toward him; it's a coy, come-hither look like his mother always gave him. The woman even looks like his mother; the shoulder length, dark hair, the large breasts. Early memories: his mother hating his father and himself. The feelings so painful, triggering so much vengeance and vindictiveness; the father always looking hurt and saying how he was justified in going out to find other women; God damn women, it's women's fault that this is so. Don't trust women, and the pages go *flip, flip, flip* and there, his daughter again, but she's younger—that's her— dressed in flare blue jeans and a maroon top with, of all things, a yellow fireplug on the front. "I told you not to wear those clothes," he whispers savagely. "I forbid you to wear those clothes. Your mother bought those for you, didn't she? Your mother is trying to steal you from me, isn't she?

My daughter, you are my most proud possession. You shall be with me always. Come, come, change into your nightgown and sit on your father's lap."

But the model in the catalog does not move. "How dare you ignore me!" he raves. "Remove those clothes. You are not your mother's child. You are *mine!*"

He sees the figure on the page blink and slowly back away; the other figures seem frozen in fear. "Yes," he whispers, "how rage gives everything life. That makes you move, doesn't it, my little wretch! Come to me, my little daughter, no more of this chase. I grow tired."

The figure runs off the page, disappearing behind a young lady in a green casual suit: dark green pants and pale green blouse; her head is tilted like she is making faces at someone; her long, blond hair hangs like a curtain around her right shoulder. The daughter disappears behind the column of information just to the left of the girl in green —

"*On this page, girls' sizes 7 to 14. (1) Egyptian screen print pant set, machine washable. (2) Beaded pant set, available in green and red. Flare legs, rises at natural waist —*"

The father paws back through the pages, past the One Stop Shop for Baby Section, past the Panties for Little Girls Section, and his rage is such, his rage to the point of almost violence that the children scream in terror and the father rips pages out in his pursuit and suddenly, on page 1137, in the section selling wheelchairs and hospital beds, he sees his wife. She looks at him with cold, hard eyes and whispers, "You're a sick man, Jake. A sick, *sick* man."

He glowers at her. "I told you never to say that."

"You don't want to hear how much you need help."

"I don't need help."

"I come home early and find my daughter in bed with you."

"What's wrong with that? What's wrong with teaching my daughter love?"

"*Love!* Oh, *Jake!* Oh, *God!*" His wife turns on her side and vomits. After she recovers, she whispers, "Do you *know* how *sick* you are? Do you *know*?"

"I never got any affection from you."

"I got tired of being raped, Jake. I got tired of being hate-fucked. I've been sitting in this catalog, waiting for you to stumble upon this page. And while I've been waiting, a song came to mind; I call it, *The Macho Love Song*. Do you want to hear it?"

"If you hadn't said those things to me, you wouldn't be in the hospital, Bitch."

"I'm going to sing you a song, Jake."

"It's too bad you escaped."

"It goes like this:
'The object of your aggression
Is to take your erection
And slam it between my legs —'"

"*Cunt!*" Jake screams.

He rips out the page, wads it up, fumbles in his pocket for a lighter, sets fire to the paper, and before the page is entirely consumed, he hears a whisper, "Your daughter hates you. Oh, how she *hates* you. Keep pursuing her and you'll see just how *much* she hates you."

The paper burns on the floor. He returns to the catalog. And there! Yes, yes, there she is, in the Executive Section. She is dressed in a pink dress with matching jacket which comes down below her hips. A red necklace dips low on her pink bodice. Her hair is elegantly styled. She stands behind a mahogany desk; she leans forward a bit, her hands touch the table via extended fingers—a decision-making stance and she looks straight out at Jake, a big window behind her framing the city of Chicago. And in this modeling, his daughter has done well—an executive image. "But," whispers the father, "that's over, you ungrateful wretch. You're coming home with Daddy, now."

Her look says otherwise. The fear is gone. It is replaced by a very intense look that says, "Fuck you."

"You'll not get away now," he says.

The fingers on the table. Again the look. "Fuck you. I dare you."

The father leaps into the picture, intending to land on the desk to grab his daughter. But she steps to the side. The window is open. The father sees the streets far below rushing up to embrace him.

Waiting

He's waiting for the snowman. It's dark outside, the snow is freshly falling and from his window, he sees the snow covering the yard, the fences, the bushes, the trees.

"Such a beautiful sight," his mother always said. "When I was a little girl living near Spokane, we always got winter early; we'd have snow on the ground by late November, sometimes earlier." He remembered his mother as a big woman, with high forehead and prominent cheekbones; Norwegian is what he always thought of in later years, she must have been beautiful when she was young. "And we always built a snowman."

A snowman.

He's looking out at the softly falling snow. It covers everything on this December night. It didn't seem that long ago that his mother died. Grey-haired, but sharp and quick to the end. "The snowman," she murmured as she slowly drifted off the never-ending winter of her life. She ways always talking, talking about the snowmen. *She loved winter*, he thought. *She loved winter. How she loved the winter. When she came to the west side of the mountains, it was like her soul remained on the east side, in those winters that came in November, lasted until March and where she built her snowmen.*

He thinks of his father. He liked snowmen too. He remembers how his father would join them in snowball fights and sledding on the golf course. *On the west side of the mountains, we never got much snow*, he thinks, *not much snow at all, but when it came, it was sledding and hot chocolate and friends over for Christmas.*

"Mr. Sandstrom," says Rebecca, the live-in nurse, "how are you feeling?"

He responds quietly, "I'm good, Becky, I'm good."

Becky is thirty-five. He pays her well. He's done well in his life. Real estate has done him a great service.

"Sure is snowing," she says: she, a little over-weight, with blond hair cut close and eyes that deep and magnetic blue as if the blueness has an extra added dimension of depth. It's rare to see eyes like that. "How are you feeling?" she asks again.

He smiles. "I like it when it snows."

"Sure is pretty," she says. "Would you like some hot chocolate?"

A memory swells up and almost breaks his heart. He's seven, and he's with another Becky and they've been walking in the snow and she lives a few blocks away, and they go into her parents' place and her mother makes them hot chocolate and they sit there on a deep blue sofa looking out the window and watching it snow. After they warm up, they go out and make a snowman. They name it Frosty. And it does indeed have a carrot nose.

"Mr. Sandstrom?"

He nods. "Yes, hot chocolate would be nice."

She turns, goes into the kitchen. *Hmmmmmmmm* — the sound of the microwave. 120 seconds. He told her, 120 seconds. That's all you need. *Clatter*, a spoon, *Riip*, a package of instant hot chocolate being opened. *Tinkletinkletinkle* — the sound of the spoon mixing the chocolate in the cup. And he stares out at the snow and sees himself and Julie walking out on a winter's evening — was it that long ago? Ten years? They were over by the park that, during the day, had a tremendous view of Lake Washington, the University of Washington campus and the Cascades in the distance, and on that snowy evening, they built a snowman, putting in dark rocks for the eyes, dark pebbles for the mouth. Somehow it seemed more sinister than funny. But they left it; it was getting cold and they had to —

"Here you go," says Becky.

"Thank you," he says. — had to — what? What? Oh, go back home. But they stopped and walked though Volunteer Park past the cross country skiers who thought they could actually do something in that less-than-dry-snow, but it made for great snowmen and he wondered, if the snow was so dry in Spokane, how could you make a snowman? The winter before Julia died of the tumor, it had snowed again and they went to the same place and Julia said, "This is the place where we made the snowman."

He remembered and nodded. "It is."

"Shall we?"

"Sure."

There was barely enough snow and it was wet, but they had indeed made another snowman. Julia became tired after a while, and they left the snowman's face blank. Slowly they made it back home and later, in bed, she said, "Shall we?"

"Yes."

And they made love, in the bed with the view out to the street, and in the darkness, they held each other, lying so both could look out to the falling snow, and she said, "There's a snowman out there — see him moving — ?"

He just kissed her, not knowing what to think of that comment, because she had been saying things like that, and he did not know what to say, but for a moment he thought he saw something move out there, too. In the morning the snow had turned to rain and Julia was saying, "Look at all the snowmen out there; they must be falling from the sky — " and he knew she wasn't joking and that afternoon, she was in the hospital and the next week —

"Mr. Sandstrom?"

"Yes?"

"Is your hot chocolate OK?"

He sips it. Even now he can remember what the hot chocolate tasted like when he was seven at Becky's house and *this* tastes of chocolate-flavored water and mind numbing aspartame. Maybe aspartame was the culprit for his wandering mind —

"Mr. Sandstrom? Are you — ?"

He turns, pats her hand. "I'm fine. Watching the snow fall brings up so many memories. Did you ever make snowmen?"

Becky looks relieved. "I've only been here a few months, Mr. Sandstrom. In San Diego, we didn't make snowmen."

"Go out and make a snowman," he says. "Get that young fellow of yours to go out with you and make a snowman." He laughs. "And the chocolate is fine. Thank you."

"Well, I just wanted to be sure you're OK."

He hears the relief in her voice.

"Anyway, I think I'm going to go to bed. Do you need anything else? Are you going to go to bed soon? It is ten o'clock." Becky moves about with that controlled energy like the evening is just beginning and it's tough that her boyfriend is away, so what is she to do but go to bed while feeling as frisky as she is?

He says, "Good night, Becky, I'm going to go to bed before long."

"You took all your pills," she says.

It really is her duty to know this but he knows she doesn't want to question him, his memory, and inadvertently insult him, so the question comes out as a face-saving statement and he says, "Yes," though he isn't always exactly sure.

There's a pause. "Oops," she says, "one more. You have to have this last one."

He doesn't say anything. He just looks out at the window to the snow. He feels her draw near and put the pill into his hand. He takes it, opens his mouth, and she gives him the water.

"Take a big swallow, Mr. Sandstrom. You have to have this one. This is a really important one."

He takes the water, swallows, and gives the cup back to her.

"I don't know how we overlooked that one Mr. Sandstrom, but it's really important to take that one to keep your blood pressure down. It's been pretty high, and the doctor will be coming by to see you tomorrow and maybe change your medication."

"Yes," he says.

"Goodnight," she says. "I'll see you in the morning."

"Yes," he says, "goodnight, Becky."

She leaves; and he takes the pill out from his mouth, as he takes them out of his mouth as often as he can, and puts it neatly in his bathrobe to flush it down the toilet later. And he sits in the dark of the room, watching the snow fall and realizes that he is waiting for something. He looks out at the softly, quietly falling snow. Waiting? Waiting—for? Suddenly, a crushing pain in his chest, and then he sees what he is waiting for: the snowman.

Harborheights Hospital Psychiatric Inpatient Service

New Admission Interview
Bruce Taylor, Interviewer

Dec. 22.

Form 747: Identification and Problem list
  Patient: Kringle, Kris, Nicholas St. (Also known as Santa Claus)
  Problem List:
  1) Possible delusions: (Patient claims he's *the real* Santa Claus.) When this doctor doubted the gentleman's claim, Mr. Claus asked, "Have you been a good little boy?" This doctor then informed Mr. Claus that the question was inappropriate, at which point Mr. Claus said "Ho, Ho, Ho." Abruptly in the lower pocket of this doctor's $250 Polo sports jacket there was one (1) lump of coal.
  2) Support system: Mr. Claus wanted to have his wife, a little girl named Virginia, and Mssr. Dasher, Dancer, Prancer, Vixen, Comet, Cupid, Donner and Blitzen to visit.
  3) Diagnosis: Manic Depression with underlying characterlogical disorder and delusions of grandeur.
  4) Disposition: Pt. claims that after he, "...distributes presents throughout the world to good little boys and girls, I'll return to the North Pole."

Form DC-10: *Record of Valuables and Clothing*
  1944 United States Navy star chart, *Life Pictorial Atlas of The world, Chandler's Latest Edition of International Air Traffic Routes,*

Texas Instrument Calculator, labeled, "Don't Touch, Programmed for Satellite Orbits." One Sony Walkman with various tapes, *Christmas With Lawrence Welk, Bing Crosby Sings White Christmas, Muzakly Yours, The Nutcracker Suite, Twisted Sisters Do Rudolph*, one large Thermos of Hot Chocolate, bags of marshmallows, Hershey Kisses and Screaming Yellow Zonkers, Doritos and onion dip, packages of Hostess Twinkies and Ding Dongs plus a zip lock bag labeled, "Sugar 'n' Spice 'n' Everything Nice" (sent to substance lab for analysis). One bottle of *Flea and Tick Off, Heavy Duty*. One red, white fur-trimmed Santa Claus suit badly singed, burned and soiled, scuffed boots, blackened and dirty cap with matted fluff of white fiberfill on end.

Form 284-3205: *Observation of Patient*

Elderly white male, rather chubby and plump, elfin in features and stature with immense beard on chin the color of snow. Pt. has broad face, with cheeks red as roses and nose like a cherry (semi-ripe Bing). Pt. dressed in burned, singed Santa Claus outfit with Adidas sport bag filled with personal articles as previously described. Pt. looks tired and anxious, nervously glancing at clock. Frequently puts finger beside nose and gives abrupt nods of head.

Orientation:

Date: "It's beginning to look a lot like Christmas."

Place: "Oh, little town of Bethlehem?" (Pt. smiled sarcastically.)

President: "Ho, ho, ho."

Assessment: Probably well oriented.

Concerns: "Where's my sleigh? My reindeer? My bag? I was just on a trial run—"

Assessment: Characterlogical Disorder. Most likely patient is feeling very guilty about something and is atoning for guilt by acting out fantasy of being perfectly good and beneficial because the core personality is seen as evil and terrible. "Santa Claus" is compensatory mechanism/reaction formation to guilt. Insistence about sleigh, reindeer and personal effects simply shows depths of denial.

Form 98109: *Harborheights Mental Health Clinical Data*

I. *Chief Complaint – Patient's Stated Reason for Seeking Help*

Brought in by Seattle Police for wandering around Columbia Center Tower yelling, "Help me! My sleigh and reindeer have crashed into the fifty-first floor!"

II. *Present Life Situations*

A. *Describe Relationships with Significant others*

Claims good relationship with wife, a little girl named Virginia, and a particularly good relationship with a Mr. Rudolph.

B. *Housing*

Pt. claims to "...live at North Pole."

C. *Education: Describe Learning Deficit and/or Strengths*

Mistletoe Academy of Packaging Design and Gift Wrapping; Cinderella Electronic Game and Toys; Nutcracker Institute of Advanced Fudge Making and Cookie Design; C.I.A. Intensive Workshop, "Nice People, Naughty People and You"; Peter Pan Academy of Doll Making and Fire Truck Design; Scrooge Institute for the Study of Year-round Christmas Merchandizing; Mr. Claus continued for another twenty minutes. Apparently no formal schooling but seems very bright.

D. *Past and Present Employment and Economic Status*

Self-Employed.

E. *Social and Societal Activities*

"Well, me and the elves get together a lot to make lots of toys for the following year. So I guess I'm a family man. Got my reindeer to take care of. I have a busy life. No, I don't have a car...no roads. No, I don't go to movies. No. No, TV. I read a lot: *A Christmas Carol, The Night Before Christmas.* I also like Edgar Allen Poe and Stephen King."

III. *Past History*

A. *Significant Developmental History (early Family, Childhood and Adolescent Problems)*

"I loved my parents. I never drank. No, I was never in jail." Patient seemed sincere. Pt. seemed lively and quick. This writer knew in a moment that it must be remembered that since patient still claimed to be Santa Claus, it would have to indicate some sort of background psychopathology.

B. *Family History*

"I don't remember much about my parents. No sir, I don't remember anything about cancer, smoking, drinking. I do remember lots of cookies and eggnog. Every day was like Christmas."

C. *Past and Current Medical History – List Major Illness, Operations and hospitalizations.*

Pt. claims none.

IV. *Review of Systems – Sleep Disturbances Weight Loss, Sexual Problems, etc.*

"I get lots of sleep 364 days of the year, but on the twenty-fourth, I stay up all night. What's today? It isn't the 24th is it? O Holy Night! Oh, Christ divine! How long does this last? I've got my sleigh and eight reindeer on the fifty-first floor of that Darth Vader building..."

Sexual: "Ho, ho, ho."

V. *Mental Status*

A. *Appearance and Behavior*

Unkempt, apprehensive; overall affect is anxiety. At times comforted self by making out lists and checking them twice. Muttered at times, "Gonna find out who's naughty and nice."

B. *Speech and Communication – Coherence, Pace, Organization.*

Obsessional: "When is this going to end? I was just doing a practice run and the smog blinded my reindeer and the loss of ozone must have affected something and I crashed into the building...you have to let me get back to my reindeer and sleigh...I have to get back to the North Pole to get things fixed up so I can get to all the good little boys and girls and give them presents...Please..." Pt. was then informed that he was on a seventy-two hour hold for being gravely disabled. At which point, patient leaped up and yelled, "You can't do that! I'm Santa Claus and Santa Claus is coming to town! The whole world is expecting me to deliver presents! I've got to get my sleigh and reindeer! I've got to get out of here!" At that point, Mr. Claus jumped up, shoved all personal effects back in bag and yanked open the door to the admitting office. He was met by fifteen staff people, a set of restraints and after much struggle was wrestled to the ground and carried to his room where he was placed in a waist restraint. Interview terminated.

Subjective: "What am I gonna do? Jingle Bells! It's Christmas! I have to get my sleigh, my reindeer. Without me, what is Christmas? Think of all the disappointed little girls and boys. How can you do this to me?"

Objective: Tearful. Later on, was quietly smoking pipe the smoke of which encircled his head like a wreath.

Assessment: Deeply rooted delusional system. Obviously sincerely believes in what he's saying. May mean long term hospitalization. The patients in group therapy, however, were obviously taken by the gentleman, many asking about his reindeer, and what it was like being Santa Claus. Efforts at refocusing the group on more fruitful subjects proved hopeless. Oddly enough, the group therapists all ended up with chunks of coal in their pockets. Most likely cause is some sort of staff hysteria for being out of control of a group. For group to be so taken in by this gentleman means impaired reality functioning.

Plan: Double all pts.' meds.

B. Tai Lor, M.D.
Attending Psychiatrist

Dec. 23

Subj. "Better watch out! Better not cry! Better watch out I'm telling you why—can't you see what a mistake you're making? I'm Santa Claus! What do I have to do to make you see?"

Obj. Intense eye contact.

Asses. In one to one contact, pt's delusional system remains intact. Pt obviously very well defended against his feelings of unworthiness because of the fear that what he *really* feels is who he is as a person, (I feel unworthy therefore I am an unworthy person.) Oddly enough, all the patients in spite of massive doses of medication, act as though Mr. Claus is, in fact, Santa. Certainly, at times, his eyes, how they twinkle, and when he laughs his stomach shakes like a bowl full of jelly.

Plan: Further evaluation.

Brucia Talorez, R.N.

Subj. "Hark! the Herald Angels sing! Angels we have heard on high!"

Obj. Pt.'s droll little mouth drawn up like a bow. Finger beside nose, turning head with a jerk.

Asses. Pt. may be hearing voices. Certainly unusual perceptions present. Pt. also claims to know not only when people are sleeping, but knows if they've been bad or good. Seems obsessively concerned about this and some of the more paranoid patients seem uneasy around Mr. Claus. May be psychotic elements present. Also, pt. engaging in compulsive giving behavior. When confronted, said, "But that's what I'm *supposed* to do." Pt. secluded in room for thirty minutes.

Plan: Start on Lithium; if delusions persist, begin Thorazine. Monitor compulsive giving behavior; pt. must also learn how to receive.

> Bruce Taylor,
> Primary Therapist

Sub. "Here comes Santa Claus; here comes Santa Claus,"

Obj. Pt. leading other pts. in singing Christmas carols during community meeting.

Asses. Pt seems to have excellent rapport with other patients. The singing became so affect laden that it became something of a clatter and other staff leaped from their chairs to see what was the matter. Mr. Claus was informed to limit the intensity of his interactions with others.

Plan: Increase pt.'s Lithium

> B. Tai Lor, M. D.
> Attending.

Dec. 24

Sub. "Oh, ho, ho, ho!"

Obj. Surprised, pleased, good affect. Pt. dressed in cleaned, pressed red Santa Claus suit.

Ass. It was the evening before Christmas, and all through the unit the patients were admiring Mr. Claus' street clothes when all of a sudden who should appear at the main door but a little girl, age eight, by the name of Virginia, who asked, "Is there a Santa Claus?" (pause) "here?" Visitor handed over to this doctor a sealed envelope. "If he's here," visitor said, "these are papers for his release." As this doctor opened door to let visitor in, abruptly visitor yelled, "Now Dasher! Now, Dancer!" Two immense, well-formed Reindeer charged the door and jammed it open. At that point, Virginia yelled to Mr. Claus, "SANTA BABY! The elves got the sleigh! Let's *go!*" Mr. Claus, surrounded by pts., was escorted to the front door and escaped. A few minutes later one of the patients pointed out the window and yelled, "Look!" And what to our therapeutic eyes should appear but an open vehicle pulled by eight reindeer.

Plan: Remove coal from pocket, take suit to dry cleaners.

> Bruce Taylor
> Primary Therapist.

Of Thumbs and Rafters

Now it was of great consternation to the citizens of the little town of M, and especially to the Ramanda family, to discover the family head, the heretofore, smiling, gregarious and rather rotund, Mr. Ramanda, hanging by his thumbs from the rafters in the attic. Now, many were affected by this event and certainly not just the family.

Dr. Johanson, an older, very well respected person in the community was the first to come up the stairs, at the urging of a hand wringing and certainly concerned Mrs. Ramanda.

"What," said Dr. Johanson, "is the meaning of this? Why are you hanging by your thumbs from the rafters?"

Mr. Ramanda merely smiled and said, "I've done many things in my life, but this is something I've never done before."

Dr. Johanson was totally shocked. "This is a scandal," he said pulling at his brown beard. "This most *certainly* is a scandal. You, a professional banker and community leader — you who run the yearly telethon for the sufferers of food allergies, you, of all people, are making a mockery of yourself, and," he drew Mr. Ramanda's child, Eric, close by, "your sickly son, who must someday leave this house to go out into the world."

Mr. Ramanda smiled benignly; "Yes, I suppose that is true," and his smile became somewhat rueful, revealing his fine, gold capped incisor, "but everyone has something that they must do and I guess this is something that I must do."

"No," said Dr. Johanson, "this is something you must *not* do. I can have you committed to the local asylum for what you are doing —" and he turned to Mr. Ramanda's wife. "Has he threatened suicide?"

Tearfully but dutifully, Mrs. Ramanda shook her head no.

"Has he threatened property damage?"

"No, no, he has not done that," said Mr. Ramanda's wife.

"Does he eat, I mean, he surely can't eat —"

"He does eat," said Mrs. Ramanda.

"Well, has he threatened young Eric here?" pointing to the six-year-old child.

"No," and again, Mrs. Ramanda shook her head.

Dr. Johanson, now very indignant at this community outrage, said, "Well, this *must* stop. I'm going to saw this beam in half—"

But Mr. Ramanda just tightened his grip on the beam with his great thumbs and said, "No. The main electrical cord to the house is fastened here; you could get electrocuted."

Dr. Johanson, simply said, "We'll remove the cord and just cut the beam."

"No," said Mr. Ramanda. "This is a very important beam. Cut it and the roof might well collapse."

Temporarily dismayed at all of this, Dr. Johanson, said, "Well, I'll pull you down then."

"No," said Mr. Ramanda, "for I will kick you."

"You kick me," said the doctor, "and not only would that be very ungentlemanly of you, but that might cause me to press charges and have you taken to jail."

"And I'll just find another beam from which to hang by my thumbs."

Mrs. Ramanda went up to her husband. "Please dear, if it was something I said..."

Mr. Ramanda looked lovingly at her and simply said, "No, no, not at all."

"I'll make your favorite desert of tapioca pudding and raisins—whenever you want it and however much you want—"

"That's quite all right," he said, "but no, I think you don't have to do that. And this really doesn't have anything to do with you—"

"Is it something I've done?" and she went up to her husband dangling by his thumbs from the rafter. "If you'd just tell me—"

But he shook his head.

Mrs. Ramanda motioned young Eric over. "But what kind of role model are you providing for Eric? He needs a father—"

"But I'm here," said Mr. Ramanda. "He can see me any time, ask me any questions. Just because I'm hanging from the rafter doesn't mean I can't be a role model to him or a good father," and he looked at his son. "Isn't that right now?"

Eric just looked a bit confused but nodded in agreement. "Yes Papa."

And Mr. Remanda smiled almost triumphantly. "See? Now what did I tell you? 'Out of the mouths of babes—'"

"Oh," said Dr. Johanson, abruptly turning, "this is too much. Too, too much. Give me polio, a cold, a bleeding ulcer, give me something I can cure, not someone who is totally deranged—oh," he said, walking downstairs, "this is too, *too* much."

And you know how it goes, other people found out quickly what had happened, and the neighbor, Mrs. Reginold, stomped up the stairs. She was a hefty lady with glasses and grey hair, and she was dressed in a blue dress with her stockings bagging above her dirty white running shoes, and she said, "Now, *what* is this? Why are you doing this? The neighbors are talking and you are presenting one awful scandal—an awful scene—in the neighborhood. Surely you know better, a brilliant industrialist and banker like you hanging by his thumbs from a rafter. Here now, I've known you for years. Come down immediately."

But Mr. Ramanda kept his place and said, "I really must not do that. I really must not. We all find our place in life and I've found mine."

Mrs. Reginold just shook her head. "Well, your thumbs are certainly going to become tired. That is very obvious."

"No," said Mr. Ramanda, "I think not. Because when you really find what you like to do, strength, my dear Mrs. Reginold, strength! You can do anything! Endurance is forever."

Mrs. Reginold, looked at Mr. Ramanda for a long time. She smiled. "Well, certain bodily functions..."

Mr. Ramanda smiled to his wife and he glanced to a white bucket nearby. "I've thought of everything. It's in foot reach."

"Oh," said Mrs Reginold, "oh, oh, my heart just can't take this. Oh, oh, my." And she stomped down the stairs, saying, "Oh, oh, oh," with every step.

Eric looked up at his father with a mixture of pride and fear. "But Papa, won't you play with me anymore?"

"Eric," said Mr. Ramanda, "we've played a lot, but there simply has to come a time when a man must make a decision about what he must do for the rest of his life. But I'll be here and I'll most certainly help you with your school work and give you pointers about how to deal with that terrible monkey-brained Billy Danas."

Meekly, Eric considered this, then the local Priest, Father Loharns, came up the stairs and looked at Mr. Ramanda for a long, long time. Father Loharns, tall as a whip, rigid as a cross, with abrupt facial features like chiseled steel, looked at Mr. Ramanda with hard, grey eyes, looking and locking into Mr. Ramanda's face like a vice grip and asked, "Do you, by any stretch of the imagination, think that by doing this, you are doing God's will?"

"With all due respect," said Mr. Ramanda, "Never said I wanted to do God's will, with all respect, most Holy Father."

"God has greater things for you to do aside from hanging by your thumbs from a rafter."

"How do I know that this isn't God's calling?" asked Mr. Ramanda.

The father took in a very deep breath, as if looking into the abominable sins of the devil's work right before him. "This cannot be the work of God."

"Well, what if it is?"

"God does not work this way."

Mr. Ramanda smiled. "Maybe He does. How do you know? It's a strange world God has created—a world of snakes, spiders, butterflies and clouds—all the strange, simultaneous faces of God. So how are you to know what order is God's order, and, given how strange this planet really is, what is not? Is what I am doing so truly strange? All is taken care of and provided for; the pension comes once a week so I don't have to work. I'm available at all times—now what harm am I doing?"

Again, Father Loharns sucked in a very deep breath. "There are certain—ahem—duties between a husband and wife—"

"We've not touched each other for a long time," said Mr. Ramanda.

"It's true," said his wife, looking down out of deep shame, "We simply are not interested in that any more. I wish it were different, but it is not."

A deep look of consternation and disgust passed over Father Loharns' face as he looked at Mr. Ramanda again. "There is your son. He needs to be touched by you—"

Mr. Ramanda smiled. "Oh, heavens, I never was much of a father, Father. Now my Brother, Jacob—he and my son have a much, much better relationship."

Eric smiled at the sound of Jacob's name. He turned to his mother. "Is he coming over again today? Is he Mother? Is he?"

"We'll, see," said Mrs. Ramanda.

Mr. Ramanda looked at the Father. "Now, what more to you need to know?"

Father Loharns just shook his head. "Brother, you must be a lonely, lonely man."

"Father," said Mr. Ramanda, "forgive me, but you must be a nosy, *nosy* man."

Father Loharns bristled as if the God within him had touched the devil's flesh. "I'll pray for you," and he abruptly turned and left.

Yes, there was no doubt about it. What Mr. Ramanda had done had indeed caused quite a stir in the neighborhood. A reporter from *The Daily* stopped by and did a feature story on "The Man with the Iron Thumbs." A Mental Health Specialist IV stopped by and tried to talk to Mr. Ramanda about the way hidden anger comes out, but Mr. Ramanda just laughed, and in a huff, the Mental Health Specialist IV stomped away. There was even a writer who stopped by and offered to write an article about this incident and claimed that he had very good credentials—that he was writer in residence at Shakespeare and Company in Paris, and had been translated and published in Germany and that he was even a member of a well-known science fiction writing association, and Mr. Ramanda laughed and said, "Go ahead," so, indeed, for the next year or so, Mr. Ramanda was getting much publicity. *Life Magazine* did a story, and there was even an article in *The New York Times* in the Tuesday edition on Science: "Thumbthing Remarkable: Mr. Ramanda Hangs On" and the story went into the amazing thumbs that Mr. Ramanda must have to be able to hold on for so long. And little Eric, as well as the rest of the family, certainly got a great deal of notoriety for this, but even such things as these, people get used to, and so, as hard as it may be to believe, even this story faded into oblivion. But young Eric, growing up with this situation, could not help but admire his father and often sought his counsel.

"Be brave, Eric," said his father, through the years. "You have to go out there in the world, and establish your place. Yes, you have to believe."

"Yes," said Eric, "but don't your thumbs ever get tired?"

"Faith," said Mr. Ramanda, "is a mighty thing."

Another time, after Eric had brought back the emptied and washed-out white bucket, his father said, "Well, now you're eighteen. So tell me, has living with a father who has hung by his thumbs for twelve years been so difficult?"

Eric set down the bucket and said, "It would have been nice to play baseball with you."

"Ah," said Mr. Ramanda, "You'd have been disappointed. I really am a terrible thrower and catcher. I really am. But at any rate, look at all this fame and fortune that has been bestowed on this family. Now surely that is worth a great deal. Just in money alone from the stories and the special on Channel Ten several years ago. And much of that money has been put into a trust fund for you to go to college if you so choose."

"Yes, father," said Eric, "I do appreciate that."

"Would you get out my pipe from my pocket, put tobacco in it, light it and give it to me?"

Eric did as requested. "Yes," said Mr. Ramanda, "it will soon be time for you to leave."

"In several weeks, actually," said Eric.

Mr. Ramanda, sucked on his pipe thoughtfully and gritting the stem between his teeth, said, "Yes, on to college. Well, just remember," he said, "just remember this: hang on, just always hang on, and most likely you'll get famous and outlast everyone. You just have to hang on. But then I've always told you that."

Eric just nodded.

Mr. Ramanda sucked on his pipe again. "Everyone is always hanging by their thumbs, you know? I've enjoyed this," he said. "Yes, I've enjoyed this. Now. Be on your way. Oh, take the pipe from my mouth, put it out, and —" he nodded with his head.

Eric did so and put the pipe back in the right pocket of his father's maroon smoking jacket, then went down the steps to finish up his papers for school.

And two weeks later, after a fond farewell, Mr. Ramanda looked out the upstairs window and saw his son, walking down the street, luggage in hand, heading for the bus that would take him away. And Mr. Ramanda laughed a good natured laugh. "Good for you my boy," and he smiled and nodded. "Good for you. Going out into the world of thumbs and rafters." And at that point, Mr. Ramanda sighed mightily, relaxed his thumbs, *crash*, fell to the floor — and died.

Morality Play

"Some things we probably can do we shouldn't do."
Bill Joy, Chief Scientist, Sun Microsystems
New York Times, 31 August 2000

"Did you know that 'Attic salt' means, 'fine and elegant wit'?" asks Jack's SemiKat, Yank. ModularVoice renders the speech soft and comforting.

"How do you know that?" Jack has to ask as he looks around to the burned out landscape from a world gone mad. Tired and exhausted, he pulls a fiberfill jacket around himself, then, distracted, he runs fingers though his black hair. *Need a haircut*, he thinks, and then laughs. *Where the hell do I find a barber?*

"Don't know," says Yank. "Guess my VQ705 Tetradyne Brain-InteractChip just likes to come up with these things."

"Too bad it taught you language and how to think and talk," laughs Jack. "Sometimes I'm not sure I wanna know your mind chatter but I gotta say, some of it's interesting...harkening back to the primitive feline in all of us? Or is it the reptilian part we're talking about?"

Contrary to Jack's comments, he knows Yank can be both very surprising and disturbing in how it thinks. "So, what do we do for dinner?" Jack asks. The clouds are low and he suspects blizzard conditions are coming again. He wonders if July has any meaning any more, or if where he is sitting, in what use to be called Denver, has any meaning, either. Jack muses, *did they* really *screw up the weather too*? *How'd they do* that?

"Did you know that human beings used to wonder how many angels danced on the head of a pin?" Yank asks. "I'm sure that contributed to human survival."

"Time on their hands, Yank," Jack says. He scratches Yank behind the plasticine ears, then strokes the head, marveling at the satin feel of the tawny VeluraDerm skin. Jack muses how Yank almost looks like a cat, kind of a large robot-cat if you will, with a feline brain, for what purpose he can't imagine—maybe to give it some sort of pet-like characteristics so it wouldn't be too alien or so that it could bond with children. It's really hard to say just what the motives were for creating a bunch of cat-robots like Yank except that—they *could*. And did. SemiKat made millionaires out of everyone—including Jack.

"What were they working on before the world fizzled?" Jack wonders out loud. "I can't remember all the stuff that was going on, though I should..."

But Yank's head is tilted up, its irises dilating. "Food," it says. A laser blasts out of Yank's mouth and a rat flies up in the air, somersaults and lands, semi-roasted. Yank finishes the cooking and then sterilizes it with UV radiation. "OK to eat," Yank says.

Jack climbs over the busted masonry and, after waiting a few minutes for dinner to cool, he gingerly picks up the rat. After a few mouthfuls, he says, "Not bad. You're good at this. Too bad there isn't much else to eat." He shrugs. "But thanks anyway."

Yank is quiet. Finally it says, "Dogs were always man's best friend, but since they've all been eaten, well, even if we aren't entirely all cat, looks like we'll have to do. But look at it this way, I'll never die."

"Maybe so," says Jack, finishing off dinner, "but right now, I gotta find shelter or I'm gonna freeze!"

"Over there," says Yank, "a sheltered place."

Moving toward a cave formed by broken slabs of a collapsed wall, Jack ponders Yank's perception and how it moves. That is indeed interesting to Jack: there *was* a cunning logic to computer implant enhancement of a cat's brain. Certainly their senses are remarkable so why not just *enhance* them? *Ah, the wisdom of bio-engineers*, thinks Jack, sarcastically. *If only there were wisdom.* He feels an immense surge of guilt and remorse. None of this was done with malicious intent, but the guilt eats away at him anyway.

Once inside the cave, Yank sanitizes the place and puts up an energy barrier to repel rodents. The bugs, however, are another story.

After settling down for the night, Jack asks, "Just how long has it been?"

"Three months," Yank answers. In the semi-darkness, Yank sits like a cat might, butt in the sand, forepaws out front and the blunted cylinder shape of the snout horizontal. The eyes Jack likes the most—pale blue and they almost really do look like the eyes of an animal.

"Three months, almost exactly," repeats Yank. Jack's glad he doesn't enumerate the days, hours, and seconds.

"Did you see it coming?" Jack asks after a while.

"Yes," says Yank, "I saw it coming."

"But—"

"No point arguing inevitability."

"Hopeless?" Jack asks.

"Pointless."

"How much time is left?"

"Not much," says Yank.

"Will it be painful?" Jack asks.

"What do you think?" Yank looks directly at Jack; animal? Machine? Nonetheless, the gaze is penetrating, intense and burns right through Jack. *Of course it's going to be painful*, thinks Jack. *What a stupid thing to ask. How could it not be painful? It's gonna be bloody awful.* Jack swallows, "How—how soon?"

"Do you wish it were sooner? Isn't life precious to you?"

Jack just stares into the darkening gloom, then closes his eyes and lets his head fill with the images he knows all too well: the shattered, busted world, the burned, broken skeletons of skyscrapers, now just jutting, rectangular bones piercing the sky; everywhere one looked there is nothing but a mammoth open burial ground.

"Not in a world like this," Jack finally says.

Yank comes out with a rumble that sounds remarkably like a purr. Then it stops. "They're coming."

Oh, shit, thinks Jack. "Where?"

Yank becomes very still: processing. "I think you're safe," Yank finally says. "It's close. Be glad you're downwind. They can't sense you." Pause. "Yet."

In the cavern of rubble, Jack can see fading daylight from a gaping crack in a wall. Quietly, he makes his way over to it and is rewarded with a view westward. At first he sees nothing, just the guts of a burned-out city. Looking down the blocky chaos of what was an arterial, he can see into the distance—then he sees them. "Fuck," he whispers, "fuck, Yank, fuck, *millions* of the fuckers. How do they eat? How the hell do they keep going? They weren't supposed to—"

"There's just enough to keep them going, but don't worry, when all the food is gone..." and Yank looks to Jack for a long second, "their numbers will crash."

"So will the planet," adds Jack.

Yank says nothing and finally muses, "The minds that created me are the same minds that created them. Just because you can do certain things doesn't mean you should do them."

"I know," Jack says, "I know. Science without conscience is no better than the *worst* Nazi atrocities..."

"Only this *is* worse than the *worst* of the Nazi atrocities—a whole planet..."

"I know," says Jack, "I *know!*"

"It's just a matter of time—they will get you, you know," says Yank. "I can protect you just so much, but I only have so much energy that I can store and regenerate."

Jack watches them. *I can't believe we* did *this*, he thinks. *I can't* fathom *how we did this.* He pauses in his thinking, *I can't imagine* why *we did this. What were we* thinking—*just because we could*—*we* did—"Fuck," he says, "look at them. Half-beetles, half-spiders, half-moths-half-wasps, flying scorpions, bugs big as rats, others as big as dogs. Oh, shit," Jack whispers, "I don't know what happened—"

Yank looks at him. "*You* were the one who began this madness—*you* gave the final OK for the bio-engineering."

"But it was all theoretical how...I didn't think..."

"Maybe that's the problem," says Yank, "you didn't think—" Yank pauses. "Uh, oh," it says.

"What?"

"Sorry to say, wind has shifted—"

The seething mass of hybrid beasts stops moving away, and suddenly—

"Oh, shit," Jack says, "oh, shit!" He turns to Yank, "Stop them!"

Yank stands, shoves its muzzle through the crack; a searing white-hot laser blasts from its mouth, but the hordes come and they come, down the streets, coming, coming, the boiling, seething mass coming as if to take revenge on their god—for their creation.

Fire

I wasn't particularly enjoying Pluto. It's such a miserable place, all cold and dark. A lot of us have only rags to wear and some of us get ill. I was lucky, I guess. I had mittens. I had rags on my feet which served as socks and I had good leather boots, although, with the cold of Pluto, the leather got hard and brittle.

But, rags or not, each shift we went out, grabbed the cables and pulled and Pluto revolved a sixth of the way. And every shift, I always take a few minutes to look at the sun, a far, far away dot in the cold, black sky and I get angry. I get so God damn angry. My cave-mate, as I, has no name. He calls me "X"; I call him "Y" and we leave it at that.

But, one day he said to me, "Whatsa matter? You look sour."

"Oh," I said, "I look sour, do I? Listen, I got better things to do than go out, yank a wire to help this fucking chunk of rock revolve. For what? For what do we do this? For what?"

Y shrugs. "Listen, so what do you got better to do?" He hunches over and spreads frostjam on his snowbread. "Not so bad here."

I stand. "How the fuck can you say that when it's all you've ever known?"

"Gotta place to sleep. Got food."

I want to say more, but the boss comes. He's a bent man with white, frozen hair and he has a cough like breaking ice and a laugh like wind through icicles. He shuffles along, moving the snow with his feet. "Eh, eh, eh," he says to me, "X, you bitchin' again? Eh?" He looks at me with ice-blue eyes; the left one is cloudy from cataract. His mouth hangs open, his attention keen as he waits for an answer.

I sit and munch my bread. Finally I say, "What do you want to hear, snowballs?"

He puts a hand on my shoulder. "Eh, eh, eh, you got a fighting spirit, boy. Maybe you'll make it."

175

I'm surprised. "Ha! You vertical pile of snowmush—you listening to me for once?"

The old man coughs. "Dunno. Whatcha want?"

I stand, furious. "Listen! I want fire. You hear me? I want the fucking fire! I'm tired of being cold." I grab the boss and shake him. "You hear me, fog fart? You hear me, vapor brain? I want the fucking fire!"

The boss looks up at me. He hasn't shaved for weeks; his breath smells like methane. He looks at me with open mouth and one eye large with wonder, the other foggy with indifference. "Eh," he says again, "you want the fire? Sure you can handle it?"

"I want it! *Now!*"

"Eh, eh, eh. It's not your time yet. Better eat your snowbread before it gets warm."

"Warm? Here? Warm? Ha!" I let go of him. He shuffles down the corridor. He returns in a few minutes, handing out ice muffins with chlorine frosting. I take one. "Hey, you old fog, these aren't bad. Once in a while you can do something right. By the way, what are you going to do about my request?"

"Eh? Eh? What request?"

"About the fire?"

He looks away, pretending to not have heard me. I throw the muffin and it bounces off his head. He turns. "All *right!* But you don't know what a mistake you're making."

"Listen," and I go up to him and put my nose almost against his, "listen, I'm tired of going out there and yanking on a cable to turn this ice ball. I'm tired of it. I'll take *anything.*"

The boss looks at me and then he clicks softly to himself. "*Klk, klk, klk;* all right, clean up and go up to the If/When Department. Ask to see Mr. Maybe."

"Is he in right now?"

"Perhaps."

"Where is the If/When Department?"

"That's indefinite. But, I'm sure you'll be able to find it." He smiles. "Eh, eh, eh."

I don't bother to clean up. I just go out and find the Administrative Cavern. When I find it, I walk in and all along each side of the vast cavern, the administrative offices rise four levels. I locate the If/When Department on the second level, only to discover that it had been moved to the Department of Probability. I looked a good time for that and finally had to stop and ask a guard who was eating an ice cream cone. "Where is the Department of Probability?"

He shrugged and pointed to the end of the cavern. "Chances are you'll find it down that way."

And I do find it; it took careful looking; the sign was obscured by a tall snow sculpture of our leader, who had just recently had a problem with a high fever. I stepped into the office. "Is Mr. Maybe around?" A young lady turned from an open filing cabinet to look at me. She shrugged. "Could be. I'll check."

She returned in a few minutes. "Mr. Maybe said that he might have a few minutes to spend with you. Perhaps you'd like to follow me."

I did. The lady showed me into an office. As soon as I walked in, Mr. Maybe turned. He was smoking a large, fat snowgar and he had on a white suit with intricate snow patterns woven in. Every flake was different. He was very fat. He looked at me shrewdly. "Yes?" Then he shrugged. "No?"

"Mr. Maybe," I began, "I want to have a chance at something else. I've been pulling planet now for a long time, and—"

"Come to the point; come to the point, although you don't have to if you don't want to. Perhaps you'd care to continue, though I can't guarantee anything, but I do want to listen, but that is subject to change without notice."

"I want the fire."

"You *what*?"

"I want the fire."

"Is it your turn?"

"I have no idea. All I know is that I want the fire."

"If there's no opening, then there's no chance of fire. Sorry."

"Is there an opening?"

"Could be. And then again, there might not be."

"Could you check?"

"Perhaps." Mr. Maybe sat down at a desk made of pure carbon dioxide. He kept it well polished. He pulled out a drawer which squeaked horribly—perhaps it was characteristic of carbon dioxide desks—I don't know. He looked at lists. Then he looked at me. He sucked on the snowgar. "Well," he finally said, "I do have something but I really don't think you'd be interested in it. You certainly wouldn't be aware of the fire—it would be *most* dreadful if you—"

I sigh. "The fire. The fire. At *all* costs. The fire."

Mr. Maybe came up to me. "Why don't you go back and pull planet and wait for your turn?"

"My turn may never come."

"That may be true—I don't know—but it would be better than forcing the issue."

"No," I say, "I want the fire. I want the fire *now*!"

Mr. Maybe looks exasperated. "All right." He looks to the list. "I'm going to give you a number. You must remember it. The number tells the *form* by which you will know the fire and how aware you are of it. It is also an indication of how many forms you must progress through before you reach Divine Humanform. Do you understand?"

"Yes," and I nod my head.

"Are you ready?"

"Yes," I say, "yes, yes, oh, yes!"

"I can say this number only once. You will repeat it to Mr. Random and that is the *only* other time it can be repeated."

"Why is that?" I ask.

"As soon as I say the number, similar slots open up. If I were to repeat the number, slots would be confirmed, *for me*. When *you* repeat it, slots are confirmed for you. Once repeated, *a slot* must be filled *within minutes* or else the system jams or overheats. Only Mr. Random has the machinery and the knowledge to fill the right slot and that is why you must confirm in his presence *only*. It also makes for a lot less confusion: *I* open the slots, *he* fills them. Now, don't forget what I told you." Mr. Maybe glances to his list. "The number you are to repeat to Mr. Random is: 191*dash*694518."

Silently, to myself, I repeat the number. I clear my throat. "I really wish you could repeat that so I could be sure—"

"Nope. Nope." He shakes his head gravely. "Can't do that. I told you why. Simply can't. It's just too confusing with all the variables and randomness we have to work with. No point in taking unnecessary chances." He chews on his snowgar. Some flakes of ash fall onto his suit and he dusts them away and the flakes sparkle in the light. "Your next step—I think maybe—" He looks puzzled for a minute, "Oh, yes, go next door and see Mr. Random. Repeat the number to him. It is up to him to slide you into the right slot and send you on your way."

I go up to Mr. Maybe to shake hands. "Thank you, thank you," I say.

But he shakes his head and waves his snowgar. "Beat it," he says, "I'm just doing this to keep peace in the camp."

I nod and leave. And enter the office next door. Mr. Random looks to me. He is throwing icicles at a dart board. He is thin, his eyes dark and calculating. In the breast pocket of his suit, a yellow slide rule. His suit is dark, yet shines like black ice. He wears a ring. The setting is white with a black question mark in the middle. He looks at me for a long time. "You're probably 'X,'" he says.

I nod.

"Chances are you're here to get the fire; is that right?"

I nod again. Mr. Random clears his throat. He then sits at a desk covered with green felt, like a game board. He stares at me for a long time. He picks up a deck of cards and shuffles them. "You're taking an awful risk," he finally says. "Go back and pull planet. This just isn't worth it."

"It's my decision," I say. "I want to know fire."

"So does everyone else up here. But you gotta wait for the right time."

"I want it *now!*"

"Is it so miserable here on Pluto?"

"*Yes,* it's miserable." I look at him. He folds his hands and stares at me as though trying to bluff me.

"You're serious, aren't you? You really intend to win."

"Yes."

Mr. Random sighs. He opens a drawer, pulls out a pad, a pencil and activates a calculator that is built in the desk top. He figures. "All right," he says, "what is the number Mr. Maybe gave you?"

Instantly I respond, "191694518."

He looks at me. "You're sure?"

I freeze. "Uh—Yes, yes that was it. Yes," I triumphantly announce.

"You're absolutely sure."

"Yes."

"Positive."

"Yes."

He turns to the calculator. He takes notes. Then he sighs once more. He looks at me. "You're crazy. You are *crazy!*" He smiles and shakes his head. "Well, you wanted to know fire." From his pants pocket he takes out a pair of dice. "As soon as seven appears, everything will be ready for your departure." He rattles the dice. Five. Again. Ten. Again. Seven. "Chance and order coincide," shouts Mr. Random. "This is it!"

A searing white light. Crash of thunder and a sensation of burning, burning, burning.

Groggy. Blurred vision. Headache. Gradually my vision clears and I realize I have eight legs. I also realize that I am terribly hungry. I rummage around in my mind to see how this life form survives — *Oh, no,* I say to myself, *oh, God, how disgusting!* I cower within myself and am suddenly aware that the mind that I share is incredibly alien to me and it does *not* want me there and, frankly, I don't want to be there. I begin to realize why others were telling me to wait. I begin to realize a lot of things. I sigh. Well, I might as well have some fun. I jiggle the web. I wave in the breeze, but as far as feeding—I put *that* thought aside and something dark in the mind that I share immediately struggles and fights. And then something lands in the web, and that dark force wants to go for it and I say, "No." Part of the intelligence I share is enraged; it is a blind, insect hate and I am horrified at the naked emotion with simple survival behind it. "No," I say again, "I find the process disgusting." The bug gets away. And I sit. If this is the fire of being, I think, it doesn't do much to warm my heart. Movement again. I look. A large bug which looks very much like me creeps down the web. Instantly within this mind, I feel the darkness alert, tense, and to *that* response I say, "No. We're going to be civil about this." I take over absolutely and wave a leg in greeting. "Hello, brother," I think, "I'm X from Pluto."

The other advances closer.

"Earth is a nice place," I think, assuming that somehow the other can hear me, "but the one thing that bothers me is the way we eat—aren't there any other choices..." My thinking trails off. There is *no* intelligence in the other's eyes. Only mindless hate. "Oh, shit," I whisper to myself. I back off and let the darkness within control. But I have not eaten and am weak and the other comes scrambling. "But, we're of the same species," I frantically think, "intelligent creatures—" It is at that point, when the other overpowers me and injects the poison that I remember what Mr. Maybe said: I wouldn't be aware of the fire. And I probably wouldn't have any knowledge of my past consciousness. Something is terribly, terribly wrong here, but I have no idea what might have happened. I can only wait and see. Abruptly I feel the intensity of hate that comes from the darkness of mind that I share. What can I say? "Sorry," I think, "I'm rather new at this. Didn't mean to interfere with your life—you know, cut it short." I can tell that my host isn't happy with me. But as the life fluids are sucked out, so is the primitive awareness. I grow sleepy.

When I awake again, I decide that I'm gonna play it smart, no matter what. I concentrate. I look around. I got fur this time. White fur. And I'm dressed in clothes and I'm in some sort of carriage. I listen. I feel a rumbling within me and discover that the mind I now share makes that noise because it's happy. Suddenly the animal intelligence is aware of me and is intensely curious. It is not frightened. But curious, puzzled, yes. I practice the voices I hear in the mind of the animal: "Meow? Mew?" And while I'm sitting there, supposedly comfortable but actually hot, two little girls come over to me. Ah, I think, gazing at the children, the Divine Humanform. How many forms must I go through before I reach it? *That* is what I want. That is what we *all* want on Pluto—to make it to Humanform, and I am so enraptured that I suddenly realize two things: since I must have made a mistake, I have no guarantee of making it. And secondly, I notice one little girl's hand lifting up my dress as she says, "Look, Susie, pussycat is a girl kitty—see? She doesn't have—"

"Yee-oowwwlll!" I scream; the feeling behind it, outrage; God damn it, don't you feel *me* up. My paw turns into five hooked daggers and I rake the girl across the arm. Blood oozes; she draws back, hurt, afraid, then angry and her open hand lands on my head. "Oh, you *bad* kitty," she says. "You hurt me!"

"Fuck you," is what I want to say, but it comes out "Fffftttt!" and, clothes and all, I leap from the carriage and hide in rose bushes, and growling with my ears back, I begin to wonder just why in hell had I left Pluto? I should have waited until my turn to be *called* rather than having to go through all *this* crap. And why didn't someone tell us that the Divine Humanform had a streak of obvious perversion? And while I'm mulling this over, I am suddenly aware of a white and gray cat coming toward me. The cat mind I share says it is my father—a mean tomcat. *Oh, shit,* I think, *oh shit.* I should have let the little monsters molest me. It might have been easier than what is probably going to happen. For I am aware that one part of me wants to purr and make it with daddy but *I* don't. No. No more of this. I take over and try to run but one paw gets caught in the sleeve of the dress and I stumble and daddy comes sprightly over to give me some help. He tries to pull the dress off with his teeth but then his glands get the best of him and he mounts me, grabbing me by the scruff of my neck and the cat part of me responds with affection, but *I'm* mad and say, "Rorrrr!" I turn, and with my claws, rake daddy's face. The cat draws back and then, then it realizes that while I may *look* like a cat, there is a part of me which is *not.* I realize that I lost it again. And the other presence, that of the cat, is bewildered. Daddy attacks. Teeth on my neck and I feel the fear, the hatred, the agony, coming from this mind that I share. But I have nothing to say. Bones snap. And still in my clothes, I twitch and gargle while daddy stands back, snarling. My vision grows dim, dim, then dark, then nothing.

When I open my eyes again, I am in a chair. Mr. Random is sitting in his chair. Across the table from him sits Mr. Maybe. They are playing Scrabble. "Is 'qwlyx' a word?" asks Mr. Random.

"Perhaps," says Mr. Maybe.

Mr. Random puts the word on the board. Mr. Maybe reaches for the dictionary. "Challenge," he says, and flips through the pages. "Nope. You lose a turn."

Mr. Random shrugs. "Calculated risk." He looks over to me. "Welcome back. Enjoy the intense and wonderful fire of earthly existence? Hum? Enjoy the wonderful and varied forms of being? Hum? Hum? Hum?"

"Uh." I close my eyes.

Mr. Maybe sucks on his snowgar. "We don't usually bring souls back until they've gone through the human phase. But we had to bring *you* back."

"Just as well," I say. I shrug. "Why?"

"You gave the wrong number sequence," says Mr. Random. "The sequence you gave me is for gods. Gods have to be omniscient, you know." He clears his throat. "They also don't interfere with a creature's basic consciousness." He sighs. "It was just random chance that slot 191*dash*694518 — non-awareness of self, and slot 191694518 — continuity of awareness and omniscience were simultaneously open."

Mr. Maybe chomps on his snowgar and stretches. "If you still insist on knowing the fire of being from any point of view, I'm sure we could work out something, although it would be far better to wait."

I lean forward and stare at the white rug with frost patterns so carefully woven in. "I'll wait," I say, "I don't want to go through all that again."

"Well," says Mr. Random, "it wouldn't be the same — you wouldn't have the continuing awareness — "

"No. No. I'll wait." I stand. "Thank you anyway."

Both men shrug and return to their game. "Is 'Xwzk' a word?" asks Mr. Random.

"Try it," says Mr. Maybe.

"Very well." Mr. Random places the word on the board.

"Challenge." Flipping the pages of a dictionary. "Nope."

"Gotta take chances," replies Mr. Random.

I turn and walk out of the office and in a few minutes leave the Administrative Cavern behind. I locate the cables and there is Y, tugging, tugging on his cable.

"Hey," he says. "Good to see you, X."

"Thanks. Good to be back."

"Really?"

"Yeah."

Y blows onto his hands and rubs them. "Have to admit, I was envious of you, going for the fire."

"Don't be," I reply. "Wait. Wait until you're called." And then, rolling up my sleeves, I grab cable and pull.

Insight

I waited for my daughter at the shuttleport. *Would she be as angry now as the day she had left? Probably. Angry, angry, so terribly, terribly angry, like a thunderhead swollen with darkness and promise of fire. Yes, yes, just like a thunderhead, building from a sense of righteous indignation, as though she had been deliberately and malintentionally hurt, slandered, poisoned and vilified and it was always a mystery to me why she was that way. But there — the attendants open the door of the connecting tunnel to the shuttle; the people walk into the waiting area and there she is, my daughter, fresh in from Jupiter's moon, Callisto, and — yes — she's looking like a thunderhead, just as she did when she left. Perhaps it was a bad trip; perhaps she's had trouble with the mining company on Callisto. She sees me. She tries to smile. Oh, how she tries to smile. Hm, I think, her mind must have been poisoned by the methane from Jupiter; perhaps she has spent time on Io and soaked up too much ionized sulphur? Hm. Look how hard she tries to smile.*

I go up to her. "Hello, darling," I say, kissing her on the forehead. She, of course, tenses.

"Hello, Dad, how you been?"

"Fine," I say, "just fine."

"I'll bet. How's your ulcer?"

"Oh, fine, fine; gets better all the time."

"Still killing yourself with alcohol?"

"Oh, no," I say, and laugh, "I've cut down a great deal."

"I'm sure you have." She sighs. "Let's get my baggage."

We walk side by side. *Such an angry lady, my daughter, so angry. I don't understand. Such a pretty lady to be so angry. Her hair is short and black; her eyes are green. Her nose is just like mine, stout, you know, a little pointy perhaps, but a good nose. So slim is her body, so large her — oh — oh — dear, oh, dear, mustn't think such things about my daughter.*

"Please remove your arm from my shoulder," she says.

"Oh," I say. "I thought you might be cold."

"You liar."

"Oh, that really hurts my feelings."

"Feelings?" she laughs. "What feelings?"

"Oh," I say, "let's not start *this* again."

"Why not?" We stop in the middle of the concourse. "Why not?" she asks again and people are looking; they see how angry she is; they notice. *I feel very sorry for her. She has no idea how she looks. And if they got to know her, surely they would realize how angry and how strange she is — imagine, a women miner on a moon of Jupiter! Surely everyone would see that as odd. Everyone would agree that she really needs a nice man to marry and settle down with and have children — yes, yes, have many children so that she would be happy and then I could see my grandchildren. It would be nice to have grandchildren, but my daughter just can't see my logic of it.*

"You spacing out on me, Pops?" she asks.

"No, of course not."

She sighs and looks away. "I wish to God I could at some point in my life get close to you but I don't think that's ever going to happen."

"Whatever are you talking about?" I ask.

"Right now, tell me what you're feeling."

"Why, I told you — I'm feeling fine —"

She shakes her head and rolls her eyes. "Why do I bother?" she says. "Why do I even bother?"

"Whatever is the matter?" I put my arm around her.

"*Please* take your hands *off* me!" she says. "Let's get my baggage."

We get the baggage. For me, it is a comfortable wait; but Meredith looks so uncomfortable; I glance at her. *Thunder and lightning. Such a storm of anger. Such a tornado of rage, a hurricane of deep resentment. She has always been like this — I cannot understand why. She's too pretty and cute to be angry; anger is such an evil thing and for a mere child to be so consumed by it is so tragic.*

"How's Mom been doing?" she asks.

"Oh, splendid. Very well."

She grits her teeth. "You make me want to puke," she says. "Everything is fucking fine, fucking splendid. You insincere son of a bitch."

All that anger. It's so sad. "I'm sorry you feel that way."

She looks at me with a look that I don't understand. "Aren't you the *least* bit offended by what I just said? I called my very own father a son of a bitch—doesn't that upset you? Aren't you angry at me? Don't you feel *anything*?"

"Of course I feel something," I reply. "I feel sorry for you."

She just looks at me. "You're a sociopath," she whispers, her eyes so big, "You're just a God damn sociopath. You can't feel anything. You're so God damn nice; you're so fucking God damn nice. Don't you realize how sick it is to be so nice? Don't you think I pick up on the hostility behind your niceness? Don't you think I feel your lust?"

"Meredith," I say with concern, "there are people watching. Don't you realize how you must look?"

She shakes her head and starts crying. "I don't *give* a rat's ass *who* or *what* people think. Can't you see how *you* appear?"

"Why—" I shake my head in dismay, "I'm terribly concerned about you."

"The *hell* you are, you manipulative, controlling son of a bitch!"

"I'm sorry you feel—"

"*Fuck* your sorriness! I don't trust you!" She sits on her suitcase. I glare at her with sympathy, my fists are clenched in concern.

She tries to control her crying. "And I suppose if I were to ask you what you were feeling right now, you'd say you were sad that I was so unhappy, right?"

I nod. "That's right."

"And I suppose if I said that you were angry that I was causing a scene and making you uncomfortable, I suppose you'd say that you simply don't understand and that maybe I'd better see Dr. Halkerson for another round of therapy."

I nod, amazed that she knew so well what I was thinking. "That's *just* what I was thinking."

"Why is it that *you* never came to see me in the hospital?"

I'm astonished. "Why, I thought the professionals knew all the answers."

"Why were you too busy to come in for family therapy?"

I don't understand this. "Your mother knew my views perfectly well."

"And, when Mom had *her* breakdown. Why didn't you see her?"

I shake my head. "Because there was nothing that I could do."

"You didn't even visit her!"

"Why, of course not. I didn't want to impede her therapy."

"Why isn't Mom here with you?"

I put my arm around Meredith, knowing this is going to be hard.

"*Get* your hands *off* me!"

"I mean only to console you," I reply. "Your mother is back in the hospital."

"Oh, Jesus," she whispers, "Oh, Jesus." She stands and, quite dramatically, turns and puts her hands over her mouth. *It's very dramatic, you realize; people turn and look at her; they feel sorry for her, they want to help her and I suppose they somehow see me as the culprit. I know they do; everyone usually does. But they don't obviously understand how terribly and tragically ill are the women in the family. I am certainly glad that I am not responsible for any of this; after all, you can't control how people will react. That they would become so ill around someone so nice as myself never ceases to amaze me. It must be genetic; my daughters and my wife must have a gene that pre-disposes them to schizophrenia.*

She looks at me, oh, that look of vulnerability, of weakness — *there she goes, trying to manipulate my feelings again.*

"And, my sister, Mary, is — is she all right?"

"I didn't tell you this," I said. "I didn't want to worry you." I sigh. *Bad news is always hard to give.* "She slashed her wrists again — and succeeded. She died three months ago."

"Oh, my God," she says; the color drains from her face. "*Oh, my God!*"

She leaps up and runs to the women's bathroom. *I do hope she'll be all right. All this emotion is hard to bear; it always makes my diabetes worse, elevates my blood pressure and I have to be careful of my asthma.* I wait. Finally, I go over to a magazine section and read the latest *Popular Mechanics*. I'm half-way through an article on Compartmentalization Theory: how units in a system can be plugged into it or unplugged from it — certainly a neat system and very efficient — I feel a tap on my shoulder.

"As soon as you can put down the magazine," says Meredith, "I need to talk to you."

"Very well," I reply.

I finish the article, very much impressed by the idea; it makes things so much easier — to plug units into a system and not to have to worry about messy wires or take apart the whole system. You just plug in and remove defective parts and the total unit works just fine. *I really should plug some money into stocks in the field. That's where the money is. I'll make my mint, unplug my investments and plug them in elsewhere.*

I sit beside my daughter.

She sighs. "While you were reading, I signed up to go out on the next ship to Syrtis Major, Mars. It leaves the station tomorrow, so I have to catch the shuttle to the station in the hour—"

"What?" I'm shocked. "Your mother has been wanting to see you and you really should visit the grave of your sister—"

"Stop it," she says, "I feel guilty enough." She closes her eyes.

"That's a bad decision," I say, gritting my teeth in sadness. "Don't you care?"

"I feel guilt-tripped," she says, "and I think I know what you want. You want me to attack you so that you can sign me into the hospital."

I suck in my breath. "I am shocked. That's not true at all. You know that's just not true."

"I'm going to Mars. It's almost far enough away from you."

"Why, I'm sorry to hear that."

"You won't destroy me like you destroyed my sister and are destroying my mother."

I shake my head in sorrow. "All that time at Bayview didn't help at all, did it?"

She comes up to me. Her teeth are remarkably white and her face wonderfully pale. "I want to hit you *so* much," she says, "but that way you'll get me. You'll not get me with your anger. You'll not use me to punish your mother for killing your father. I won't be used like that."

And a voice comes from somewhere, but I know not where; it sort of sounds like mine, but it can't be because I don't have those feelings in me. But the voice says, "You God damn mother-fucking little bitch!" And then a hand—it sort of looks like mine but it can't be—comes out from nowhere and strikes her. Right in the mouth. The guards come running. *And why they grab me is beyond my understanding.* I keep insisting that *she's* responsible for what happened. But so many people are saying, "sure, sure" and "uh-huh" and someone says they will sign statements. *I don't understand at all. It's my daughter, my daughter that has all the anger. Why, she looks like a thunderhead all puffed up and all and flashing and booming from rage – that's not my problem. In no way am I responsible for that. She needs the treatment and yet – they're going to allow her to go to Mars? Don't they understand they can't let someone like her roam free? They have the wrong person! It's so obvious who has the problem! It's so obvious who is ill! I just don't understand this. And most of all, I don't understand her smile. I just don't understand her smile.*

Insult to Injury

Now, in the town of S, Mr. N. awoke one morning to a very strange fate. His house was gone. He was still under the blankets, the top quilt made by his aunt, showing, ironically, a town with houses and the house in the middle, along the main route, looked very much like his, but in reality, his house was quite gone. He nudged his wife. "Dear," he said, "I think we've been robbed."

"—um—" she murmured, then she opened those great, brown eyes of hers and said, "What *happened*?!" She pulled the covers up. They looked around. But, yes, it was true, their house was definitely—gone.

"Gone," said little Enrique Smith who lived next door and he pointed this way and that. "Gone. Your house is gone."

The day came on like a drunken brat. The police came and Mr. N. and his wife were still in the basement in their bed and in their pajamas beneath the blankets. Some neighbors had brought over some milk, bowls and Rice Krispies®. The police examined the area. "Can you describe the house?"

Mr. N. nodded. "One story, one and a half baths, two bedrooms. It answers to the name of 'Our Place'."

The police officer pushed his hat back and pondered the report he was filling out. "This is going to sound awfully strange," he said. He sighed, looked about. "Oh, well," he said, "at least it's a nice day for something like this to happen. What if it had been raining?"

"True," said Mr. N., "but we would like our house back."

The policeman, rather overweight and for some incomprehensible reason, somewhat put out about all this, said, "Well, we'll just have to look for it—" he looked around. "I guess..."

Via the cellar steps, another officer came into the basement. "No reports of any strange noises, like helicopters or—" and he looked down, obviously embarrassed, "'flying saucers.' Some neighbors were up all night and didn't see anything unusual, but some heard—" and he looked down again, still obviously very embarrassed, "some—uh—well—"

"Well," said the other policeman, striking a pose of 'no nonsense here,' "let's get on with it."

"Well," said the second policeman, "some reported hearing a heavy thudding and stomping at about three a.m., like something big walking..."

"Something big, as in a house walking?" asked the first officer.

The other man hunched his shoulders a bit and shifted his weight. "Uh—um, yes, yes—um—yes."

The first policeman cleared his throat. "Yes," he said, "ah—yes, well, are there any other conclusions to draw here?"

"Big indentations in the ground, heading south-southeast, toward the forest."

"Houseprints?" the first policeman grimaced at the word.

"Maybe a trail."

Out of acute discomfort, the policeman said nothing about what it was they had to do. As they left the basement, neighbors were setting up an umbrella tent in the basement bedroom so that at least Mr. N. and his wife had privacy to get up and get dressed. In a few minutes, they accompanied the two officers.

"We really don't know how this could have happened," said Mrs. N., once they were in the police car. "Goodness knows what would have happened if we were sleeping on the main floor instead of in the basement bedroom. I guess we chose a good time to turn the upper bedroom into a study."

The policeman tried to be as indifferent about this as possible. "What color was the house when you last saw it?"

"Brown with fading yellow trim. Some bricks were gone from the front porch and the roof needed repair."

"Also," said Mrs. N., "we needed a new refrigerator and the toilet was cracked and leaking—"

"Sort of in disrepair," said Mr. N., "but we were getting ready to get a loan to fix it up."

The police officers didn't say anything, but they followed the trail of cracked roadway, an occasional crushed car, a broken fire hydrant fountaining, several toppled trees, broken power lines and a ransacked hardware store.

"Oh, dear," said Mrs. N., "I'm afraid our house did a lot of damage."

Mr. N. looked unhappy. "I wonder if this is covered by insurance."

"I wonder if all the china in the kitchen is broken," said Mrs. N. "Certainly the refrigerator is a mess by now."

For a few minutes, as they all drove the streets in the general direction of the trail, no one said anything. Finally, the trail had to be followed by foot. They quietly walked and before long, found the house nestled in the forest. As they approached, they heard a heavy, booming voice, "Leave me alone! Go home!"

Mr. N. called back, "Uh—but we *are* home—you are our home."

Pause. "Go home to *another* home."

"You're the *only* home we have," said Mr. N.

"Not anymore," boomed the voice.

"Would you mind telling us what we did?" asked Mrs. N.

Pause. "It's what you *didn't* do. Ants in my foundation and you knew about them for the last three years. And my plumbing was bad and rotting my infrastructure. The roof leaked and I was falling apart. It was a matter of self-preservation."

"But—" said Mr. N., spreading his hands, "didn't you hear me the other night? I sat right in the kitchen talking about getting a loan to take care of all of that."

"You said that before."

"Well, this time I meant it."

"You said *that* before, too."

"Won't you give us another try?" asked Mrs. N. "Please?"

"No!" said the house. Somewhere a door slammed.

The police scratched their heads. "We don't know *what* to do. This isn't covered in our procedures. We can deal with abusive situations, and runaway children—" and he puffed out his cheeks and blew out slowly, "but we've never had to deal with an abused house."

"Well," said Mrs. N. wringing her hands, "it wasn't *conscious* abuse."

"Abuse is abuse," rumbled the house. A window slammed.

"But—but—but," said Mr. N. "We *own* you. You're *ours*."

"Not anymore."

"Look," said the first police officer, "what are you going to do here? Without care, you're simply going to fall apart that much faster."

"Not as fast as I would with *their* help—or non-help as the case may be."

Mrs. N. pleaded. "Oh, won't you reconsider? Don't you have any good memories? Didn't we treat you better than the last occupants?"

A long pause. "No."

The four of them sat on a log and considered what to do. And after a while, they came to the conclusion that they didn't know *what* to do. "We certainly can't force it back," said the first officer. "It might splinter. Almost your best bet would be to try to bring new materials here as a good will measure."

Mr. N. stood up, cupped his hands to his mouth and yelled, "How about that? How about if we bring all the materials here and repair you now as an act of good faith?"

A long, long pause. "No. Because if you leave, I'll have to go through this all over again. No." Another window slammed shut.

Mrs. N. called, "Can we come in and at least get some personal items? Clothes? Jewelry?"

After a minute, the front door opened and the house virtually vomited clothing, articles, razors, soap, shoes, jewelry. Mr. and Mrs. N. were buried, and *wham* the door slammed shut.

For the next few minutes, they gathered up their personal belongings and stood looking at the house.

"What about our cat, Fluffy? Have you seen her?" called Mrs. N.

"She stays with me. At least she appreciated my warm rooms and wide windowsills. Now, beat it!" yelled the house. A frying pan sailed through the air. The police and Mr. and Mrs. N. jumped back toward the police car.

"Well," said Mr. N., "maybe what we can do is put a roof over the basement. We'll have to do that; I don't know what else to do."

The police officers looked to each other. "We don't either. We're going to have to have a new category for investigation: 'Abandonment of Owners by House.' And how we investigate this is going to be interesting indeed. What if the house wants to sue?"

From the forest, the house yelled, "I'm considering it!"

Mrs. N. said, "I didn't know it had such good hearing."

"Now you know!" yelled the house. A coffee pot came flying through the air; *chink*, it landed nearby.

"Well," said the officer, taking his hat off and wearily massaging his forehead, "the one saving aspect of all of this is—thank God this doesn't happen—"

At that point, they all heard a great commotion. Turning, they saw the county court house striding down the street, followed by a frantic, yelling crowd of judges and lawyers.

Mr. and Mrs. N. and the police stepped aside to let it all go by. The police sighed. Mr. and Mrs. N. looked at their hands. After a few minutes, they resumed walking, saying not a word.

When they finally got back to the cellar of Mr. and Mrs. N. the police drove off and Mr. and Mrs. N. looked at the cellar with the tent. The neighbors had set up a table and a portable gas stove. After a dinner of stew, Mr. and Mrs. N. soon retired to bed. And as Mr. N. began to finally doze and drift off to sleep, *Thud, thud, thud, thud, thud.* He and his wife sat bolt upright. "What is *that?*" asked Mrs. N., terrified. The ground shook around them. They pulled aside the flap of the tent, to see their house standing nearby in the twilight. Fluffy came sailing through the air and landed on a nearby pile of clothes.

Skree! it screeched and dashed to hide beneath a nearby dresser.

"You can have your damn cat back," boomed the house. "Just *like* you to forget to put kitty litter out for her. Shit all over the closet floor! What a mess!"

And with that, *thud, thud, thud, thud,* the house stomped off into the night.

Jessica's Place

Now, Miss Jessica Wingate, at sixty or so, with curling white hair and lively green eyes and a body that seemed to not show age at all, ran a little store called, Jessica's Place. And oh, such a place was Jessica's Place; you could get someone or yourself the most perfect gift, for Jessica had the knack of a being a giftmatcher supreme. Where she obtained all the gifts, well, sometimes she confessed that even she wasn't too sure; after all, at her age, you can't account for every second, and everything that does come your way and sometimes people came in having to sell the most perfect thing that someone else most surely could use.

Now, her shop couldn't be said to be the neatest of worlds, what with bookcases all sagging with trinkets and treasures, vases and bowls and small figurines that occasionally got up, muttered a bit and, dusting themselves off, sat down again. Oh, yes, a *most* unusual place was Jessica's Place. And Jessica herself was a bit of a wonder—ah, how she hurried about, unpacking a box here and saying, perhaps, to herself, "Oh, but this is nice! Just bet Mary Hawthorne could use this for her rambunctious son!" (Now it has to be mentioned what was rambunctious about Mary Hawthorne's young son, all of, perhaps eight, who, of late, had developed a habit of Cookie Jar-itis, and it need not be said what *that's* all about.) And Mary Hawthorne liked to have cookies on hand for guests who dropped in, but whenever she looked, alas, the jar had been emptied, *again*, and it was just on that day when Jessica had opened the box that Mary Hawthorne walked in and, shaking her head, said, "What can I do? I simply can't win—"

And Jessica smiled a bright, clever smile and gave Mary a tube of Cookie Surprise®, the label of which said, (and Jessica read), "Especially designed for eight-year-olds of the Hawthorne Clan. Just squeeze this invisible fluid on outside of jar after you've placed wonderful cookies within."

Mary Hawthorne, a bit puzzled and eager and curious and wary, finally settled on the feeling of most profound, puzzled hope. "Well, exactly what does it do?" She turned the tube over and over again.

"Well," said Jessica, folding her hands in front of herself in a sign of definite assurance, "I'm not real sure; I've not sold this before. But," and she pointed expertly to a seal on the tube, "it is guaranteed by Good Spellkeeping. Satisfaction or double your magic back."

Mary Hawthorne looked more reassured. "Well," she nodded, "that *is* a good sign. I could always use magic here and there."

"Give it a try," Jessica said, "and don't pay me until you're absolutely and totally pleased."

"Why, thank you, Ms. Wingate."

"Oh!" and Jessica made a sharp snapping move with her fingers, like the stroke of a wing, "It's Jessica! *Jessica!* Now how many times need I remind you? Jessica, please!"

"Oh," said Mary Hawthorne, "I'm sorry. Well, anyway, Jessica, thank you so much. I'll have a chance to try it today."

"Do let me know?"

"Oh, I shall, I shall. Believe me, I shall."

And she left. The next day she returned with a box full of cookies and a crisp ten dollar bill. Grinning and smiling, she said, "Oh, my goodness! Why, it worked like a charm! Poor little Alex; he was thoroughly alarmed when he reached for a cookie and suddenly there were ten. He took another and then there were twenty. He took another and then there were forty and he took another and then there were eighty and all different types: oatmeal, and peanut butter, vanilla and animal crackers, some with cream fillings and some with orange sprinkles and they overflowed the cookie jar and onto the floor and he absolutely could not take any more. He tried to eat all that he had and then he got sick—" She laughed and laughed.

And Jessica, sampling a vanilla wafer, said, "That did the trick, but the ten dollars *is* a bit much."

"No," said Mary Hawthorne, "please, it's so worth it to me."

"Well," said Jessica, pondering this and sampling that, "why thank you. I am so pleased it worked."

And, smiling, Mary Hawthorne left Jessica's Place while Jessica sampled a chocolate chip cookie.

Such were some of the gifts at Jessica's Place. It was as though, as soon as a customer walked through the door, Jessica could look and think to herself, *Ah, I know just what he needs.*

So it was when a small, dismal-looking man walked into the shop. He was short and stooped with heavy black eyebrows and lips turned down in an expression of gloom. He wore a dark raincoat, though it was sunny outside, and a dark hat with a brim that seemed incredibly wide, as if this gentleman had somehow been trapped by another time and was unable to draw some sort of metaphysical line between here and then. This man shuffled into the shop, looked about, then walked up and plopped his hands on the counter. He sighed. "I don't like what I need," he said, "but I guess for now I'm this way and I think you got what I need."

Jessica nodded her head. "I suppose I do," and she *tsked* and she *tsked* and brought out a plastic bag filled with darkness. "You sure?" she asked.

Glumly, the little man nodded. "When things get better, can I trade it in?"

Jessica nodded and popped the bag with a pin and the darkness rushed out, gathered itself over the little man's head and in seconds he was drenched in a very wet storm. Little lightning bolts flashed and there were the miniature sounds of thunder, while a little rain blew in his face. The man sighed, "That's fine. That's what I want just for now. How much?"

Jessica shook her head. "No, no, I'll let that be free. I just can't see charging you for that damp little tempest of pure misery."

He nodded. "Thank you," he said, and he shuffled out, while above him the lightning flashed and the miniature thunder boomed and crashed. Jessica thought, *At least he knows what he needs right now. But a smile and a hug would most likely help more. After all, that's what they're for, to help us learn to love, or at least be more comfortable with our inner selves.*

Then in walked a stranger in a bit of a fix, or so it might, at first, appear. To anyone else, the sight of the stranger would cause a great deal of fear, for the man had no face. Everything else was really quite right and the clothes showed excellent taste, but without a face, such a stranger is stranger indeed and what was more disconcerting to one (if naïve), was that the man carried a plant of silver trunk and metallic blue leaves. The plant seemed to bear some sort of translucent fruit. The gentleman placed the plant on the counter, and faced (if you will) Jessica.

Now Jessica looked at him and, very calm and serene, said, "Well now, bless me, looks like what stands here is mysterious indeed. You'd like a face? You've come to sell me a plant? You've come to barter? To trade? Have you lost face? Have you come to retrace your way?"

The man pointed to a fruit on the small bush; the opacity faded and an image became clear. Jessica leaned over and saw what appeared to be a dark-haired young girl riding a pony through pastures and Jessica sighed, "Ah, yes, my pony Buttercup. How old was I? Perhaps five? My, oh, my, such a time ago *that* was. Oh, dear, dear, I'd almost forgotten—"

The scene dissolved. The stranger pointed to yet another fruit and when it had cleared, Jessica saw herself, perhaps twenty-five, walking those lovely beaches in Spain with her husband-friend-lover, John Spencer, tall and tanned with a smile that turned any place into somewhere unique. He turned house into palace, hill into mountain, pond into ocean; ah, such a person, such a person, John Spencer.

And again the fruit turned into round mist and Jessica nodded and gently whispered, "Ah, yes, John Spencer; how my world broke when he died. Oh, how I cried." Then Jessica looked up at the man without a face. "How do you know these secrets of mine? Oh, stranger, stranger, who is becoming stranger than dreams, what is it you want? Usually anyone who walks in here, I can always read: their hopes, their problems, their terrible misdeeds, but this—" she waved at the strange plant, "just where does *this* lead?" She gazed back at the strange plant. "Oh, but what I've so far seen is poignant indeed, so much so that I've forgotten—"

The man gently pushed the plant toward her; his intent was very clear.

"For me?" asked Jessica. "Why—" she stammered, "oh, dear, such a gift, such a switch this is. Do you want me to pay you? Something like this will command a very high price."

The man touched yet another small fruit and it slowly cleared and there appeared a face.

"John," whispered Jessica. "John Spencer—" and then her voice failed and her skin, Lord knows how, her white skin paled and she grabbed the edge of the counter and stared at the fruit.

Though the image was small, the voice was not, "Ah, Jessica, Jessica, this gift is for you. When I died I did not have the chance to ever say how much I loved you and treasured our friendship. Ah, I would have come sooner, but, oh, the Universe is *such* a big place. It's taken this long to finally track down where our paths parted and where you went from there, and I had to find you again. I could not rest until I found you again and gave you this, for this says it best: for being my friend and sharing my life. Ah, Jessica, Jessica, yes, we were blest—the memories I have, yes, they are the best."

"Oh, John," whispered Jessica, standing as if held up simply by her clothes, "such a gift, oh, such a wonderful gift. How can I thank you—"

"You already have—in so many ways."

And then Jessica, breathing in deeply, said in a low but strong voice, "I am going to ask of you something. Perhaps I am wrong, and if that is the case—"

There came gentle laughter. "Ah, the strength, the willingness to see that which others would see as incomprehensible. Ah wonderful, so brave, even now. Very well. I grant you your wish."

And then, when Jessica looked to the well-dressed man, gazing at his face she saw—"Planets," she whispered, "comets and galaxies and stars and moons—"

The voice of John, "This is now my face. I embody now the raw stuff of space."

"Oh, John, John," sighed Jessica sadly, "how I've missed you, and longed to be with you—"

A gentle laugh. "Ah, Jessica, that will happen; it will happen all soon enough. Enjoy the magician you've turned out to be; enjoy the memory of magic between you and me. There is so much more I'd love to say, but now—" and he sighed, "and now, I must go." And again a sigh. "But now I can rest. I'm so glad I found you and now I must go."

"John, thank you—oh, John—" was all she could say as she sadly watched John, with the Universe for his face, slowly walk out of her shop, Jessica's Place.

Metamorphosis Blues

You're standing in line, waiting for your coffee at the espresso stand. You notice that it's a wonderful day; the sky is blue, you're comfortable in your jeans and tee-shirt, with the picture of Kafka on the front and a caption beneath that reads, "I Love Cockroaches."

When you get to the counter, you notice that the person behind the counter who is making the drinks sure looks a lot like Kafka.

He looks at you. "What'll it be?" he asks, "Latte? Americano? Cockroaches over ice?"

You gulp.

For whatever reason, you look down at your shirt; the image of Kafka is looking at you; the lips move: "Double-shot with hazelnut," he says.

Looking back up, you watch as the counterperson slowly changes into a cockroach.

This does not look good.

"You are my abusive father," says the counter-person-turning-cockroach. "I've always been afraid of you. I've written a 47 page letter to you which I will mail to you tomorrow which will tell you why I'm so frightened of you."

"Whoa," you say, "I ain't your daddy."

"Hurry up with the damn drink," says the image of Kafka on your shirt, clearly impatient. "I need a jolt of Java before I go buggy," he smiles, "pun intended," he adds.

You look around. The sunlight is fading fast; dark clouds have rolled in and the sun shines in a way that cloud edges glow like molten pewter. You don't have a clue how this happens, and when you look at the counter of the espresso stand, there is a cockroach on it, on its back, legs flailing. It's still wearing a minute, blue apron and you can make out tiny, white lettering that reads "Kafkabucks Coffee."

"I still want my drink," says the image of Kafka on your tee-shirt.

You go behind the stand, and without really knowing how, you make yourself a drink and you listen to the image of Kafka on your shirt: "Anything is possible," he says, "we're all mad in some way—nonetheless, we still create the Universe in the image of our subconscious and how we see it largely determines what we think the world is about."

You gulp. "Wasn't it Jung who said that the unconscious, when it is not recognized, appears to us as fate?"

"*Drink*, please?" says the image on your shirt.

You start to drink through the straw.

"That's *my* drink," says Kafka-on-your-shirt. "Make your own damn drink."

You don't know what to do with this.

"*Put the fucking straw in my mouth, stupid!*"

"Oh, yes—" you say, and doing so, you hear Kafka suck noisily at the drink.

Numbly, you make a drink for yourself with one hand, while, with the other, you hold a drink up to Kafka's mouth. You never dreamed that this could be so awkward but you manage to do it.

"Not bad," says Kafka.

You look at the counter with the cockroach struggling on its back and you remember how miserable the cockroach was. You could kill it— *would that be doing Kafka a favor?* you wonder.

"I know what you're thinking," says Kafka, "don't you *dare*."

You feel your tee-shirt suddenly tighten and it feels like your upper body is clenched in a fist, as if the tee-shirt has suddenly shrunk six sizes. You feel the air *whoosh* out of your lungs. You notice it's gotten even darker; a cold wind blows, no lights come on anywhere, and then you say, in a high-pitched voice, "I wasn't going to do it—think of all that wouldn't have been written—" You want to say more, but you've just run out of what little air you had left.

The shirt relaxes. "Damn right," says Kafka. At that point, you seize the opportunity and tear the tee-shirt off only to discover—Kafka is emblazoned on your chest. You stare, stunned.

"Good try," says Kafka. The lips form a sneer. "We're all Kafka, hence his lasting appeal—the unconscious is alive and well and all the Prozac, coffee and coke will never kill it—kill it, *never*."

You look to the cockroach on its back, and feel a sudden burst of compassion—before you run flailing, stumbling, into that dark night.

Movies

Alex, his parents and sister sit in the back of a dark theatre in the lounge chairs. They are fighting again. Alex glances to the screen and the screen hasn't changed. It is dark blue with familiar constellations on the screen: Cassiopeia, the Big Dipper, the Southern Cross. Alex wonders if this is going to be a foreign film. He glances to his father — a tall man, big-boned, big-jowled and his grey hair is in a crew cut. His nose is off-side a bit, broken from a scuffle while waiting in line for an earlier movie. He's gesturing to Alex's mother, a stout lady whose jaw line is firm as granite. Her black hair is curly and cut close and she doesn't say anything.

"I toldya, ya shoulda bought the tickets first," he says. "We almost didn't make it to this show because of that dumb mistake."

"We got in, didn't we?" says Alex's mother finally. "So what's your problem?"

"Yeah," Alex says. He's sitting between his mother and father. "Yeah, what's the big deal here?"

"Lissen," his father says, leaning real close to Alex, "you keep outa this."

Missa, Alex's sister, sits on the right of Alex's mother. She looks like her mother, that firm face, those eyes staring ahead, watching the movie screen and the tranquility of it and the never-changing constellations.

Down in the front, a family has started to sing but they abruptly go off-key and laugh. In another part of the theatre, someone is crying, then sobbing hysterically. But Alex pays little attention to that. "You're always picking on Mom," he says. "Why don't you leave her alone?"

"Listen, buster, you keep outa this. This is between me and my wife, your mother; you got that, twerp?"

Just then, Alex's grandfather turns around. "You don't call Alex a twerp. You've been petty all your life. Why don't you just shut up and watch the screen?"

Alex's father explodes. "What is this? Pick on Daddy day? She made a mistake and how can I watch the screen when I'm upset? You want I should sit on my anger like on a turd all evening?"

Missa laughs and Alex's mother turns, seething. "I'll not have you use that language in public at this theatre."

"Oh, Jee-zuz Christ you dumb bitch—"

Someone in the back row throws popcorn on Alex's father. "Sexist pig!" someone whispers.

"Hey, looky there," says someone down front. "Boy, ain't that a scene?"

Alex looks around but can't tell what the person is referring to. The screen remains blank except for the constellations.

"God damn it, who threw that popcorn?" Alex's father turns around in his seat and glares into the darkness.

Someone else whispers in the back, "Turn around, bozo, and quit being such an asshole."

Alex's father stands, turns around again, and, yanking up a frail old woman with round glasses and black veil by the arm, he then stares. "Oh," he says, "sorry Sister."

"Jesus be good to you," she says. "Young man," she continues, "you must learn to control that temper."

"Fuck you, Sister."

Alex shoves his father down in the seat. "Jesus Christ, Dad, are you nuts?"

Down front, there is hysterical laughter, which changes to a sob.

"Don't you God damn shove me, you little asshole," and Alex's father shoves back.

"Oh," says the mother, "can't we just watch the show? It's always like this. All this fighting. Can't we stop the fighting?"

"Hey," says Alex's father, "I grew up in the front row. I fought all my life. I fought for the seats, the place in the ticket line. You gotta fight to survive; gotta be tough. This movie house here don't do nobody favors, got it? No favors, no way." He folds his arms across his chest in the darkness, obviously self-righteous. Finally he says, "Oh, hell, who wants popcorn?"

But everyone is angry at him and nobody says anything. "Oh, hell," he says again, "the silent treatment. I'm supposed to feel shitty now, huh?"

He gets up and goes for the popcorn. In the rest of the theatre, another argument breaks out, this time, between kids. It turns into a fight and The Management comes flapping down the aisles whispering urgently, "Shush, we can't have this fighting. You can argue all you want, but you can't fight like this. Not in this theatre, and since this is the only theatre there is, we can't have fights."

"Bullshit!" someone yells. "People fight all the time here. Always have. Always will. You know it. Take your flashlight and stick it up your ass."

Alex's dad returns with a big bowl of popcorn. For himself. "Greedy son of a bitch," says Alex. "God, you're greedy."

"Bullshit, you long haired frog. I asked you if you wanted popcorn. You didn't say anything. What's your problem?"

The mother shakes her head. "You two are always fighting. Can't you stop fighting?"

"Sure," says Alex, "when Dad grows up and stops being such a God damn buttfucker."

The father laughs. "Boy. That's a joke; I mean, who's the one who has to grow up around here? Hey, punk," and then the father leans over, "want popcorn? Here." The father takes a handful and dumps it on Alex's head.

"God damn it!" screams Alex, and he yanks the popcorn away from his father and sends it flying, spilling out over the audience.

"God damn it!" someone yells.

"Whoopee!" yells someone else.

Somewhere else, someone has taken up the guitar and plays a lovely Spanish ballad. The father turns to Alex and grabs him by the collar. "Listen sonny boy, you're gettin' too big for your britches. I don't care if you *are* just fourteen, and I don't give a fuck what the laws are here, but you've just pushed a little too far and —"

There is applause. The main show has begun. And both Alex and his father turn to watch — turn to see a ghostly blue hand come drifting out from the screen, over the audience to Alex. The hand engulfs Alex, then crushes him; his eyeballs pop out of his skull and arc high out over the audience. The hand turns a deep red and pulls back into the screen while Alex's father screams, "Oh, no, oh, no, one less person to fight with! Oh, no!" And the rest of the audience cheers wildly and enthusiastically. A couple dances in the aisle.

"Great show," someone yells.

"Four stars!" yells someone else. And the applause is deafening.

Mr. Wetzel and His Wurlitzer

He had been driving slowly a long, long time. Alone, he drove a 1953 Chevrolet truck, painted pale blue. In the open bed of the truck was a Mighty Wurlitzer jukebox.

Before the event, when he had breath, he was thin, lean and inclined to smoke a pipe. His white hair was sparse, his skin tan, and he'd liked wearing a jean jacket and jean overalls. Now he drove his Chevrolet across the featureless plain, beneath the dark and starless sky, driving forever to the pale horizon.

"Get there someday," he frequently said as he drove. "Don't know what's there, but I'm gonna get there someday. Who knows when?"

He drove in a daze for long periods of time. He never looked at the dashboard because the gauges did not work and he never ran out of gas.

Finally, he stopped. "This is a good place," he mused. Automatically, the truck stopped, and the engine turned off as Mr. Wetzel got out of the truck. He slammed the door, climbed into the bed of the truck and sat in a rocking chair. The Mighty Wurlitzer jukebox lit up and on came *Sentimental Journey.*

He liked the song; he liked all the songs—they were songs that he knew well and as he sat and listened to *Sentimental Journey...*

...little Johnny Jenkins from down the street came running into the store. "Mr. Wetzel! Mr. Wetzel! Can you fix my bike, Mr. Wetzel? Please?"

"Sure can," said Mr. Wetzel, and he came out from behind the counter of Wetzel's Grocery.

In the humid afternoon, in the hot Florida sun, Mr. Wetzel fixed Johnny Jenkins' tire.

Johnny was eager to help; for a six year old, he was pretty strong. Deftly, he used a wrench to undo the nut on the front wheel. Once the wheel was off, Mr. Wetzel removed the tire and patched the inner tube.

In the background, his jukebox played *Sentimental Journey*.

After the tire was fixed, Johnny came in, went to the cooler, got a bottle of orange pop and plopped down ten cents for it. It was actually fifteen cents, but Mr. Wetzel said, "Perfect; right on the money."

And Johnny left, slamming the screen door with the diagonal "Hires Root Beer" sign across the bottom of it. He yelled back, "Thanks, Mr. Wetzel!" and he waved.

"Okay, Johnny!" yelled Mr. Wetzel and he began to write out his order.

Next, Bud Williamson came in. He wore a straw hat that he kept pushed back. He was very Florida brown and wore his light blue shirt open and the long sleeves rolled up. Mr. Wetzel always wondered why, in this hot place, didn't he wear something cooler? Why the shirt? The heavy work jeans?

Bud's hair was black, his eyes pale blue and he chewed gum.

"Hi, Gus," he said, "how goes?"

"Pretty good, Bud," said Mr. Wetzel.

Bud went over to another cooler and got out a six pack of Hamms. He sauntered over to the counter and easily reached back and pulled out a wallet. "Another hot one," he said.

"Yup," said Mr. Wetzel. "Sure feels like it." He rang up the beer. "Ninety cents."

"Good 'nuff," said Bud. He opened the coin compartment of the black wallet, counted out the change and let it slowly flow from his palm to Gus's.

"Ah," said Mr. Wetzel, looking at a new, 1955 dime, "first new dime I've seen this year."

"Hm," said Bud. "If I don't get some work, it may be the *last* dime you'll see from me for a while."

"If I hear of anything, I'll let you know," said Mr. Wetzel.

"Thanks. 'Preciate that." And swinging the beer like a slow pendulum, Bud sauntered out the door.

Sentimental Journey played all day long; Gus Wetzel dusted, arranged, put away stock.

Mary Jean Saxton, sixteen-year-old daughter of the sheriff of the small town of Whittonville, wandered in, wearing a dark red bathing suit. "Hi, Gus," she said; her dark hair was stringy from swimming and she had a dark blue beach towel draped around her brown shoulders. Her feet went *slap-slap-slap* against the green and white tile floor.

"Hello, Mary Jean. How you doing?"

"Pretty good." She went to the cooler and yanked back the top to peer into the depths of bottle and ice. "You got any Honey Dew?"

"Sure. Should be some in there."

"Oh, there it is." She pulled the bottle to the side and down the rails.

"Been swimming, eh?" said Mr. Wetzel.

"Yeah," and Mary Jean's smile was wonderful. "Great day for it."

She counted out fifteen cents from a small, plastic purse (even now he knew the details of it: the gold trim along the opening where two nub-bins of metal, like stubby fingers, cross when the purse is closed. He remembered the yellow flowers on the outside of the purse; how bright they were against the white background!). After she put the money on the counter, *snap*; she closed the purse.

"How's your dad?" asked Mr. Wetzel.

"He's better," she said. "Can you believe it?" She went over to the cooler and snapped off the lid. "Someone backs over his foot! Can you believe it?"

Mr. Wetzel shook his head. "Can't say that I do."

She pulled long on the Honey Dew. "Wow! That's good." She then turned around and waved. "You take care."

"Thank you," said Mr. Wetzel. "You, too." He watched her leave, watched the shoulders, the tanned and strong legs and loved the red bathing suit.

Later on, he sat outside on the porch and watched the fireflies flicker on, flicker off. He sat out there, drank a beer and sighed contentedly. There came the screams of the Watson kids next door, there was the smell of fried chicken. Rex, the old German shepherd loped along the sidewalk, favoring his left rear leg.

Across the street, Mr. and Mrs. Hawthorne walked slowly; a retired couple, they stayed rather distant from others, but superficially, they were friendly enough.

And Mr. Wetzel drank his beer and in the background, the tune of the day, *Sentimental Journey*, played and played, never stopping, just going on and on.

About ten o'clock, Mr. Wetzel went inside the store, shut out the lights and just stared at the Mighty Wurlitzer jukebox. He stared at it, listened to it, became captured by it, carried by it and exactly at midnight—it stopped. The lights went out and...

Mr. Wetzel opened his eyes. He sighed, and patted the jukebox affectionately. "Mighty nice," he said, "mighty, mighty nice. It's nice to go back and visit." Then, getting up, he climbed out of the back of the truck, opened the front door; the truck started up immediately and he drove his Chevrolet across the featureless plain, beneath the dark and starless sky, driving forever to the pale horizon.

Of Love, Beasts, and Burning Webs

Lara runs. It is night on the planet Knull. Lara runs through the darkness; she runs blindly, flailing, falling, stumbling. She falls against a tree trunk, slippery with frost; the cold bites her stomach, numbs her breasts. She gasps. She wraps the cloak around her again and listens. Silence. She looks to the stars — cold, impersonal as the frost. The gaunt winter fingers of trees clutch the sky.

One of the moons of Knull lifts over far and sharp peaks. The tops of trees become color of bone, of calcium. Lara scoots to the dark side of the tree. In the shadows, she feels safer. She tries to breathe quietly, to still her pounding heart.

She peers through the forest but cannot see the Spires of Knull. She wonders — perhaps her mother, the Queen, has not discovered her missing. Yet.

She draws her knees up to her breasts and huddles in the cloak. How will she survive out here? She had no food. And to be out on Knull at any time was dangerous. *And yet*, she thinks, *I cannot stay with my mother at the Spires of Knull. What choice do I have? What choice is there? I have to leave — I cannot — I cannot* — and Lara shakes her head in confusion and misery. She places her forehead on her arms and shivers, shakes in despair.

The moon rises higher.

Suddenly Lara leans forward as she feels the empathetic rage of her mother at her leaving. Lara holds her stomach. She knows what her mother is saying; she knows her mother now so well: "Lara, my darling," oh, the anger, the cunning behind the sweetness, "Lara, my own, to leave me is to abandon me to your father. Do you not remember his injustices against me? How many times have I told you of that viciousness of his: that he would cast me away to Darkplain if I broke off relations with my father who seduced me when I was but a child? Lara, my darling, my

213

sweet, my angel, come back, come back and help me fight your father, who insisted, for the sake of inheritance, that I be nice to my father though I loathed the air he expelled, though I sought to spit upon the ground he trod."

Lara crumbles from fear, from intimidation and from guilt at leaving her mother with her father. Part of Lara wishes to return, part of her rebels at the thought and says, "No! No! I cannot. I *will* not!"

Lara feels the hate and anger of her mother flow from the Spires. She hears the message drifting down through the night: "Come back, little daughter, come back, come back, we have a battle to fight. *You* must become the Queen of the Spires. *We* must have your brother rebel against your father; if you leave, your brother will take control—I—*we* cannot have that. We will not allow that, will we, my daughter, my daughter, my most precious and prized possession?"

Pain! Lara yanks her head back, her mouth opens and she sobs; the fingers of hate, of absorption, of the fusion of the will of purpose of mother and daughter—the fingers flow, like darkmist, flow—a bleak river through the calcium white forest, over the ground, coming, slowly and as purposefully as a strange and tenuous serpent toward helpless prey.

"NO!" screams Lara. "No! You cannot! You will *not* use me so!"

She springs to her feet. "All my life you have sought to make me into your image; you have sought to infuse me with your values, your purpose, your will. No more!"

"Ah, daughter, daughter," comes the whisper through the forest, "how you hurt me with your wicked little tongue. How nasty you are to hurt your mother so. To hurt, to abandon the one who bore you, suckled you, wiped the shit from between your legs and told you of the awful blood, the cross of womanhood—you ungrateful daughter—come back and give a poor mother the love that she has given you."

Lara covers her ears and screams and runs. She stumbles in her blindness and her confusion of her guilt yet her profound conviction of what she must do. And the hate and clutch mist of the Queen rises and looks about the tortured, rough land as might a serpent, then it drops to the ground and moves on. Lara picks herself up from a fall and runs, runs from being swallowed, engulfed; runs from the guilt of abandonment to the guilt of her wanting her life as her own, running into the uncertainty, the darkness, the cold. She again stops, this time on top of a hill. She looks back, but the Spires of Knull are lost in the distance. She looks up. The moon is high. A second moon rises.

The hatemist, the clutch fog condenses into a darkform of yellow eyes, white teeth and claws that go *click* on the stones.

The Queen's anger feeds the Darkform and the Darkform snarls with intent and knowledge.

Click-click, click-click. The Darkform follows Lara.

"Bring her," says the Queen. "Bring her back to me, my creature."

Click-click, click-click.

Again, Lara stops. She gulps air, wraps her robe tightly about her, hides between sharp, cold boulders left by a lobe of ice from the mountains an unthinkable time span ago. She closes her eyes. A dream? Hallucination?

She sees Darta, her brother; she sees herself, standing in her room. Her brother is tall, with dark hair down to his shoulders. His dark eyes are so wide that the iris seems lost and he shakes his head in horror. "What you tell me," he whispers, "what you tell me cannot be so!"

She sees herself sobbing, then on her bed and hitting it, pounding it again and again. "Yes!" she sobs, "yes, yes, it is so. I was with Motoros, a high-ranking young man in the defense of the Spire—"

"Yes," says Darta, "I know him so well. A wonderful person though temperamental, it's true. But nonetheless, a responsible—"

"Oh, Darta—we were on the main spire overlooking the Darkland when my mother appeared, took me by the arm and said to Motoros, 'She is much too busy today to be company. Perhaps some other time you may visit.' And then she said to me, 'You are *not* to see him again. You are to see *no one* unless you speak of it to me!' And I said to her, 'But, I like Motoros—' and she said, 'But, *I* do not! He is too strong willed and independent—just like your father—' Oh, Darta, it was then that I understood everything, everything and now I know that I must leave."

Darta swallows. "Leave? Leave? Leave the Spires of Knull? But where will you go? There are no safe places in Darkland to hide!"

Lara sobs again. "But what is there for me *here?* I have no say in my own future, in my own being, my fate!"

Darta shakes his head again. "But, if you leave—what will you find? Surely you will die—stay here, stay here; when you have the power, you will be able to decide the right fate for you."

Lara leaps to her feet. "No! Another instant in this evil place is a lifetime for me. I leave *now*!"

And, wrapping a cloak about her, she hops over the low ledge of a window and out into the night.

Hiding amidst boulders, she remembers the scene and shivers again. She wants to know—but cannot know what happened after she fled: that Darta ran from the room to find his father, King of the Spires, in counsel with the Defense.

"Father!" said Darta, "I must speak with you *now*!"

The father, looking alarmed, said a few words to his Counsel and stepped away. "What is it, my son?"

"Lara—Lara—she has left! Run away to the Darkplain!"

The King looked long at his son. His eyes were grey-green, intense, piercing. He then looked beyond Darta. He folded his hands behind him; his robes, dark green—pulled back to fully reveal the soft yellow of the delicate clothes; the bright red sash of royalty about his ample waist.

The lines in his face seemed to deepen; almost absently he began to stroke his beard; he walked to a window that had a view of the night of Darkplain. Still stroking his beard he said, "And so. Somewhere out there, Lara moves." He sighed. "Your mother drove her away as surely as she drove me away."

Darta ran up to his father. "Father! Do you not realize? My sister—*your daughter*—Lara! *Lara* is out there on Darkplain. We can still rescue her, bring her back!"

"No," the King turned and stared at his son, "no, we cannot. I wish Lara well, but no, no, she cannot be saved."

Darta was aghast. "Father! My sister—your daughter! Does that mean nothing?"

"I'll tell you exactly what that means! Your mother has lost. You are now inheritor of the Spires of Knull."

"No," says Darta, "that is too high a price to pay."

"*Darta!*" says the King, his voice, oh, yes, honed, honed by an anger so keen and patience so thin, "This kingdom is best when run by a male. Know you this, my son, about women, especially women who aspire for power: that their love and affection are mere ways of getting that which they wish. There is payment for pleasures of bed, my son. By giving or withholding of pleasures, they claw at men's souls be they peasant or king. Your mother has not slept with me for so long a time that I begin to wonder if we were ever bedded together at all. Already your mother has probably poisoned her daughter's mind—your sister—telling her lies about males."

Darta backs away. "And *you* say that my mother has filled my sister's head with mistruths about men. If you and my mother are so miserable together, what, then, dear father, is *your* part in such a miserable bond?"

"Enough!" says the King. "You accuse me of lying?"

"I accuse you of dishonesty to yourself." Darta stands defiant.

The King glares. "Do *not* disagree with me!"

"And why shall I *not* disagree with you? Is your knowledge of the world so perfect that it cannot be challenged?"

"Enough!" And the King steps close to his son; the counselors have stopped talking and turn to watch with eyes opened wide.

"We—my son—*we, you* and *I*—have won this battle against two women. Together, you and I, we shall dominate the Spires of Knull."

Darta stands. "What if I choose not to rule?"

"You will!"

"I will not!"

The father stares. Abruptly he turns. "Guards! Solitary! Perhaps, dear son, confinement will weaken your foolish resolve."

The guards, surprised, hesitate just a moment too long and in that moment Darta suddenly sees enough of what he needs to see to make his decision. He turns, runs from the chamber.

"Seize him!" the King yells; the guards come running, but not fast enough. An open window. Darta leaps, stumbles, falls upon landing, but then, quickly now, to his feet, and running again, over another ledge, falling, landing on the steep slope of the mountain on which rest the Spires of Knull.

Head over feet, an ungainly ball, Darta rolls down the slope until stopped by thick brush. And not giving thought to the pain, Darta manages a limping run; the thought that it is evening, that he heads toward the Darkplain, such does not stop him. His only concern: he *must* get away.

Darta stumbles. Yet, not for a minute does he stop, for he knows, he knows by the empathetic tug in his guts: his father is after him.

Yes, the mist, the clutching darkmist creeps after Darta. It whispers, "Come, come dear son." Oh, the sweetness, the cunning sweetness behind which, the claws: "How dare you leave me, my son, my son, my most prized possession? Did I not teach you of your body, your strength? When your mother turned against us, was it not I who took care of you? Who showed you what it meant to be a man? Who showed you what sweet words made ladies spread their thighs for you and your royal amusement?"

Darta screams in his mind, "Oh, father, if this is proof of your love, you may have it. I would soon find love amidst the stones and the moss and bugs rather than have the love *you* speak of."

"You whining, runny-nosed little bastard," comes the empathetic message, comes the mist prowling, sniffing out the trail of Darta. "You ungrateful she-bitch in disguise. You cowering, queen-brained, daughter-minded wretch who paraded before me as a son with proud rod 'tween your legs. Had I known that this was your mind, I'd have taken your rod and given it to Darkplain beast where at least something would appreciate the heritage that a king passes on."

"Oh, Father," screams Darta's feeling/mind, "your anger brings out the vileness of you; something I've long sensed but that which you have carefully concealed from all like a running sore in the crack of your butt."

"Insolent son!"

Darta squeezes his eyes closed from the massive guilt: the guilt that he is unfair toward his father, the guilt that it is wrong that he should live his own life. But he knows that he cannot return; better the guilt that it is wrong that he should live his own life. And he knows that he cannot return; better the guilt of him being his own person than the guilt of self-hatred of battle in which he does not believe.

And the mist coalesces and forms, yes, yes, the yellow eyes, yes, yes, the brilliant white teeth that shine in the moonlight, yes, the scales, the powerful muscles that rip and shred and *click-click, click-click,* the nails on the stones.

"Bring him," says the King. "Bring him back."

And silently, Darkbeast's mouth opens in silent snarl; the yellow eyes widen in purpose and the nostrils sniff—the trail—smell of sweat, trace of adrenalin—oh, there, ah, yes, *click-click, click-click.*

Lara wakens.

Click-click, click-click.

Startled, she looks about. The sky is bright with the two moons. She holds her breath.

Click-click, click-click.

It is yet distant, but it draws closer, closer. And Lara knows; up on her feet and running, running again. The land slopes up now and she finds herself in a stilled avalanche of boulders beneath cliffs. She climbs between the massive angular stones, finally pausing, trying to quiet her beating heart, her labored breathing. Silence. Suddenly a hand covers her mouth; then, "Sister! Lara!"

She turns her head, eyes widening in surprise. Darta removes his hand.

"Darta—what—"

"Sh!" Then, in a husky whisper, "I did not mean to frighten you. I will tell you all but not now; something wicked follows me."

Lara nods. "Yes, yes, I know. Something hideous follows me." She looks about. "Where are we safe?"

"Up higher. We need a place to hide and see our enemy."

Carefully, quietly, they warily pick a trail up through the rock fall; oh, do not dislodge one stone; no, no, not the slightest noise. Make the beasts which follow have little to go on; let them battle for their own path through the ragged and broken rock.

Lara and Darta pause in the shadow of a rock.

From one direction, faintly, *click-click.*

And from another direction, the way which Darta had come, *click-click.*

"There—" points Lara. The top of the rock fall, an angular granite slab, a shield behind which to hide yet see the clearing at the base of the rock fall.

On the right, below, *click-click, click-click.*

On the left, below, *click-click, click-click.*

And in the bright light of the two moons of Knull, the two beasts arrive at the clearing at the same time. They stop, turn, stare at each other.

Lara shudders; they are such ugly beasts, like short, brutish lizards with thick, scaly skin, white and sharp teeth and eyes that flash white in the moonlight. The beasts circle and circle each other; both snarling and hissing at the other. Suddenly one attacks and, grabbing the other by the neck, mounts and tries to penetrate. The other screams, kicks the attacker away, turns and with a mighty slash of claw, rips away the organ. The attacker howls, then it attacks again; they struggle; the shining teeth, the claws that shred, the howls, the shrieks. Lara cannot look; Darta turns and vomits. When he recovers and can look again, there is no movement. Both creatures lie still.

Lara points. "Look."

Darta strains to see. "What—" he whispers; then he says no more. The two carcasses glow, melt and form a sphere. It glows like quicksilver. For a time it is quiet. Abruptly the sphere shakes and ruptures; a creature emerges—a creature with six legs of silver, bulbous body of gold and eyes of jade. In the light, the creature sparkles and turns and looks up the rockslide. "Hiss," it whispers, "whose wickedness is this? What love be so distorted as to create me?" The creature pauses. "Love? Did I say love? Ha. By hate am I created. Whose hatred? Yours? Then you shall pay—"

"No," Darta responds, "it is from hate we flee. It is from the corruption of love we run to Darkplain, to hide, escape—"

The creature continues to watch Lara and Darta. "Yes," it finally says, "yes, I feel your minds and I also know from whom you run. And I seek payment. I seek revenge that I, the sacred Will To Be, am born of hate. There shall be payment for this bastardization, this humiliation of my divinity, for until I am released from this carnal form, *this* universe is still. There will be *no* creation until *I am released!*"

Darta swallows. "How is it that you shall be released?"

"By seeking the destruction of those by whose hatred I am born: to be aborted is far, far kinder than being born of, and suckled by, hatred. Take me to your mother and father—and my mother and father."

Lara shakes her head. "We can't do that. To be part of their death is unthinkable."

The creature laughs. "To destroy evil is unthinkable."

"They don't *mean* to be evil," Lara says.

"Your compassion shall destroy you," says the creature. "Your hearts are pure and your minds kind; you are easy prey for evil just as evil is prey for itself."

Darta hefts a stone up over his head. "We shall destroy you."

The creature laughs again. "You destroy me and you destroy the Universe. Which is it? Our mother and father or the fate of creation?"

Lara falls to her knees, her hands covering her face. Darta holds the stone for a long time. Finally he lowers it, drops it. "We will wait here," Darta says.

"You will not. You shall come with me."

"No," Darta says, "do not ask us to do this."

The moonlight glitters off the gold, the silver, the jade. "You must," says the creature. "You must come back and see for yourselves."

Darta sobs. He pounds his fists on the granite. "You cannot ask us to do this. To see those who bore us—our parents—destroyed—"

"Even though they destroy you?" asks the creature. "You're too, too kind to your enemies. Do you not understand that if they stay free, they will seek you and seek you until they capture and confine you, until you do just as they say? Until they break your will and your self respect like an ax cuts noble trees. Can you not understand what it is that you say?"

"Can you not," Darta sobs, "understand what it is *you* ask us to do?"

"I understand very well," says the creature. "Come with me; I'll show you *how* well I *do* understand."

Slowly, reluctantly, Lara and Darta make their way down through the rocks. When they reach the creature, they realize how large it is. The many eyes of the creature regard them impersonally. "Climb on my back," it says. It lowers itself close to the ground and Lara and Darta climb on the back. Both discover how cold is the metal. Neither says anything to the other on the journey back. Lara holds onto Darta; her head rests on his back. Darta holds his head down. The two moons light the land and the high white trees clutch the air with bone thin branches. The ground sparkles and sparkles with frost and the barren granite mountains are pale grey in the distance. Soon the land begins to rise; they come to the top of a hill, and a short distance away, the upsweep of a mountain crowned by the multiple Spires of Knull, ringing the hill like thorns in a crown. And in the middle of the crown, two high spires, the West and East Spires; how white, like bone, they are.

"And so," whispers the creature below them, "the Spires of Knull, the corrupted kingdom."

"Yes," sighs Darta, "where love and shit are the same."

The creature moves on. Deftly, deftly, up the slope the creature moves, over a wall between spires of the outer ring, then to the plaza between the two main spires. The creature stops. Lara whispers to Darta, "Oh, dark, dark is this moment."

"Stay on my back," says the creature. Then it taps the tip of a front leg four times on the stone of the square: *click-click, click-click.* The sound echoes.

And again, *click-click, click-click.*

A door in the East Spire opens. The Queen comes out, dressed in dark, filmy clothing. She comes up to the creature and admires the silver, the gold, the keen jade eyes. Lara is surprised that her mother is not afraid. The Queen smiles. "Ah, dear daughter, you return and you return on the back of a creature that will be of great use to me."

Lara and Darta watch, amazed. For her words form threads — silver threads that adhere to the spire opposite.

The creature taps a leg tip against the stone. *Click-click, click click.* Again the sound echoes. A door in the west tower opens. The King of the Spires appears. *Click-click, click-click.*

The King draws near and looks to his son. "Ah, Darta, you return. You remember the obligation to your father. And you bring back such an elegant creature." The father touches the silver. "How useful this, against the viciousness of the Queen who would take the empire into her hands." And the King's words form silver threads that adhere to the opposite spire.

Click-click, click-click. The King taps the leg of the creature.

Click-click, click-click. The Queen taps the creature. And then Queen and King face each other. The King smiles. "Darta is back, you Queen of the Frost, ungrateful wretch who gives me no peaceful mind. Darta is back," and the King laughs, and as he speaks and laughs, more silver threads form the words, "Darta is back and the kingdom is mine."

The Queen sneers. "My daughter is here. My daughter is back to seduce and destroy any plans you'll ever make. The way of you and yours is through your rod; your intelligence comes in spurts and is gone; the keen minds and plans replaced by lethargy and withdrawal; the deep thrusts of your wit and your stiffness of will become flaccid and limp." And her words form threads and as both of them speak, a web forms out of their words; it forms between the two spires.

The creature does not move.

Lara and Darta say nothing. Aghast, they listen and watch the web form.

"—how typical of your race, you dry bitch; with your passion and love as nurturing as a diseased teat," says the King and he walks closer to the Queen. He is glaring and mocking. "What tenderness you have you save for Darkbeasts that stalk through your dreams." As his words come out, the silver strands wrap about him until he is covered by thick, sticky silver.

The Queen laughs. "You foolish man; you accuse me of that which you do. Is this a sign of your intelligence, too?"

And as the Queen talks, her words wrap about her until she is enshrouded by the sticky silver silk of her words. They both fall to the ground and continue to deride one another until they are utterly bound in their own silk; they look like cocoons and finally become totally silent.

"You may get off now," says the creature.

Lara and Darta climb down.

"You see how it is?" asks the creature. "No matter how much compassion, or how much love you have, they cannot pause in their struggle long enough to listen or feel."

"And now?" asks Lara.

"Watch," says the creature. It takes the loose end threads from the cocoons and holds them in its jaws and thus drags the bodies along the plaza to the vast and shimmering web between the two spires. The creature deposits the two cocoons in the center of the web and then returns to Lara and Darta. The creature taps the end of a leg on the cold stones; *click-click, click-click.*

Immediately, the cocoons wriggle and move; two forms emerge from the shining silver shrouds; two forms that are duplicates of the creature; the legs of silver, the bodies of gold and as soon as they discard the cocoons, they attack each other.

"It is as it should be," the creature says. "Hate and cruelty such as theirs makes them as ugly as the survival-based minds of the creatures they have become. They've no room for compassion or love, only lust and survival and mindless hate. I've done nothing to them; I've only let them be as they truly are. Do you still have compassion for them?"

Lara and Darta numbly watch the two creatures in the web, a despairing dance of glitter and movement that shakes the web, makes it sparkle in the light of the two moons.

"So weirdly beautiful," murmurs Darta, "yet so deadly and ill. Each unable to stop the poison within them that drives them to grapple and hate and destroy."

"It is sadness," whispers Lara, "sadness and sorrow."

Suddenly, simultaneously, both creatures bite each other and slowly become still. And when at last, neither moves, Lara and Darta hear a voice behind them: "Ah, it is over; now it is done."

Lara and Darta turn to see the creature of gold and silver with eyes of jade—turn transparent. With wonder, they look inside—in the belly of the creature, a pool of water. And there comes a voice: "I am known by many names, and sacred is every name." In the pool, a plant, all green and growing. "All I seek is an expression of my Will To Be." A flash; when it fades, the plant is gone and there is a beautiful fish that changes colors: red to gold to silver to blue. "I am the will of being in love with being; those who bore me with hate shall be destroyed." Another flash. The fish and water vanish and the belly is filled with mist that suddenly coalesces into creatures of scales and claws that go *click-click, click-click* in the belly. The creatures are dressed in royal robes; they suddenly attack and maul each other until they are still. "No, no," comes the voice, "you will not use me to clutch and hold and possess; I am the will of Life, of Being and can no more be held or possessed than the sky, air, water, land or flame. What I seek and always seek is the expression of myself in all the forms ready to be touched by magic. And as chance and circumstance allow this, I give the gift of replication and the wondrous knowledge that life is dependent and interdependent. I forever define myself by the forms in which I exist, with which I exist. To try to separate oneself from this, to try to own it, to somehow rise above it—is to hate oneself, and in turn, hate life. For life, in its love of self-expression, joins." Another flash: a golden bird with bright blue eyes. "Lara and Darta, know what love is: it is knowing what is best for you; it is living your dreams based on self-pride and with respect and with reverence toward others. They who love you will help you become your dream; yes, they will encourage it as you encourage those whom you love. And those who would do evil do them-selves evil." There is a long pause. Then, "And for now, The Good—that which loves, enhances and generates life—triumphs. And I am free!" The golden bird grows in the belly of the creature and suddenly unfolds its wings. *Wham!* The shell of the creature breaks and the bird furiously beats shining wings. Up, up, the bird goes higher, higher, soaring, cir-cling—abruptly, it becomes the sun. The web and creatures burst into flame and there comes the voice of the sun, "Lara, Lara, look upon my disk and tell me what you see."

Lara gazes into the light. She steps back. "I see my face!"

"Darta, Darta, look upon my disk and tell me what you see."

Darta does so. "Oh, stars!" he whispers. "I see *my* face."

"Be as my light," whispers the sun, "fill yourselves with light and warmth and flow, travel, wherever you may. All I ask is that in your travels, you pause and appreciate the will of being, of myself, that I chose your form in which to express myself."

"Yes," says Lara, "to this will of our being we offer our praise."

Darta raises his hands to the sun. "Praise be to the Will To Be, that it chooses uncountable paths to express itself. Praise be to the Will that it chose me as a path."

"Go," says the sun, "go, and in the light and time that is yours and in the form that is yours, enjoy and respect and love this life that is yours."

Lara and Darta walk away from the Spires of Knull. They walk into the light and leave the burning web behind them, behind them, so far, far behind them.

Satan Claus

Hee, hee, hee. No, not ho, ho, ho, but hee, hee, hee. Make no mistake about it, I'm nasty. You don't hear about me. Not officially. Oh, no. Everyone hears the music of Tchaikovsky, the "Nutcracker" business. Oh, yeah. And everyone hears of "Oh, Holy Night," and "Away in a Manger," but they never hear about *me*. Oh, no. I'm the shadow. I'm Santa's dirty underwear. I'm the toadstool growing beneath the Messiah's bed.

Crunch! Aww. Your expensive one-of-a-kind ornament just got broken and the glass fragments got ground into the shag rug? You say it's a hundred years old? Tsk. What else would you expect of Satan Claus? Old St. Prick? I got horns, man, and they may be covered with tinsel and lights, but, hey, baby, they are still horns. Uh-huh. And the tail? You say it doesn't look like Rudolph's tail? Very good. That's because it's not. Turkey got all burned? Who, me? Better believe it. I do all *sorts* of nasty things befitting a devil.

Love to mess things up. Just listen to the kinds of things I do. Family gatherings are a specialty of mine.

"Oh, Martha," the overweight woman says, "I'm on a diet. I really can't have chocolates."

"Nanette, it's Christmas. One or two pieces won't kill you."

"I really shouldn't—I have to stay on this diet!"

"Nanette, don't be silly, you stay on a diet for 364 days a year; one day won't kill you."

"Oh, Martha, shame on you! Don't tempt me. Aren't you on a diet, too?"

"Well, yes, but I haven't lost any weight. *You* are looking really thin—I can't believe a piece of chocolate would hurt you. Look. I'll have one and then *you* can have one."

"No, really, I shouldn't—I really shouldn't—"

"But this is really wonderful chocolate. You'll hurt my feelings if you don't have a piece."

"Oh, Martha—don't tempt me. I couldn't possibly hurt your feelings by not having any."

"You *will*, you'll hurt my feelings! Now have a piece—"

"Well—"

"Just one—"

"But—"

"It won't hurt you."

"Well, all right."

"What are friends for?"

"Yum. That was good."

"Oh, look, I bet this one has caramel inside—you've always loved caramel, haven't you?"

"Martha—I said *one*—"

"Nanette, how could another hurt you?"

"Martha, you *devil*, you!"

Hee, hee, hee. You can say *that* again. Boy, she got *that* right. Told you I was mean. Take great pride in it. Oops! That fifty-dollar tree has a nest of spider eggs that decides early Christmas morning is a great time to hatch and surprise you with a thousand crawling gifts. Hmmmm. What *fun*. What a delicious mingling of odors, pumpkin pie, turkey and Raid. And so what if your husband is arachnophobic and faints every time he sees spiders? Hey, it's *Christmas*. Time for surprises. Santa comes down the chimney with his sack of goodies; I come up the toilet with my bag of tricks. Like so:

"Excuse me, but I bought this raincoat for a gift and it's torn."

"Well?"

"I want my money back."

"I'm sorry, it's a sale item; you can't have your money back. Next, please—"

"Wait a minute—I've waited in line an hour and I want this taken care of. I didn't pay a hundred bucks to buy a torn coat."

"Should have been more careful. Sale item. Buyer beware. Next!"

"No, sir, no! I want my money back! I want to see the manager!"

"I am the manager. Next!"

Hee, hee, hee. Say you drove fifty miles to pick up your uncle at the airport only to discover that he has the flu? Say he got sick in the car on the way back and you got a flat tire and you discovered you forgot to check the spare and it's flat? Say that it's beginning to blizzard—oh, I could go on, and on and on. Oh, I could—I *love* being nasty. It's in my blood; it's in my nature. Santa takes delight in bringing joy. I take delight in bringing pain. What's that old saying? Without pain, how can you know joy? So you see, when I'm not making life miserable, you should really try to experience as much joy as you can, because I will visit you sometime, somewhere during Christmas. After all, I *am* the Christmas devil, Satan Claus, and I have a duty to uphold, misery to bestow. 'Cause I'm mean: I'm the $200 sweater with that hole you didn't notice, the puzzle with pieces from another puzzle that will never fit, the drunk brother-in-law who stumbles and falls into the Christmas tree. Alas. An ornament a *tad* too large, it seems. I'm the family bickering at a time when everyone is supposed to be forgiving, right? Right?

"Well, Sam, it's been ten years since we've seen each other but I'm glad I made the overture to call you up and invite you over—"

"Well, hey, dear brother, I called *you* up last year and you never returned my call."

"No you didn't. You didn't call me. How could you? I was in New Jersey."

"I left the message on your answering machine."

"Well, I played back the messages when I got home and I never heard your message."

"I left one."

"You couldn't have. I would have heard it."

"You calling me a liar?"

"Look, it's Christmas. Let's not fight. We're together; let bygones be bygones, even if we messed it up last year."

"No, you messed it up last year."

"Well, I didn't mean to—and as far as messing it up goes, look who's messing it up now!"

"Well, it wouldn't be messed up now if you hadn't messed it up then."

"You know something? You're being as much of a jerk now as you've been all your life. No wonder we got out of contact—maybe we should get out of contact more often."

"Yeah, maybe ten years wasn't long enough."

"Apparently not. There's your coat."

"Thanks. I was getting ready to leave."

"Good."

"By the way, Merry Christmas, *jerk!*" *Slam!*

Ah, the joy of misery. The gift of sharing darkness. And I'm out there doing my bit to make Christmas memorable. *So* memorable. You better believe it!

Hee, hee, hee.

"The Ear of Ozone"

The Last, Ultimate and Final Worst Amateurish Science Fiction Story Ever Written

(With deep apologies — sort of — to the author(s) of the infamous "The Eye of Argon.")[1]

"Hee, hee, hee," said the horrible, oozing, smelly, obnoxious, putrid, pulsating, malodorous, evil, slimy, but also handsome, alien.

"Eek," ejaculated the young, semi-clad, blond-haired, blue-eyed, peaches-and-cream-complexioned, breathless young girl. Her breasts strained mightily against her state-of-the-art, finely crafted Jantzen Beach tee shirt. ($8.95, available at fine stores everywhere.)

"Hee, hee, hee," yelled the alien, advancing slowly but hastily, its filthy, pulsating, pubescent pseudopods extended in hateful loving clutches. "Hee, hee, hee," it chortled gleefully, outrageously, delightfully, sadly, lost in its lustful vision of a new, terrible, malodorous, nauseating, but in some way handsome, race of new, improved creatures, born of this young, throbbing, vital, strong, beautiful female from Earth who happened to come to the filthy, degenerated, dingy, turgid, dank, miserable, but in some way beautiful, planet Krudencorruption.

"What do you want from me? My life savings?" babbled the young female incoherently. "What do you want from me?" She held her hands up to her face and noticed curiously that the time was midnight, Earth time, on her fantastic waterproof, dustproof, Krudencorruption-proof Casio watch, with the built in miniature TV screen, thermometer, and appointment calendar. (Available at all K-mart stores in seven galaxies.) Idly, she pressed the button and noticed with some chagrin that it was her father's birthday and she had intended to come to this planet for

---

[1] Punctuation added so reader can readily see just how bad a story can be.

231

some Dilithium crystals for him. *Shoot,* she thought, *I'll be late for dinner and The Force knows when I'll be able to gift wrap them.*

"Hee, hee, hee," extrapolated the alien, feeling left out and reminding the girl where she was.

"Eeek," mumbled the girl as she suddenly remembered where she was. "What do you want from me?" The girl, stumbling backwards, catching her breath, stubbing her toe, catching herself against a slimy, bug-infested tree, asked.

"Hee, hee, hee," said the alien, turning all sorts of icky and unwell colors.

"Oh," said the girl, "oh, you can't want *that.* What would my boy-friend say? I mean, we promised to be faithful to each other—oh, oh, oh, oh, oh, oh, how can you do this to me? Oh."

"Oh, ho, ho, ho," said the alien uncharacteristically. It moved closer, its deeply crinkled and smooth skin sweated an oily, putrid, nauseating, disgusting, filthy, malodorous, but not altogether unpleasant, stench.

Just then, two game officers from the Krudencorruption Outdoor Life Improvement Program stopped and saw what was going down.

"Look, Frank," said Larry, who looked like Frank's father at age nine-teen, "it's a scantily clad stock character and a dreadful shock-feature creature, who, as you know, is placed in bad science fiction stories so the reader will stay interested in the story because the plot is so inherently lousy that it has to have external devices to keep people reading."

"Yes," said Frank, who looked like Larry's brother did after he had twenty two and a half sessions of shock therapy, a prefrontal lobotomy and 5000 milligrams of Thorazine. "You are right. And as you know, Larry," said Frank, looking wistfully at the moon, "since we were just passing through, we have to decide whether or not we should get in-volved, because, dear reader, the awful stock character shock-feature creature is actually bisexual. But we all know that, as far as this story goes, it has to be implied that it is heterosexual."

"Yes," said Frank, "before we can do anything, we should talk to our lawyer. We have to remember the Prime Directive."

"Yes," said Larry, "the Prime Directive."

"And we all know what the Prime Directive is."

"Yes," crooned Frank. "We all know that."

"Yes," added on and rejoined Larry, "we all know that the Prime Di-rective is 'No parking any time.'"

"No," gesticulated Frank. "That is not the Prime Directive."

"'Things go better with Coke?'" articulated Larry.

"No," yawned Frank out loud.

"'Yield right of way?'" offered Larry.

"No," negated Frank. "The Prime Directive is—"

"Yes," said Larry breathlessly. "Yes? Yes? Yes?"

"'Use birth control.' That is always the Prime Directive—along with, of course, 'Consult your attorney,' not to mention 'Yield right of way,' and 'God bless America.' Anyway, if this is still going on in a day or so, we may be able to do something—or at least take some pictures for evidence."

"Yes—" ejaculated Frank, cautiously. Then both men cast their eyes down the road and darkly, Larry asked, "Shall we go?"

"I don't see why not," said Frank. And blinded by the awful truth of something or other, they went on their way.

Meanwhile, the young, scantily clad maiden, her wonderful, undulating, pulsating cantalopean breasts straining at her training bra said, "Oh, will this never end?"

"Hee, hee, hee," said the putrid, fetid, smelly, malodorous, snotty, slimy, turgid, but not altogether unhandsome, beast. "Hee, hee, hee, hee, hee."

Meanwhile, back at the ranch, Cowboy Joe stuffed some snuff between his gum and lower lip and looked at the sun setting in the west. His faithful, fearless full time friend, an Indian named Pinkeye, of the Flatfoot tribe, looked at the sunset and said, "Huh. 'Red sky at night, sailors' delight'."

Cowboy Joe looked to the west and said, "Yep."

Pinkeye stared at the sun. "Huh," he pontificated, "Me heard that woolly caterpillars with narrow band mean cold winters."

Cowboy Joe spat a wad. "Yep."

Pinkeye looked around, running his fingers through his long, natural, dark, Flatfoot Indian hair which he washed daily with Ivory soap, down at the creek which ran across Cowboy Joe's property on which Pinkeye set up his teepee in which he lived along with his pony, Frank, his pet crow, Poe, and his Sanyo Ghetto Blaster with four by six speakers and dual tape drive with CD player Extra Bass Boost which he picked up free for Raleigh coupons but which can also be purchased at any Sears store. Pinkeye thought a long minute and then said, "'Red in the morning, sailors take warning.'"

Cowboy Joe looked at his horse and liked how it stood. "Yep," he ejaculated, then cleaned himself off.

Pinkeye rubbed the top of the corral fence with a stealthy and studied hand and idly wondered about the composition of matter and what relevancy it had to the atmospheric currents in Saturn's moon, Titan. He had long since wondered about such things: why aluminum beer cans always seem to bend in the middle, why male dogs lift their legs to pee, why pi equals 3.14, and as he rubbed his hand on the wood, he wondered why Cowboy Joe existed and what cruel joke brought him to this place, this time. *Was there a God?* he wondered. *Is there Interdimensional Time Space between galaxies? Must the real square root of Quantum Mass times the linear aspect of Sidereal Time of the Universe always yield blue marshmallows? Was it all a lie? Was the entire Universe just a forked Tongue? Was firewater really fire? Could rocks with flat surfaces facing east accurately foretell the absence of potatoes next year?* With all this on his mind, he turned to Cowboy Joe, took a deep breath and said, "Huh."

Cowboy Joe also took a deep breath, hocked mightily, and cleverly, trajectorially, and almost magically, was able to aim an immense ball of chewed up crud—*patooie*—and hit his other horse, Startrek—right in the butt. "Yep," he rambled.

Just then, Sally, Cowboy Joe's sweet, angelic, homey, plain, but good-hearted, humanitarian, loving, five-foot-two, eyes of blue, wife, with the smell of fresh bread, corn and chicken shit approached Cowboy Joe, a letter waving in her hand like a piece of steel. She came up to him and smiling said, "Shithead, dear, an interstellar spacegram from the Krudencorruption Outdoor Life Improvement Program just came—your little whore of a daughter is stuck on the planet Krudencorruption and for a minor fee of a million dollars, the Outdoor Life Improvement Program will pay off some alien trying to get his tentacle or organ or reproductive thingie or weenie into her slit. Take care of it, Bozo. She's your daughter."

"Yep," said Cowboy Joe.

Pinkeye looked up in the gathering, enfolding, oncoming, deepening night. "Ring around the sun mean rain in 48 hours. Sometimes six."

"Yep," said Cowboy Joe, stuffing another wad of chewing tobacco between his lip and lower gum. He did it carefully, with loving care. This habit he had for many years. It was his statement to the Universe. About why things should be this way. Tobacco. As meaningful and as beautiful as a toad sunbathing. It was the all. Yes, tobacco, snuff to be rolled up into a ball of *whuck,* the ultimate statement of—

"Well, Fuckbrains," said his smiling, handsome, wholesome wife who he had met coming out west lo, those many years ago, when they had big dreams about having a large ranch, a herd of cattle, and a pond of bullfrogs with the ultimate dream of having a chain of restaurants across the country of *Cowboy Joe's South Dakota Fried Bullfrog Balls* until the ultimate truth hit about just how many—and how small—and he sighed at the lost dreams and his wife took the letter and stuffed it in Cowboy Joe's shirt and said, "If you ever get your shit together, send your little whore tart some money."

"Yep," mused Cowboy Joe.

"Huh," said Pinkeye, "When the frost is on the punkin..."

"Yep," elaborated Cowboy Joe, making up his mind that he would have to talk to his daughter about these things; the neighbors were getting suspicious of all the UFO's around his house recently, and his bank account was getting as low as his sperm count.

"Huh," said Pinkeye, for no particular reason.

Meanwhile, the alien approached the young maiden and as he came closer, his pseudopods quivered in wanton, naked, shamefaced and actually, not unreasonable, lust. "Hee, hee, hee," it gelatinized.

"Eeek," said the young, scantily clad maiden, her breath coming in gasps, and her buxom bosom unabashedly bursting brazenly at her brown and dainty brassiere. "What do you want from me?" she whimpered. "If it's money, I'm sure American Express will come to the rescue. And you can have my Goodyear Tire credit card, my Texaco credit card—you can even have my birth certificate which maybe you can use if you apply for a driver's license."

"Hee, hee, hee." The alien moved even closer, seething in naked, unvarnished, unshellacked, undenatured, unhydrogenated, undulating, polyunsaturated, disgusting lust.

The young maiden, against a rock and a hard place, made a last stand. From the depths of her superficial soul, she said, "But there's one thing you can't have..."

Undaunted and unheeding, the alien poised to leap upon the maiden, its tentacles hard, turgid, waiting to paw, to tickle, to stroke, to penetrate, to fondle, to flagellumate.

"You can't have my virginity," she wantonly said.

"Hee, hee, hee," said the alien, rising to the occasion.

"Because I haven't got any."

"Hee—" the alien stopped. "Hee?"

"I admit it," ejaculated the maiden, head fervently turning to and fro in damnation and desperation. "Freddy and I went too far one night in his '97 Pontiac...he said he'd just put it in a little way..."

"Ho?"

"But no," sobbed the young lady, crying, mouth working, big tears coursing, tidal-waving down her face. "no, that prick went all the way—so now you know—"

"Hum," the alien backed away.

"Yes," the girl said, "yes, I'm a ruined woman, it's true. It's true," she sobbed, she shrieked, she rationalized. "So, if you want me, here I am." And she lunged for the creature, she lurched into the abyss of her womanly downfallen misery and she lunged toward the alien to complete this unholy and ungodly and no doubt fascinating bonding.

But the alien backed away. And then it ran as fast as it could pseudo-podly ooze. "Eeek!" it screamed. "Eeek! Eeek! Eeek!"

The girl ran after it, "Come here you little pussy; aren't I good enough for you? Come on, the chance of a lifetime! Come and get it!"

"Eeek!" murmured the alien, blithely, quickly, adroitly and swiftly and gently sliming away.

"Hee, hee, hee!" said the young girl, with her feminine breasts pushing and twisting against her Jantzen Beach tee-shirt. "Hee, hee, hee, hee, hee."

"Eeek!" ejaculated the alien, "Eeek, eek, eek, eek, eek!"

And with that, the young maiden woke up. It had all been a dream. Very disappointed, she placed a hand between her legs—and masturbated violently.

The Mall

The man walks. As he walks, his footfall leaves no impression on the frost-covered sands. He is naked, yet he does not shiver, nor does his breath hang in the air. Yet, the man walks. He is bald, like an ancient baby. And he walks beneath a dark and starless sky, then he stops. His blue eyes search the horizon. He turns his head this way, that. *Ah,* he finally thinks, *there it is.* He changes his course, goes down an ancient, dry creek bed that leads him through a narrow canyon. Once through it, he walks around a boulder and there it is.

The Mall, he thinks. *Yes, the Mall.*

He goes up to the doors, they open, and immediately someone seizes him by the hand, puts him in clothes. He tries to speak, but the words are incomprehensible.

"It's all right," comes the voice, "right now you just got here; don't hurry yourself." The man looks at the one who speaks: a woman and much taller than he is. *Just before he came to the Mall,* he wonders, *he didn't seem so small.*

"I'm sure you have many questions," says the woman. "Everybody does."

A man joins the woman. "And like all questions," the man says, "most are unanswerable."

"By the way," the woman says, smiling and stopping, "my name is Dorothy, this gentleman is my friend Andrew and your name is—" she thinks for a minute and looks up at her friend, "Would William be all right? Billy. How about Billy?"

The man nods, still unable to speak.

Andrew, who takes on more and more characteristics as Billy's eyes get used to the lighting and the Mall, turns out to be tanned, with abundant black hair, an easy smile and much warmth. Billy decides that he likes Andrew. The woman, who also has become more defined, has brown eyes, yellow hair and very long fingers.

"You've probably been walking a very long time," says the man, Andrew. "No one I've ever met in the Mall knows how long a time it takes of walking before a person finds this place. I think you'll discover it to be quite a place, so many shops—but first, let's sit somewhere. You just listen to us and you'll get the hang of it all."

The three of them walk to a café by a lake in one of the larger shops. The trees are big and full. Billy guesses the Mall is quite large and has certainly been there for a while. They are served strange eggs, round and with water and land covering the outside of the egg. Billy looks. Dare he eat anything so delicate? So wonderful?

Andrew notices Billy's hesitation as he, Andrew, expertly splits the wonderful egg in half and lets the boiling red insides ooze and steam over his plate. "Yes, I suppose at first they are strange, Billy, but they are here for us to enjoy, so eat them and be happy."

Billy, with sadness that is unexplainable to him, cracks open the eggs and eats. Somehow, he has the sense of eating his own body, but surely such a sense must be ridiculous. The woman, Dorothy, looks to Andrew. "Oh, dear, I'd forgotten how difficult it is; he hasn't learned how to objectify the objects around him. He's still far too sensitive and sees too much kinship and linkage in himself to the soil and the world."

The man, Andrew, smiles. "You know, in one shop in the Mall, there are people who say they are sorry to the animals they eat. So primitive. That's why they never progressed to any sort of ownership in the Mall. You have to objectify things, put things in boxes. Separate yourself. He will learn."

Billy hears the man, but abruptly realizes that Andrew is not being honest; Andrew does not want to recognize his linkage and to see Billy knowing the linkage makes Andrew very uncomfortable. With sorrow, Billy eats the eggs, realizing that there is something terribly wrong here, that neither the man nor the woman wants to talk of it and automatically, Billy feels as a stranger to them.

After lunch, they continue on. They come to another shop. Dorothy points to the interior. "This is a very important shop, Billy; let us sit down and watch." They all sit on the grass and look at the inside of the shop, which, as far as Billy is concerned, seems empty—it is simply a room filled with blue. But then the blue changes to white and the white changes to black. Vivid white light flashes out of the room and there is a terrible roar. Billy covers his ears. Dorothy laughs; Andrew shakes his head. "Boy's frightened," says Andrew. "That will never do. Afraid of the Weather Shop." He shakes his head.

Billy is beginning to dislike Andrew and he is not sure why. The blackness in the Weather Shop abates and a beautiful rainbow fills the shop. Billy claps his hands in delight.

"You like this shop," says Dorothy.

"Very much," says Billy, suddenly surprised at his own voice.

"Ah," says Dorothy, "language; how quickly you learn." She smiles at him and hugs him. "You're a bright one. Shall we go on?"

"Yes, I'd like that."

They walk farther. They come to another shop. "Let's sit here," Dorothy says.

Andrew seems reluctant, but sits. Billy tries to get close to him, but Andrew seems distant and Billy withdraws, simultaneously hating himself for feeling that somehow he has done something wrong, that he is no longer loveable to the man, yet hating the man because he would not talk. He senses what the problem is: could it be that Andrew is jealous of him? That because Dorothy is paying so much attention to him, Andrew feels left out and angry and is therefore withdrawing from Billy? Punishing him? Billy sighs. Dare he say anything? What if he only gets rejected? He finds himself sitting closer to Dorothy and, as he does so, Andrew seems to emotionally distance himself even farther.

"Look," says Dorothy, pointing into the shop.

Billy does. At first it is just dark in the shop.

"What is this shop?"

"Not going to tell you," says Dorothy. "You're bright, and you'll be able to know. You just watch now."

Billy is excited and glances to Andrew who sits, sullen, almost glaring into the shop. Billy wants to ask him what is wrong, what is he feeling, but he holds back. There is something terribly wrong here, and though he has his ideas, somehow, Andrew feels unapproachable. And even though Billy feels enraged at Andrew, he also feels fearful of him, and very sorry for him, for he can tell that even Dorothy is withdrawing from Andrew. He looks back into the store and the darkness is changing to a deep blue, a pale blue and then an unbelievable light pours out from the store.

"Sunrise!" exclaims Billy and he claps his hands.

"Yes," says Dorothy, "and something else."

The light continues to pour out of the store and then, in the middle of the shop, something begins to form and the light seems to coalesce into a figure, made of brilliant light, standing, looking skyward, hands outstretched. Billy feels a tingling of his flesh, a desire to cry, to touch the figure. "Such a special shop," he whispers. "The Shop of Hope?"

"Yes," says Dorothy. "The Shop of the Sunrise is also the Shop of Hope, because as hurtful and hard as the Mall can be sometimes, our place in it is somehow safe, beautiful and there are so many reasons to explore all the shops."

Billy stares at the figure, the figure made as though of sun. "Yes," says Billy, "I understand why this store is so wonderful. So much warmth here. So much joy. Let us go on."

He and Dorothy stand; already Andrew is standing, obviously impatient.

Dorothy looks at him, her anger obvious. "I take it that this is not the store for you."

Andrew looks disdainful. "I think there are other stores of more value," he says, obviously smug.

"What is more important than the magic of every sunrise? The ability to hope?"

Andrew shakes his head. "Finding enough to eat. Hope never did much for an empty stomach. You never were one for practicality."

Dorothy looks hurt and goes to Andrew, touching him on the arm, "Something is wrong. Ever since Billy joined us, you've become so distant. Is this the way it is to be for the rest of our time here at the Mall?"

Billy looks entreatingly at Andrew. *Please,* he thinks, and the image of hope, of fire, suddenly touches him in a way that brings tears to his eyes. *Please,* he thinks, *all the wonder about us means so little if we are not happy, and do not know how to love and be loveable. Nothing means anything at all if we are not open to ourselves, to others. Please —*

Andrew hesitates. *He wants to be open, yet what is wrong with him? What is wrong? Does he see openness as a weakness? As something to be shunned? Loathed? As if he is strong for being able to cover?* Andrew smiles. "Nothing is wrong," he says.

And Billy hates Andrew. Dorothy looks dismayed, disappointed and hurt. Andrew turns. "Here's a good shop over here," he says, pointing.

And Billy and Dorothy look at each other, the message the same between them: for Andrew there is no hope, as he has closed himself off and there is nothing to be done. Nonetheless, they follow after on the slim hope...on the slim hope...

Andrew sits on a stone bench in front of a strange shop. Dorothy and Billy approach the shop but keep their distance. "Now *this* store I find interesting," Andrew says.

Both Billy and Dorothy look warily at Andrew, but then focus their attention on the store: it is a scene of a jungle, of rampant growth, of flowers, birds, smells exotic and erotic; a primeval moist, sour and musky smell, the smell of earth, of rotting and living vegetation, permeates the atmosphere. But then something strange begins to happen.

"Look!" whispers Dorothy to Billy. "The leaves are withering and falling away."

Indeed. And the flowers wither and tree limbs, once full and plump and fleshy as thighs, twist, dry and break. The air becomes dry and in the distance a sand dune approaches; sand fills the store, and where once was dense and tropical forest, now it is desert.

"Ah," says Andrew. "How amazing. And how simple it makes everything."

Dorothy looks at Andrew. "And you prefer this, this *dying*, to hope?"

"It's refreshing," says Andrew. Billy notices how Andrew avoids eye contact with both him and Dorothy. "Or this shop," says Andrew. "Now *this* has always been interesting to me."

The shop is dark, but Billy, looking closely, is both frightened and amazed. All the surface area of the shop is covered with creatures that look like huge insects, but they are mechanical. Each one has little headlights that stab the darkness. And the insects crawl over each other, occasionally one destroying the other, then moving on, or, after destroying it, cannibalizing it, and either using the parts of the insect for something else, or devouring it entirely.

In the back of the shop is a very large mechanical insect and Andrew stares into the darkness, as though entranced by what he sees.

Dorothy goes up to him. "Andrew. It's true that this shop is also part of the Mall, but you need not be attracted to it."

Andrew does not look at her. "You are attracted to hope, but you fail to realize how impractical hope is. Look at this. Some great intelligence is at work here, guiding, controlling, powerful."

"Andrew," says Dorothy, imploring, "come, talk with us. Something is gone between us. And what is in this shop is a poor replacement. What is in this shop is *no* replacement." She tries to turn him to look at her.

"Turn away from this shop. Let us go back to the Shop of Hope; let us try to rediscover—"

Andrew goes closer to the store. "There is nothing left to rediscover. You have Billy now."

Dorothy looks shocked. "Is that it? You've drawn away because you are jealous? But you are acting on feelings instead of talking of them—"

Billy is dumbfounded; he simultaneously feels guilty, yet sorry for Andrew, and has a sense that Andrew has damaged himself too much. Andrew takes Dorothy's hand away, and walks into the store.

"No," says Dorothy, "we can talk! I understand! Please do not go—"

But it is as though Andrew does not hear. He walks into the shop, into the darkness, in with the strange insects, to the strange power beyond.

"What will happen to him?" asks Billy, terribly frightened.

"I know and I don't want to know. And you will see," she points, "right now."

The strange insects stop moving. After a minute, they organize; they turn slowly about and face one direction—toward the front of the store. The insects slowly grow larger, larger until they are as large as Billy. And then they move out of the store.

Dorothy and Billy back away. The strange army approaches them until they are at the center of the Mall, and it is then that something even more peculiar happens. From down the Mall in the direction from which they have come, a white, a brilliant light flows. The strange creatures turn away from Dorothy and Billy, turn away and begin to move toward the light. As soon as the light touches the strange creatures, all the creatures explode into darkness, and the individual darknesses grow and merge into a sphere, a black star, and coming from that black star is a horizontal flow of darkness.

Where the light and the darkness touch, there are explosions, smoke, and screaming.

Dorothy and Billy stand transfixed, staring at the volatile surfaces where light and dark meet. The light is flashing like lightning.

Billy points.

"Oh, my," says Dorothy, "oh, my."

Straddling the boundary between the light and the dark is Andrew: in pain, but joy, hopeful yet despairing, calm and violent, half of him perfect, the other half mutilated and hideously disfigured, half of him loving, half of him hateful; he is being pulled into the light, sucked into the darkness, over and over again, ripped apart and healed, expressions of wonder, expressions of blind, insect hate.

"Ah, Andrew, Andrew," says Dorothy, shaking her head. "Why you? That you should become the battlefield of all that is holy and all that is ugly and evil."

Billy looks to Dorothy; Billy looks to her, to the vast and strange Mall with the strange stores, looks to Andrew torn and saved, healed and ravaged, and knows that while he fears for Andrew, he begins to also fear — for himself.

The Well

Now just why or how these things happen, it is hard to say. One minute, Edward, age 40, thin with abundant black hair and slate grey eyes, is driving his little red sports car down the highway in the country, and the next minute, for some unexplainable reason, he decides to turn off onto a road that he has never been on before in his life. And even Edward does not know why he is doing so. The road is secondary, paved, winding through lush, evergreen-choked countryside, typical Pacific Northwest countryside—grasses, ferns, maples, fir trees and on hills where the road climbs, expansive views of mountains. Edward drives on, comes around a curve—*flash!* A blinding light and *bang!* There is Edward, smack dab in the middle of what has to be a small town in Mexico: the white adobe walls of buildings, the red tile roofs, the brown, unpaved and dusty soil and the damp heat.

Edward stops the car. He is somewhat surprised and looks about, this way, that. There is no one else around. "Well," says Edward, more to himself than anyone, and, given he is by himself, it would in fact have to be to himself, he says, "this is interesting." And he drives a little ways down the narrow street, comes around a corner and there is a plaza, in the middle of it, a well. *You know*, he thinks to himself, *something tells me*—He gets out of the car and goes over to the wide, broad-rimmed well. He leans over. Darkness. He reaches into his pocket, finds a penny and tosses it in. It drops for a second, then bursts into flame, looking like a miniature meteor, and then goes out. But in the flash, Edward sees rungs on the side of the well. He sits on the rim and looks into the darkness. "I don't think I understand this too much," says Edward. "I don't know why I turned off the main road. This does not look like Seattle, Portland or Vancouver; I don't know what I'm doing here; this does not look like a normal well; my car won't start and I don't know what to do." He sighs.

"Dream," comes a voice.

Edward looks around. There is no one else there. "Dream," says Edward.

"Dream," comes the voice.

Edward glances into the well. "Is there someone down there?" asks Edward, peering into the darkness.

"Yes and no," comes the voice.

Edward tries to place the voice and the best he can do is the sound of wind through trees, water over stones. It is a voice—but it is hardly a voice that Edward would call human.

"To whom am I speaking?" asks Edward.

"Time," comes the voice. "So much time. And so little of it. So much hope. Yet virtually none. All the risks to take, nothing to risk at all, yet everything to risk."

Edward looks away. "All I asked was a simple question and I get back a verbal jigsaw puzzle. Helpful."

"Cynic," says the voice. Then, "Excuse me."

Abruptly, there is much wailing and sobbing and a woman climbs out of the depths of the well. Slowly she makes it to the top rung and, oblivious to Edward, with tears streaming down her face, her black hair in disarray, she weeps and walks away.

"Oh," says Edward, sighing, "I see. You don't dispense water. You dispense misery. Just what I need."

"You misunderstand," says the well. "I dispense only what people expect."

"Who *are* you?" asks Edward, looking back down into the well.

Silence.

Edward looks up. A little child approaches; a gay, smiling little girl. She tosses a wooden bucket over the rim. *Splash!* In a moment, the little girl pulls up a bucket of—

"Pardon me," says Edward.

"¿Qué?" asks the girl, smiling with eyes very bright.

"What have you there?" And realizing that the girl does not understand, Edward points to the bucket.

Eagerly, the little girl lifts the bucket; inside, there appear to be large soap bubbles. And Edward looks closely: in one bubble, the little girl is running somewhere, running with another little girl—on a hill—through grass and flowers, overlooking a bright blue sea. Another bubble: the girl, older, appears in a very nice, long white dress, clean, made of coarse cloth but elegantly woven. A gentleman is with her; someone of dark mustache, dark eyes and well-dressed. The scene is a beach at daybreak. And in another bubble, the girl and her parents at a market, all very happy. The girl lowers her bucket and Edward nods. Then the girl runs off, in spite of the full bucket—it is as though feather light.

Edward sits, arms folded, staring after the girl. "A bucket of dreams?" he muses. "Realities?"

"Sometimes they are the same," says the well.

"Not always," replies Edward.

"But often enough," says the well, "if you so believe."

Edward thinks for a minute. And as he sits on the wall of the well, an old man approaches the well and looks in. He sighs. He has a shoulder bag. With great effort and very slowly, he takes it off and lays it on the broad rim of the well. And with obvious pain, he lowers himself over the rim and climbs down the rungs. Edward watches; as the man climbs down, the well takes on an aquamarine color inside and the man, as he climbs down, slowly becomes transparent and the more transparent he becomes, the deeper the hue in the well. Then the man vanishes. Abruptly, there is a wild movement in the old man's satchel, and a beautiful butterfly, maroon of body, aquamarine of wings, emerges as though coming from a cocoon—and moving about as though admiring itself, the butterfly beats its wings furiously and flutters away.

"Impressive," says Edward, nodding appreciatively, "very impressive."

"Thank you," says the well.

"Now," says Edward, turning and looking into the now dark again depths of the well, "what about me? I take it you have me here for a purpose."

"No," replies the well, "you brought yourself here."

"I don't see how," says Edward. "Just on impulse I—" and abruptly stops.

"You knew which road to take," says the well, "because you were ready."

Edward says nothing and almost distractedly, he watches his hand seemingly float up to his sports jacket, go for the inside pocket and produce a letter. He opens it and reads it out loud:

Dear Meredith:

Last time I heard from you was seventeen years ago. You were going to be married, and sent me a wedding invitation. I did not respond. I never heard from you again. I did not respond not because I did not care, but because I guess I could not bear the thought of you marrying someone else. So, after 17 years, I guess I just wanted to say that I did care but maybe didn't express it very well. Even now I think of you and care about you and I just want you to know that and I hope your life is joyful and good. I wish I would have been the person then that I am now. But that's the way it is. You need not reply to this letter. Just know that you meant a lot to me those many years ago and I wish the best for you now.

Edward

Edward gulps and, in spite of himself, feels a tear rolling down his cheek, then into the well.

And in the well there occurs the softest most wonderful color possible—a deep maroon of sunset, the color of a butterfly. And the letter abruptly leaves Edward's hand and drifts down into the well.

"Dreams," whispers the well, "dreams, dreams, dreams. How many dreams have I given? Taken? Yet the power of dreams awes me still. Eon after eon, millennia after millennia, dreams, oh, the lovely power and magic of dreams."

Flash! And Edward is sitting in his car on the side of the road, overlooking a broad river valley to the mountains beyond. He is just a short distance from the road on which he turned off. Dazed, he looks about. It is near sunset and the color of the sky is the softest, most wonderful color possible: a deep maroon of sunset, the delicate colors of a butterfly. He looks about the car and on the seat, an envelope. His name is on it. He opens it.

Dear Edward:

What a surprise to get your letter after all these years. I thought sure I'd never see or hear from you again. I am still married, have two rambunctious teenage sons and am content. I've often thought about you as well, hoped the best for you and certainly missed you at the wedding. Now I understand why. Thank you for sharing that. There is no greater gift than knowing that someone cares. I wish you well, my friend, and thank you *so* much. God bless.

Love, Meredith

Edward holds the letter, looks out over the landscape and says to himself, "Thank you, well."

And somewhere he hears the sound of wind, of water flowing over stones and the familiar voice, "Dreams. Dreams, dreams, dreams. How many dreams have I given? How many dreams have I taken? Yet the power of dreams awes me still. Eon after eon, millennia after millennia, dreams, dreams, dreams, oh, the lovely power and magic of dreams."

And Edward sighs, looks into the sunset, as he comes to know the power and magic of dreams.

You Know Who I Am by the Song That I Sing

She comes to me in my dreams—she's engulfed in yellow flames and when she walks, white sparks fly from her feet: *click-spark-click-spark*—and she walks down that long, dark hallway—

At first, I cannot comprehend the nature of the dreams. My good buddy, Jake, we sit drinking beer. He's 45, got black hair, blue eyes, thin face with prominent cheek bones. "Yeah," he says, "yeah, it's tough all right. Two kids, need dental work and man, they just don't pay enough—"

I sip my Bud, I hear him, but I'm kinda lost in my own thoughts. I'm abruptly aware he's quiet.

"Sorry," I say, "it's gotta be tough—everyone is making more but somehow we're all making less."

He nods. "Pisser," he says. "How you doin'?"

I shrug. "Same old. Kathy is doing OK; likes her new job."

"Manager," says Jake.

"Yeah. She likes it. Nordstroms treats her OK. Good bennies."

"You?" says Jake.

"OK," I sip my Bud. "Having these fucking dreams, though."

"About?" Jake's eyebrows arch in that "tell-me-more" look.

"Ah—well," I begin; I don't know about this, but I take a deep breath. "It involves this picture of a woman on fire coming down a dark hallway—"

Jake grins. "On fire, huh? Boy, whatcha doin' to Kathy these days, stud?"

I feel myself glower. "Not really all that funny," I say. "Scary."

Jake still grins. "So, what's in a dream, buddy, eh? Random neural firings, or so that's what Martin says."

Martin, mutual friend who's a counselor. I realize if anyone would know about dreams, he would. I don't say anything. So, what is in a dream, anyway? What is in a dream?

We finish our beers. He goes home to Angie and their kids, I go home to Kathy and go to bed and it's OK...at first...

...she comes to me in my dreams, flaming, her feet tap against the floor, *click, flash, click, flash* and the sparks change to bursts of flame. Her hair is burning orange and she says something—*something* to me—

"What," asks Martin, "do you suppose she's trying to say?"

He looks older than his forty years; lined face, gray hair, a little overweight, dressed in blue shirt, gray slacks. I sit in his office. I've talked to him off and on throughout the years about stuff. We've known each other since high school.

I shake my head. "Don't know," I say. "Just don't know."

"Let's try hypnosis," Martin says. "It may be able to help you focus and concentrate—take in a long, deep breath—"

I do.

"Let it out slowly."

I do.

"Another long, deep breath—three, two, and let your breath out slowly—"

I do.

"One. Sleep deeply—"

And I'm gone, sinking into this sleep where I'm floating, drifting, comfortable and I hear Martin's disembodied voice—like it's coming from a long, long way off—"do you suppose she's...saying...?"

What—who... then I see her. She's trying to talk to me but I can't understand—

"...nothing..." I whisper in the trance state, "—can't understand her..."

"Imagine a blackboard," Martin says. "See her standing before it with a piece of chalk. She's writing you a message—"

I see her put the chalk to the board; it squeals against the slate and I experience it like fingernails across a blackboard and I wake with a start.

"What—" says Martin.

"You're behind the times. You should have had me use a dry marker," I say, rubbing my eyes. "The chalk squeaked; woke me up."

Martin nods. "Let's try again, this time using dry marker on an e-z erase board."

"No," I say, "let me come back after I dream again. Maybe I can hear what she has to say."

Martin thinks for a moment then nods. "OK," he says.

She comes to me, all flame, but more intense, almost blinding now. Her footfall—lightning flashes. I feel the heat and she comes to me—my clothes blacken, shrivel, burn. Her mouth moves and I see bright light in her mouth as she talks. I hear her, but it's like inside my head. "You know who I am—"

Mentally, I complete it, "—by the song that I sing."

Suddenly, I'm on my back, flat against the cold marble floor. She walks around me, a pillar of fire now, and when she walks, her footfall is continuous, unrelenting lightning.

Another session with Martin. He taps the eraser end of a pencil against his chin as he leans back in a black swivel recliner. He regards me as if I'm a puzzle shy a few pieces. "So, she says to you, 'You know who I am by the song that I sing.' So, what's it mean?"

I sit, staring at my knuckles. "Don't know," I finally say without looking up. "But I don't like this."

"Processing dream," says Martin. "You're processing something. It's unfolding before you."

"Is that why the hypnosis wouldn't work?" I respond.

Martin just regards me with a mixture of friendship and professional concern.

"What do I do next?" I ask.

Martin chews the end of the pencil. "Let's let it play out. Where's it go?"

"Hopefully, someplace good," I respond.

"Ever have a dream of falling off a cliff?" he says.

I nod.

"Ever experience yourself hitting the ground?"

"No."

"Nor will you. You always wake up." Martin leans forward, totally convinced of this. "So, you'll wake up for this. The body always protects itself."

"Hope so," I say. "I don't wanna hit the ground."

"You'll wake up before that happens."

I feel heartened by this but also unsure.

I'm on my back again on the cold marble floor and she's there. She walks around me, her feet flashing fire, and I hear her say, "You know who I am —"

"By the song that I sing," I whisper. "What song do you sing?"

I don't know how she does it but she somehow walks over me and when she walks flames burn, searing heat, and suddenly in my head I hear her song: it is the song of the damned. It is the song of life disturbed, burned, ripped apart, tortured. It is the song of napalmed children, kittens thrown against brick walls; of dreams shattered, broken, unfulfilled, the sledgehammer against the skulls of cattle; life tortured, life destroyed. The horrible unfairness of life giving up life long before it should have to.

"You know who I am," she sings.

"By the song that I sing," I reply.

"And, what song do *you* sing?" she muses.

Fire rips up through me, from my bowels, through my stomach, through my heart, searing my mind. "I've not done what I've meant to do with my life."

She then dances over me and my body incinerates into smoke and I'm beyond pain, beyond screaming, beyond tears and I know the song that she sings and I know I've fallen over the cliff — and I'm not waking up.

Panther

It is a dreamscape. The clouds are dark gray and roiling over a landscape that is pale gray, monotonous—like a vast plain that stretches off into the distance. A surprisingly warm wind blows; it also feels like it's rather humid and you wonder how such a landscape that is so bleak, so—disturbing—can be so warm, and you fancy you can smell the scent of flowers—lilac, rose, honeysuckle.

You wonder what you are doing here. If it's a dreamscape, then it is a dream. You close your eyes. "I will wake up." You open your eyes. Nothing has changed. You kneel. "How did I get here?" you wonder. "If this is a dream, I can wake up," but you are not waking up. You touch the ground—it has a smooth, surprisingly smooth, texture and it's warm. You weren't expecting that. The clouds continue to move, roil overhead, like you're beneath the guts of a thunderstorm, and you're waiting for the lighting to flash, the thunder to crash, but nothing happens, just a steady wind. And it's *so* warm.

You decide to walk. You walk for long time but the landscape remains the same. You stop, look around, look back the way you came and it looks no different. You sit. Out of your shirt pocket you pull out a Snickers bar; you unwrap slowly, munch it thoughtfully. You don't know what to do with the wrapper; you place it on the ground and in seconds, it sprouts little hands and feet. It raises a fist to you, curses, and then runs off screaming. You aren't really frightened. Disoriented, maybe, but not frightened. You just wonder where you are.

Abruptly, there is a vivid flash of lightning, which strikes nearby but holds for a minute, long enough for you to see in the incandescent glow an image of Elvis in his later years. There is no thunder, just Elvis in that burning moment, saying, "Thunk yew, thunk yew, thunk yew ver, ver, much—" and then, gone. Then it begins to rain, but it abruptly turns to large hailstones. You look down only to discover the hailstones are actually miniature Beatle dolls, hopping and jiving about and you hear high pitched snippets of Beatle songs: "Help," "Can't Buy Me Love," "Hey, Jude," "Paperback Writer" and as you sit, the songs vie and merge, vie and merge with each other and you fancy, after a few minutes, you've heard all of them. All around you, for as far as you can see, the little minute Beatle dolls hop, jive about and you hear that weird, high pitched singing. Then slowly, just like hail, it all melts and the songs slowly fade away and you're left with that vast plain again. In the distance, you see something bright. It's a figure running to you, no, toward you, and then it passes by: it's Richard Nixon on fire, screaming, "I'm not a crook. I'm not a crook! I'm *not* a crook!" and then he disappears off into the distance. You look up and the sky slowly clears; two bright stars reveal themselves and the clearing in the sky takes on a shape. You realize what it is: you see the color of it. Blacker than the sky. A panther. It steps down from the sky, with the stars for the eyes and it looks at you curiously. It paces around you, circles you and finally sits, looking at you with those burning star-eyes. "You're a brave one," it whispers, "hanging around in a dream."

"Can't leave," you say, "can't seem to get out of this dream."

"We all can leave," says the panther. "The question is, what price do we pay."

"For — ?"

"Leaving. Staying. Always a price to pay."

The panther finally sits, like The Sphinx, paws outstretched in front of it, looking down on you with those burning eyes.

"Your eyes are very large," you say.

"Suns make large eyes. I could make a pun about enlightenment, but I'd rather chat," it says.

"Who are you?"

"Panther," the panther replies.

"Why are you here?" you ask.

The panther begins purring. "Not the question. Why are *you* here?"

"I don't know," you say. "It's like I'm in a dream and I can't get out."

"Do you want to get out?" asks the panther. "Do you really want to get out?"

"I want to get back to my life," you say.

"What was your life?" asks the panther. "Tell me about your life."

Funny how, at such times, you think of simple things and the dream changes: you're standing in vast melting fields of different flavors of chocolate, and in the distance, melting mounds of vanilla and chocolate ice cream create molten mountain ranges. But suddenly, you're back, looking at the panther and it says again, "Tell me about your life."

Overhead, the clouds have become low and mean-looking and the wind blows harder and you know you're dealing with something awful. Is it the devil in disguise? Is it death? What is it that you look at? The panther lords above you, looks down at you with those burning stars for eyes, and you say the thing that you know is true. "Compassion," you say, "compassion. It is all that life is; it can be the only thing that matters. Compassion."

The wind has picked up and suddenly the clouds descend and you are enveloped in a thick and dark seething mass of clouds and the blackest fog.

"Compassion," comes the voice. "Tell me of compassion."

With the wind blowing you around and the grit flying in the air, grit from where you cannot guess, you are also aware of how utterly quiet it is and you say, "What else is life but compassion? Compassion for self, compassion for others. What is life without it?"

Suddenly, all is still. You look around, the low clouds are still engulfing you but it's like they are frozen in place. Grit is suspended, not moving. A newspaper has been lifted by the wind and hangs in front of your face; it self-illuminates and you can read the name of the newspaper: *Dreamscape Times.* You read the lead headlines of the stories on the first page: *What Else Matters? Lessons Take Forever to Learn, Buddha Remembered.* And as you glance around, abruptly all disappears; the clouds vanish, as does the paper, the winds and — the panther. You look up to a sky filled, glowing with stars and you hear something whisper to you, the panther? The voice of the Universe? You don't know, but you listen, for you cannot help but listen: "If you have learned compassion, then you have learned the only thing that matters."

And off to the east, you see sunlight touching the edge of the world.

Acknowledgments

To the memories of Marie Landis, founder of the writing and critique group I've been a part of for over 26 years and to her husband, Si. You taught me that the object of life isn't wealth. The object of life is the wealth of life.

To the former members of the above mentioned group: Phyllis Hiefield, Joel Davis, Brian Herbert and wife Jan and to the memory of Cal Clawson.

To the present, dedicated members of present critique now known as the Landis Review in honor of Marie Landis: Linda Shepherd, Roberta Gregory, Sarah Blum and Art Gomez and Jim Bartlett — and to success, to love, laughter, connection, and a wonderful sense of a full and vibrant life well lived. What better definition of success do you need than that?

Thank you Pippin Sardo and Nancy Lou Polk for work done on the early version of this work and a big thank you to Bear Lightfoot for amazing computer work getting different formats coordinated and updated. That was as lot of work and you did it well. Thank you very much!

Many thanks to my good friend and former agent, Ben Bova whose suggestions in regard to the "bigger picture" of this work has proven to be most correct.

And with deepest gratitude and thanks to Andrew Burt and ReAnimus Press for publishing new editions of my earlier works as well as publishing new titles. I am so delighted!

Last, but certainly not least, to Roberta Gregory, my partner, my friend, who, with infinite compassion and forbearance, offered great solace and a superb eye for detail, and suggestions in the difficulties around my being challenged by computers and the proofreading of this manuscript. Such are these people, upon entering one's life, you know that no matter how many times you say, "Thank you," it never seems enough. But that being said, "Thank you. Thank you all, thank you so much."

Bruce Taylor
Seattle, Washington
February, 2017

Publication history:

"Bats," *Vampires Crypt 24,* (Fall, 2001)

"The Bauble," *Magic Realism,* Vol. 5.1, #10, (Winter, 1995-96)

"The Ear of Ozone," *Pulphouse: The Report,* (magazine ceased publication before story published)

"Eggs," *Science Fiction Jahrbuch, 1985,* Moewig Science Fiction, Germany

"Growing up: Rocked and Rolled," *13 phantgastische Rock-Stories,* Fantasy Productions, Germany, (1988) "Insight," *Alternate Realities Webzine,* (2001)

"The Little Black Box of San Manuel," *Naughty Bits #40,* Fantagraphic Books, Inc., (2004)

"The Mall," *Shillelagh,* Pyx Press. (project cancelled before story published)

"Morality Play," *Continuum Science Fiction,* (Fall, 2005)

"Mr. Wetzel and His Wurlitzer," *Ellipsis,* (magazine ceased publication before story published)

"One Afternoon in the Sears Catalogue," *Stigmata,* (1997)

"Planetary Loves," *ConAdian Souvenir Book,* The 52nd World Science Fiction Convention, (1994)

"Satan Claus," *Heliocentric Net,* (1996)

"Spiders," *Talebones,* (July, 1996)

"You Can Hardly Wait," *Northwest Passages: A Cascadian Odyssey,* Windstorm Creative, (2005)

"You Know Who I Am," *Talebones,* (May, 2001)

The first chapter of *The Tails of Alleymanderous*...was originally published in a different form, as a short story, "Alternate Reality 578.5" in *Pulphouse*, (September/October 1992)

A Dilly of a Dally of a Day, Waiting, Jessica's Place, Mr. Wetzel and His Wurlitzer, Of Love, Beasts and Burning Webs, The Ear of Ozone, The Well, Metamorphosis Blues, Panther originally appeared in the collection, "Metamorphosis Blues" published by Fantastic Planet Books, c. 2011.

About the Author

Bruce Taylor, known as Mr. Magic Realism, was born in 1947 in Seattle, Washington, where he currently lives. He was a student at the Clarion West Science Fiction/Fantasy writing program at the University of Washington, where he studied under such writers as Avram Davidson, Robert Silverberg, Ursula K. LeGuin, and Frank Herbert. Bruce has been involved in the advancement of the genre of magic realism, founding the Magic Realism Writers International Network, and collaborating with Tamara Sellman on *MARGIN* (*http://www.magical-realism.com*www.magical-realism.com). Recently, he co-edited, with Elton Elliott, former editor of Science Fiction Review, an anthology titled, *Like Water for Quarks*, which examines the blending of magic realism with science fiction, with work by Ray Bradbury, Ursula K. LeGuin, Brian Herbert, Connie Willis, Greg Bear, William F. Nolan, among others. Elton Elliott has said that "(Bruce) is the transformational figure for science fiction."

His works have been published in such places as *The Twilight Zone*, *Talebones*, *The Seattle P.I., Darke Phantastique* and *New Dimensions*. His first collection, *The Final Trick of Funnyman and Other Stories* (available from Fairwood Press) recently received high praise from William F. Nolan, who said that some of his stores were "as rich and poetic as Bradbury at his best."

In 2007, borrowing and giving credit to author Karel Capek (*War with the Newts*), Bruce published *EDWARD: Dancing on the Edge of Infinity*, a tale told largely through footnotes about a young man discovering his purpose in life through his dreams.

With Brian Herbert, son of Frank Herbert of *Dune* fame, he wrote *Stormworld*, a short novel about global warming.

Two other books (*Mountains of the Night, Magic of Wild places*) have been published and are part of a "spiritual trilogy." (The third book, *Majesty of the World*, is presently being written.)

A sequel to *Kafka's Uncle (Kafka's Uncle: the Unfortunate Sequel and Other Insults to the Morally Perfect)*, as well as the prequel *(Kafka's Uncle: the Ghastly Prequel and Other Tales of Love and Pathos from the World's Most Powerful, Third-World Banana Republic)* were published in 2016. *Industrial Carpet Drag,* a weird and funny look at global warming and environmental decay, was released in 2014.

Other published titles are, *Mr. Magic Realism* and *Metamorphosis Blues.*

Of course, he has already taken on several other projects which he hopes will see publication: *My False Memories With Myshkin Dostoyevsky-Kat,* and *The Tales of Alleymanderous* as well as going through some 800 unpublished stories to assemble more collections; over 40 years, Bruce has written about 1000 short stories, 200 of which have been published.

Bruce was writer in residence at Shakespeare & Company, Paris. If not writing, Bruce is either hiking or can be found in the loft of his vast condo, awestruck at the smashing view of Mt. Rainier with his partner, artist and writer Roberta Gregory and their "mews," Roo-Prrt.

More books from Bruce Taylor are available at:
http://ReAnimus.com/store/?author=Bruce Taylor

ReAnimus Press

Breathing Life into Great Books

If you enjoyed this book we hope you'll tell others or write a review! We also invite you to subscribe to our newsletter to learn about our new releases and join our affiliate program (where you earn 12% of sales you recommend) at
www.ReAnimus.com.

Here are more ebooks you'll enjoy from ReAnimus Press, available from ReAnimus Press's web site, Amazon.com, bn.com, etc.:

Kafka's Uncle and Other Strange Tales, by Bruce Taylor

Kafka's Uncle: The Unfortunate Sequel, by Bruce Taylor

Kafka's Uncle: The Ghastly Prequel, by Bruce Taylor

Edward: Dancing on the Edge of Infinity, by Bruce Taylor

Alleymanderous and Other Magical Realities, by Bruce Taylor

Magic of Wild Places, by Bruce Taylor

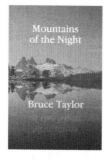

Mountains of the Night, by Bruce Taylor

Side Effects, by Harvey Jacobs

American Goliath, by Harvey Jacobs

Biff America: Steep Deep & Dyslexic, by Jeffrey
Bergeron (AKA Biff America)

A Knife In The Mind, by Craig Strete

The Angry Dead, by Craig Strete

The Game of Cat and Eagle, by Craig Strete

My Gun Is Not So Quick, by Craig Strete

The Bleeding Man and Other Science Fiction Stories,
by Craig Strete

Death Chants, by Craig Strete

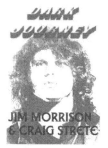

Dark Journey, by Jim Morrison and Craig Strete

When Grandfather Journeys Into Winter, by Craig
Strete

If All Else Fails, by Craig Strete

Dreams That Burn in the Night, by Craig Strete

Burn Down the Night, by Craig Strete

Wyoming Sun, by Edward Bryant

Cinnabar, by Edward Bryant

Fetish, by Edward Bryant

Neon Twilight, by Edward Bryant

Predators and Other Stories, by Edward Bryant

Trilobyte, by Edward Bryant

Darker Passions, by Edward Bryant

Among the Dead and Other Events Leading to the Apocalypse, by Edward Bryant

Particle Theory, by Edward Bryant

The Baku: Tales of the Nuclear Age, by Edward Bryant

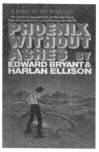

Phoenix Without Ashes, by Harlan Ellison and Edward Bryant

In Hollow Lands, by Sophie Masson

Journals of the Plague Years, by Norman Spinrad

Fragments of America, by Norman Spinrad

Pictures at 11, by Norman Spinrad

The Men from the Jungle, by Norman Spinrad

Greenhouse Summer, by Norman Spinrad

Passing Through the Flame, by Norman Spinrad

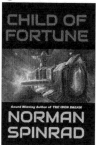

Child of Fortune, by Norman Spinrad

Mexica, by Norman Spinrad

Songs from the Stars, by Norman Spinrad

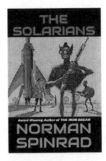

The Solarians, by Norman Spinrad

The Void Captain's Tale, by Norman Spinrad

Staying Alive - A Writer's Guide, by Norman Spinrad

The Mind Game, by Norman Spinrad

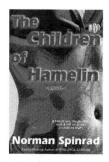

The Children of Hamelin, by Norman Spinrad

The Iron Dream, by Norman Spinrad

Bug Jack Barron, by Norman Spinrad

Experiment Perilous: The 'Bug Jack Barron' Papers, by Norman Spinrad

The Last Hurrah of the Golden Horde, by Norman Spinrad

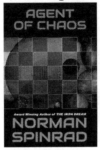

Agent of Chaos, by Norman Spinrad

Russian Spring, by Norman Spinrad

Little Heroes, by Norman Spinrad

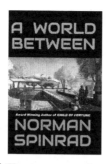

A World Between, by Norman Spinrad

Anthopology 101: Reflections, Inspections and Dissections of SF Anthologies, by Bud Webster

Past Masters, by Bud Webster

Of Worlds Beyond, by Lloyd Arthur Eshbach, ed.

The Issue at Hand, by James Blish (as William Atheling, Jr.)

More Issues at Hand, by James Blish (as William Atheling, Jr.)

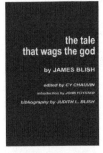

The Tale that Wags the God, by James Blish

The Exiles Trilogy, by Ben Bova

The Star Conquerors (Collectors' Edition), by Ben
Bova

Colony, by Ben Bova

The Kinsman Saga, by Ben Bova

Star Watchmen, by Ben Bova

As on a Darkling Plain, by Ben Bova

The Winds of Altair, by Ben Bova

Test of Fire, by Ben Bova

The Weathermakers, by Ben Bova

The Dueling Machine, by Ben Bova

The Multiple Man, by Ben Bova

Escape!, by Ben Bova

Forward in Time, by Ben Bova

Maxwell's Demons, by Ben Bova

Twice Seven, by Ben Bova

The Astral Mirror, by Ben Bova

The Story of Light, by Ben Bova

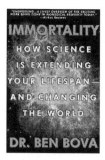

Immortality, by Ben Bova

Space Travel - A Science Fiction Writer's Guide, by
Ben Bova

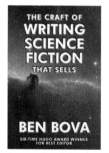

The Craft of Writing Science Fiction that Sells, by Ben
Bova

How To Improve Your Speculative Fiction Openings,
by Robert Qualkinbush

Ghosts of Engines Past, by Sean McMullen

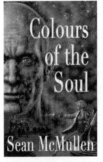

Colours of the Soul, by Sean McMullen

The Cure for Everything, by Severna Park

The Sweet Taste of Regret, by Karen Haber

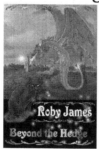

Beyond the Hedge, by Roby James

Commencement, by Roby James

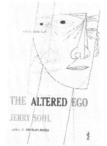

The Altered Ego, by Jerry Sohl

The Odious Ones, by Jerry Sohl

Prelude to Peril, by Jerry Sohl

The Spun Sugar Hole, by Jerry Sohl

The Lemon Eaters, by Jerry Sohl

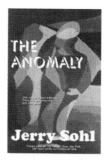

The Anomaly, by Jerry Sohl

I, Aleppo, by Jerry Sohl

Death Sleep, by Jerry Sohl

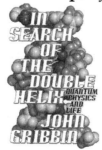

In Search of the Double Helix, by John Gribbin

Fire on Earth, by John and Mary Gribbin

Q is for Quantum, by John Gribbin

In Search of the Big Bang, by John Gribbin

Ice Age, by John and Mary Gribbin

FitzRoy, by John and Mary Gribbin

Cosmic Coincidences, by John Gribbin and Martin Rees

The Sad Happy Story of Aberystwyth the Bat, by Ben Gribbin

A Guide to Barsoom, by John Flint Roy

The Gilded Basilisk, by Chet Gottfried

William J. Hypperbone, or The Will of an Eccentric,
by Jules Verne

The Futurians, by Damon Knight

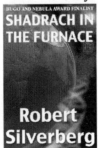

Shadrach in the Furnace, by Robert Silverberg

Xenostorm: Rising, by Brian Clegg

Bloom, by Wil McCarthy

Aggressor Six, by Wil McCarthy

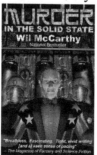

Murder in the Solid State, by Wil McCarthy

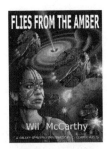

Flies from the Amber, by Wil McCarthy

Dear America: Letters Home from Vietnam, by edited
by Bernard Edelman for The New York Vietnam Veterans
Memorial Commission

I've Never Been To Me, by Charlene Oliver

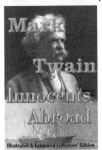

Innocents Abroad (Fully Illustrated & Enhanced Collectors' Edition), by Mark Twain

Local Knowledge (A Kieran Lenahan Mystery), by
Conor Daly

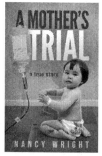

A Mother's Trial, by Nancy Wright

Bad Karma: A True Story of Obsession and Murder,
by Deborah Blum

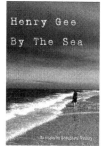

By The Sea, by Henry Gee

The Sigil Trilogy (Omnibus vol.1-3), by Henry Gee

Made in the USA
San Bernardino, CA
18 May 2017